MOUNTAIN MAGIC

"Relax, my little love. Open your mouth a bit," Raven urged. His tongue played over Misty's lips in fiery strokes, then skillfully slipped between them. By now, what was left of her natural resistance had been swept away, and she felt as if she were drowning in a great undertow of passion.

Though he'd made love to dozens of women, Raven had never kissed anyone like Misty, and exultation now burst within him like a shower of stars. Consumed with passion, he fiercely molded her feminine softness against him, deepening the kiss, and delving his fingers into her silken hair.

Then, like a dull ache, his strong sense of responsibility gradually began to trickle back, reminding him of how different they were. His family was rich; hers was indigent. He'd attended a university and was highly educated; she could scarcely read. On top of that, he'd lived in the great city and was sophisticated in the ways of the world, while she'd never been out of the Ozarks and was utterly innocent.

Even if the alliance wasn't wrong, surely it wasn't prudent. How could it be otherwise? Their families had been feuding for more than a century, and any connection between them was star-crossed and utterly doomed from the beginning.

FROST FLOWER

SONYA BIRMINGHAM

LEISURE BOOKS NEW YORK CITY

Frost Flower is dedicated to my good friend Steven Wann, an Arkansan whose keen sense of adventure is only matched by his love for the old times and the old tales. A true outdoorsman, his spirituality, wry humor, and steadfast strength are a source of constant joy. Years ago in the quiet of the scarlet woods, he learned to appreciate what was special in each thing and person. He has never forgotten.

Steven—may your game be abundant, your trail clear, and your aim true.

A heartfelt thanks to Col. and Mrs. H.T. Tucker, my beloved parents, who accompanied me to the Ozarks to research this book.

Chapter One

The Ozark Mountains—October, 1885

Dead.

Yes, the man was dead . . . he had to be.

Misty Malone's heart began an uneasy thud as she rose from the spot where she'd been gathering herbs and stared in the direction of the glowing sunset. She pulled in a breath of fresh, pine-scented air and focused on a point about fifty yards up the mountain trail. There, sprawled under a huge oak, lay the body of a man . . . a large, naked man.

Her throat tightening with emotion, she dropped her herb sack and glanced behind her. Her friend Lukie walked along the same trail, leading a belled pony that pulled a shallow cart filled with bundles of wild herbs. The girls had been walking for three hours and the cart was brimming over with horsemint, bosenet, camel root, and dozens of other plants useful in making healing potions.

Misty started to cry out, but she stopped herself. No, she wouldn't alarm Lukie . . . not just yet. Perhaps the startling sight was just a trick of the dim light.

Hearing a rustling noise, she saw her pet raccoon scatter leaves as he scampered toward her, and without thinking, she bent and scooped his warm, furry body into her arms. She straightened and disentangled Rollo's paws from her fringed buckskin jacket, then returned her attention to the big oak, darkly silhouetted against the red sky. Cautiously, she moved up the road. If there *was* a dead man up the trail, she wanted to see him!

Misty's heart fluttered anew as she neared the oak, for indeed, there under its sheltering limbs sprawled a body. Shocked, she placed Rollo on the ground, then sank to her knees and gave a soft cry. At that moment a shaft of golden sunlight streamed over the man, illuminating him.

His arm thrown over his head, he was lying on his back atop a bed of scarlet leaves. His hair was disheveled, its inky color a vibrant contrast against the bright leaves. Mesmerized, Misty inched her gaze over his huge form, noticing an unaccustomed heat suddenly flush her skin.

As an herb doctor, she had seen her share of naked men, but somehow this one affected her differently. Pine needles had blown over his powerful chest and now clung to muscular legs and slim hips. At the juncture of his thighs, wiry black hair clustered about his manhood, which even now seemed large and rather imposing.

Misty responded to the man with her innermost feelings. *Precious Jesus,* she thought, sorrow flooding through her. *What had happened to him?* Her heart aching, she trailed her fingers over his cheekbone, feeling the fine stubble of his beard. He was so strikingly handsome . . . what a shame he was dead! His square face was clean-cut and strong; his lashes thick and dark against his bronzed cheek; his lips full and sensuous. She was saddened by how huge but strangely helpless he looked.

How perfectly still he was . . . how silent.

Noticing the crackle of dry leaves, she rose and saw that Lukie had timidly followed and was now a few paces behind her. Dressed in a worn calico gown, the plain girl had a freckled face, a shock of carrot-red hair, and large eyes that now looked terrified. For as long as Misty could remember, Lukie had lived with her grandfather, an old preacher the people of Red Oak Hollow called Brother Jubal, and for as long as Misty could remember, the girl had been her best friend.

Lukie seemed petrified, looking as if her eyes might pop right out of her head. Together the girls stood motionless, staring at the lifeless form.

"Look at the size of him," Misty breathed. "He sure has a big chest, doesn't he? And big arms and legs, too."

Lukie blushed deep red, then averted her eyes. "That ain't all he has big," she drawled.

"Maybe he's still alive," Misty said, regarding her friend. "Maybe I can help him."

Lukie shook her head. "No, he ain't movin'. That man's dead—*graveyard* dead." She surveyed the shadowy forest, even now stirring with quiet night sounds. "We ain't goin' to find no more herbs

13

this afternoon. Why, it's nearly sunset now." She stepped back and twisted the end of her long apron. "We sure don't want to be standin' here in the dark. *Let's just go.*"

Misty transferred her attention back to the man's chest, and seeing a movement, she knelt beside him. "Well, I'll be flamboozled," she murmured. "I think he's still breathing." Hope glowed within her as she gently shook his shoulder. When he groaned, her heart lurched with excitement. The beautiful man was alive; he was alive and needed saving.

Misty looked at her friend and grinned. "See, he isn't dead—and he's pretty enough to be one of the Lord's own angels!" Thoughtfully biting her lip, she worked her fingertips through the man's hair. "Why, he's got a knot bigger than a goose egg on the back of his head." She feathered back his hair and studied his chiseled features. "I've never set eyes on him before . . . he's a stranger for sure."

"How do you suppose he got here?"

"I suspect he rode out from Eureka Springs. That trash that's been plaguing the hollow probably knocked him on the head, then stripped him and stole his horse."

As she looked at the man's bold face, caution and a kind of wild exhilaration battled within her. She often tried to save animals caught in traps, but surely this was the most dangerous thing she'd ever done. Why just finding him had already altered her life and he was still unconscious.

Lukie shot her a disapproving glower. "You ain't thinkin' about bringin' him home with Ezra gone, are you? Why, you don't have any notion who he is"—she ran her eyes over the man's muscled

14

body—"and he don't have on any clothes to tell you. He might wake up in the mornin' and snap your neck like a dry stick!"

Misty took the man's big square hand and spread it open, its warmth buoying her hope. Finding no callouses, she deduced that he wasn't a laboring man. Her pulse raced a little faster as she caressed his ring finger. There was no white place there from wearing a wedding band, so he must be unattached. She scanned his face again, which to her held a kind of nobility. Yes, she thought excitedly, he had the look of a gentleman about him. Bravely casting aside the remainder of her caution, she stood and eyed Lukie. "Fetch that cart up here while I straighten out his arms and legs. I'm gonna take him home and doctor him."

Lukie scowled. "What if he's an outlaw or a revenuer man?"

"That doesn't matter. He can't lay out here all night knocked out of his senses. The varmints will get him. Don't you remember the story from the Good Book about the man who was left for dead beside the road? If the Good Samaritan hadn't happened along, I guess he'd still be laying there. Good Samaritans being scarce as snake feathers around here, it's up to us to save this fellow!"

For a moment, there was only the sound of the wind in the pines and the tinkling of the pony's bell. "Why do you have to be bringin' up the Good Book at a time like this?" Lukie moaned. "The Good Book don't say nothin' 'bout takin' care of no naked men."

Misty looked at her friend, knowing that despite her protest, she would do the right thing. Their years together had taught her that most of Lukie's complaining was for show and that the girl possessed great strength and was unshakably loyal.

She smiled as Lukie turned and walked to the cart, all the while muttering softly under her breath about murderers and revenuer men.

By the time Lukie returned, Misty had worked her hands under the man's shoulders and was trying to lift him from the ground. She met her friend's frightened eyes. "Well, come on. Help me. He's heavy as a sack of iron skillets!"

Lukie hung back. "I ain't ever touched a naked man before."

Misty gave an exasperated sigh. *"He's knocked in the head.* He won't know you're touching him. Now, come on and help me get him in the cart."

Still grumbling, Lukie reluctantly hoisted the flatlander's legs while Misty struggled to lift his torso. With a round of grunts and groans, they finally managed to place him in the cart, where his arms flopped over the low sides and his legs dangled from the open end.

Squinting, Lukie picked up some of the brilliant leaves and scattered them strategically over his groin. She stood back to view her handiwork, then opened one eye and nodded. "Yep. He looks a heap better now."

Misty dusted off her hands and took her place beside the pony's head. "We'd better be moving on," she declared, looking down the dusky trail. "The shadows are getting longer by the minute." As she took the bridle, Rollo jumped into the cart and perched on the man's stomach. Misty glanced back at her friend. "Follow behind, and see that he doesn't slide off those herbs and hit the ground." She squared her shoulders. "Are you ready?"

Lukie tossed a few more leaves over the man's groin and took a deep breath. "I'm as ready as I'll ever be. But I don't like it at all. Not at all."

Misty pulled as hard as she could on the pony's bridle, and with a rush of relief, felt the cart move beside her. For a while the girls kept to the trail, then they followed a small footpath into the woods. The shuddering cart squeaked and groaned, and the man shook like a rag doll as the conveyance bounced over the rough countryside.

Rollo, enjoying the ride, scampered about and occasionally posed on the flatlander's chest. The cart creaked so loudly that Misty feared it would burst apart, but when the sun was just slipping behind the mountains in fiery splendor, they turned a bend and, nestled in a close of dark pines, her ramshackle log home and its outbuildings loomed into sight.

After dropping the patient on the ground several times, the girls finally lugged him into the cabin, then placed him on a sagging bed.

Lukie stood back and wiped an arm over her brow. "I'd better be leavin'. It's dark and my granddaddy will be worryin' over me." At the cabin door, she paused and looked back at her friend. "Will you be all right? You ain't skeared?"

Misty gave her an encouraging smile. "I'll be all right." She scanned her charge. "He's a big one all right, but there's something in his face that tells me he's a gentleman."

Lukie groaned her displeasure. "Lord, your brother would pitch a fit if he knew about this!"

Misty raised her brows. "What Ezra doesn't know won't hurt him, will it?"

Lukie slipped from the cabin, and after the door had closed, Misty knelt by the bed.

Sonya Birmingham

Tenderly, she brushed back her patient's hair and studied his elegant features, thinking they were almost perfect. Who was this big stranger? Where was he from? Why had he ridden into her hollow, and what was his business? Lord, how she ached to know the answers to these questions!

If he'd been bleeding, she would have put a spider web on the cut, or if he'd been burned, she would have put the scrapings of a potato on his flesh to draw out the fire. These cures would have produced quick results, and she would have had the answers to her questions. But as Red Oak Hollow's best herb doctor, she knew that when someone had been knocked unconscious, there was nothing to do but wait.

Filled with a sense of tingling anticipation, Misty pulled a quilt over the man's body and did just that.

As Adam Davenport drifted into consciousness, the sounds of soft music and an angelic voice filtered into his ears. At first he wondered if he'd died and gone to heaven; then, as he flicked open his eyes, he realized that he was definitely not in heaven, for it seemed a hundred demons were pounding on his head. Furthermore, a raccoon was nestled on his chest, the animal's glistening black eyes filled with wonder. Blinking, Adam stared back at the furry ball and attempted to sit up, thinking there wasn't an inch of his skull that didn't ache.

The angelic singing came to an abrupt stop. "Rollo, get off the stranger's chest!" came a command from across the room.

When the raccoon bounded to the floor, Adam propped himself up on one elbow, feeling weak and empty with hunger. His vision bleary, he looked across a room furnished with crude puncheon tables, cupboards, and block cheer beds. Then as his eyes fully focused, he noticed a beautiful girl sitting by the window, dressed in fringed buckskins. Afternoon light washed over her. She immediately laid aside a stringed instrument and stood, her face radiant with happiness.

She had a dewy complexion, a generous mouth, long, luxurious brown hair, and green eyes that held a glint of concern. A deep opening slashed the front of her buckskin shirt, revealing the creamy swell of her bosom, which even in his groggy state caught his attention. If Adam had ever seen a more desirable woman in his twenty-eight years, he couldn't remember who she might be.

"I thought you were an angel playing a harp," he muttered in a rough voice.

The angel in buckskins laughed softly. "I'm no angel. I'm Misty Malone. And that was a dulcimer I was playing."

Adam's memory quickened at the mention of the Malone name. His grandfather originally hailed from the Ozarks, and with a jolt of surprise, he recalled that years ago his ancestors had been feuding with the Malones. In fact, the feud had provided story material for many of the old man's colorful tales.

Before Adam could fully sort out his present situation, Misty broke into a friendly smile, showing pearly-white teeth. "Welcome, stranger," she said in a cordial tone. After moving to the blackened hearth where a pot of beef broth sat on the grate, she knelt to ladle the richly scented liquid into a tin cup. "Here's something to warm your innards," she said as she rose and walked across the cabin. "I thought you'd be waking up hungry enough to eat a horned frog backwards."

Misty gazed at her patient, feeling a weight lifted from her heart now that he'd regained consciousness. She'd supposed he would be filled with a powerful life force when he woke, but what a joy it was to see that moment arrive. She had scarcely slept the night before, often rising from her own bed to check on him, and he now radiated a potent magnetism, drawing her to him. A smile flashed on his face and lit his features with such warmth that she noticed a thrill within her.

Sitting down on the side of the bed, she placed the broth on a nearby keg to cool, then laid her hand on his forehead. His expression was strongly sensual and even in his weakened state, he projected an air of easy confidence. She instinctively sensed the danger of becoming involved with an outsider, but as his dark eyes swept over her, a delicious sensation flooded through her. "I guess you should feel better now," she said teasingly, searching his strong, commanding features. "You've slept a night and most of the next day."

Adam glanced down at his partially uncovered loins, and tilting a brow, pulled the quilt over his muscular frame.

She moved her hand away and chuckled lightly. "Don't let being naked bother you, stranger. Doctoring comes as natural to me as praying to a preacher man. I don't take any more notice of a man's backside than his face." Her smile broadened. "Besides, I figured you'd be stove up like a rusty pump, so I washed you and rubbed you down with leopard's bane salve to ease your tight muscles. If you ever had any private places, they're not private anymore."

She took his pulse, and when their gazes locked, she saw a gleam in his eyes that prompted a staggering flash of pleasure deep within her. She ignored the exciting feelings his presence elicited and studied those eyes, thinking they were the color of spring storm clouds—all dark and tinged with living fire.

To Adam's mingled consternation and delight, Misty released his wrist and leaned over him, revealing more of her satiny breasts. "Are you feeling better?" she asked solicitously. "Someone gave you a real whack on the head. Do you know who it was?"

Still half dazed, he rubbed a hand over his temple, as if to clear his mind. "Late yesterday afternoon, I spotted two masked riders galloping behind me at full tilt," he said in a thick voice. "My mount barreled around a bend . . . then a low-hanging limb loomed out of the mists. I ducked"—he gingerly touched the tender lump on his head—"but evidently too late. The last thing I remember was a flash of pain and a patch of whirling sky . . . then everything went black."

Misty sat back and nodded wisely. "I'll bet it was those no-accounts who've been robbing folks on the Eureka Springs road. My friend Lukie and I found you about twilight late yesterday afternoon, and on first sight we knew you weren't from hereabouts." Her eyes sparkling with curiosity, she grazed her fingertips over his face. "Where do you call home, stranger?"

Adam rolled his tight shoulders, thinking that despite Misty's administrations, he still ached as if he'd been beaten with sticks. "Saint Louis.

I came to Eureka Springs by train yesterday, then bought a horse and decided to explore the area," he said casually. "I rode several miles out of town . . . and then, you know the rest."

She arched a delicate brow. "Why would a fancy city fellow like you want to come to the mountains anyway?"

He gave a light shrug. "My grandfather came from the Ozarks," he explained. "I'd never been here, and I wanted to see where he was born."

She surveyed him thoughtfully. "You must be rich as a king to just pick up and leave like that."

"Not really," he said with a touch of laughter in his voice. "I'm a doctor."

Her eyes shone with happiness. "Well, I'll be flamboozled. So am I—at least, I'm an herb doctor!" A smile hovering on her lips, she picked up the tin cup and pressed it into his hand. "Here, drink this while we talk. You must be hollow down to your toes."

Adam gulped some of the warm, tasty broth, all the while trying to decide how he would break the news that he was a Davenport. Damnation! he thought, what an awkward situation this had turned out to be. He'd been rescued by his supposed enemy, but with that lovely face and spirited personality, she certainly didn't seem like an enemy to him. But what would she do if she knew who he really was?

Her eyes large, Misty scooted closer to his side. "My granny was the one that taught me doctoring, you know. She was the best granny-woman in the Ozarks." She rose fluidly and walked across the cabin, her silky hair bouncing with every step. "My granny was a plump little chicken of a woman with a smile so sweet it just melted your heart to look at it," she threw over her shoulder. "When we went hunting herbs, she'd say, 'Look at these sweetbriar hips. They're good for curing a cold. And look at the leaves of this little bird-on-the-wing plant. They'll make a fine tonic for the flu.'" She turned and sent him a dazzling smile. "She could cure everything from whooping cough to an ingrown toenail. And she knew everything about the woods around Red Oak Hollow."

"Is that where I am . . . Red Oak Hollow?"

Her green eyes danced. "Yep. I been living in this hollow all my life," she stated proudly. "I was born here, and after Mama and Papa died, my granny raised me and Ezra here. Granny went to her reward a few years ago, so now there's only the two of us."

"Ezra is your brother?"

Misty nodded. "That's who he is, all right. But right now, he's twenty-five miles away, down on the White River cutting pine at a logging camp. He goes down there every fall to earn money to tide us over the winter." She frowned lightly. "I reckon we're gonna have a terrible bad winter this year cause the woolly worms have a thick coat and the laurel leaves have already started rolling up."

Adam studied her large, expressive eyes, which shone with the sheer joy of living. He'd never met anyone like her before and her soft backwoods drawl made him want to smile. "You're not afraid of living here by yourself?" he asked quietly.

She swung an incredulous gaze over him. "Shoot, no. I'm not a helpless citified female. I can kill a deer, tan a hide, chop down a tree, and put a bullet 'tween the eyes of the first rabbit-twister that bothers me."

With a beguiling grin, she scooped Rollo from the floor and sauntered back to the bed. "I reckon you want to get word to your family back in Saint Louis. When you're better, you can borrow my mule and go into Eureka Springs. They've got a post office there."

Adam frowned. "Believe me, the last thing I want right now is to get word to anyone in Saint Louis."

Misty raised a questioning brow. "Lord, didn't you leave word with anyone where you were going?"

He shook his head and sighed. "Yes, my brother knows where I am." A silence fell between them, and feeling he'd been too free with his words, he quickly changed the subject, "Don't you get lonely here by yourself?"

"Nope. Lukie and Brother Jubal live just a hoop and a holler from here, and I've got my coon to keep me company." She caressed her pet's head before putting him down, then glanced at the hearth, where the fire crackled pleasantly. "And at night I lay on that braided rug by the fire and read my doctoring books."

He put the soup aside and suppressed a smile. *"Doctoring books?"*

She pulled several homemade books from a little shelf above the bed, and with the eagerness of a child, handed them to him. He scanned the volumes, thinking they reminded him more of recipe books than anything else. Bound together with rawhide thongs and written in highly un-grammatical English, the books contained cures for everything from bee stings to kidney trouble

24

to sweaty feet. Adam smiled as he read: *For lice, wash your head in kerosene, then sprinkle it with salt and whiskey. Let it stay on for two days. Don't smoke or go near the fire.* Lord, if the girl used cures like this for her patients, it was a wonder she hadn't killed someone!

Misty assessed him as he leafed through her books, and without understanding why, felt a strange warmth for him. She'd seen only a few people who had come from the world beyond the Ozarks, but deep down in the pit of her stomach she instinctively knew this stranger was special . . . very special. And it had nothing to do with his dashing good looks or the smooth way he spoke; it was something inside his heart and mind that made him special, and the thought of it made her blood race. Keenly aware of the sexual tension between them, she knew it would be best if he moved on, but at the same time she prayed he wouldn't. Her hand brushed his as she took the books from him, and she felt a pleasurable fire race up her arm.

She stretched over the bed to return the books to their shelf. "I've been doctoring folks for years out of these little books. My granny put them together using her curing recipes and her mama's curing recipes. You're sure lucky that I'm the one that found you, me being a doctor and all."

Adam eyed Misty's curvaceous form as she shoved the little volumes in place, then walked to the foot of his bed. By the grace of God, this spunky mountain girl had found him on the road and been brave enough to take him in when she had no idea who he was. If he'd lain naked on the road all night, he might have caught pneumonia or been attacked by a mountain lion. No doubt, she'd saved his life.

"You know, stranger," she said with a little frown, "we've been talking all this time, and you still haven't told me your name."

Adam groaned inwardly, realizing that the moment he dreaded had arrived. According to his grandfather's stories, the bitter feud between her family and his had started more than a hundred years ago. As he looked into Misty's soft green eyes, he wondered what she would think if she knew a Davenport had finally returned to the hills. To him the quarrel meant nothing, but from his grandfather's stories he knew that mountain folks still took their feuds dead seriously. Forced to do some quick thinking, he decided to give her a false name. After all, there was no reason to offend her after she'd saved his life.

"I said what's your name, stranger?" Misty's voice held a note of impatience.

Adam wrapped the quilt about himself and slowly stood, noticing a throbbing pain at his temple. Somewhat light-headed, he tried to gather his wits and think of a suitable name.

Behind him, he felt her warm breath on his shoulder and her palm sliding over his arm like satin. "Well, what is it?" she prompted.

Still groggy, all he could dredge up was the name of the last patient he'd treated before he left his Saint Louis practice in the hands of a capable colleague. The balding, spindly-legged gentleman had a case of phlebitis and his name had been Hershel Hepplewhite. "My . . . my name is Hershel Hepplewhite," he blurted out, hardly believing he'd uttered the words.

Misty moved before him and let out her breath in a rush. "*Hershel Hepplewhite?* Lord, that's the worst-fitting name I ever heard!"

Trying to change the subject, he hastily surveyed the cabin, still feeling weak from his blow on the head. "I need to find some clothes, then return to the spot where you found me," he said, glancing at her concerned face. "Maybe the tracks will tell me something about the highwaymen."

Misty bit her lip and glanced down uncomfortably. "Sorry, *Her-shel*," she offered, mouthing the name as if she couldn't believe it belonged to him. With sad eyes, she looked up. "It rained last night while you were sleeping, and it's bound to have washed everything away."

What unbelievably bad luck! Adam thought. He'd been robbed, stripped naked, and his horse stolen—and it now looked as if he had little chance of finding the men who did it. All at once, pain flashed over his forehead and made him ease down on the bed again.

Her touch as light as a butterfly's Misty placed her cool hand on his shoulder. "Don't worry. I'll get you some of Ezra's clothes and fix you some mustard leaf tea for your headache," she offered, smiling into his eyes. "Then later I'll make us some bacon and biscuits and white sop gravy. You're bound to be a little shaky from being knocked out so long." She tipped her head to the side. "'Pears to me that someone needs to care for you for a day or two. Since we're both doctors, it only seems fitting that you stay 'til you're stronger."

As Adam ran his gaze over her gorgeous face, he decided that maybe his luck wasn't so bad after all. He'd been abducted, but he'd been rescued by a vision in buckskins, which meant his visit to the Ozarks might prove interesting indeed. Gradually his spirits rose and he felt himself relax measurably. Instead of rushing off like a damned fool to chase bandits who'd left no trail, why didn't he enjoy the hand fate had dealt him and linger until he was fully recovered? After all, Misty didn't have to know she was offering hospitality to her family's blood enemy . . . at least not for a while.

"All right," Misty said, tossing back her curls. "Tell me what you would do for a bee sting." She cocked her head, studying Adam's bemused expression. They'd been drinking coffee and talking about cures half the morning, with Misty affirming the merits of herbal healing over conventional medicine. Feeling he'd gotten the best of the discussion so far, she just had to try a few more questions.

Adam's eyes glinted with mirth and he smiled, showing strong white teeth. "I'd remove the stinger with a sterilized knife tip, then apply ice, followed with alcohol and calamine lotion." He leaned forward and inclined his head in an elegant manner. "What treatment would you suggest, Dr. Malone?"

She gave a thoughtful sigh. "Well, if I was in the woods, the first thing I'd do is crush some leaves and rub the resin over the sting to ease the pain. Then I'd slap some cool mud on top of that." She grazed a knuckle over her chin. "If I had the patient inside, I'd make a poltice out of an onion slice, then rub the sting with apple cider vinegar."

Adam stood, and carrying his coffee, walked about the cabin. He easily filled out Ezra's clothes, his powerful shoulders tapering into a broad chest, trim stomach, slim hips, and long legs which were encased in dark, close-fitting breeches. His glossy black hair, square, aggressive chin, and the sheer strength of will marking his rugged face gave him an allure that almost made Misty forget how aggravated she was at him.

Adam's mouth quirked upward. "I suppose that would work if you didn't smother the wretch with onion and vinegar fumes."

She raised her chin a little higher. "All righty then, Mr. Saint Louis-Big-City-Doctor. . . . *warts*." She snapped her fingers. "Quick, tell me what you'd do for a good old-fashioned case of warts?"

Laugh lines fanned out from Adam's eyes, and he took his seat again. "I'd apply salicylic acid and bandage tightly." He arched a wondering brow. *"And you?"* he parried smoothly.

She sat back and laced her fingers. "Well, real green stump water drawn up under a full moon would make mighty fine medicine, but if I couldn't find that, I'd doctor the warts three times a day with dandelion sap. Or I'd sop them with fig juice." When Adam gave a derisive chortle, she leaned forward and piped up, "What are you laughing at? I've seen that remedy work many a time." Misty's emotions were all topsy-turvy. She recalled the rush of pleasure she'd experienced yesterday afternoon when Adam had decided to stay, yet at the same time, it nettled her when he scoffed at her cures!

"And what would you do if the fig juice didn't work," he asked.

"If it didn't work, I'd use mind medicine."

29

"Mind medicine?" he echoed, openly surprised.

She rose, and crossing her arms beneath her breasts, walked about the table. "Yep. One time I took the warts off a little girl's hand with mind medicine. I rubbed them with fig juice, then I counted the warts and tied a knot in a string for every wart she had. We buried the string, and I told her we were burying the warts, and they would go away. Sure enough, the next time I came to see her, they were gone."

He waved his hand in a gesture of dismissal. "It could have been a coincidence."

"I guess it could, but the mind holds the most powerful medicine of all"—she sighed wistfully—"and there's a special magic in these old hills. It almost floats on the air." When his doubtful gaze drifted toward her, she brushed back her hair and asked, "Is your pa a doctor, too?"

Adam searched her curious face, then purposefully placed his cup aside, feeling wonderfully relaxed in her presence. True to her prediction, she'd cured his pounding headache with mustard leaf tea, and except for occasional spells of dizziness, he felt much stronger today. "No, my father, John"—he stared to say Davenport, but bit his tongue just in time—"my father, John Hepplewhite, owns the Missouri and North Arkansas Railroad."

Misty sank to her chair, her fine features alive with amazement. "The Missouri and North Arkansas Railroad?" She whistled low under her breath. "Your pa *owns* the Missouri and North Arkansas Railroad!"

He slowly nodded his head.

"Did you tell them railroad folks at Eureka Springs who you were?"

"No . . . it didn't seem important at the time."

She blinked her eyes. "I still can't get over your pa owning a whole railroad. He must be a powerful, rich man!"

Adam leaned back and stroked his chin. "Yes, I suppose he is."

"How does one man come to own a whole railroad?" Misty asked in an awed tone.

"It all started with my grandfather," Adam said matter-of-factly. "Do you remember I told you he came from the Ozarks?"

"Yep, I remember."

"Well, when the old man came to Saint Louis, he was shrewd enough to buy a stack of cheap railroad stock. By the time my father was a young man, he was the heir to a great fortune."

"So then your grandpappy died and left it all to your pa?"

Adam sighed heavily. "Not exactly. Ezekiel and my father constantly fought about manners and money. You see, the old man never lost his country ways and John was always ashamed of him. John also kept badgering him for control of all the money." He sat back and steepled his hands. "My father bought a palatial estate on Garrick Street. He claimed he wanted to mingle with the upper crust." Adam was surprised to find himself revealing his family history to Misty, but she was so open and unpretentious that the words just rolled from his tongue.

She gave him a half smile. "Well, you still haven't told me what happened to your grandpappy."

He pulled in a deep breath. "One day Ezekiel surprised us all. He took a great part of the fortune and simply vanished."

She blinked her eyes. "He just vanished?"

"Yes . . . without a word." Adam felt a heaviness about his heart. "I suppose he was simply tired of arguing with John. Ezekiel was a spiritual person and something of an eccentric. He cared little for worldly comforts and would have been just as happy living in a shack as a mansion. A few years ago, I received an unsigned letter from the Ozarks saying Ezekiel had died and was already buried. John came to investigate, but no one knew anything about Ezekiel or the money. Although we don't know what happened to the fortune he took with him, I'm more worried about what happened to my grandfather." He sat there silently, regretting he'd never had the chance to say good-by to the old mountaineer.

Misty rose, her eyes moist with compassion, and clasped his shoulder. "Your grandpappy meant a lot to you, didn't he?"

"Yes, I suppose he did," Adam replied. "He taught me how to fight and shoot when I was a boy, and he filled my head with wonderful mountain tales." A frown tightened his brow. "John was always too busy for things like that," he added woodenly.

Misty sat down and propped her elbow on the table. "Well, *go on*. Tell me about this brother of yours."

"Warren is a few years younger than me," Adam replied. "He's supposed to be John's assistant, but he's more like his servant." He found his hand slowly tightening into a fist. "He follows John's orders implicitly."

"Maybe your pa is just trying to help him," Misty suggested kindly.

Adam observed her innocent expression. "Yes, that's what he always told us. I can hear his words now. *'Can't you see I'm trying to help you? I have social ambitions for myself and my sons!'* "

He stood and, raking a hand through his hair, paced about the cabin. "Unfortunately his ambitions for *me* include a fancy society wife—someone with *impeccable bloodlines.*"

"Sounds like he had a gal all picked out for you," Misty returned, following his movements with her eyes.

Adam paused to steal a look at her. "He does. Her name is Priscilla Lindsey."

Misty sat back, momentarily baffled, then said, "Well, if Priscilla Lindsey doesn't strike your fancy, it seems you could find *someone* you'd want to marry in Saint Louis. I've heard there's a passel of beautiful women living up there." She stood and clasped the back of her chair. "What are you looking for in a woman, anyway?"

Adam opened his heart to her, briefly wondering why he would do such an impulsive thing. "I want a woman I can love . . . a woman I can respect . . . someone who has other interests in life than fashions and mindless balls."

She tossed him a sly grin. "I'll bet this so called *trip* of yours has something to do with your pa wanting you to take a wife."

Adam rubbed the back of his neck. "Yes, John has been pressuring me to wed Priscilla," he said tightly. "A few days ago, I found out he'd actually started a rumor among his friends that we were getting married this winter," he announced, hurling out the words contemptuously.

Misty stared at him with parted lips.

"I'd been considering taking a trip for a long while," he went on, "and this seemed to be the perfect time to desert the Saint Louis social scene." A smile crept over his mouth. "Abandoning Priscilla during the holiday season should squash rumors that I'm marrying the chit."

Misty spread her slender fingers. "Couldn't you just tell everyone you weren't marrying her?"

Adam shook his head. "It's not as simple as that. I left because I was sick of girls like Priscilla and their mothers trying to trap me into marriage, and I was sick of John badgering me to give up my practice."

Her eyes darkened with surprise. "*Give up your practice?* Why in thunderation would he want you to do that? Being a doctor is a wonderful profession."

"I agree. Medicine means the world to me, and I've always dreamed of being a hospital chief-of-staff, but none of my aspirations mean anything to John," he answered roughly. "With him, my profession is a matter of expediency. You see, he's afraid Warren doesn't have the spine to take over the Missouri and North Arkansas when he's gone—he wants to groom *me* for the job."

"Seems like your pa is a bit overbearing," Misty offered with a chuckle.

Adam blew out his breath. "Yes. Sometimes he's like a man possessed, but unfortunately not like a man possessed of a great deal of understanding."

Misty walked to him, the beginning of a smile brightening her countenance. "No wonder you don't want to get word to those Saint Louis folks. You came to the mountains to get away . . . to look for your heart's ease. A lot of folks have done that . . . and a lot of folks have found it." Her face softened. "You can help me rob my honey tree this afternoon, then later we'll go by one of the mineral springs. A little fresh air will do you good."

Adam remembered Misty's words about the mountains being filled with magic. Perhaps, just perhaps, he thought, his spirits rising a bit, he *would* be lucky enough to find his heart's ease here in the Ozarks.

Chapter Two

About three o'clock that afternoon, Adam and Misty set out. Carrying a rifle and a tin pail with a lid, they headed for her honey tree. Chirruping his satisfaction, Rollo trailed behind, scampering through the dry leaves and enjoying the golden autumn sunshine.

When they were about fifty yards into the woods, Misty stopped and trailed her hand over an axe half-buried in the side of a great tree. "This oak is my great-grandpappy's witness tree," she said, her voice threaded with pride. "He put the axe into this oak over a hundred years ago. The handle is rotted away, but the axe head is still here just like it was the day he drove it into the tree."

Adam shifted the rifle and drank in the sight of her. The fresh air had pinked her cheeks with color, and when she smiled as she did now, she was a picture of wild, sensuous beauty. "Why do you call it a witness tree?" he asked, fascinated with the artless way she expressed herself.

"It's bearing witness to his claim now just like it did then," she said, her eyes shining with happiness. "Way back in 1773, Daniel Malone and his wife Mary Ann came all the way from Kentucky leading a packhorse that carried everything they had in the world."

Warmth sped through Adam's veins as he gazed at her standing there tall and graceful, her supple buckskins outlining her willowy body.

"When old Daniel saw this oak," she went on, "he knew this was the place he was looking for. He put the axe into the tree to show everybody that all the land hereabouts belonged to him. Then he threw up a half-faced camp. A few months later, he built a log cabin, and he and Mary Ann started bringing children into the world."

Her eyes took on a soft, dreamy look. "A Malone has lived on this land for over a hundred years— for as long as anybody can remember. And I wouldn't want to live anywhere else. Just thinking about living cramped up in a town gives me the all-overs. I've never seen any place that can compare with my own little cove."

She offered him a dimpled smile. "Come on," she urged with a teasing light in her eyes. "I'll take you to my honey tree, and we'll fetch us something sweet for supper!"

Lithe as a fawn, Misty set a swift pace through the woods, where the scent of decaying leaves perfumed the air and bright foliage trembled like flashes of gold. About a mile into the forest, they came to a small clearing, and he saw another ancient oak with a great hole in its side. Scarlet leaves clung to the tree's thick branches, and bees drifted lazily about the gaping opening. Misty wet her finger and stuck it in the air, testing the direction of the wind; then she put down her pail and tugged a length of netting from her deep jacket pocket.

With growing interest, Adam watched her lightly wrap the netting about her head. "How did you find this tree, anyway?" he asked.

"Last summer I just dropped a little honey on a warm rock to attract some bees," she explained, a grin sliding across her lips. "When the bees found it, they nearly went crazy trying to carry it back to their hive. I followed them and found this old hollow oak."

The soles of their boots crunching over the dry leaves, Adam and Misty walked closer to the tree. "I've got this oak marked now, and everybody in the hollow knows the honey belongs to me," she said in a pleased tone.

On closer inspection, Adam noticed she'd indeed carved her initials upon the tree. He now saw her take a pair of long leather gloves from her pocket and pull them on. "You look like a knight in medieval armor," he said jokingly. "All you need is a sword." He smiled, and spreading his arms expansively, started reciting lines as if he were on stage. "What noise is this? Give me my long sword, ho! My sword, I say! Old Montague is come."

Her questioning eyes roamed over him. "What kind of words are those? They sound like they came out of a book."

"They came from a play called *Romeo and Juliet,* written by a man named Shakespeare," Adam explained, realizing the opportunity at hand. "The story is about a young Italian couple

38

who love each other, but their families are feuding."

She passed him an astonished look. "Feuding?" she echoed after a little hesitation. "Well, that Romeo and Juliet had a problem, all right. Feuds are serious business—real serious business."

Adam noted her disapproving eyes, thinking this was the first time he'd seen her frown.

Then her mood changing as swiftly as a child's, and her face brightened once more. "And all this time I thought the Ozarks was the only place where we had that sort of trouble."

"No," he commented, giving silent thanks that he'd held back his real name, "they have that kind of trouble everyplace." Privately he thought, *And if you only knew it, so do we.*

Suddenly a bee darted from the hole and buzzed around Misty's lustrous hair, making her duck. "There's a whole passel of bees in that tree, huddled up together in a winter hive keeping warm," she cried. "If they fly in the wrong direction, I'll need more than a sword to keep from getting stung!"

Adam leaned the rifle against a tree trunk and crossed his arms. "And how *are* you planning on getting the honey without disturbing all those bees?" he asked, amused by her determination.

She knelt and picked up a saucer-shaped piece of bark and filled it with twigs, then added green pine needles atop the dry twigs. "I'm going to smoke them out," she answered, reaching into her pocket for a long wooden match. Striking it on a rock, she lit the kindling, which burned rapidly. When the flames reached the green pine needles, sweet-smelling smoke billowed up from the bark container.

"Better stand back," she warned, giving Adam a saucy look. "When those bees get a whiff of this smoke, they'll come sailing out of that tree like a bull going through a cobweb." At the oak, she put the smoking bark on the ground just beneath the opening, then raced back to stand by his side.

Bluish smoke soon floated into the tree and, wafting outward, gently drifted toward them. Seconds later, a horde of buzzing bees streaked from the oak and darted into the woods. A few smoke-addled insects still hovered about the tree.

Adam chuckled. "Very impressive, indeed. How did you know the bees wouldn't come in our direction?"

Her eyes kindled with satisfaction. "By the way the wind was blowing," she replied lightly. "They always fly away from the smoke."

Adam felt a great respect for her ingenuity and her knowledge of the woods, and sensed she had great wisdom about the important things in life. And how refreshing she was compared to the dull society debutantes his father tried to force upon him! They were all so stiff and boring, so unlike this mountain girl, who was not only amusing but mentally stimulating. With Adam, women had always been delightful diversions to enjoy and cast aside. Now new emotions stirred within him—emotions he didn't understand.

When Misty had removed her netting veil, she and Adam went to the tree and stamped out the smoking twigs. Then she gingerly lifted out the dripping honeycomb, dropped it into the pail, and snapped on a lid. "We'd better be getting out of here," she said, swinging her gleaming hair about her shoulders. "Those bees are stupefied from the smoke right now, but they'll begin drifting back soon."

After Misty and Adam had gathered their things, they took a different path through the woods, with the mischievous raccoon waddling behind. Soon they came to a little spring, which gurgled from the side of a small bluff and formed a lapping pool beneath it. With an air of pleasure, Misty fell to her knees and dipped her fingers into the sparkling water.

Adam knelt beside her and drank from his hand, thinking the clear, icy water had a wonderful taste. Interest perked through him as he remembered his grandfather's words about the springs' reported healing powers, and he thought of his own family. Lord, how he wished there *was* some magic here, some magic in the water to restore Warren's broken spirit and bring John to understand that love was more important than money or social position.

When she'd quenched her thirst, Misty walked to an oak and sat down, leaning against the wide trunk. Her mind alive with questions, she studied the man who had entered her life like a comet plunging from the sky. Lord, he was an imposing figure . . . broad at the shoulder and lean at the hip, with dark eyes that could shake any woman's heart. Why had fate chosen to put this big-city doctor with his easy manners and fine way of talking into her life? she wondered. Surely a man such as himself had loved many women— elegant city women who made her seem plain and countrified.

All at once she realized that she'd been staring at him, and when he glanced her way, she nervously lowered her eyes. Still, when he rose from the pool, she couldn't help notice how his snug breeches emphasized the strength of his powerful thighs, and she blushed, adding to her embarrassment.

With a nonchalant grace, he strode toward the tree, then eased down beside her, his muscles rippling under the buckskin jacket.

Struck with his preoccupied expression, she sent him an absent smile. "There's over fifty springs hereabouts. The Osage Indians say the waters have healing powers and can make ailing folks get well," she informed him, feeling warm and flustered. "I do believe there isn't any water better than Ozark spring water."

Silent, Adam tossed a pebble toward the spring, and Misty studied his clear-cut profile with a twinge of concern. "Are you thinking about Saint Louis?" she ventured. "Are you worrying about that brother of yours?"

Slowly turning, he looked at her, a hint of sadness gathering in his eyes. "Yes," he answered roughly. He scooped up another pebble and hurled it into the water.

Misty put her hand on his huge shoulder and felt the tension in his muscles; there must be something terribly wrong between his father and brother and himself. *Despite the great family fortune, they are all unhappy,* she thought sadly. With a tilt of her head, she smiled making an attempt to lift his spirits. "While you're in the mountains, just leave your past in the flatlands."

He regarded her again, his eyes lighting with humor. "Just leave my past in the flatlands?"

She laughed throatily. "Yep. Just like it was a sack of 'taters!" She relaxed against the oak and gave him a slow grin. "You know, I think getting knocked on the head and marooned here was the best thing that ever happened to you. You're a real lucky man!"

He studied her with amused wonder. "What do you mean by that?"

"I mean, lots of folks would like to forget their troubles, but they can't get away from them. It seems it would be a great easement to know you were free from everybody and everything for a while." She searched his twinkling eyes. "What do you think about that?"

He leaned close, a dazzling smile streaking across his sun-bronzed face. "I think you're very wise," he said quietly, caressing her shoulder and sending tingles down her arm.

His deep-timbered voice held a tinge of sensuality, and she found his nearness both disquieting and arousing. As their gazes locked, excitement swirled in the pit of her stomach, and she felt her emotions welling up within her, ready to spill forth. In the distance, she could hear the lapping spring and bird calls enlivening the air . . . and a sensual magic lingered about them like the aroma of the pine-scented forest itself. Despite the risks their involvement presented, she felt herself almost irresistibly drawn to him.

Her senses reeling, she noticed the glint in his eyes, which prompted feelings she didn't want to face. "A-Are you tired? do you want to start back?" she stammered.

A roguish grin hung on the corner of Adam's mouth, then he trailed his fingers down her arm and tightened them around her wrist in a gesture that made her tremble with pleasure. "I'm feeling fine," he said huskily. "But sitting here with you for a while longer would make me feel even better." He was so close that the heat of his body washed over her, and in his rugged features, she noticed a hunger that reflected her own.

He lifted her hand and pressed his warm lips against her fingers, leaving her speechless. Confusion swept through her. Had his fine words disarmed her? "What are you doing?" she finally managed.

He placed feather-light kisses over her wrist and up her arm. "Kissing your phalanges, and your carpus, and your radius, and your ulna, of course."

A blush stung her cheeks and she started to turn her head, but he caught her chin. Feeling soft and vulnerable inside, she met his passion-heavy eyes. She anticipated that his lips would brush hers, and she shivered with fear and delight, craving the kiss, but at the same time overcome with shyness.

A sigh caught in her throat. Lord, if only she knew more about this good-looking flatlander. She already believed him to be the finest gentleman she'd ever met, yet a stubborn, practical part of her mind warned her that she was in dangerous territory. Perhaps he was only toying with her affections. How could this well-educated stranger, who doubtless had a host of lovely debutantes vying for his attentions, have any feelings for a simple mountain girl like herself?

Suddenly there was a loud trill at the spring, claiming her attention. Glancing that way, she saw that Rollo had dislodged a frog from his hiding place. He looked so comical as he followed the splashing frog through the water, trying to catch it, that she and Adam both laughed.

When the frog had escaped the raccoon, Misty glanced back at Adam, noticing a look of regret in his eyes. She felt a rush of relief that the romantic encounter had been interrupted, yet at the same time, just the thought of what might have been sent sweet tremors through her body.

Disturbing thoughts plaguing her mind, she fought the wave of passionate feelings his closeness aroused. She must be careful . . . so very careful. He was a city man and would always be a city man. Why should she surrender to his arms when she knew she could never leave the mountains with him? Worse yet, what if he stole her heart, then returned to the city, leaving her yearning for him the rest of her days?

Hot and flushed, she smiled weakly, then rose and picked up her pail with a quaking hand. "I think we'd better be going," she said, her voice unsteady. "It'll be getting dark soon, and we need to shoot something for supper tonight."

Adam stood. Looking into her eyes, he knew they'd only been a heartbeat away from a kiss. With a resigned sigh, he realized that the golden moment could not be forced, but was bound to come again. Sensing her unease, he guided her away from the tree. "You make hunting sound as easy as a trip to the butcher shop," he remarked with wonder.

The wind stirred and Misty's hair blew about her like polished amber. "It is. The forest is full of game just there for the taking."

As they returned to the woods, walking side by side, Adam studied her young, finely molded body and felt a shudder of excitement pass through him. She was so intelligent, so feisty and free-spirited, so warm and unpredictable. A man would have to be made of stone not to appreciate how well that softly curved body filled out her buckskins. Totally innocent of sophisticated ways, this enticing girl

Sonya Birmingham

had an extravagant beauty that intrigued him mightily.

They followed a little creek that babbled through the cove, its waters bright with color from the overhanging trees crowding its shores. The cool air was redolent with the scent of moss and moist earth, and as they strolled along, Misty pointed at a clump of poison ivy. "Look at that, Mr. Saint Louis-Big-City-Doctor—*poison ivy*. What would you do for a hard case of poison ivy?" she asked teasingly.

It amused Adam that she constantly tested his medical knowledge, always hinting that hers was better. "I'd use oatmeal baths and cold compresses," he replied matter-of-factly.

She rolled her eyes heavenward. "*Oatmeal baths and cold compresses?* Is that all you can think of?"

Adam cocked a brow. "And pray tell what is wrong with that prescription, Doctor Malone?"

If looks could kill, he'd have been a dead man.

"It isn't enough—that's what's wrong with it," Misty answered loftily. "I'd roll the patient in hardwood ashes, bathe him in buttermilk, then give him a hard rub-down with vinegar, raw rhubarb, and horse pee." She smiled proudly. "I'd give him the full treatment!"

Adam burst out laughing. "Yes, I'm sure you would. I'm just thankful the poor devil didn't have shingles."

Not long after they passed the poison ivy, a squirrel scampered across the trail and rustled up a tree. Adam shouldered the rifle and took aim, but Misty stood on tiptoe and tapped his arm. "Let me show you how we do it mountain-style," she said with a wink. After setting down the

46

pail, she braced the rifle butt against her shoulder and, holding her breath, squeezed the trigger. A moment later, the squirrel toppled from the tree like a falling nut.

Adam chuckled. "I would have sworn you missed him."

"I did," she said mirthfully. "I hit the limb right beside him and *barked* him out of the tree. It was the concussion, not the bullet, that killed the little critter."

During the next half hour, Misty claimed three more squirrels, and as she and Adam rounded a bend, her cabin came into sight, the surrounding pines standing dark against a sky sprinkled with stars that gleamed and winked like a swirl of sparkling diamonds. A chill rode the air, and from the woods came the soft, quavering call of a whippoorwill.

She looked up at Adam, and with a warm grin suggested, "Let's go home and fry up this meat. I'll make us some biscuits to go with the honey, and after supper, we'll have a drink or two of my applejack. It's crystal clear, simon pure, double run, and three times twisted." She took a deep breath. "And it's pretty strong stuff!"

"Lord, you make liquor, too?" Adam asked in an astonished tone.

Her expression brimmed with amusement. "Sure. Nearly everybody hereabouts makes some kind of spirits, you know."

"What you're planning sounds like a special occasion," he remarked lightly. "Is there some local holiday I don't know about?"

She glanced at him, and even in the gloom he could tell her eyes held a glint of mischief. "There sure is. I'm gonna name you tonight."

47

"Name me? I told you my name was Hershel Hepplewhite."

A wry smile touched her lips. "Pardon me saying so, but that's about the *ugliest* name I ever heard. I'd hate mighty much to keep calling you Hershel much longer 'cause it doesn't fit you at all." Her eyes flashed with humor. "Before the night is over, you're gonna have a good mountain name!"

Misty and Adam had just finished supper, and the delicious scent of fried meat and warm biscuits still lingered in the cabin. The cozy room was illuminated by the fire's glow and the light of a grease lamp, no more than a small bowl full of oil with a twisted wick hanging over the side of the vessel. As the pair sat talking and drinking applejack, a loud crash reverberated from the other side of the room.

With startled eyes, Misty rose from her chair and stared at the hearth, where she'd placed the honey pail on a keg for safekeeping. "I'll be flamboozled, you're the orneriest coon I've ever seen!" she cried, hurrying to the overturned pail, where, with a rapturous look in his eyes, Rollo licked honey from his paws.

Adam had noticed that Rollo was very sensitive to Misty's tone of voice, and he chuckled as the abashed raccoon lowered his head and padded away from the sticky mess.

Misty swept up the animal by the scruff of the neck and carried him toward the cabin door. "Just truckle on down to the creek and clean yourself up," she ordered, opening the door and putting him outside. "And don't be coming back 'til you've got all that honey off yourself."

After closing the door, she cleaned the pail and stowed it away beside some cooking staples.

With a weary sigh, she returned to the table and reclaimed her seat. "Sometimes that coon can sure be troublesome! He's always getting into things and he prowls at night."

"That's because he's nocturnal," Adam explained.

A blush crept across her cheeks, making her even prettier. "He is? I thought he was just a coon. One thing about him, he's been around folks so much, most of the time he stays awake during the day just like us."

"Where did you get him?" Adam inquired with a chuckle.

"I found him in a den tree near the creek one spring a few years back. I guess his mama and brothers had ventured out and got killed." She shook her head. "When I first saw him, I thought he wouldn't make it either. He was whimpering and crying, so I stuck him in my jacket and brought him home and fed him on a rag tit sopped in warm milk." She chuckled softly. "He sucked that rag like he was starving to death. Pretty soon he began to pick up, then he started getting fat and sassy and following me around like a regular lap baby. I named him Rollo 'cause he's so roly-poly."

She grinned and Adam felt his chest fill with an unexpected warmth. As blithe as a ray of golden sunlight, this young woman who was really no more than a stranger had managed to work her way into his emotions without even trying. "How did you get *your* name?" he asked, suppressing an urge to touch her mass of silken hair that glinted auburn in the firelight.

A warm look came into her eyes. "Well, my granny named me three days after I was born.

Y'see, Mama died birthing me, and Papa was terribly grieved at the time. My granny said there was no use grieving, that everybody had to go on living the best they could. That's what Mama would have wanted."

Charmed with her drawling voice, Adam crossed his arms, leaned back, and listened to her story.

"On the day when they were fixing to bury Mama," she went on, "it was so misty they could hardly see to walk to the graveyard. Granny had me wrapped up in a blanket carrying me, and that's when she thought of naming me Misty. Papa said he liked it fine. He thought Misty Malone had a right pretty ring to it."

She ran a graceful hand through her hair. "From the time I was little, Papa and Ezra taught me to ride and hunt and shoot and do all sort of boy things. Granny allowed it wasn't a natural raising for a girl, but Papa said I'd be better off for it. Granny taught me her healing ways and how to do woman chores. She talked about the Good Book a lot, and if there's something good in me, it was my granny that put it there."

Her eyes soft with memories, she sipped a little of her applejack. "It took a lot out of Papa when Mama died, and he started failing more every passing year. He went to join her when I was ten years old. Life was a struggle without him, but Ezra was fifteen by then and big enough to work alongside full-grown men cutting logs."

She traced a fingertip over the scarred table top. "We were dirt poor, but we didn't think of ourselves as being poor." She gave him a gentle smile. "Granny and I tended a little garden and we had potatoes and carrots and onions laid away, and sun-dried fruit, and chickens and a milk cow. Ezra is a good shot, and he kept us stocked with meat." She sighed heavily. "Granny's gone now, so there's just the two of us," she finished, her lips trembling. Everything was quiet for a moment, and a suggestion of pain shadowed her eyes.

Her words about losing a grandparent made Adam think of Ezekiel, and at that moment, he promised himself that he would find the old man's grave before he left the mountains.

He grinned quickly, wanting to cheer her up. "Have you ever wanted to visit a city . . . to be a fine lady just for a day?"

She shook back her hair, showing her white neck. "Wearing pretty dresses might be fun for a little while," she said in a brighter voice, "but even if I had slathers of money, I'd get bored just sitting in a house all the time." Her eyes glistened with emotion. "Here in the Ozarks, a chilly wind moves down from the pines in the fall, and the oaks blaze with color like a leaping fire. And in the spring, when all the world comes to surge, everything turns a soft green, and the scent of dogwoods lies so heavy and sweet in the hollows, it nearly takes your breath away."

She looked directly into his eyes. "I'd miss that, living in a town, and I don't think Rollo would fit into city living real good either. I've never heard of a coon living in the city."

Adam laughed. "No, I haven't either."

She stood and moved to his side, her curves swelling beneath her buckskins. "I saw a big town once. Ezra took me to Berryville. The streets were crowded and everyone was hurrying and going no place." She tilted a brow. "Seems town folks are living so fast, they don't have time to notice a cardinal bright against the snow like we do in the mountains."

"You make the Ozarks sound like Utopia."

She quirked her brow. "Is that someplace in the flatlands?"

He clasped her slim fingers, thinking they were as soft as a child's. "No. It's a made-up place," he answered softly. "A place that a man once wrote about where life approaches perfection."

The touch of his hand sent Misty's pulses racing, and as he floated a bold gaze over her, something intense flared up within her as it had earlier at the spring. "I'd like to read what that man wrote about this Utopia town," she remarked in a shy voice. "Sounds like it would be a right interesting place."

Adam stood and moved his hand up her arm, leaving her skin tingling. "I hope you *can* read about it someday," he said quietly. "Where did you learn to read? From the Bible?"

"How'd you guess that?" she asked, still a little shaky from his touch. She slipped her hand from his, then returned to the table with a tattered copy of the Scriptures, eager to begin finding him a name. "Granny taught me reading from the Good Book. 'Course sometimes I still get tangled up on the Ammonites and the Jebusites and the Amlekites. Those Children of Israel were always wandering around on the desert fighting with some of those folks."

She creased open the New Testament and studied his warmly erotic eyes. "I know how to find you a name. We'll go to the Begets." She sat down and ruffled through the book's dog-eared pages.

Adam sank onto his chair. "The Begets?" he echoed, a stunned look on his face. "I never heard of that book of the Bible before."

She narrowed her eyes at him. *"Didn't your granny teach you anything? It isn't a book, it's a place in Matthew. You know, Abraham begat Isaac, and Isaac begat Jacob and so on. There's a whole passel of good names in there. We might find something you like."* She raced her finger down the slick page. "How do you like Amminadab?"

He bit off a smile. *"Amminadab is better than Hershel?"*

She waved her hand impatiently. "Well, how about Rehoboam or Zerubbabel?"

He shot her an amused frown. "Perhaps something a little shorter?"

With growing irritation, she sat forward and ruffled the thin pages. "All right then, if you want something plumb modern, how about Obadiah or Zephaniah or Zechariah? They're all good names."

Adam's frown turned into a scowl.

She snapped the Bible closed. "It seems you're a speck hard to please. It isn't every man that gets to help name himself."

As Adam moved, the fire flared up, and a shaft of golden light fell across him, highlighting his glossy black hair.

Happiness singing through her, Misty rose to her feet. "I know what I'm going to name you. The Lord just gave me a sign!"

Adam's brows shot up. "He did?"

"He sure did. The firelight just shone on your head while I was holding the Good Book in my hands. It was like the Lord was showing me your hair special. I'm going to name you Raven, 'cause your hair is black as a raven's wing. 'Course Raven isn't a Bible name, less you count the raven that flew out of Noah's ark, but I think it fits you like a new boot." She blinked thoughtfully. "What do you think about being called Raven?"

A faint smile curved his lips. "Raven. I like it. It sounds like a name Sir Walter Scott might have used."

"Is he a flatlander, too?"

Adam laughed deeply. "No, he was an Englishman who wrote books." He pushed back from the table and flashed her a serious look. "Am I to be just Raven? What about a last name?"

"You don't need one," she said with a careless shrug. "Raven is strong and good, and that's enough."

"Don't you think people might ask—"

"No," she answered flatly. "Plenty of people have come to the mountains carrying one name, and they weren't asked any questions. If a stranger isn't a federal man, mountain folks are right trusting toward him."

Guilt shafted through Adam as he digested her words, and he stifled an urge to tell her his last name was Davenport. Then, remembering her reaction at the honey tree when he'd mentioned feuding, he decided he shouldn't. After all, why should he upset her when he wouldn't be in Red Oak Hollow that long anyway? He smiled to himself. If it pleased the girl to call him Raven, what was the harm in humoring her?

For a while, he and Misty sat at the table and talked of the people who lived in the hollow. Then, as the fire crackled low, Rollo returned to the cabin and scratched on the door. After Misty let him in, he padded to his box by the hearth and, with a satisfied *chirr*, climbed in and settled down for sleep.

Later, as Adam lay in Ezra's bed, he clasped his arms behind his head and, staring up at the darkness, listened to the popping fire. Warm and relaxed, he recalled the magical moment by the spring, remembering how tantalizing Misty had looked with her eyes closed and her rosy lips slightly parted seconds before their kiss was interrupted.

He grinned as he thought of her naming him Raven. Lord, what a charming little baggage she really was! Thoroughly amused, he voiced the name several times, liking it more and more each time.

As he was drifting into sleep, he heard Misty turn over in her bed and softly say, "Raven, you know something?"

"What?" he replied gently.

"You're mine now 'cause I named you. Granny said when you name something, it's yours then. I named Rollo when I took him in, and now I've named you too."

Adam chuckled softly. "Good night, Misty."

"Night, Raven."

And from that moment, Adam Davenport started thinking of himself as simply Raven.

Chapter Three

Raven, who'd worn his mountain name for almost a day, shouldered Ezra's rifle, took aim, and squeezed the trigger. Dark smoke blossomed in the air, and the weapon's retort echoed through the hills. With some pride, he saw that he'd hit the bottle Misty had placed on a stump to test his shooting skill.

Standing in front of the cabin by Lukie, she swept a mirthful gaze over him. "That was pretty good shooting for a city man," she remarked. "I suppose you can be trusted to bring in your share of squirrels this afternoon." She'd been in a teasing mood all day, and a wry smile tugged at her lips. "How did you learn to shoot like that, anyway?"

Raven cradled the rifle and shrugged negligently. "I've already told you—Ezekiel taught me. In his day, the old man was quiet a marksman."

An impish grin raced over Misty's mouth. "Well, you may be good, but I'll bet you can't hit a nail at sixty yards," she remarked in a challenging tone.

"Of course he can't," Lukie chortled. "There's only one or two men in all the Ozarks that can do that!"

Raven fought an urge to smile as he scanned the scrawny, red-headed girl, who today wore a calico dress with a full skirt and scuffed boots. For some reason he couldn't understand, she would often look at him and blush, then giggle and cover her face with her hands.

He was feeling especially good today and enjoyed bantering with the girls. "Actually, I've made that shot several times myself," he commented, a smile pursing his lips.

The fringe on her buckskins swinging, Misty sauntered toward him, pointing her finger. "Wait a minute," she said, punctuating every few words with a tap on his chest. "Are you telling me that a Saint Louis-Big-City-Doctor like you can shoot better than a hillman? How can *you* do something like that?"

He swept a slow gaze over her, purposefully eyeing her figure. "I assure you, I can do lots of things better than a hillman. As they say, practice makes perfect with a weapon—and I've had *lots* of practice."

The comment's strong sexual overtones brought a blush to Misty's face, but making a quick recovery, she gave him a cheeky grin. "All righty— if a man makes a claim like that, I figure he ought to back it up," she prodded, her own meaning plain. She pointed to a post about sixty yards in the distance. "See that post with the big nail sticking out of the top?" she asked.

He narrowed his eyes against the sunlight, then nodded. "I see it."

"Well, we'll just see how handy with a weapon you really are. I'll bet you a whole silver dollar you can't hit that nail head."

Lukie giggled and shook her head. "He can't do that. I've never seen *anybody* do that."

Raven slowly shouldered the rifle, then shot, sending another retort through the hills. When the acrid-smelling smoke cleared, the amused expression had faded from Misty's face to be replaced by a look of wonder, and she whistled low under her breath. "You nicked out a piece of wood next to the nail," she exclaimed in a shaky voice. "I can hardly believe it. I've never got that close myself. Ezra neither."

After taking careful aim, Raven shot again, and as the gun barked, a bullet nipped off the nail head with a loud metallic *twang*. "You owe me a silver dollar," he said, looking at Misty, who gasped softly.

"Well, I'll be flamboozled," she breathed. "You've done it, sure as a goose goes barefoot! I've heard of it being done at sixty yards, but I've never seen it." She stared at him with puzzled eyes. "Why'd you let me shoot those squirrels yesterday when you could have done it yourself?"

Raven grinned. "I was having too much fun watching you."

Giggling with excitement, Lukie came up to him. "That's fine shootin'—the finest shootin' I ever saw. If you was in a turkey shoot, you'd win the first prize for sure!"

Misty placed a chicken egg on the post and Raven shot it off; then, five yards farther out, she put a bottle on a stump and he also shot that. For ten minutes, the target practice went on, and all the while the rifle's sound reverberated through the cove.

As Raven paused to reload, he heard the sound of trotting horses and, turning about, spotted four scruffy-looking men riding into the clearing, trailed by a pair of yapping coon dogs. Wearing floppy hats that shaded their keen eyes, the bearded mountaineers were unkempt and loose-jointed, and their faded overalls and broken boots showed signs of much wear.

Without waiting for an invitation, the oldest and most slovenly of the men dismounted and expelled a stream of tobacco juice on the ground. Gray stubble covered his jowls, and his fingernails were dirty and broken. Giving a sour grin that showed rotten teeth, he narrowed his eyes suspiciously. "What's all the shootin' about?" he inquired, tilting his large head, which seemed a little too big for his body. "We was goin' to the mill and heared a rifle barkin' over here."

Misty drew herself up importantly, and her snapping green eyes told Raven she was well acquainted with the man. "Nothing special is happening, Sloppy," she answered firmly, pausing after the sentence to give her words authority. "Raven was just shooting a few targets."

Sloppy Brewster threw Raven a suspicious glance. "Folks seen you and Misty in the woods together. We've been a-wonderin' who you was. You a flatlander, come to the hills lookin' for somethin'?"

Raven appraised the slack-jawed men and noticed something flickering far back in their eyes. *They've come to challenge an outsider,* he thought, noting the look of marked distrust on their lean faces. The situation was not good—not good at all.

Before he could reply, Misty raised her chin and announced, "Lukie and me found Raven after he'd been attacked on the road." She spoke bravely, but he heard a quaver in her voice. "He's a doctor and he's from Saint Louis."

The men nudged one another and guffawed with laughter.

"Sure he ain't just funnin' with you, gal?" Sloppy asked, leaning forward.

Seething with anger, Misty stepped forward to confront the worst bully in Red Oak Hollow, but she felt Raven's warm hand on her arm, firmly holding her back. A slight smile hovered on his lips and he looked as cool as ice, but she could sense the tension within him.

A disparaging laugh burst from Sloppy's loose mouth. "Let's see you shoot, mister," he jibed, winking at his companions. "I never seen a flatlander that could hit nothin' yet."

"All right," Raven answered in an easy manner, his eyes narrowing on Sloppy's red face. "What do you want me to hit?"

The hillman pointed a grubby finger toward the post. "See if you can hit that there nail," he taunted.

With great deliberation, Raven shouldered the rifle, squeezed the trigger, and zinged off the remainder of the nail. His eyes twinkling with amusement, he scanned Sloppy's startled face, then purposefully handed the rifle to Misty.

After a second of stunned silence, a murmur rippled among the woodsmen. "Why, he ain't a doctor! I never seen a doctor shoot like that. He's a revenuer man!" one of them called out.

The accusation hung heavily in the air, and the raw hostility Misty saw in Sloppy's eyes made her throat tighten.

"He's a federal man, and he's come to the holler to spy on us—to sniff out stills," he said heatedly. "You done took in a revenuer, gal!" His eyes like chips of glass, he strode toward Raven, balling his hand into a fist. "You ain't no doctor. You're a federal man, ain't you!" he thundered, taking a swing at Raven.

Quickly, Raven blocked the attack, then slammed his fist against the man's jaw with a loud *crack*. He followed it with a blow to the hillman's soft gut, sending him stumbling backward. When Sloppy regained his footing, he lunged forward, but Raven rammed another sharp blow to his face, and he fell to the earth like a heavy sack of grain. The mountaineer clutched his nose and groaned as blood squeezed out between his fingers. His pride at stake, he clumsily struggled to his feet, only to be met with another powerful blow to the stomach.

As the fight continued, Raven had the best of Sloppy, but then, one by one, the rest of the woodsmen piled on him, swinging at him from all sides while the dogs barked and yapped in the background. Even with the added men hammering their fists into Raven, he managed to hold his own for a long time, but finally by sheer weight and numbers they pulled him down.

Her eyes wide with fear, Lukie danced around the rolling ball of men on the ground, crying and wringing her hands. "They're killin' Raven. They're killin' him!"

Sonya Birmingham

A sick rage rose within Misty like a scalding tide. She'd be damned if she'd let this rabble intimidate her and beat Raven to death! Lifting the rifle to her shoulder, she rushed to the men and shot above their heads.

As the sound of the bullet shattered the air, the mountaineers fell atop Raven, then glared up at her with stunned faces.

"You ridge-runners stop beating Raven or I'm gonna shoot you!" she cried, her voice quavering with disdain.

Slowly getting to his knees, Sloppy hollered, "Hoooeee, listen to that, boys. She's a-fixin' to shoot us. I'm shore skeared. Ain't you!"

They all hooted with laughter.

Misty, shaking with rage, suddenly cracked Sloppy on the side of the head with the rifle barrel and knocked him to the ground. She felt all hot and sickish inside, but she knew she couldn't show it. The others stared at her in open-mouthed wonder as she slapped the rifle butt against her shoulder once again. "I've had a churnful of you peckerwoods," she cried, hearing the erratic throbbing of her own heart in her ears. "Just pick up and ride out of here, or I'm sending the next bullet through Sloppy's head!"

Bright blood trickling down his brow, the mountaineer struggled to his knees and clasped his head. "You're a right gutty gal, but somebody needs to give you a good tannin', missy!"

Misty swallowed the lump in her throat and stepped forward, cocking the rifle. From the corner of her eye she could see Raven struggling against the men and Lukie trembling with fear. "Ezra will be back soon," Misty warned in a loud voice. "Why don't you take that up with him?"

One of the other woodsmen grabbed Sloppy's arm. "Let's go. We don't want to be foolin' with Ezra Malone. He can whup any man in the holler!"

The bully stood and waved his beefy arm. "All right, come on, boys," he growled. "We'll be leavin'—*at least for now.*" As he lumbered away, slapping the dust from his hat, he wheeled and jabbed a finger at Raven, who rose to his knees. "You just watch yourself, 'cause we ain't through with you yet, federal man!" Then, his eyes hot and angry, he glared at Misty. "A different story would have been told here if we'd been huntin' and had our rifles. You better lay low, gal, 'cause I've got a score to settle with you." He gave a dark, ugly laugh. "Somethin' real bad may jest happen to you before that brother of yours gets home!"

After the ruffians had mounted and galloped away, relief flooded through Misty, leaving her limp and weak-kneed. With trembling steps, she moved to Raven, who was on his feet, wiping blood from his mouth. "Come on," she said hoarsely, tears pricking her eyes. "Let's get you into the cabin so I can patch you up. You look like you tangled with the wrong end of a wildcat."

With Misty on one side of him and Lukie on the other, he limped toward the cabin. "You know," he replied, with a grin, "I always wondered which was the *right* end of a wildcat."

Several nights later, Raven lounged in a chair by the glowing hearth and watched Misty play her dulcimer. It was late, and the grease lamp being extinguished, the room was awash in dancing shadows and filled with the sweet scent of wood smoke. Her eyes shining with concentration, she sat on the braided rug with Rollo, who was already asleep, snuggled by her side.

With nimble fingers, she strummed the instrument with a turkey quill while depressing the melody string with a small stick. Flooding the cabin with its sweet music, the dulcimer produced a lush plaintive sound, reminiscent of a harp.

After the poignant ballad was finished, she put the instrument aside and fixed a soft gaze on Raven. "Ezra bought me this dulcimer with money he earned cutting logs. He gave it to me one Christmas when I was a little girl. That was 'Mist on the Mountain' I just played."

"You seem to know all the notes very well."

She skimmed a white hand over Rollo, then looked up again. "There aren't any notes on a dulcimer . . . you just play it," she replied simply.

Raven chuckled. "Are all the Malones musically inclined?"

"Yep. Uncle Fuzzy over in Russell's Hollow plays a fiddle just about as old as he is, and his wife, Aunt Izzy, plays a banjo. And Ezra can make a guitar cluck like a hen, if he has a mind to."

She leaned to the side and placed her pet in his box, then, straightening, scanned Raven with concerned eyes. "Sit down on this rag rug and I'll get my potions and doctor your face again," she suggested, patting a place beside her. She rose gracefully and gazed down at him with warm eyes. "You're healing pretty good, but you still have a ways to go."

Raven moved to the rug and watched her as she brought a little leather satchel bulging with bottles of homemade potions. The first night after the beating, she'd lovingly doctored his cuts and scrapes with yellowroot salve from the same satchel and given him moonshine to ease his pain.

Raven thought of Sloppy and hardened his jaw. He realized that the bully had only left because Misty was holding a rifle on him. He was the type to arrange an accident for her in the woods, then deny all knowledge of it—or worse yet, come back to her cabin.

Like an unexpected piece of bad news, Sloppy and his gang had rearranged Raven's life, making it imperative that he linger in the hollow until Ezra's return. As the object of his wrath, Misty needed protection that could not be provided by Lukie and her aged grandfather. Raven realized that he might be jeopardizing her reputation by staying with her, but had decided that under the circumstances, her safety was more important.

As she dabbed the cool medicine on his face with a bit of wadded rag, he casually asked, "What do you think about me staying with you until Ezra gets back?"

Her eyes wide, she dropped her hand and locked gazes with him. "If you think you need to protect me from Sloppy and that bunch of no-accounts, you can forget it. I'm not afraid of those peckerwoods!"

Raven chuckled lightly, thinking she'd reacted just as he expected. "I wasn't thinking about Sloppy," he lied. "I thought I might teach you some medical procedures. Give you a little—"

"And what's wrong with my doctoring now?" she interrupted hotly. "Everybody for miles around says I'm the best herb doctor in the hollow."

"And that you are," he quickly added. "But I can teach you how to suture a wound properly and—"

"I already know," she cut in, dabbing at his face.

"Can you do it so it will hardly leave a scar?"

She stopped and slowly hung her head. "Well, I . . ." She trailed off.

He lifted her chin, studying her obstinate face. "And I can teach you to set a bone properly and tell if a child is malnourished and so many other things that would help the people here. Don't you want to learn those things?"

Her eyes sparked with interest, and Raven could tell that she really wanted him to stay, but the war of whose medicine was the best still raged between them. "Perhaps you could teach me about some of your herbs," he said to ease her pride. "I didn't get much of that kind of thing in medical school."

She ran a speculative gaze over him, her countenance brightening. "Sure, I could do that. I could teach you about every herb in the forest if you want to know."

"Good, then that's settled," he said with a ring of finality, relieved that she'd agreed to the proposal.

The wind had risen, making the temperature drop outside, and as Misty returned to her work, the cooling cabin made popping sounds. "Hear that noise?" she asked, smoothing medicine over his bruised cheek. "Some folks would say that was ghosts, but I know it isn't."

"People here are steeped in superstitions, aren't they?"

With a sigh, she stoppered the potion and turned to put it and the rag away. "Yep. Lots of people won't set out a cedar tree, 'cause they say when it grows tall enough to cast a shadow long as a coffin, somebody in the family will die," she answered, closing the satchel.

66

She reached into the wood box and tossed a pine knot into the flames, making it flare and light up the cabin for a few moments. Then, her eyes full of wonder, she glanced sideways at him. "There are stories about ghost panthers and mad dogs and all such like. And folks believe it's bad luck to rock an empty chair or sing before breakfast or cut a baby's hair till he's a year old." Her face softened and she gave him a smile that touched his heart. "But it's real good luck if you see a red bird on Christmas day or find a cricket in your cabin."

As shadows engulfed the room once more, he looked at her childlike face, realizing that the Ozark people were reverent of both religion and superstition, that it was wound about their hearts and could not be separated from them. He reached out and took her small hand in his. "Do you believe all these things?" he asked quietly, feeling the deepening intimacy between them as he had at the spring.

She chuckled. "I believe a person can make himself sick by his thinking, and if you believe in a cure hard enough, there's a good chance of it working. The mountain folks are bedcord strong on signs, and lots believe that life is all laid out for them, that there isn't anything they can do to change it."

He searched her delicate face, now gilded with golden firelight. "What do you think about that?" he asked, grazing his thumb over her soft hand.

"I think a person *can* change his life. Otherwise the Lord wouldn't have given him hands to work with and a mind to think with and a heart to hope with."

Enjoying the fire's warmth, Raven let her smooth hand slip away from him and stretched out on the rug, thoroughly amused at her tales. "What do the mountaineers talk about when they've recounted all the ghost tales?" he asked, crossing his arms behind his head.

Her eyes became large. "They talk about the feuds, of course. I guess there's more feuds in these mountains than anyplace else in the whole world."

Raven's heart pumped a little faster, and slowly sitting up, he reached out and cupped her chin. "And who are the Malones feuding with?" he asked, eager to hear her reply.

"The Davenports, of course. Remember how I told you about Daniel Malone coming here with his wife and marking a witness tree?"

He brushed back a stray curl on her cheek and nodded, anticipating the story he knew was to come. He'd heard his grandfather recite the tale many times and wondered how the Malones viewed the original incident.

"Well, way back then, Daniel Malone and Jeremiah Davenport began feuding over a little meadow that snaked out of Daniel's land onto Jeremiah's land. It was on the west side of the creek, and most folks accepted that everything to the west side of the creek belonged to Daniel."

Raven dropped his hand and she leaned back and rested on her elbows. "One day Daniel's boy Lem was plowing the land so he could plant corn. Everybody carried rifles in those days 'cause of the Indians. Jeremiah tried to stop him, and there was a shooting over it and Lem was killed. Old Daniel nearly went crazy when he heard Jeremiah had killed his boy, then everybody got to fussing and more Malones and Davenports were killed."

Raven remembered that in the Davenport version of the story, the neck of land legally belonged to them and Lem was trespassing. "Are there still Davenports in Red Oak Hollow?" he queried, trying to sound more casual than he felt.

She answered with a leisurely wag of her head. "Granny said the best she could remember, the last Davenport sold out a long time ago and moved to Missouri someplace. I don't know his name or what happened to him."

His name was Ezekiel, thought Raven, *and he was my grandfather*, but he said nothing. "Do you know if any of them have ever returned to the hills?" he asked, wondering if she might have seen Ezekiel before he died.

She looked at him thoughtfully. "No, not that I know about."

Raven knew there were many hollows about Eureka Springs, and he decided that upon Ezekiel's return, he'd simply chosen to live in one that Misty didn't frequent.

She sat up and hugged her slender arms about her knees. "'Course the first shooting was way before breakfast, but Ezra is still mighty touchy about that feud. It gnaws at his guts that so many Malones were killed by Davenports, and he hates the Davenports worse than poison. He says that hell is so full of Davenports you can see their feet sticking out of the windows."

A deep laugh rumbled from Raven's chest. "Why is something that happened a hundred years ago so important to him?" he asked, running his fingers over her arm.

"Papa used to talk about it a lot, and he planted it in Ezra's head that keeping up the feud was part of being a man. He's got his pride all tangled up in defending the Malone name."

His hand moved to her shoulder, tenderly caressing it. "But there is nothing to defend anymore. If a Davenport did return to the mountains, he wouldn't have anything to do with the old feuding. That's all in the past."

Misty tilted her head and sighed. "Being a flatlander, you'd think that way. But to a mountain man, a feud is a feud, no matter how old it is. Feuding is in a mountain man's blood and stays with him till he dies. They hold strong to an eye for an eye and a tooth for a tooth."

He touched her face. "Living so close together, it seems that over the years some of the Malones and Davenports would have fallen in love and married."

Her expressive face went blank with surprise. "*Married?*" she exclaimed in an incredulous tone. "It's like that Romeo and Juliet story—there's too many hard feelings between the families for them to marry into each other. If I married a Davenport, or kissed a Davenport, or even *looked* at a Davenport, Ezra would kill him for sure!"

Raven wryly reflected that he was waiting for this same man's return. "How do you feel about that yourself?" he asked, trailing his fingers over her smooth cheek.

"I don't know if I'd shoot a Davenport on sight, like Ezra would," she replied, her large eyes moist with emotion, "but I'd stand by the Malone name and cut a wide path around any Davenports I met."

Raven experienced a sinking feeling, but was once again thankful he'd kept his identity a secret. Evidently the isolation of the Ozarks had preserved old customs and beliefs that had faded away in other places, and the mountain people had a code of honor that he couldn't understand. At that moment he began to realize that he was not only hundreds of miles from the nearest city; it was as if he'd been whisked a hundred years into the past.

Misty gazed into the fire. "Sometimes when Rollo and me are resting before that fire on winter nights, I do some long thinking about everything. I wonder why I was born here in the Ozarks. And I wonder why I was born a girl, and why the Lord took Mama, and why Ezra is filled with such hate, still looking for Davenports to kill." She looked back at him, her satiny lips quivering a bit. "I try to piece it together . . . but it just doesn't make sense."

As he studied her finely molded face, the sound of the moaning wind and snapping flames softly enveloped them. Her bewildered gaze pricked his heart, and it seemed the most natural thing in the world to take her into his arms and caress her back. She came willingly, and the sight of her green eyes, shimmering with confusion and desire, touched his emotions as strongly as the warmth of her body through the buckskins enflamed his passion.

For one moment, common sense reared its head and he started to move her away, but an almost overpowering need flashed through him, for he ached to possess what lay so tantalizingly before him. Lord, he'd squired every beautiful woman in Saint Louis, but none of them could compare with this innocent mountain girl. *God help him, how he desired her.* With a pounding heart, he pulled her closer, enjoying the fresh scent of her loose hair.

"You're so lovely," he whispered against her silky cheek. "So very lovely."

What had happened to him? Raven wondered. How had this mere slip of a girl burrowed herself so deeply into his emotions in only a few days? For a man who prided himself on his discipline, he knew he was being foolish, reckless even, but he was so lost in the moment that he couldn't hold himself back. With a low groan, he tightened his arms about her, feeling her heart hammer and her breath come in ragged gasps.

Misty looked into his passion-dark eyes and the hunger she saw there sped liquid fire through her veins, surprising and delighting her at the same time. As he caressed her shoulders with strong fingers, warmth radiated over her back and prompted a sense of well-being to flood up within her.

Her heart raced as he appraised her with a lazy gaze and raised her chin in his strong hand. At the spring she'd told herself she must guard her emotions carefully, but how could she when just the sight of him made her heart flutter like a butterfly trapped in her cupped hands? Never had she felt like this . . . as if sweet music was welling up inside her and filling her soul with its glory. Surely this feeling wasn't wrong—it had to be special, very special indeed.

When he lowered his head and feathered little kisses over her cheeks, her breath caught in her throat, and she seemed to be floating away on waves of exquisite pleasure. She could feel the stubble of his beard against her face, and the very air seemed heady with the scent of his manly aroma. Her senses whirling out of control, she put her trembling arms about his neck and clutched his powerful shoulders, wanting him desperately but also instinctively understanding that she was at great emotional risk.

Hot desire leapt up within her as his lips brushed hers, softly at first, then with more insistence as he roughly clutched her closer and slanted his mouth over hers. His tongue flicked lightly over her lips, and she inwardly fought the commanding kiss, but slowly noticed her resistance melting. What were these thrilling new sensations? she wondered, feeling wonderfully relaxed and languorous. What was this over-powering passion, this tremulous urgency that warmed the very core of her being, and at the same time left her shivering with delight?

"Relax, my little love. Open your mouth a bit," he urged. His tongue played over her lips in fiery strokes, then skillfully slipped between them. By now, what was left of her natural resistance had been swept away, and she felt as if she were drowning in a great undertow of passion.

As he explored her mouth, her nipples hardened and strained against the smooth buckskin. His breath came hot against her cheek as he traced an aching nipple in a circular motion, searing it with pleasure. Her head reeling, she felt a warm pulse begin to swell between her thighs, then throb with a bursting pleasure. It was as if her whole body had become one fiery bundle of sensation and her very joints were melting with desire.

Though he'd made love to dozens of women, Raven had never kissed anyone like Misty, and exultation now burst within him like a shower of stars. This little mountain flower had refreshed his spirit, made him feel young and whole again. With her, he'd captured something very tender and fresh. Consumed with passion, he fiercely molded her feminine softness against him, deepening the kiss and delving his fingers into her silky hair.

Then, like a dull ache, his strong sense of responsibility gradually began to trickle back, reminding him of how different they were. His family was rich; hers was indigent. He'd attended a university and was highly educated; she could scarcely read. On top of that, he'd lived in the great city and was sophisticated in the ways of the world, while she'd never been out of the Ozarks and was utterly innocent.

Even if the alliance wasn't wrong, surely it wasn't prudent. How could it be otherwise? Their families had been feuding for more than a century, and any connection between them was star-crossed and utterly doomed from the beginning.

Dredging up his discipline, he tamped down his raging desire and gently eased her warm body away from him. A muscle flicking in his jaw, he studied her lovely green eyes, which were now soft and dreamy with emotion. "I think we should call it a night," he said in a thick voice, feeling a great emptiness even as he spoke.

She started to speak, but he put a finger over her tender lips, then impulsively held her against him again, breathing in her sweet, womanly scent, and remembering the picture of her exquisite face in the firelight. Damnation! he thought, cursing the twist of fate that decreed his name should be Davenport and hers Malone. Why should this girl who touched his spirit and evoked such wild cravings in him be his enemy!

He knew he would be kissing her again if he held her much longer, so he slowly stood, bringing her to her feet. He took a steadying breath and glanced at the corner of the cabin where she slept. A quilt was draped over a rope in front of her bed for privacy, and the flickering fire now cast dancing shadows over the patchwork coverlet.

He let his gaze move to her radiant face, burnished with the fire's glow. Her eyes glistened with suppressed sensuality, and her face was so tender and sweet, he couldn't resist brushing her cheek with a last kiss. "Good night, Misty," he said huskily, pressing her soft hand against his lips. "Sleep well."

She drew in a deep, shuddering breath. "'Night, Raven," she whispered with trembling lips.

As she melted into the shadows, he turned and fixed his gaze on the flames. He heard slow footsteps, and later the soft sound of her buckskins hitting the cabin floor. Finally there was only the wind's moan and the whisper of the fire. His mind racing with thoughts, he slowly sank into a chair by the hearth and sat there without moving until he heard her regular breathing.

After a good while, he rose and walked to the cabin window where, bracing his arm against the side facing, he paused to stare at the moon-silvered forest. Doing some long thinking himself, he raked a hand through his hair, then let his arm drop heavily to his side. Why in the hell had he been set upon here in Red Oak Hollow, where people still believed in magic and charms, and a hundred-year-old feud continued to be a matter of honor? he wondered angrily. Maybe it was coincidence; maybe it was fate; anyway you looked at it, it was an emotional disaster.

He considered the soft-faced girl whose laughter was as bright as sparkling water. Why had Misty, of all people, found him? More important, why was he letting himself become attached to her, when he knew it was a terrible mistake? What would happen when Ezra returned and found she'd taken him into her cabin? Surely there was only heartache in store for everyone if the mountaineer found out he was a Davenport.

It had all started so simply.

He'd only intended to stay a day or so. But the fact remained that he'd been here many more and now intended to stay longer. In his heart of hearts, he asked himself if he was staying to protect her, or only using that as an excuse to be near her. Although he still couldn't sort out all of his feelings for Misty, he knew he'd discovered an exquisite flower that moved him as no other woman ever had. To be honest, something deep within him passionately rejected the idea of never seeing her again.

Lord, he thought, his loins quickening at the very thought of her. *What a devil of a predicament I'm in now.*

Chapter Four

"Oh, look . . . there's some gilly root!" Misty cried as she hurried toward a patch of spiky-leafed vegetation, a delicate green in the thin afternoon light.

After Sloppy's threat, Raven had been reluctant to let Misty wander the woods, but after she'd produced an old hog-leg pistol, he'd strapped it on and agreed to her pleas for one last herb-gathering expedition before the snow flew.

He now watched as she knelt and pulled some herbs from the loamy forest floor, then slipped them into a soft suede pouch attached to her belt. Rollo, who'd been trailing behind them, emerged into the small clearing and meandered to the herbs, his nose twitching with interest.

Three days had passed since Misty and Raven's intimate moment before the fire. As if by mutual consent, neither of them had mentioned the incident, but he'd noticed an almost palpable sense of sexual tension between them. How could it be otherwise when she was always so temptingly before him? he thought as he sat down a few feet from her under the feathery shade of a huge oak. "And what miraculous cure is this?" he asked, observing the scraggly gilly root with amused disdain.

Her eyes bright with enthusiasm, she looked up from her work. "It isn't a miraculous cure, but it *is* worth a lot of money."

Raven heard her out with an indulgent smile. "You can actually sell these weedy-looking plants? What do they do?" he inquired in a jesting tone. "Cure a fatty liver or grow hair?"

A grin played over her mouth. "Neither, Mr. Saint Louis-Big-City-Doctor. The mountain girls use them to color their cheeks." With a heavy sigh, she sat down and crossed her buckskin-clad legs. "I suppose since you're so ignorant about mountain things, I'll have to show you." She cracked open a stem, revealing a reddish sap, then smoothed it on her cheeks, bringing out their rosy color.

Fascinated with the results, he grazed his fingertips over her soft face.

"Yes sir-ree-bob," she commented, her eyes alight with excitement, "this little *weedy-looking plant* has lured many a man into some woman's snare."

"So, you sell cosmetics as well as herbs," Raven came back, enjoying the affectionate teasing.

"Sure," she informed him as she knelt and returned to her work again. "Beautifying herbs fetch a fine price. Gals around these parts put sassafras tea on their faces and cherry bark tonic on their hair." She paused, and her gaze glided back to him. "You know what else they'll do?"

He leaned back against the wide tree trunk. "I've been resisting the temptation to ask."

"Well, mountain gals are so interested in catching a fellow," she rattled on, "sometimes they'll even swallow a chicken heart."

Raven laughed in sheer surprise. *"Swallow a chicken heart?"*

"Yep. Swallowing a chicken heart will make a gal pretty even if she looks like the dogs had her under the house." A puzzled look swept over her features. "At least, most of the time. Alviny Huffsetter swallowed them for years, but she's still as freckled as a turkey egg."

He chuckled a little. "Who in the devil is Alviny Huffsetter?"

"She's just a gal from the holler, but her family is kind of high-toned for mountain folk. Her pa is a three-mule man and the family's got a two-seater outhouse. I guess they're about the richest folks around."

Raven suppressed a smile. "With three mules and a two-seater outhouse, I can certainly see why."

"Yep, but all those riches haven't lured Alviny a husband yet. She's got the marrying sickness worse than any gal I ever saw." She rose and brushed her hands over her breeches. "The hill folks say if a match burns to the bottom without breaking, a gal is gonna get married before the end of the year." Her eyes glinted with merriment. "Alviny burned up two boxes of them before her ma made her stop."

With an appreciative chuckle, Raven stood and adjusted the rucksack on his back. Soon they were deep in the autumn woods, surrounded with the aroma of mellow leaves. Clearly enjoying the cool weather, Rollo scampered ahead of them.

Humor flickered across Misty's face as Raven clasped her hand. "Alviny made herself a love potion and wore it in a carved peach stone around her neck to make herself more alluring," she chattered on, "but she *still* didn't catch any men."

He looked down at her. "Maybe she just didn't stick with it long enough."

She widened her eyes. "She stuck to it like a lean tick to a fat kitten! Some of the old grannies say if a gal's skirt catches on the briars, she's gonna catch a husband soon. Alviny used to run through the briar patches trying to catch her skirt, just hoping the charm would work." Her voice was thick with mirth. "Why, I guess she'd run through a briar patch *jaybird-naked* if she could catch a husband."

Raven's mouth quirked upward at the thought.

"I knew she wouldn't catch a man," Misty went on loftily. "I saw her take the last piece of corn bread off the plate one time. Most educated people know that's a sure sign a gal is gonna be an old maid."

"And what does it signify if a *man* takes the last piece of corn bread?"

"Why, he gets to kiss the cook, of course."

Raven arched a brow. "Somehow, I have a feeling that a man made up these old superstitions," he said, feeling laughter well in his throat, "but whoever he was, I'm beginning to like him."

A cooler, damper air blew through the woods, stirring deliciously musky scents. Overhead, the sky was a smooth gray, throwing the tall fir trees into stark relief. Nothing was audible but the crisp crunch of dry vegetation underfoot and the occasional call of a crested wren.

At a sheltered nook, they relaxed under a hoary oak and, after unpacking the rucksack, ate a meal of thinly sliced ham sandwiches between split biscuits. Misty had included a jug of cider to quench their thirst, and for dessert she'd made little half-moon fried pies filled with wild peaches she'd put up herself.

When they'd finished eating, she reached into her pocket and, producing a small packet, offered a toothpick to Raven. "Want a toothpick?"

He good-naturedly accepted it, by now realizing that most mountain people considered the gesture polite.

"I have scadoodles of them," Misty went on. "I bought them from a power doctor in Russel's Hollow. They're made from a lightning-struck tree, and they're sure good for keeping your teeth strong."

Raven found benefit in many of Misty's cures, while others made him laugh. Her latest offering left him stunned. "*A lighting-struck tree?* Surely you don't believe there's any magic in toothpicks from a tree that's been struck by lightning."

"And why not?" she asked assuming an air of dignity. "Jed Mellows is the best power doctor in these parts. Why, he—"

Raven put out a hand to silence her. "Hold on a minute," he ordered in an exasperated tone. "What are power doctors, anyway?

She shifted uncomfortably. "Why, they're just healers like me, but they depend on charms and spells to do their work."

Raven let out a slow breath, realizing once

again what a primitive people the mountain folk really were. He'd worked with Misty for the last several days, teaching her better methods to treat wounds, and she'd impressed him greatly with her quick mind. Now, just as he thought he was making progress, he understood that he hadn't touched that child-like part of her that still believed in magical cures. And he was beginning to wonder if he ever would. "That's just the problem," he explained, his patience wearing thin. "Healing is based on scientific knowledge, not charms and amulets and mumbo-jumbo. Can't you understand that?"

Surprise touched Misty's features. "I can understand what works. Folks who use these toothpicks have strong teeth and hardly ever lose them."

Raven laughed. "Yes, but don't you see that's because the toothpicks help to keep their teeth clean?" he asked in a kinder tone. "It has nothing to do with the foolishness of a tree being struck by lightning."

A hurt look gathered in Misty's eyes. "Well, what harm does it do if folks think something is special?" she asked, her feelings plainly crushed.

He took her hand, knowing he'd offended her. "The harm lies in the fact that their belief may prevent them from getting treatment that could really help them."

Her expression darkened. "Is all you believe what you can see and hear and touch?"

"Yes. Pretty much," he replied thoughtfully. "And this is something I want to teach you about medicine while I'm here. You must observe and reason, and above all, trust your intellect."

She gave him a sly grin. "What about trusting your heart?"

The question caught him off guard, and for a moment he was at a loss for words. "I don't think trusting your heart applies to the realm of medicine," he countered.

A smile broke over her face. "Why, I'd think it would apply to all of life. Maybe folks don't believe in trusting their hearts in Saint Louis, but the hillman knows that the heart is the truest compass ever. And I do believe the heart is often smarter than the head."

Raven looked at her silently, knowing there was no way he could change her obstinate mind on that subject—especially today. He studied her twinkling eyes. There wasn't a day that he didn't ache to tell her who he really was, but deep within him he sensed that the time just wasn't right. Things would go along smoothly for a while, then they'd have an argument about something as trivial as lightning-struck toothpicks. Something as important as revealing his true identity would just have to wait until they were on surer footing.

The wind gusted dry leaves about them, and Misty glanced at the sky, which all afternoon had been dull and gray and was now filled with dismal, overhanging clouds. "Come on, Saint Louis-Big-City-Doctor," she said, returning to a lighter mood. "I've got work to do, and by the look of that sky, it's going to snow like all hickory in a few hours."

After packing the rucksack, they moved through the woods, which were heavy with the scent of moist earth and spicy pine. The flame of autumn leaves was almost gone, but in places scarlet leaves still clung tenaciously to the stately oaks and elms.

Sonya Birmingham

They paused now and then for Misty to gather herbs, and near a patch of sang root, Raven surveyed the mountains where clouds crept downward, half-covering the rocky crags. When the dark openings to some caves were revealed by the parting mist, he asked her about them.

"Yep. Those old Indian caves have been there long as anyone can remember," she offered, her gaze circling the hills. "No one goes there any more. Why are you interested in them?"

"When I was a boy, my grandfather used to tell me wild stories about the caves. According to him, Indians attacked him there several times, but he always out-fought them." Raven chuckled at the memory. "He said they made him an honorary chief for his bravery."

Misty tilted her head back and grinned. "It sounds like your grandpappy liked to saw off a whopper now and then."

An hour later the herb gathering was finished and the pair stood on a bluff as twilight shadowed the mountains, which had taken on a lovely bluish hue. A swift stream spanned by a foot log rushed below them. The frothy water swirled over white rocks, then raced on to a little falls, fifty feet farther down the stream.

Near the edge of the bluff, Raven watched Misty stand on her toes to crack a twig from a low-hanging tree limb. "What are you up to now?" he inquired, moving to her side.

She handed him a pert look. "I'm gonna use this twig as a balance stick when I cross that foot log."

"Umm . . . sounds interesting," he commented. "It isn't often a person gets to cross a slippery foot log over an icy creek—in October, no less. What

84

about that little bridge we used this morning?"

"Oh, we'd have to backtrack for miles to use that bridge. It would be dark before we got home." She grinned. "Let's just run over this foot log. I've done it hundreds of times."

Not believing what he was hearing, Raven stared at the cold water, then regarded her carefully. "Hundreds of times, you say?"

"Yep. Maybe two hundred! There isn't anything to it. Here," she said, breaking off another twig and giving it to him. "Just put this little stick between your teeth. It'll help you get across."

Raven eyed the twig and laughed. "But that isn't logical. It doesn't make sense. It—"

"Never mind that," she interrupted, already heading for the foot log with Rollo at her heels. She glanced back and winked. "It's mountain magic and this is one of those situations where you've got to trust your heart and not your head."

Actually Misty had only been over the foot log twice, and she fought back a dizzy feeling as she looked down into the water. Girding up her nerve, she shoved the stick between her teeth, held out her arms, and gingerly put one foot on the log. With a deep breath, she ventured forward, noticing the spray of the falls on her face and hearing Rollo nimbly scampering after her. Once she'd reached the far bank, she leaped forward, her feet sinking in the loose earth. Then, with an exhilarated whoop, she laughed and whirled about.

"Now it's your turn," she shouted over the roar of the foamy stream. "Put that stick between your teeth and come on across." She watched Raven clench the twig in his mouth and step forward. He did well until he reached the center of the log, where he began teetering back and forth. With rising anxiety, she scanned the bubbling water, then her gaze clung to Raven, who was still trying to get his balance. Her heart lurched as he almost fell—but throwing out an arm, he managed to right himself and move forward. When he reached the end of the log, he took a bounding leap and, hurling away the twig, scrambled up the soft incline.

Misty rushed toward him.

A light in his eyes, he shrugged off the rucksack. "Balance stick indeed," he chided, clasping her hands and holding her at arm's length.

Misty met his glinting eyes, and as they laughed with relief, tender feelings rose up within her. "That little twig probably saved your life," she observed with a chuckle. "It's a good thing you had it." In a spirited mood, she glanced over her shoulder and acted as if she might run into the woods.

"Not so fast, you little minx," he ordered, easily pulling her toward him. "If you're declaring war, I'm accepting the challenge." He shot her a lopsided grin. "Just wait until I get my hands on you!"

For moments they engaged in a playful tussle, Misty shrieking with laughter. Then, without realizing how it had happened, he'd locked his sinewed arms about her and fitted her against his hard frame. The warmth of his body penetrated her clothing, and the man scent of him sloughed over her, quickening her desire.

Their gazes locked and, his face marked with tender concern, he asked, "Are you cold?"

"No," she whispered, and it was then she knew she was trembling from desire instead of the chilly wind. She also knew he was trying to rein in his passions but temporarily failing. She felt a tug in her womanhood and a flutter in the pit of her stomach. In that heart-thudding moment, she understood that this man she barely knew was now as necessary to her as food and drink, as essential to her spirit as the hazy mountains themselves.

His eyes sparking with desire, Raven touched her cheek and she noticed a vibration deep within her. Groaning hoarsely, he lowered his lips to her face. He kissed her forehead, her eyelids, and the hollow of her throat, all the while caressing her body with a tender urgency that snatched her breath away.

"Misty . . . beautiful, beautiful Misty," he murmured, his resonant voice shimmering with an emotion that sent her blood racing. As he took her mouth in a deep kiss, rapture swept through her like a swirling wind, blocking out all thought and reason. Her insides trembled, and for that moment nothing existed but the emotions that flowed between them. She heard herself moan with pleasure, but the sound was lost in the rushing noise of the waterfall.

Gradually at first, then more quickly, a threatening fear grew within her, marring her euphoria. She wasn't physically afraid of Raven, but afraid of her own feelings and what could result from their emotional involvement. She'd always possessed the ability to control her simple world and work out her problems, but she'd never faced a situation like this—a situation filled with such emotional risk.

An inner voice warned her that she had to get control over herself and not let him know how much she cared. This man belonged to the city and would surely go back to the city. She could try with all her might to hold him to the mountains, but if she failed, she'd be left in lonely grief the rest of her days. And what of Ezra? she wondered. He'd be returning in a matter of weeks. Surely he'd disapprove of the smooth-talking flatlander as *not our kind.*

Suddenly feeling vulnerable and self-conscious, she eased away from him and studied his puzzled eyes. Snow now peppered down and she could see it on Raven's black hair and feel its chill on her shoulders. "We'd better get back to the cabin," she suggested hollowly, taking a step backwards. "The wind is picking up, and the snow will be coming down hard and fast."

Raven's longing gaze joined hers. "Yes, I expect you're right," he murmured, a resigned note in his voice. With an air of regret, he picked up the rucksack and, placing a hand on her back, guided her away from the stream.

Wordlessly, they walked into the vast woods, Rollo moving along beside them, his glossy coat sprinkled with snow. Misty felt a stab of sadness that she'd broken their embrace, but she told herself it was the only sensible thing to do. After all, if she didn't guard her heart, who would?

They found a woodcutter's path that led in the right direction, and within thirty minutes Misty spotted the snowy outline of her cabin. As they left the forest, she heard the crack of a tree branch in the wind, then caught sight of something that made her heart leap. There on the ground ahead of them nestled a cluster of delicate frost flowers, glittering icily in the last light.

Frost Flower

Awe rose within her as she knelt and cradled one of them in her hand. "I haven't seen one of these since I was a child," she remarked quietly.

A questioning smile on his lips, Raven stooped and cupped her hand in his, examining the little flower. By now, snow coated his hair and clung to his jacket sleeves.

"It's a frost flower," she whispered reverently. "Sometimes a summer flower dies, but there's still water in its roots. When it freezes, ice pushes out of the roots and makes these twisty flowers." With a rush of satisfaction, she smiled at him. "It's real lucky we happened onto this, 'cause you can stick a powerful wish on a frost flower."

"And what would you wish, if you could have anything in the world?" Raven asked, his eyes gleaming with warm admiration.

His voice was soft, and as she looked at his face, deep understanding flooded through her.

Despite the danger it presented, what she wanted more than anything in the world was his love. And deep inside her she was aware that she had the strength to take the risk that love entailed. At that moment, she realized that she could no longer guard her heart, for she'd already lost it.

She closed her eyes and wished harder than she had ever wished in her life. With the fervor of a child, she wished that this handsome stranger would stay in the mountains and love her—*love her until she died*. And the wish was so strong, it became a prayer—not a prayer as one offers from a pew, but the kind of prayer that comes from the deepest part of the heart and is spoken under the stars.

After she'd made her wish, she placed the frost

flower where she'd found it, then rose, flushed with new hope.

Raven stood and cupped her chin in his hand. "What did you wish?" he questioned gently. "Won't you tell me?"

She put a saucy smile on her face. "Maybe I'll tell you some other time," she answered lightly. "If I tell you now, the wish won't come true."

Filled with an exuberance she hadn't experienced since childhood, she turned and hurried toward the cabin, half sliding over the new-fallen snow. Rollo, leaving little tracks, scampered along beside her. "I'll race you home, Saint Louis-Big-City-Doctor!" she called over her shoulder. She saw Raven smile, then move out after her.

At that moment she was outrageously happy and blissfully alive. She was in love, she thought, quivering with delight. *She had to be.* This wild, crazy feeling, as if she could sprout wings and fly over the forest like a red bird, had to be love. *But it was so dangerous.* Far more dangerous than robbing a honey tree or walking over a foot log.

But then she'd found a frost flower, and everyone knew that was a powerful, good omen!

Misty had often wondered what Raven would think of her appearance in a dress, and the next Sunday morning she found out. With a deep, satisfied breath, she tossed back her hair and turned to find him watching her. He'd just entered the cabin from outdoors and held an armload of kindling. His black hair fell over his forehead appealingly, and a light stubble shadowed his square chin. His face registered surprised delight.

"Well, this is something I never expected to

see," he murmured in a meaningful tone.

"It's just flour sacks," she commented, glancing down at the dark print trimmed in cheap lace. But the compliment warmed her heart. "I saved 'em for months to get enough material to make the dress."

Raven tumbled the wood into the kindling box, then took her hand and twirled her about. In her brother's simple Sunday-go-to-meeting clothes, his abdomen was flat and firm, and beneath a dark jacket his white shirt was open a bit, revealing a broad chest liberally sprinkled with black hair. He looked at her uncertainly. "With you looking so fetching, I may have to wear a pistol to church just to protect you."

She laughed and clasped his arm. "Of course you won't. Folks are always real mannerly at Sunday morning meeting. Why, the whole holler will be there, just waiting to meet you."

Concern sketching his features, he dropped his hand to stroke her hair where it lay on her shoulder. "Yes, that's just the problem, isn't it?" Ever so gently, he took her shoulders and, searching her face, sighed heavily. "Misty . . . I know you mean well, but you can't force the people of Red Oak Hollow to accept me. It won't work."

She realized that, being an outsider, he simply lacked her faith in the mountain people; but knowing their innate goodness, she was sure they wouldn't fail her, and she placed her spread hand on his chest. "Don't you see," she stated earnestly, "once they *see* you and *hear* you, they'll *know* you're a fine, educated gentleman—a doctor, not a revenuer man like Sloppy wants everyone to believe." She looked into his doubtful eyes. "Won't you please come?" she urged in a pleading tone. More softly, she added, "It would mean a heap to me."

He circled her waist with his arms, his expression still hesitant. "Are you sure this is what you want?"

She leaned back and grinned. "Does a whole sack of flour make a big biscuit?"

Raven chuckled, and the indulgent look in his eyes told her he'd agreed to her plans. Obviously he was only humoring her, but she was confident that once the parishioners met him, they would like him—and the very thought made joy sing through her veins.

She pushed on an old hat, festooned with faded blue trimming, that had belonged to her mother, then tied the ribbons under her chin. Reaching for a heavy knitted shawl, she slipped her arm through his and strolled to the cabin door, letting her gaze roam over his magnificent body.

And that face. It was funny, she thought, how some men gave you shivers just looking at them, and Raven was definitely one of those men. "Well, Sloppy may have convinced the menfolk you're a revenuer man," she said with a half-laugh, "but the women are going to take a liking to you for sure—and Alviny Huffsetter is going to turn green as a gourd!"

Chapter Five

Raven helped Misty from the wagon, then scanned Brother Jubal's log church, situated in a leafy hollow and sheltered by tall firs and great oaks. Although October had turned into November, the heavy snowfall of a few days past had melted away, and only patches of white frosted the clearing about the building. As they walked closer to the little church that was surrounded by wagons and mules and even a few sleeping hounds, the muffled strains of "Amazing Grace" floated toward them.

Misty cocked her head, the ribbons under her chin whipping in the breeze. "Now remember, Lukie already told her grandpappy we were coming and he's expecting us. He'll set everybody straight about who you are."

Raven doubted that *setting everybody straight* would be as easy as she expected, but seeing the look of childlike hope on her face, he remained silent. Moments later, Lukie emerged from the church and, hurrying down the rough-hewn steps, eagerly clasped her friend's hand. A print dress clothed the girl's thin body, and today she'd pushed her unruly red hair under a bonnet whose stiff brim shaded her freckled face. "I've been watchin' out the window for you," she whispered, her eyes shining with excitement. "Come on inside. Church has already started."

The floorboards creaked and popped under their feet, and once they were all inside the building, which was heated by a potbellied stove in a front corner, the hymn slowed considerably. With a chorus of scraping boots, the parishioners turned about to fix their startled eyes upon Raven. The collection of shabbily dressed mountaineers stared at him as if he might have been Lucifer himself, some of them dropping their hymn books in surprise.

Raven ran his gaze over Brother Jubal, who stood behind a crude pulpit, leading the singing. His bushy eyebrows and the shock of snow-white hair that crowned his head and stood out on the sides gave him a look of wild intensity, and a black frock suit, shiny with wear, garbed his frail body. The weight of eighty-three hard years bent his shoulders, but a fiery light still glinted in his eyes behind little half-spectacles.

At last the singing stumbled to a complete halt, and in a firm voice, the old preacher announced, "That'll be all the singin' for this mornin', brethren. We'll go directly to the sermon." He gave a dry cough and waited for the wide-eyed mountaineers to turn around and grace him with their attention. "We have a stranger among us today," he offered encouragingly, "and I want you to welcome him to our midst."

Lukie, who'd been standing beside Misty, cut her eyes at one of the home-made pews that smelled of pine resin and indicated that the three of them should take a seat. As they did, a string of parishioners sent them a hard glare, then vacated their seats and moved several rows up, leaving the trio by themselves.

With a spurt of surprise, Raven noticed that one of the women had forgotten a small boy of about two. The appealing child, who sat on the floor playing with a small whittled horse that just fit into the palm of his hand, had soft brown hair, dark eyes, and an angelic face. Raven, stretching his arm along the back of the pew, leaned toward Misty, sitting at his side. "Who is the little boy?" he asked quietly.

"That's Tommy. He's Sloppy Brewster's young'un. And there sits his wife over yonder with that bunch that left this row."

Raven glanced in the direction she indicated and noticed a thin, cowed-looking woman trying to corral a group of fidgety children. Two toddlers clung to her ragged skirts while their giggling brothers and sisters poked and prodded at each other. No wonder she hadn't missed this child yet, Raven thought with some amusement.

Swinging his gaze back to Misty, he noted her astonished face. "You look surprised to see the woman."

"I am. Sloppy has kept her under his thumb for ten years, keeping her away from town and hardly letting her go to church."

Raven regarded the boy again, thinking it was hard to believe that Sloppy could have sired such a fine-looking son. With an artless grace, the child favored him with an infectious grin, then went back to playing with his whittled horse.

As Brother Jubal ruffled through the Bible, reading scriptures, Raven studied the crowd, observing how poor and malnourished they were. Many of the men had botched haircuts, and their lanky frames were garbed in mismatched suits, some hopelessly out of date. A few of the woodsmen wore their everyday clothes, including rough buckskins and moccasins. A passel of quiet, gingham-clad mothers huddled frail children to their sides, wrapping them in their tattered shawls to ward off the chill hanging in the poorly heated building. A family in the first row sported cheap mail-order clothes, and by their daughter's jealous glances, he knew it must be the Huffsetters of double-seater outhouse fame.

At this moment Sloppy's wife realized that she was a child short, and with an expression of horror, she rose and made her way to Tommy, who played near Raven's legs. With tight lips, she tugged her son to his feet, and in the process he dropped the toy, which rattled to the floor. Raven picked it up and held it toward him. Casually raising his gaze from the boy, he locked eyes with the woman, and in their deeply troubled depths he saw stark fear and suspicion. After Tommy clasped the trinket, the mother hoisted him to her hip and hurriedly returned to her restless brood.

When she'd reseated herself, a sour-faced youth stared at Raven, acting as if he greatly resented his presence.

With surprising swiftness, the preacher smacked his bony fist on the pulpit. "Now brethren," he stated in a strong voice that belied his aged appearance, "there's somethin' we need to talk about. It seems that we've got a bunch a pokeweed Christians around here. Now you all know what I mean," he droned ominously. "A poke weed will shoot up afore you can bat your eyes, then it'll wither and die just as quick." He swept a stern gaze over the crowd. "I reckon that's what happened to a bunch of you folks. You went to one of them lightnin'-bug revivals last summer and thought you got saved—*but your dippin' didn't take.* We don't need no jimsonweed Christians or cockleburr saints around here, who ain't got a drop of hospitality in their souls!"

The young fellow stood up and wagged a long finger at Raven. "And we don't need no federal men a-pokin' around our holler tryin' to stir up trouble, either," he exclaimed with hot eyes. "They ain't welcome!"

The encounter with the populace of Red Oak Hollow had gone about as Raven expected, but as he leaned forward to leave, Misty put her hand on his sleeve. "*Wait,*" she whispered, her eyes glistening anxiously.

Brother Jubal narrowed his gaze at the woodsman. "Sir, don't you know we might be entertain' an angel unawares in our holler? The Bible speaks of such things." He nodded at Raven affirmatively. "I reckon that man is the doctor he claims to be." He chuckled and adjusted his glasses. "And he might be a right handy feller to have around if any of us needed him!"

A murmur ran over the group, then a rough-looking sort stood up and tilted his head at Raven. "Sloppy's done told us about you hittin' that nail head at sixty yards," he said, thoughtfully rubbing his hollow cheek. "I ain't never heared of no doctor bein' able to do somethin' like that. I figure nobody can do that but outlaws and federal men." He sent Raven a level look. "Just which one are you?"

Pew backs creaked as other men got to their feet. "Let's see how handy you are with your fists, federal man," a beefy man challenged, hitching up his britches. He elbowed his friend and chuckled. "Me and Zeb will be glad to try you out."

Brother Jubal ripped off his spectacles and pounded the podium. "Brethren we're in the House of the Lord, not a Fayetteville saloon. Take your seats!"

A glance at the old man's worried face told Raven that it was time to leave before the situation became explosive and further disrupted the religious service. Slowly rising, he inched his gaze over the angry men. "Another time . . . another place, gentlemen." Before leaving the pew, he met Misty's sad eyes, then moments later heard her footsteps behind him as she followed him from the church.

Once outside the building, he pulled in a breath of cool air and, never looking behind him, strode toward her wagon and mule. How he regretted his decision to humor Misty and attend the service! He reached for the animal's reins, which he'd wrapped around a hitching post. From the corner of his eye, he saw her standing at the base of the church steps, a stricken look on her face, while Lukie clasped her shoulders. By now the rest of the parishioners milled from the church, trailed by Brother Jubal, who still clutched a Bible in his gnarled hand.

Raven untied the reins and clenched his jaw, thoroughly disgusted with the truculent lot. It seemed that speaking to them like a reasonable man was damn-near impossible. They were steadfastly set in their own way of life—a way of life that harbored fear and distrust of all strangers.

A babble of voices rose above the church yard, and a few of the dogs began yapping nervously. Then the man who had challenged Raven proudly ambled up to him and spat at his feet. "I say you're yeller," he taunted, a flush darkening his face. "I say you ain't got the guts to fight!"

All the irritation and anger Raven had felt since he came to the Ozarks welled up in his chest, demanding release, and he hurled down the reins. He'd had a belly full of these suspicious mountaineers. Enough of this—if they wanted a fight, a fight they would have! His temper flaring, he stripped off his jacket and, striding to the center of the church yard, tossed it on the ground and started rolling up his sleeves.

His grinning challenger followed him, taking off his own coat. Followed by their barking hounds, many of the mountaineers gathered about the pair, eager for the fight to begin. Concern welling within him, Raven spotted Misty's white face in the crowd, then the rumble of a wagon claimed his attention, forcing him to momentarily glance at the road leading into the clearing.

He stared at the neighing horses until he spied a fat, unkempt man holding the reins. With a shaft of disgust, he recognized Sloppy Brewster's coarse features. He couldn't have arrived at a worse time.

The mountaineer's jaw fell as he stared at Raven; then, his face hardening, he shot a threatening glare at Misty.

Sloppy's scornful eyes made Misty's stomach draw up in a knot. As was so often the custom in the mountains, he didn't attend church himself but was there to pick up his wife, who kept up the family's religious duties. Misty told herself she should have expected him, for like many hillmen he was fiercely jealous of his wife and didn't want her to speak to another man, even at church.

With a loose grin, Sloppy twirled his reins around the wagon's brake lever, then stood and glanced at Raven with acid mockery. "Well, looky here," he declared, laughing and showing missing teeth at the side of his mouth. "It's the revenuer man come to Sunday meetin'." He shoved back his shabby hat. "By the looks of things, he came a little late for the preachin'!"

Some of the other men joined in the laughter.

A speculative glint in his eyes, Sloppy lumbered to the ground and nodded at Raven's opponent. "I don't believe in buttin' into another man's business, but if you need any help whippin' this flatlander, I'll be more than glad to oblige."

The lout grinned and, trying to show off, took a clumsy swing at Raven, who easily stepped out of the way.

Misty's limbs trembled from nervous excitement as she studied Raven's bronzed face and broad shoulders, bulging under the homespun shirt. At first glance, he looked calm, but from the tension in his bunched muscles and the fire in his eyes, she knew he was on the verge of beating the slow-moving hillman into the ground.

Brother Jubal, who watched the proceedings with sharp eyes, now moved down the church steps, his pace stiff but purposeful. His eyes shimmering with emotion, he pushed through the noisy crowd.

As Raven and the mountaineer squared off for the fight, the old preacher held up his Bible. *"I'll not have it!"* he cried, interposing himself between them and holding out his arms like a thin scarecrow. "I'll not have a fight in front of the Lord's House on Sunday morning!" He glared from beneath wild brows at the man who'd called out Raven. "How dare you challenge an innocent man!"

Sloppy lumbered forward belligerently, taking up the hillman's side. "Don't let this flatlander misfool you, preacher," he warned, holding out a fleshy hand. "How do you know he's what he claims to be?"

Brother Jubal thumbed the Bible. "This book tells me to accept a man in good faith 'till he proves me wrong." He peered at Sloppy, his eyes burning with indignation. "Can you prove Raven *ain't* a doctor?"

The hillman blew out his breath. "No, but—"

"No, but nothin'! Get back on that wagon seat and quit eggin' on a fight!"

With a dull glower, Sloppy assessed the crowd, his watchful eyes appraising the power the frail preacher held over his flock. Misty could see confidence spilling from Sloppy like grain pouring from a sack as he slowly backed off, obviously deciding that he'd chosen the wrong spot to incite a fracas.

When the woodsman had situated himself on the wagon seat again, Brother Jubal raked a fiery gaze over his parishioners. "It's a sin to the dogs. Respectable people challengin' an innocent man at Sunday mornin' meetin'." He shook his head, his silvery hair gleaming in the sunlight. "I reckon Old Scratch is happy this mornin', you all actin' like foolish children." He jerked his thumb in the direction of the woods. "*Go home*. Just go on back to your cabins and ask the Lord to forgive you for actin' so bad."

Many of the women and children meandered toward the wagons, and some of the men coughed and hung their heads.

Sloppy motioned sharply at his wife and brood of children who, with frightened eyes, obediently climbed onto his rattletrap wagon. With an amused sneer, he nodded at Raven. "We'll be meetin' again, revenuer man. You can't hide behind the preacher forever. I'll catch you in the woods some day," he warned, a vein throbbing in his forehead, "then we'll see who's the best man."

Raven flexed his shoulders and ran a hand through his crisp black hair. His glittering eyes and hard jaw told Misty that only his respect for the preacher kept him from tearing into Sloppy.

A derisive chuckle erupting from his mouth, the mountaineer cast a last look at Raven, then snapped his reins and wheeled the rattling wagon into the woods. After the conveyance had jostled away, Raven picked up his jacket and with quick, clean strides walked to Misty's mule, gathering up its dangling reins.

Once again, Misty felt Lukie's comforting hand on her arm, but after glancing at her compassionate eyes, she hurried after Raven. He'd been right. Her people, the people she'd grown up with and known all her life, had let her down. They had disappointed her bitterly.

As Misty watched him mount the spring seat, blood stung her cheeks that he'd been treated in such a fashion. How she ached for him. At the same time, agonizing and frightening questions welled up within her. How could Raven spend his life with her in the mountains if the people wouldn't accept him? And what would happen now that he'd been challenged yet again by the hillmen? Would this final insult force him to desert the Ozarks and leave her bereft of hope?

Everything had gone so wrong, she thought, biting back her tears. So terribly, terribly wrong! Trembling at the very thought of his departure, she ran to the wagon, knowing that somehow, someway, she must clear her eyes of the mist that had suddenly invaded them. Once they were back at the cabin, she must comfort Raven and force herself to think of a way to make the mountaineers accept him. And above all she must not cry.

Five days later, Raven scowled, then leaned forward and gazed at Jasper, who sat across the table from him. "You use a tonic made of wahoo bark and snakeroot to treat rheumatism?" he asked, certain that old man's perplexed look was nothing compared to his own.

"Yeah," the mountaineer replied, hooking his thumbs under his overall straps. "Can't figure it out. It's always worked afore."

After the episode at church, Raven had assumed the parishioners would shun Misty and himself, but it seemed their medical needs had overridden their prejudices and they continued to appear at the cabin, seeking cures. He expected more trouble from the countrified lot, but silently vowed he'd never ride away and abandon Misty to Sloppy's vengeance, no matter how much they provoked him.

Once again dressed in her supple buckskins, Misty stooped by the old man's side and gently rubbed his swollen hands. "Was the wahoo bark fresh, Jasper?"

"Why, sure," the woodsman retorted. "I cut the bark when the moon was full just like you taught me, and I gathered the snakeroot the same way. Then, I left 'em in a jar of water in the sunshine for several days to get a tonic." A frown creased his brow. "But this time the tonic didn't do no good, and my hands are painin' me somethin' awful." He looked at Misty with a pleading expression in his rheumy eyes. "Can you help me a'tall?"

She slanted her eyes at Raven. "Sure. I'm probably the only one who can," she replied, placing her hands on her hips.

Raven smiled to himself, her underlying meaning not lost on him. He knew that Misty's friends had hurt her deeply, and he'd noticed her unaccustomed quietness, but this afternoon, as she helped the sick, her strong spirit had resurfaced along with her sense of humor.

The old fellow chuckled and squeezed her arm. "There ain't nobody that can doctor like you, gal."

"Well, it isn't any credit to me," she said, pleasure wreathing her face. "It was Granny teaching me and writing down all her recipes."

Raven watched her amble to her satchel and rummage through its contents. He'd toyed with the idea of exploring the Indian caves today, but instead he'd found himself helping Misty see her patients, and as usual, lively arguments had erupted, his university-learned skills at odds with her country doctoring.

Compassion darkening her eyes, Misty assessed the elderly hillman. "You took the old cure so much that it isn't working on you no more," she advised with an air of authority. "You need somethin' more powerful this time." She sighed and pressed her lips together. "I sure wish I had some ant eggs!"

Raven stood and blinked his eyes. "*Ant eggs?*"

"Yeah, those or saltpeter," she remarked thoughtfully. "Sometimes that works just as well."

Obviously pleased with herself, she brought a little bottle of brown liquid back to her patient. "Now this is a make-do remedy 'cause I couldn't get any ant eggs or saltpeter. This cure is in the trying-out stage."

The old man leaned back and stared at her. "Who you tryin' it out on?"

"*You,*" she answered, her eyes twinkling. "The first batch of this cure I mixed last summer smoked a little, but I think it was mixing the moonshine with the gunpowder. I left the gunpowder out of this and added bitters, and I think it'll work now."

Raven burst out laughing. "That concoction will cure rheumatism?"

She looked at him as if he were a dense child. "Of course it will."

He smiled and grazed a knuckle across his chin, pleased that she was back to her feisty self. "Well, thank you for telling me," he said dryly. "I didn't know."

"Oh, that's all right," she parried, a slightly superior edge to her voice. "If a professional doctor like me didn't tell you, how *would* you know?"

Turning her attention to Jasper, she laid the small bottle in his cracked palm. "Take a dose of this morning and night," she said kindly. "It'll ease the pain."

Both stunned and amused by what he was seeing, Raven skimmed his gaze over both of them. "Do you really expect this to work?" he inquired in an interested tone.

The old hillman, apparently unsettled by Raven's doubts, craned his neck to look him over, then scanned Misty. "You sure this here feller is a doctor?" he asked, jabbing his thumb in Raven's direction.

Hardly believing he was defending his medical credentials to a man who'd accepted the dose Misty had just described, Raven smiled tightly. "Let me assure you that I've attended medical school," he stated in a calm tone, thinking of the society women, their fingers glittering with diamonds, that he'd attended for this same condition. "I would just prescribe a somewhat different cure for your complaint."

Misty tossed back her hair. "And what might that be, Mr. Saint Louis-Big-City-Doctor?" With flashing eyes, she folded her arms under her bosom and waited for his pronouncement.

His eyes never leaving her face, he paced about the cabin, trying to work off his growing frustration. "Like most physicians, I would advise a trip to a warm, dry climate and rest for the affected joints," he came back, his voice threaded with irritation.

Jasper chuckled deeply. "Now that don't make no sense a'tall. We just had a hot, dry summer. And how is a man to rest his hands when he has to use them?" He shook his grizzled head. "How could I go off like some high-falutin' city folks and have all my chickens die on me?" He turned to Misty with a grunt. "What do you say, gal?"

"I say this new cure I mixed up will make you feel a heap better," she answered, patting him on the shoulder.

"I think I'm already feelin' better," he said with conviction.

She slid a significant look in Raven's direction. "Sure you are. You know you've got a fine doctor working on your case."

The wizened old man slowly rose to go, then glanced sideways at Raven, making it clear that he considered Misty the better doctor. "It's a good thing you landed here so you can learn some real doctorin'," he counseled, running his doubtful eyes over him again.

Jasper hobbled from the cabin, then spied a gangly lad who sat on the porch steps waiting for treatment. Wondering if the old man could even make it down the steps without help, Raven strode to the open door and saw the old-timer laugh and slap his leg. "That city feller in there told me I needed a dry, warm climate—*and rest*," he told the boy with a chuckle. "If that don't beat all!"

Exasperated with the string of difficult mountain patients, Raven lounged against the door frame, his arms crossed, and watched the old man limp into the woods. He decided that his mind just wasn't on medicine this afternoon. All day he'd wrestled with the mystery of how Ezekiel had died, and deep in his heart he expected he might find a clue to the old man's past at the caves.

Feeling Misty's gaze upon him, he turned, and she lowered her eyes and began to hastily crush herbs with a mortar and pestle, releasing their spicy fragrance into the cabin.

At his approach, her lashes fluttered up and she graced him with a sly smile. "What's bothering you today?" she softly asked. "You're touchy as a bear with a sore foot, and I can hear the wheels grinding in your head all the way from here."

There was a moment of silence, then Raven sighed and squared his shoulders. "I think I'll go back to the caves we saw the other day."

"Ezekiel," she said, surprise touching her face. "So that's where your mind has been all day. I knew you were thinking on *something* heavy." Through the open door, she eyed the boy on her porch, then regarded Raven, her countenance now sweet and tender. "Go on then. I'll tend to the boy."

His mind already working overtime with ideas about Ezekiel, Raven shrugged into his buckskin jacket and strode to the cabin door. Then he walked back to Misty and put a finger under her chin. His mouth quirked as he tilted her head and searched her delicate features. "Friends, Doctor Malone?" he inquired in a husky voice.

She blushed, and there was a soft light in her clear green eyes. "Friends, Doctor Raven."

An hour later, Raven reached the dark opening of the first cave, which was tucked neatly into the rocky mountainside. The room-sized chamber emitted a dank, earthy scent, and long stalactites hung from overhead. Aided by the wavering light at the entrance, he traced his fingers over the cold, rocky wall, inspecting some Indian drawings. In places, water dripped from the high ceiling, and as he returned to the glowing light, his slow footsteps echoed hollowly.

The afternoon slipped past quickly as Raven explored more of the caves. Some were hardly more than hollowed-out spots in the mountain wall, while others were as large as the first cave or bigger. It was outside one of these huge caves, amid some ferns, that a light-colored piece of wood caught his eye. He bent to investigate, and pushing back the feathery fonds, found a crude wooden cross, marking a grave covered in stones.

A heavy feeling in his stomach, he knelt and tried to read what was written on the cross. His heart sank at the words: *Here lies Ezekiel Tyler, born in these hills on December 3rd, 1801, died March 14th, 1880.*

Profound sorrow filtered through Raven. At his feet were the remains of the man who had meant so much to him. He'd always wondered exactly when Ezekiel had died, and he now had an answer to his question. He forced back his emotions, yet a hollow, lonely feeling moved through him. He wished he'd been here in the mountains to comfort Ezekiel as he died, and he wished he'd been able to stand by the grave until the last shovelful of dirt was thrown in.

But to his great regret, he had not.

Still, peace warmed his spirit now that he knew his grandfather's final resting place was here amid the quiet, tree-covered slopes that he'd loved so much. A slow smile crept over Raven's lips as he re-examined the marker. He knew that Tyler was the old mountaineer's middle name and guessed that, being the crafty fox he was, he'd used it as a last name when he returned to the Ozarks to avoid reopening the feud with the Malones. Since everyone from his younger days had died and there was no one to recognize him, the scheme would have worked perfectly.

But where had Ezekiel lived, and what sickness had snuffed out his vibrant life? Raven wondered, his mind still full of questions. Who'd buried him and erected this crude memorial, and who'd sent the letter to Saint Louis, saying he'd passed away? And what had happened to the great fortune he'd brought to the Ozarks with him?

His heart stirring with poignant memories, Raven stared at the grave for long minutes before a rustling in the bushes broke his pensive reverie. He scanned the area about him, but when the soft noise faded away, he told himself it had been made by a shy fawn.

He returned to his thoughts and was lost deep within them until he heard a familiar voice call his name from a distance. Warmth rushing through him, he rose and spied Misty walking up the incline toward him, her wind-tangled hair fired by rays of slanting sunlight.

A hand shielding her eyes, Misty paused to ease the catch in her side and gaze at the dark caves surrounded by white boulders. By one of them, she could see Raven standing with feet apart, holding up an arm to catch her attention. She waved, then continued up the mountain, feeling the sharp stones beneath her soles.

She'd quickly finished with the boy and decided to join Raven, and now, thankful for the cooling breeze on her face as she climbed upward, she thought about the incident last Sunday at church. Of course, she expected no better from Sloppy, but such treatment from people she'd considered her friends shook her belief in humanity. After she and Raven had talked about the confrontation, he'd seemingly put it aside, having the good grace not to mention that he'd warned her against the enterprise in the first place.

She might argue good-naturedly with him as she had today over some cure, but in her heart she knew he was a fine doctor. Still, if he was to stay with her in the mountains, the people must accept him, and try as she might, she couldn't think of a way to make this happen. Even now, the realization that the people of her hollow might have driven Raven off made her tremble inside.

Her heart pounding with exertion, she reached the top of the slope, and when she paused to get her breath, Raven caught her eye and glanced down at what appeared to be a grave, sheltered with ferns. Her boots crunching over dry pine needles, she joined him.

"I've found him," he said quietly, nodding at the cross as she came to stand beside him.

Why have I never seen this before? Misty wondered, thoroughly surprised to find the grave there. She hadn't been to the caves for years, but embarrassment warmed her cheeks that she, who knew so much about the woods, had missed the site.

Blinking, she studied the marker, realizing that something was amiss. "It says Ezekiel *Tyler*," she mused out loud. "I wonder why the folks that buried him didn't write Ezekiel Hepplewhite. That was his last name, wasn't it?" She studied Raven's veiled expression, feeling he was keeping something back from her. She'd seen that look in his eyes before when they talked about his kin, and it rankled her that he was so secretive about them.

"Tyler was his middle name," Raven explained, carefully measuring her with his gaze. "Who

111

knows why his last name isn't on the marker. Perhaps whoever buried him simply forgot it. Or maybe he wanted it that way. Ezekiel never felt bound by the rules of society." His firm tone made it clear that the subject was closed, and a strange emptiness encompassed her, but she instinctively knew that she shouldn't challenge him about his secretiveness here beside his grandfather's grave.

She ran her hand over his muscled shoulder, genuinely sorry for his loss. Why, anyone would notice the way his eyes lit up when he talked about the old man. "I'm sorry that he's gone," she offered gently. Raven's eyes traveled over the grave, and as he knelt to arrange some dislodged stones, she added, "From what you've told me, I would have liked him."

He turned his head, a faint smile lighting his countenance. "Yes," he replied thoughtfully, "you two would have gotten along perfectly."

After he'd put the last rock in place, he stood and looked at Misty's gentle face, regretting that he'd been forced to deceive her. But how in the devil could he tell her that Ezekiel had dropped his last name when he returned to the hills to prevent a feud with her own kin?

Putting his arm about her waist, he guided her away from the caves. As they made their way down the steep incline, Raven thought of the old man, recalling that the mountaineer had given him his only happy boyhood days in an otherwise grim youth, overshadowed by John's obsession with status. At the foot of the mountain, a sense of accomplishment glowed within him that he'd found his grandfather's resting place as he'd intended, and tranquility replaced some of the uneasiness he'd carried for years.

The day began to draw to a close now, and a mist meandered down from the lofty ridges, bringing with it the chill of the evening. Misty talked about light-hearted things as they headed through a shadowy meadow following a woodcutter's road. Raven smiled, thinking that even though she could frustrate him beyond words with her childish beliefs and wild cures, her optimistic outlook on life always raised his spirits.

When they entered a little draw, he glanced up to see how much sun was left, and as he scanned a nearby ridge, a prickle of surprise ran through him. There, shrouded in the enveloping mist, stood a heavily cloaked figure silhouetted on the horizon. Garbed in a long coat and a floppy hat, and carrying a rifle, the man walked along the top of the ridge, disappearing now and then behind the tall pines, then reappearing once again, his face always in shadow.

Raven watched the figure carefully just to make sure his eyes weren't deceiving him. Gently he touched Misty's arm and pointed toward the blurry skyline. "Take a look at that," he murmured, his tone carrying a note of concern. "Someone is following us."

She studied the horizon, then turned her eyes to him. "Maybe it's Sloppy," she ventured, her eyes large and dilated. "We better be getting home!"

Raven peered through the fading light, sizing up the figure. "No. I don't think it's Sloppy. This person is a lot smaller and more agile, but there's a chance it might be one of his friends."

The ground rose, but he noticed that the figure still trailed them, pausing when they paused and moving on when they started out again. As they quickened their pace, preparing to leave the draw, he glanced at the ridge just as the sun slid behind its edge.

Who was the mysterious figure standing out dark and threatening against the purplish sky? Raven wondered with growing unease. And what did the determined man want of them?

Chapter Six

A hint of pale moon had already risen as Raven and Misty hurried along the woodcutters' path, trying to make it back to her cabin before dark. Raven was still thinking of the man on the ridge, and try as he might, he couldn't shrug off a feeling that something was amiss. One look through the lengthening shadows at Misty's tense face told him that she felt the same way.

After they'd put a hundred yards behind them, Raven heard a noise that made his skin crawl. It was the soft thud of horses' hooves. He ran to Misty, but before he could move her to the concealing foliage, a group of riders rounded the bend, their dark forms silhouetted against the dusky sky. He could make out Sloppy's burly shape, surrounded by at least a half-dozen men, all loafers and no-accounts. *Damn*, what a time to be alone and unarmed, he thought uneasily.

As Sloppy and the others reined in their whinnying horses, Raven saw the sunset gleaming off the ruffian's rifle, and he instinctively gathered Misty in his arms. "Easy," he said, caressing her trembling shoulder. "I'll take care of this."

For a few moments everyone froze, poised for action. Only the sound of the blowing horses and the chilly wind sighing through the trees broke the silence. Then Sloppy leaned forward in his saddle and jabbed a finger at Raven. "You!" he shouted loud and clear. "It seems a man can't ride into town for a little fun without runnin' into a federal man nowadays." He swung from his mount, and with creaking saddles, the other mountaineers followed suit.

Raven felt his insides grow taut as he scanned the men. Clad in worn clothes, jackets, and flat boots, the hillmen looked mean and bitter. He guessed the men had once been good enough, but hard work, hard luck, and hard weather had all worked to defeat them and steal their pride. Now there wasn't much left for them but swapping stories, hunting and drinking, and defending their territory from outsiders—namely him. In their faces he found no warmth, only cold indifference and thinly veiled hatred.

Sloppy tilted his head toward Misty, then at a tall, thick-set man with a full beard. In an instant, that man and another mountaineer closed in on Misty and grabbed her arms. Raven swung at the bearded man and connected with his jaw, but the other slammed a rifle butt into his stomach, cutting off his breath and forcing him backward. At the same time, the bearded man pinned Misty's arms behind her back and dragged her away as she struggled and kicked at his legs.

Hot anger rose in Raven's chest and he moved toward her, but before he could reach her, his attacker cocked his rifle and took aim. "Take another step this way, and I'll gut-shoot you for sure, federal man!" the lout chortled through tobacco-stained teeth. "And Jake there will make it real hard on the girl."

"Please . . . stay where you are," Misty cried, flashing her eyes at Raven. "They'll kill you."

Raven assessed the long-faced man with the rifle, knowing she was right. From his murderous look, Raven knew the idler had a taste of blood in his mouth, and killing an outsider would give him something to brag about around the winter fires. Worse than that, he realized that if he took another step, the brute holding Misty's arm might break it. Two other men rushed up with poised rifles, and Raven was surrounded.

With an ugly grin, Sloppy came forward until he was only a few feet away and narrowed his hard, close-set eyes. At close range, Raven could see that the woodsman wore an open-necked shirt with a greasy collar, and a threadbare mackinaw with missing buttons. "There ain't no preacher out here in the woods to butt into our business," Sloppy rasped, his feet planted apart, "and I'm gonna kill you, federal man—put you under the ground where you belong."

Misty kicked and struggled in her captor's arms. "You half-wit! I've already told you he isn't a federal man. He's a doctor!"

Sloppy threw her a fiery glare. "Hesh up!" he shouted. "You think I'm gonna believe you? He may have you fooled, but I know what he is." He turned to face Raven again, his eyes hot and mean. "Are you scared now, city man?" he taunted, taking several bullets from his jacket pocket and shoving them into the rifle with a loud *ka-twang, ka-twang.* "'Cause if you ain't, you ought to be."

His friends chuckled with derision.

For moments there was only the sound of the wind scattering dry leaves over the path, and the mounting tension was almost unbearable. Then, with a burst of action, Sloppy fired a shot at the ground, spraying Raven's boots with dirt.

The hillmen laughed raucously.

Raven pulled in a deep, steadying breath and held his ground quietly. From his peripheral vision he saw that the rifleman was still on the ridge and guessed the bystander was probably one of Sloppy's hunting companions and would naturally be on his side. Even if he could somehow overpower Sloppy, how could he and Misty escape when the rogue on the hill would undoubtedly put a bullet in them? Still, anger flashed through him at the thought of standing motionless, and he couldn't resist baiting the woodsman. "You'd better make the next shot count because you're not going to get a third," he warned without a smile.

"Better listen. He's tellin' you, Sloppy," one of his cohorts jibed with a nervous laugh.

Sloppy shook his beefy fist at Raven. "I won't need another shot, federal man, 'cause I'm gonna beat you to death with my bare hands."

Suddenly a rifle cut loose with a tremendous roar, and the dirt flew up at Sloppy's feet.

Raven blinked, wondering what was happening; then he eyed the ridge, realizing in a flash that the stranger was a friend.

The surprised group glanced around in confusion. "Where in the hell did that come from?" the woodsman holding Misty hollered.

His companion shoved back his hat and pointed at the ridge. "There's a feller on that ridge, and he's got a rifle!"

"Pick him off!" someone cried.

"I can't," his friend replied, "he ducked behind a tree."

The figure on the ridge now zinged bullets all around the mountaineers, spraying dirt and gravel into the air. There was no arguing with the constant bombardment, and with a terrified face, the man holding Misty backed off. "Hellfire, he's got a repeating rifle, and he's gonna kill us all!" he shouted before scrambling for his rearing horse.

Misty picked up a dirt clod and chunked it at his head, where it burst into pieces. "Take that, you peckerwood. You come near me again, and it'll be bullets I'm flinging at you instead of dirt!"

There were more startled cries and the noise of boots running, as the other men leaped on their wild-eyed mounts and, leaning crooked in their saddles, galloped away.

When Sloppy saw he was deserted, he turned to join his friends, and at that moment the man on the ridge cracked a bullet so close to him, it made him jump. The ruffian clutched his rifle and took out like a frightened bear, lumbering to his whinnying horse and mounting clumsily.

Raven ran after him and lunged at his leg, nearly pulling him from the saddle, but Sloppy spurred his horse and, barely righting himself, rode away. With blazing eyes, Misty slung a dirt clod at him, which fell short of its moving target. "You ignorant moonshiner. You don't have the sense God gave an addled chicken!"

119

Hardly believing their luck, Raven hurried to Misty. Putting his arm about her, he searched the hazy ridge. In the last of the light, he spotted the lone figure who'd rescued them and wondered who he might be. The wispy fog cleared for a moment, revealing the man more clearly, then the figure vanished in a breath, slipping into the winter woods like a fleeing specter.

Misty's lips parted in surprise. "Well, I'll be flamboozled," she muttered in an awed tone. "I know who that fellow is."

Standing by the hearth, Raven watched Misty measure out coffee for the pot. They'd just returned to the cabin, and she still shivered with the evening chill and the excitement of their run-in with the hillmen.

"I'm shaking like a leaf," she said as she placed the pot on the fireplace grate, then rubbed her hands together. Raven glanced at her as he knelt to add kindling to the freshly made fire. "Do you think Sloppy might come poking around the cabin, looking for more trouble?" she asked, her eyes bright with anxiety. "If he does, there'll be hell to pay."

Raven stood and tossed the last of the wood on the fire. Then, taking a few steps, he picked up Misty's rifle from the scarred table top where it lay surrounded by scattered ammunition. "If he does, he'll get quite a reception," he answered, snapping several bullets into the magazine and returning the weapon to the table. He scanned her concerned face, then walked to her and gently caressed her arm. "I doubt they'll show up tonight," he replied in a smooth voice, brushing back her hair. A smile lifted the corner of his mouth. "I'd be willing to bet they're in Eureka Springs drinking off a fair case of nerves right now."

Misty chuckled. "Did you see them lighting a shuck down that road?" The tension had melted away from her face, and amusement now snapped in her eyes. "Those rascals scattered like a covey of quails when that old hermit started spraying bullets down from the ridge."

She'd told Raven a little about their rescuer on the way to the cabin, but at this point, he only knew the sketchiest of facts about him. He drew her to the table. "Can you tell me more about this old man?" he asked as they sat down across from each other.

She tossed back the windblown hair that gleamed in the lamplight. "Sure," she said, lacing her fingers together before her. "He came to the hills several years ago, but he stays to himself." She leaned forward, and her eyes grew large and earnest. "No one knows his real name, and some folks are right scared of him."

"Where does he live?"

She sighed and relaxed against the chair. "No one knows," she continued, a note of compassion in her voice. "I suppose I've run into him more than most, since I'm out gathering herbs so much." She lowered her voice as if she were telling a secret. "One time I came on him sleeping under a big oak. I got a real good look at him then," she said quietly, "and one night he came to my cabin asking for some healing herbs. I gave them to him along with a bit of meat and some bread. He didn't say anything, just stood back in the shadows." She smiled faintly and shrugged, then stared at the fire as if remembering the scene. "He paid me for the herbs, then thanked me kindly for the vittles and went on his way."

The pungent scent of coffee now flooded the cabin, and Misty rose and poured the dark liquid into two chipped cups. After giving Raven his coffee, she walked about the cabin, sipping the brew, a reflective look softening her face. "I reckon a lot of folks don't like him because he stays off by himself so much, but I don't see any harm in him."

Raven scraped a hand over his stubbled jaw. "I still don't know how you could tell who he was in the gloom and the mist."

She threw him a mildly amused look. "It was easy. He's the only one in the hollow who wears a red muffler all winter. I saw it flashing out in the dusk as he disappeared."

"Does this old hermit have a name?"

She put her cup on the table and her eyes kindled with warmth. "Billy Red Scarf—that's what folks here in the hollow call him. And I reckon we were awful lucky the old fellow was about today."

Raven frowned. "Yes," he answered thoughtfully, "but it was strange—him following us along the ridge that way and taking our side against Sloppy."

"I suppose he wanted to take a good look at you, you being a flatlander and all," she said. "And I reckon he decided he'd just even up the odds with that old repeating rifle of his."

It made Raven's blood race faster when she looked at him as she was now, and the stirring in his loins reminded him how long it had been since he'd given in to his sexual desires. As he finished his coffee, he took in the snug fit of her buckskins and the curve of her ample breasts, but what really fired his passion was her lovely face with those moist lips, and those silky curls tousled about her finely-molded cheeks.

He placed the cup on the table, walked to her, and lightly enfolded her in his arms. "You're very special, you know," he said, sweeping back her bright hair. "Your face, your smile, everything you do and say. And I'm sure I've never met a kinder-hearted person." He took her small, smooth hand and grazed his thumb over it, surprised by the tingle of desire the simple action produced. "See what you're doing to me," he said, putting her hand on his chest so she could feel the thumping of his heart.

She blushed, and her green eyes became languorous with passion. Their near escape in the woods made him realize how much she meant to him and how he cherished her. What if he'd never been able to touch her again? With a will of their own, his hands slipped to her back, and he started massaging her shoulders as one fondles a precious object. Then they strayed down her back, his fingers working in firm circles over the spine.

"Mmmm . . . that feels mighty fine," she whispered with a sigh.

"As fine as this?" he asked huskily, drawing her closer. His lips caressed the throbbing pulse at the base of her throat, and a fire sparked somewhere deep inside of him. When his lips brushed over hers, he felt a surge of excitement course through him with startling force. Although he'd daily ached with longing for her, he'd never permitted himself to dream that he might make love to her. Now he felt as if a dam had burst inside him and he could contain his raging passion no longer. "Misty," he mumbled, hungrily fluttering feather-light kisses over her face. "It wasn't supposed to happen like this. I—"

"Shhh," she mumbled, placing a white finger over his lips. Her eyes shining with mischief, she encircled his shoulders with her slender arms and raised her brows. "You know, you're some good kisser . . . for a flatlander, that is."

Raven chuckled deeply and, pulling her closer yet, rained kisses over her sweet-smelling hair and buried his hand in its softness. In his heart of hearts, he knew that their relationship was highly risky, but there was some deep, relentless emotion inside of him, that he couldn't ignore. With a hoarse moan, he threw caution aside and aggressively covered her mouth with his.

As his kiss became more insistent, Misty felt the warmth of his wandering hands through her clothing and noticed the thud of his heart against her breast. Wild sensations clamored through her and she pressed herself against him, her desire careening out of control.

A few moments later she eased away and looked into his dark, passionate eyes. "Well, I'll be dogged," she whispered, "If you don't have the mountain boys plumb backed out of the woods on this kissing business."

He laughed, and her arms inching upward, she reclaimed his lips and impulsively wound her fingers in the long hair at the nape of his neck. As she did so, he unfastened her breeches with gentle hands and pulled them over her buttocks, kneading their rounded cheeks with his hands.

A hot blush rolled up from Misty's bosom as her breeches fell to the floor and she stepped out of them, yet at the same time, her heart swelled with emotion. From somewhere deep within her, she heard a warning voice, telling her to guard her emotions, but the voice became dimmer, less distinct, until it vanished altogether. All she could think of was that she needed Raven the way the mountain laurel needed the sun and the rain, and in a moment of wild abandon, she totally let down her guard. *Yes*, she told herself. She was finally ready to challenge the future, to risk her happiness. This very moment was what she'd secretly desired and feared for so long.

As he skimmed his palms over her bare hips, she gasped with pleasure and, to her surprise, found herself fumbling with the buttons on his shirt, her hands trembling with desire. With a shaft of surprised delight, she parted her lips for his thrusting tongue as he continued caressing and kneading her buttocks. Then, leaving a trail of fire, he moved one hand forward to the moist tangle between her thighs and began a tender exploration. When his fingers insistently caressed her seat of desire, she shivered, thinking she would faint with passion.

Ever so gently, Raven scooped her up and carried her to the rug before the hearth. The small fire he'd lit earlier cracked and popped, barely illuminating the shadowy cabin. The glow of the flames lent a seductive glint to his eyes as he reverently laid her on the rug, his gaze never leaving hers. After raising her arms, he slipped the deeply slashed buckskin shirt over her head, then lightly tossed it aside, sending it to the floor with a soft *whoosh*. As her breasts spilled forth, he lay beside her to nuzzle her nipples with warm lips and swirl his tongue about them. Then he

125

leaned across her to skitter kisses down her body, arousing a raging fire within her.

Misty felt the soft rug against her back. Raven's warm hands and lips were everywhere, kissing and caressing her from head to toe, provoking her passion. Her heart fluttered wildly as she considered what was happening, but lost in the mesmerizing taste and feel and scent of him, she bit her bottom lip and sighed with pleasure.

A shudder passed through her, and she felt her skin glowing under Raven's touch as he traced a path back up her body, finally kissing her lingeringly on the mouth. When she thought she would cry out with need, he reluctantly stood, and in one languid movement, pulled his buckskin shirt over his head and tossed it aside. As he discarded his boots and stripped off his breeches, she let her eyes roam over his magnificent face, softly highlighted by the fire's orange glow. In the wavering light, she drank in his manly features: the black hair falling appealingly over his forehead; the firm jaw, shadowed with a fine stubble; the determined mouth; the glittering eyes, dark and intense with desire.

After he'd divested himself of his clothing, she ran her gaze over his huge shoulders, sinewed arms, and matted chest that tapered into a flat belly and slim hips. Heat flushed her face as in the shadows she caught a glimpse of his proud manhood, rising long and firm from his finely haired groin.

Impulsively she reached out a welcoming hand, and he took it in his strong grasp and lay down beside her again. He was such a fine, educated man, she thought, secretly wondering if she was worthy of him. And could she, who'd never tasted the delights of lovemaking, surrender to a man she hardly knew? And would he still care for her when his ardor had cooled?

Then she told herself that he was happy here, and they shared the same passion for healing. Finally, as he gathered her into his arms, she put all the troubling questions aside, and in an effort to block out reality, totally lost herself in their lovemaking.

Now he pressed her against his chest so they lay touching, and he began making exquisite love to her, caressing her body with gentle but fiery strokes of his hand. As he smoothed his fingers down her arm, leaving it tingling, his hard maleness brushed against her thigh, and her womanhood throbbed with pleasure, already moist and ready.

His breath warm upon her, he scattered soft kisses over her cheeks and eyelids and nuzzled a path to her hairline where, with expert movements, he explored the crevices of her ear with his tongue. Misty shivered with anticipation and clung to his broad shoulders, rocked by waves of passion. "Raven," she whispered as he nipped at her lobe. Her pulse quickened as his tongue invaded her mouth and his arms tightened about her. Instinctively, she traced the bunched muscles of his back, then ran her fingers over his lean hips, feeling the concentrated power within him. Then, with sure, thrusting movements of his tongue, he intimately explored the moist recesses of her mouth, making her world tilt to the side.

Before she knew what was happening, her hand instinctively reached for his hard manhood and she felt him stir under her fingers. Ecstasy spiraled through her as he covered her hand with his and, caressing it, showed her how to pleasure him.

With a groan, he moved his lips away from hers. "Surely you have bewitched me," he murmured hoarsely. "I want you so badly."

Raven brushed back Misty's stray locks and ran his eyes over her, trying to absorb her beauty. Her reddish-brown hair was fanned out over the rug and its silky luster brought out the fineness of her white skin and the blush of her cheeks. Her features were perfect, and in the flickering firelight, her face held an almost incandescent glow. With her air of innocence and trembling lips, she looked so vulnerable, but the smoky glint in her eyes told him that she wanted him as much as he wanted her. Deep within him, he knew their coupling would very likely have disastrous ends, but for a second time that evening, he turned his back on his better judgment. *Lord, I want her, want her as I have never wanted another woman, and consequences be damned,* he thought, his loins aching with longing.

Her creamy bosom trembled against his chest, and she was so quiet that he could almost hear the blood racing in her veins, almost hear her thoughts. How beautiful she was with the soft light burnishing her flat stomach, gently curving hips, and long legs. As she continued her tender ministrations, making him groan with pleasure, he put his hand over the soft heart of her femininity and aroused her there until she sucked in her breath and closed her trembling eyelids, her lashes casting long shadows on her cheeks.

Misty glanced up at his rugged face as he took her mouth once more and cupped her breast in his hand. Her heart lurched as she pulled him to her. Her nipple ached for his touch while an overwhelming passion began to boil up deep inside her, demanding release. His tongue plunged into her mouth, and welcoming it, she met it with her own, her body ablaze with the fiery sensation of his touch. A white-hot longing now swept through her, and she raised her hips and moved against him, her senses filled with the texture of his skin, the scent of his moist seed, and the feel of his breath against her face.

"Misty, sweet Misty," he groaned, his voice thick and intense as he trailed his mouth over her breast.

Deep inside her, she understood that the statement was really a question. Her heart beating rapidly, she answered him by running her fingers over his back and pressing him more tightly against her.

His eyes glittered with need, and he kissed her ravenously again. She could taste him and feel the satin of his darting tongue as he rolled her aching nipple between his fingers, then slid his hand between her legs and caressed her there until she thought she would explode with pleasure.

When he moved his lips away from hers, her breath came fast and hard, for she saw him lift himself a bit to protect her from his weight, then position himself over her. The glow of the fire illuminated his damp face, and she heard his raspy breath and felt his manhood's velvety tip brushing against her. Driven by a deep, primeval force, she spread her quivering legs and he lowered himself over her, then settled the tip of his shaft against her womanhood. Teasing her with entry, he insistently grazed it against her, making her heart flutter crazily.

"Are you ready for me, my darling?" he asked.

"*Yes* . . . make love to me." Accommodating him instinctively, she arched herself toward him. Her head spun with pleasure as she moved her hands down his muscled back and pressed them against his tight buttocks, thinking she couldn't wait a moment longer.

"*Misty,*" he groaned, settling into her. She murmured with surprise as he powerfully entered her womanhood. Then, as he stroked her deeply, deliberately, lovingly, she clutched his shoulders and, casting aside the last of her fear, was swept away on a tide of pleasure. A languid satisfaction stole through her as he began a mesmerizing movement that satisfied her more with each masterful stroke. Her heart beat deeply and steadily, and melding her body with his, she met the faster pace and sighed with an exaltation she'd never known. As he relentlessly continued, waves of ecstasy throbbed through her, taking her inside the gates of paradise itself.

At last, her ever-building passion could be contained no longer, and brimming with ecstasy, Misty exploded in a firestorm of exquisite pleasure that lasted until the only sound in the room was her own throaty gasps of desire. Afterward Raven kissed her hair until their racing hearts resumed a natural rhythm, then he eased to his side and pressed her against him.

An afterglow rippled through Misty's body, making her feel luxuriously satisfied and relaxed. As Raven placed tender kisses over her face, a peaceful feeling swept through her. Wrapped in his arms, she felt that their spirits were one. She knew it might have been the hunger of their bodies that had given birth to this moment, but it was love pure and simple that had transformed this physical act into something that was not only beautiful, but magical as well.

Raven watched firelight gather in Misty's long auburn hair and touch her creamy skin with warm colors, and he was shaken with a deep emotion he couldn't express. Her bosom rose and fell evenly, her long lashes fluttered drowsily, and just watching her, a passionate tenderness coursed through him.

In the half shadows, her nude body had an ethereal quality that stirred Raven's desire yet again, and he knew that nothing could keep him from taking her with him when he went back to Saint Louis. She'd become too important to him. At this point he had no idea how he could get her out of the Ozarks, but deep in his heart he knew that decency demanded that he tell her who he really was. And he must tell her soon.

Chapter Seven

The next morning, Raven's day started badly and got worse. He'd stubbed his toe when he got up, misplaced his knife, then later found out they'd run out of salt. And when he'd dressed and gone outside, the latch had broken off the outhouse, enabling a cold wind to blow the small chamber's door wide open and bang it back and forth.

Now as he stood in the middle of the cabin drinking coffee, he knew that once and for all he must confess to Misty that he was really a Davenport. Gathering his courage, he watched her kneeling at the hearth in her buckskins, frying a skillet of thinly sliced ham. Determined to have the confession off his mind, he placed his coffee on the table, then strode to her, took the frying pan from her hands, and pushed it to the cool side of the grate. When she glanced at him with

132

wide eyes, he brought her to her feet and gently gathered her in his arms.

Still flushed with sleep, she sighed and put her arms about his neck, a sly smile on her lips. "I reckon you don't believe in wasting any time, do you?" she teased, her surprised gaze flickering over him.

Raven steeled himself to the distasteful task at hand. "I have something to tell you," he blurted out, brushing his fingertips against her rosy cheek.

"Mmmm . . . you do?" she replied in a husky voice, her eyes straying over his shoulder to the table. "Well, let's sit down then."

Crossing the room, she pulled back a cane-bottomed chair, then surveyed him as he stood at the hearth. "My great Uncle Jesse Malone made this chair," she began, warming up for what Raven knew would be a long story. "My granny used to talk about him all the time," she added, sinking onto the chair. A thoughtful look crossed her face. "He could do anything with wood, and he built the best porch-sitting chairs in the Ozarks." A frown suddenly raced over her smooth brow. "It's sure a shame the way he died."

Raven walked to the table and braced himself for what he was afraid he was going to hear. "What happened to him?" he inquired, knowing he'd now be forced to let her have her say before he began his involved confession.

"Well, way back there before the Davenports left the Ozarks, they killed him," she replied, her mood now veering from nostalgia to anger. She slid him a dark look. "Yes sir," she stated, raking a hand through her hair. "Those rascals killed him *graveyard dead*."

Raven sank to his own chair, greatly disliking the turn the conversation had taken. He wondered how *graveyard dead* differed from just plain dead, but knew better than to ask. "Oh . . . I see," he remarked stiffly.

"Course he ain't all they killed," she added in a bitter tone. "The same year they killed my great Uncle Ephraim Malone. Some of those Davenport scoundrels snuck up on him and shot him in the back while he was out hunting. And they killed Elmer Malone, too," she added, her voice rising. "One winter they shot his horse out from under him when he was a far piece from his cabin, and he froze to death before he could get home."

Raven took a deep breath and released it slowly, knowing there was no way in hell he could tell her his real name today.

She banged her small fist on the table, rattling the sugar bowl. "Sometimes it makes me almost think that Ezra is right in what he says."

Raven forced a faint smile, wishing he was back in Saint Louis or Paris, France, or any place away from this cabin. "And what is that?"

She pulled her brows together. "He always says the only good Davenport is a dead Davenport!" Misty now stood, her green eyes flashing dangerously, and paced around the cabin, continuing her tirade against the Davenports.

So impassioned were her words that Raven actually began to wonder if he could calm her. Then, with a sudden brainstorm, he rose and strode to her. Wrapping his arms about her, he took her mouth in a wild kiss, muffling her voice. As he deepened the fiery kiss, tightening his arms about her, she closed her eyes and became silent and he felt her body relaxing. Soon she melted into his embrace, and with a little moan, slipped her arms about his shoulders.

After that, there were no more words about Davenports, and he felt her nipples harden and swell under the buckskin shirt and heard the rhythm of her racing heart. The kiss continued until her muscles became devoid of tension, and half-opening her eyes, she eased her mouth away from his. Peering through long lashes, she looked at him passionately. "I plumb forgot," she murmured in a lazy drawl. "There was something you wanted to tell me. What was it?"

Raven told himself he'd rather walk barefooted over blackberry thorns or swim the mighty Mississippi at its widest point with his hands tied than divulge his true identity to the woman he held in his arms.

"Well, what is it?" she asked insistently. "I figure if we skip breakfast, we can make love four or five times before noon—that is, if we don't talk all morning."

Raven coughed and glanced around the cabin, wondering what he was going to say.

"Well?" she prompted, raising her brows. "You're as quiet as a mouse wetting on a boll of cotton. Cat got your tongue?"

Still choosing his words, Raven coughed again. "No. I m-mean," he stuttered as his roaming gaze finally came to rest on a keg of cornmeal. Licking his lips, he nodded in the direction of the keg. "That corn meal over there has weevils in it. I saw them yesterday."

Misty blinked her eyes in astonishment. "*That's* what you wanted to tell me? *The meal has weevils in it?*"

"That's right," he replied a little nervously. "We'll

135

have to throw the whole lot out. I doubt if we can cook with it at all."

A smile grazed her lips and she held him tighter. "We'll worry about what's cooking in the kitchen later. Right now we've got more exciting things cooking right here."

Taking his cue, Raven lowered his head and kissed her again, thankful that he'd got out of the sticky situation so easily. But what would happen next time he tried to bring up the subject of his ancestors? he wondered with rising anxiety. He hadn't envisioned the troubling chain of events he'd started when he told her just one white lie to protect them both. But like a condemned man, he knew his day of reckoning couldn't be postponed forever, and he felt as if the hangman had already tightened the noose about his neck.

Now he was only waiting for him to throw the trap door.

That afternoon Raven decided he'd take advantage of Misty's decision to visit Lukie and indulge himself in a long private bath and some private thoughts. He'd put several buckets of water on the fireplace grate to warm and now, buck-naked, he poured the heated water into a number-three washtub. He placed the buckets by the hearth, splashed a bar of homemade lye soap into the tub, then stepped into the soothing water and sank into it. With a large *ahhh*, he leaned his head back, luxuriating in the hot water and rubbing the soap over his chest.

As he washed himself, he once again wrestled with the seemingly unsolvable problem of how he was going to tell Misty who he was. He also suddenly realized that he'd never told her he loved her. Somehow the words had never come to his mind or sprung from his lips. With a flicker of guilt, he knew that Misty had felt him worthy of the gift of her virginity and was in love with him.

While he cared for her deeply, he wasn't sure he understood what real love was. Passion he understood, desire he understood, but verbally expressing romantic love was a horse of another color. Vaguely he guessed it all had something to do with his past, but at this point he couldn't understand any of his confused emotions. He felt as twisted up inside as a ball of tangled twine.

Suddenly, laughing voices rang outside the cabin. Realizing that Misty had returned and Lukie was with her, he lurched to an upright position, churning up the bath water and nearly knocking over the tub. Water streaming from his body, he hastily looked about and, cursing under his breath, saw that he'd left the flour-sack towel on the other side of the room. The door rattled ominously, and with only one option left, Raven shot back into the water just as the giggling girls burst into the room, letting in a rush of icy air.

With the bearing of a princess, Misty flounced into the cabin bundled to the chin in a ragged jacket. "What's the matter?" she asked, looking at him with a wide grin. "You look a might upset."

Caught off guard, he stared at her tongue-tied for a moment, then he echoed, *"A might upset?"*

Misty shifted her gaze to Lukie. "Close the door. I reckon it's a might airish in here for him."

Raven splashed the soap into the water, thinking that this was the first time he'd ever held a three-way discussion while one of the participants was nude. "Airish, hell! Can't you see I'm taking a bath!"

"Well just keep on taking it," Misty advised with a devilish glint in her eyes. "We won't bother you none." Lukie slammed the door and the girls proceeded to a carved cedar chest on the other side of the room and knelt down before it. A look of anticipation brightening her face, Misty opened the leather-strapped chest, filling the cabin with a pleasant cedar aroma.

"*Misty!*" Raven yelled.

Her eyes large, she jerked up her head and glanced over her shoulder. "You want me to wash your back or something?"

"No," he retorted, feeling his temper flare. "I want you both to leave so I can step out of the tub and dress!"

Misty tossed some tissue paper from the chest, then lifted out a long white dress and drew her hand over it caressingly. "We're not looking at you none," she told him, focusing her attention on the old-fashioned gown. "Just go on with your bathing."

"Have you ever heard the word *privacy?*" he ground out, wondering what mountain protocol was for this particular situation. "Do you have any idea what the word means?"

"Sure I know what it means," she answered, fluffing out the gown so it made a lovely swishing sound, "but I've already seen everything you've got." She inspected the buttons down the back of the garment, seeing if they were all there. "I saw it last night when we were rolling around on that rag rug."

"Well, Lukie hasn't!"

Misty turned about and observed him with a

sweet, reflective look. "Sure she has. She saw you naked as the day you was born the night we brought you to my cabin. So you don't have to carry no worries about nothing." She sighed and gazed at him as if she were speaking to a slow-minded child. "Look, if you've got something that she hasn't seen before, she won't know what it is, and if she's already seen it, it won't matter—so you're covered on all accounts."

Lukie, who was dressed against the cold in a long skirt and jacket and a woolen head scarf, covered her mouth and giggled. "You ain't got nothin' to be ashamed of, Mister Raven. You're a right handsome man"—she blushed deep red—"in all respects."

Raven huffed out his breath. "What are you two doing in here, anyway?" he inquired, feeling a vein throbbing in his temple.

Misty tossed the gown over the lid of the open cedar chest, then sashayed toward him. "We're looking at my wedding dress," she explained pleasantly. "Of course, it used to belong to Mama and it's a might big, but Lukie and me can take it in." Her face lit with faint amusement. "I'm not saying that sometimes we don't get the cart before the horse in the mountains, just like they do in the flatlands, but when that happens, most of us try to straighten things out."

Raven's heart lurched his chest. Lord, the girl was talking about marriage—*their marriage*. His mind was clattering like a threshing machine, and the dreamlike existence he'd lived since he came to Red Oak Hollow came to earth with a loud thunk. It wasn't that he minded spending the rest of his life with Misty; what bothered him was the realization that by marrying her he was upping the stakes for potential disaster when he broke the news that he was a Davenport. And the sting of it all was that he didn't have anyone to blame for his situation but himself!

He wanted to stand up and say that they could never get married, that their star-crossed relationship would never survive, that relatives from both families would object and come to blows, that the stars themselves would explode if a Malone and a Davenport were wed—but considering last night and his current state of undress, he was in no shape to argue.

Hands on her hips, Misty marched back and forth in front of the washtub. "'Course we'll have to let Alviny sing. Brother Jubal will say it's the right thing to do." She paused and, leaning toward him, held her hand to one side of her mouth and whispered, "Her having no suitors, singing is about the only outlet she gets, if you know what I mean."

Seeing Lukie approach, Raven swept his gaze about the room, finally seeing a ripped-open flour sack. "Pitch me that towel," he ordered, glancing at the skinny redhead, who stared at him with an innocent grin.

After she'd returned, he caught the tattered cloth and strategically draped it over his vital parts. The rest of his exposed flesh he tried to garb with an air of dignity.

A satisfied smile spread over Misty's lips. "We'll be married in true mountain style. Brother Jubal will tie a knot that's bull strong and hog tight." She knelt down by the tub, to be followed by Lukie, who didn't seem to be bothered by carrying on a conversation with a naked man in a washtub.

"My Granddaddy does a real pretty weddin'

ceremony," she chimed in, grasping the rim of the tub. "And like he always says, '*Happy is the wooin' that's not long a-doin'!*'"

Rollo chose this moment to wake up and scamper from his box, and attracted by the shiny tin wash tub, he waddled to it. Standing on his hind legs, he twitched his whiskers and splashed a slender paw into the bath water. With a loud groan, Raven pushed him away, while the girls laughed and eased back, brushing water droplets from themselves.

Raven felt as if he might be dreaming the whole thing, and with a sense of unreality he studied Misty's face, which seemed to glow with happiness.

"You know, I do believe this whole marriage was preordained," she speculated, moving back to the tub again. Her eyes were adrift in pools of great wonderment. "I heard a mocking bird singing after dark a few days before we found you sprawled on the road, and that's a sure sign that a person is getting married."

Lukie looked at her and nodded in agreement. "Remember that butterfly that lit on your head last summer? That's another sign that a marriage is a-comin'."

Misty snapped her fingers. "That's right," she came back with a laugh. "How could I have forgotten that?" She leaned over the tub and put her hand on Raven's bare shoulder. "I hope you don't mind us telling you these things," she said kindly. "We don't want you to be ignorant around the weddiners when they start asking you questions."

"Weddiners?"

"You know—the folks coming to the wedding."

Lukie suddenly got to her feet, hurried across the room and, snatching a calendar from the wall, brought it back to the tub. "Looky here," she said excitedly, falling on her knees again and pointing at a lunar indication.

A smile broke on Misty's face. "Well, I'll be flamboozled. We'll be coming into a full moon by the end of the week. It's awful good luck to be married in the full of the moon."

As the girls rattled on about the wedding plans, Raven retreated into his own thoughts. How in the devil did all of this happen! he wondered, his mind spinning with the suddenness of it all. In Saint Louis, he and Priscilla would have been married in the largest cathedral in town. Later they would have received guests at a reception held at the palatial St. Regis Hotel, where an army of servants would have served champagne and caviar, followed by Kansas City steaks and lobster tails. A forty piece orchestra would have provided Strauss waltzes, and the glittering guests would have danced until dawn. Now his marriage plans were decided as he sat in a tub of cooling water in a tumble-down Ozark cabin—with plans being made for white lightning and corndodgers.

After Misty had rattled on for almost ten minutes, she rose and heaved a great sigh. "Well, I guess that about covers everything." She ran a concerned gaze over Raven. "You got any questions before we get spliced?"

"*When?*" he asked dully.

"Saturday afternoon," she answered, pulling a note from her pocket and handing it to him. "Here. See if you can find these medical supplies for me today. With the wedding coming on so fast, I won't have time to look for them."

With a stab of surprise, he glanced at the long written list and started to rise, but remembered what he was doing and sat back down just in the nick of time.

Misty sauntered to the cedar chest and tossed the dress over her arm. "We're going over to Lukie's to work on this sewing," she announced, swishing past the tub once more. "You can take all the baths you want." At the door where her friend already waited, she whirled and shot him a saucy grin. "Well, don't just sit there batting your eyes like a frog eating fire—get out of that cold bath water. Being a doctor, you should know that a thing like that isn't good for a person!"

After the girls had left, Raven let the towel splash into the water, experiencing a feeling of disbelief. Then, his lips twisting with exasperation, he got out of the tub and strode to the hearth to read the note again. When he heard Rollo following him, he turned and gazed into his beady eyes. "Where in the hell am I going to find lizard eggs and scorpion stingers in the dead of winter?" he muttered, water streaming down his body. Then, as he paced back and forth before the fire, he suddenly realized that he was discussing the problem with a raccoon; he slapped a hand on his head and moaned.

He didn't have any idea where he could get the supplies, and he didn't have any idea how he was going to handle his present predicament either. What he *did* have was a mountain girl who wanted to marry him and the prospect of a new brother-in-law whose very name struck profound fear into the local populace. Taking another look at the ridiculous note, he balled it up and threw it on the floor, then he let out a long frustrated breath.

Lord, he thought. Sometimes it just didn't pay for a man to get up in the morning!

Afternoon sunlight poured into the wagon where Misty sat on the spring seat, watching Rollo creep toward her with pleading eyes. "Well come on, then, if you're going. Don't poke along like a hen with a busted lay sack," she told him. *Lord, what a predicament!* She was almost late for her own wedding and forced to contend with a raccoon who didn't want to stay at the cabin alone. According to mountain custom, Raven had gone on ahead with Brother Jubal to wait for his bride at the church.

Needing no more encouragement, Rollo scampered onto the seat beside Lukie, who, dressed in a green wool gown and deep-brimmed bonnet, held the reins in her hands. Misty hastily tucked the animal under the long shawl she'd thrown over her wedding dress, then glanced at her friend's freckled face. "Don't worry," she said, seeing Lukie's troubled eyes. "I'll make him wait in the wagon so he won't disturb the weddiners."

"Lord, I never heard of a 'coon goin' to a weddin'," Lukie exclaimed, wheeling away from the cabin. Still mumbling her displeasure, she guided the trotting mule onto the woodcutter's path, where new-fallen snow glittered on the bare-limbed trees.

For an interval, there was only the jangle of the mule's harness and the creak of the wagon wheels, and Misty thought of Ezra, who should be giving her away this clear, cold day. Doubtless he would be angry and confused when he returned to find that she'd married a man that he'd never met, an outlander who was so different from himself.

And surely her prospective father-in-law wouldn't approve of her county ways. But pushing her anxieties into the future, Misty told herself that she was marrying Raven today, and that was all that mattered.

Then the weather-beaten log church loomed into sight, and Misty's heart lurched in her chest. She'd seen the building hundreds of times, but somehow, with smoke billowing from its snow-frosted roof, it looked a little frightening today. As the rattling conveyance slowed and finally came to a stop, she marveled at the long line of horses, mules, and wagons. Knowing how the populace of Red Oak Hollow felt about Raven, she was surprised to see such a big turn-out. Evidently the wedding promised so much entertainment that the curious mountaineers just couldn't stay away.

Turning on the seat, Misty squinted her eyes at Rollo and tried to sound stern. "You stay in this wagon and don't move a hair until I get back." She shook her finger at him. "Do you hear?" she asked, gathering up her skirt and climbing out of the conveyance. The raccoon covered his nose with his paws and blinked at her. At the same time, her friend tied the mule, then held up the back of Misty's full skirt as they both hurried down the shoveled path and up the church steps.

When Lukie threw open the doors, warmth from the pot-bellied stove at the front of the building rushed over them, and a hush fell over the assembled parishioners. Misty entered the church and heard the doors close behind her as she surveyed the crowd, who were dressed in their Sunday best, the ladies in calicos and shawls, the men in mismatched jackets with their hair slicked down.

There before the alter, holding a Bible in his veined hand, stood kindly Brother Jubal garbed in his threadbare black clothes. And when Raven rose from the first pew and met her gaze, a great tenderness welled up within her. Dressed in Ezra's dark suit, which emphasized his broad shoulders and trim form, and wearing a starched white shirt and string tie that set off his tanned face, he held her eyes and took his place by the frail minister.

As Misty studied Raven's face, she was shaken by his spectacular good looks as strongly as she'd been the first time she saw him lying under the great oak tree. But what was going on behind those dark eyes? she wondered. She could detect a secret there—a secret that she couldn't fathom. Was he regretting that he'd agreed to marry her?

At that moment, she spotted Alviny Huffsetter sitting in the front row with her parents. The homely girl sported another new mail-order hat with red cherries that had to be the envy of all the other country girls, who wore cheap homemade bonnets. From the haughty glint in Alviny's eyes, Misty knew she was jealous that she hadn't snared Raven herself; she also realized that as painful as the loss might have been, her pride wouldn't let her miss an opportunity to perform.

Before Misty could fathom what was happening, Lukie removed her shawl, then Brother Jubal's voice rang from the front of the church, "Everyone stand for the bride, please!"

With a pounding heart, Misty realized that she was stepping from one world to another, and when she left the alter, she would be Raven's wife.

Chapter Eight

A great shuffling of feet arose, and when Alviny began singing "Oh, Promise Me" in an off key, Misty started walking down the aisle. When Raven caught her gaze, the compelling power she saw in his eyes gave her courage to continue. Trying to mask her inner turmoil, she proceeded to the altar, her skirt swishing quietly while her steps sounded on the bare floor.

Click-click, click-click, click-click.

With a sick feeling, Misty recognized Rollo's nails scratching down the aisle behind her. It was obvious from Raven's expression and the children's twinkling eyes and smothered giggles that the raccoon had crept in while the doors were open and was now trailing her. Well, there was nothing she could do now, she told herself. Nothing but hope the varmint behaved himself.

When she at last reached the altar, Alviny stopped her caterwauling, and a blessed peace fell over the small church. After nervously scanning the crowd to see if she had their attention, the singer finally sat down, and Misty faced the minister.

Raven was beside her, standing so close that she could smell the freshly washed scent of him, feel his body heat, and sense the physical bond between them. As he tightened his brown hand over hers, the amused glint in his eyes buoyed her spirits, and when she slanted her gaze to find that Rollo had sprawled by the front pew to take a nap, she allowed herself to relax and temporarily forget that he was even there.

Brother Jubal adjusted his spectacles and waved his slim hand. "Everyone may be seated."

The parishioners re-seated themselves and the old minister cleared his throat and began to speak. "Marriage is a noble institution," he drawled.

Raven looked into the depths of Misty's emerald-green eyes, wondering how he'd managed to get himself so entangled. How amazed he was that things had come to this point. Here he was saying wedding vows when he'd left Saint Louis to escape the same fate! How could he have let himself concoct the wild fantasy that had got him into so much trouble? In his heart he knew the answer—he'd followed his emotions and told one white lie that had grown and grown until he was now caught in a tidal wave of events he couldn't stop.

He swept his gaze over Misty and his heart beat a little faster, for she was a sight to behold. No powder or lip salve had touched her face, but the excitement of the occasion had brought out her color and lent a sparkle to her eyes; with her hair loose, she looked very fresh and appealing. He'd thought her fetching in her buckskins, but with its sweeping curves, the V-waisted gown belonging to her mother accentuated her femininity and added an exquisite touch to her natural beauty. Sadness twinged through him as he spied boots peeking from the hem of the full-skirted gown, and he promised himself that one day he'd buy her a closetful of fashionable shoes.

The preacher droned on, finally saying, "Who gives this woman to be married?"

Not anticipating the question, Raven glanced at Misty and was surprised to hear her pipe up, "I give myself." A murmur ran through the crowd, but understanding her spirit, Raven felt the answer quite appropriate.

Brother Jubal asked Misty to repeat her vows, and looking up with shining eyes, she said, "Whither thou goest, I will go. Whither thou lodgest, I will lodge." She squeezed Raven's hand and in a heartfelt tone added, "Thy people will be my people, and my people will be thy people."

Knowing their families had been at odds for over a hundred years, he felt a tightness about his heart and desperately wished he could relive the last few months, but now that the lie had been told, he could not recall it. At the same time, he knew that John Davenport would shout and splutter and turn red in the face at this very moment if he knew what was happening inside the humble log church.

Other words were said, then Brother Jubal peered at Raven over his half-spectacles, and with his old eyes full of meaning, asked, "Do you promise to love, honor, and cherish Misty in sickness and in health all the days of your life, so help you God?"

Raven was aware of the dark stares that had followed him as he entered the building. Now he was aware of all eyes upon him, waiting for him to speak. "I do," he said loud and clear, watching a smile play around Misty's mouth. Although he knew that many mountain people never owned a ring in their lives, he regretted that he didn't have a wedding band to give her, and in the back of his mind he made plans to buy her one as soon as possible.

Then, to everyone's astonishment, Misty interrupted Brother Jubal and asked if she could add some words of her own to the wedding vows. Winter sunshine poured through the little church windows and made her upturned face almost incandescent as she said: "Raven, I found you on the road left for dead, and like the Good Samaritan I doctored and cared for you till you were well." She fluttered her long dark lashes. "Well, I'm gonna care for you and love you all my life like that—till the great White River runs dry, till these old mountains crumble down and the Ozarks are flat as a flitter, till it doesn't snow in January or get hot in July, till chickens don't lay and hound dogs don't hunt, till mamas don't sing to their babies and daddies aren't proud of them." Raven felt her hand tremble in his as she added, "And I'll be as constant in my love as the sun in its course." Her eyes twinkled. "And if some gal comes between us, I'll put a mark on her that won't rub off, 'cause I'm gonna hold on to you forever, even if I have to tear the stars out of the sky to do it."

Raven's throat tightened, for he wasn't used to speaking from his heart, but this time he did, and his words were simple and true. "I'll stand by you as long as I live," he promised in a deep, velvety voice.

A heartbeat later, Brother Jubal narrowed his eyes and scanned the crowd. "Anybody here gonna start shootin' if I marry these two?" An embarrassed silence hung over the audience, and some of the men hung their heads and shuffled their feet. "Anybody here gonna start shootin' if I *don't?*" the old man asked, challenging them once more. Light laughter now tittered through the audience. The old preacher looked at the bride and groom with shining eyes. "All right, then. You're hitched!" He winked at Raven and slapped him on the back. "Go ahead and kiss her, man. She's yourn."

Raven grinned and, getting into the spirit of the occasion, crushed Misty against him, kissing her so fiercely that she began to go limp in his arms. Applause burst out and a few roughly dressed woodsmen in the back whistled and stamped their feet. At last he broke the passionate kiss, but still pressed her against him, gazing at her surprised face. He'd almost forgotten that Rollo was in the building, but hearing a shriek, he glanced to the side and saw that the raccoon had climbed onto the back of the Huffsetters' pew.

A *thwack, thwack, thwack* echoed through the church as Rollo tried to bite into the rock-hard cherries decorating Alviny's hat, then tossed them disgustedly on the floor. Alviny squealed and held onto her hat with all her might. Misty widened her eyes as the girl shot to her feet and, turning bright red, stared at her father and wailed, "Pa, that coon picked the cherries off my new hat!"

As if he understood he was the center of attention, Rollo nimbly leaped to the church floor and darted toward the altar. Old man Huffsetter stood up, his face blotched with color. "Somebody get that coon!" he ordered, jabbing a finger at the scurrying animal. Brother Jubal stooped and swiped at him, but the ring-tailed wonder dodged his hands and kept going, now heading for the pot-bellied stove.

Children laughed and stood on the pews. Caught up in the excitement, a gangly lad of twelve tore out after the raccoon, frightening him behind the stove. The boy knelt and swiped at Rollo, but the animal was too quick for him. Alviny moved behind the boy, urging him on. *"Get him . . . get him,"* she cried. "He ruined my hat!"

Misty, breaking away from Raven, ran to the stove herself and scolded Rollo, who finally darted forth and leapt for the protection of her outstretched arms. Raven, thinking a quick departure advisable, clasped her hand and looked at the back of the building. He was relieved to see that Lukie had already opened the double doors for them. As he hurried Misty and Rollo down the aisle, Alviny cried, "Misty Malone, that coon of yourn ruined my new hat. I want something done about him! I—"

At that moment a loud crash reverberated from the front of the building, and Raven turned and saw that the clumsy lad had fallen against the stove pipe, which belched soot all over him and Alviny. The unfortunate girl, who now reminded him of a minstrel man he'd once seen in Saint Louis, was covered with black ashes, except for two white rings about her startled eyes. Always the man of peace, Brother Jubal rushed to the pair to assist them with the tumbling stove pipe, which now broke into sections, causing more havoc.

Braving the icy air, the newlyweds half-ran for their wagon. Raven helped Misty onto the seat, then quickly moved to the other side of the conveyance, where Lukie waited to hand him the reins. Once in the driver's position, he gave a sharp whistle, and the animal pulled forward, jostling the wagon over the rutted snow.

He saw children spill from the open doors into the church yard, where they began a snowball fight. Then a small black figure, standing out in clear relief against the whiteness, ran out and shook a clenched fist high in the air. As Raven urged the trotting mule over the icy road, the last voice he heard was Alviny's. "I'll get you and that coon yet, Misty Malone. I swear I will!"

Being a man of science, Raven generally left signs and portents to fortune tellers, but even an unbeliever like himself realized that starting a marriage with a riot at the church couldn't be auspicious. Now that he'd taken on the responsibility of a mountain spitfire and a rambunctious raccoon as well, he knew that his troubles had escalated. How many complications lay ahead of him? He really didn't want to know, but deep down in his gut he had a bad feeling that he was going to find out soon.

At the stroke of midnight, Raven blew out the kerosene lamp, plunging the cabin into darkness; then he walked to the window and pushed back the flour-sack curtains. "Listen to that racket," he told Misty, bracing a hand on the window and peering through the frosty pane. "I can't believe they've been going on like this for three hours."

Through the falling snow, he could see heavily clothed hillmen milling about in the clearing just outside the cabin. The men, who'd brought moonshine in their wagons to keep them warm, were shooting guns, beating tin pans, ringing bells, chucking rocks at the roof, and generally creating enough noise to raise the dead.

He glanced back at Misty, who was lying in bed, propped up on her elbow. "How long do you think this ruckus will go on?" he asked in an irritated tone, rolling his eyes upward as another rock hit the roof.

She grinned and tugged the quilt over her bare shoulder. "Not much longer now," she said softly. "Most mannerly folks know it's not polite to shivaree past midnight. Things will be dying down soon."

Raven strode back to the bed, thinking he'd never understand mountain ways. He could understand Brother Jubal and Lukie bringing them a fine wedding dinner and sharing it with them. But considering his unpopularity, he was surprised to see so many people at the wedding itself, and even more surprised when two dozen woodsmen arrived at the clearing in wagons and on horses, determined to raise enough noise to shake the rafters.

Only after Misty had explained that weddings and shivarees were entertainments not to be missed, as well as social events, did he begin to get an insight into Ozark logic. "Are all newlyweds blessed with such lengthy shivarees?" he inquired in a dry tone as he sank to the mattress and tugged off his boots.

"Well, of course," Misty explained. "It's not like they were picking on us special," she added, making it clear that she thought him a little dense.

"Oh, they pick on everyone this way?" he asked, shrugging off his shirt and tossing it aside.

Misty laughed and ran a silky hand over his bare shoulder. "Nobody gets married in the mountains without a shivaree. I reckon the custom is as old as the hills themselves, and you being a city man just makes it all the sweeter for them."

Raven stripped off his breeches and swung into bed with her, noticing that, as she'd said, the noise had started abating. Turning his head, he listened to the mountaineers' shouted farewells, thinking that *good night, ya'll* had to be the most beautiful words in the English language, even when they were pronounced with a heavy Appalachian drawl.

His gaze now strayed to Misty's bare shoulders and full breasts which, during the course of their conversation, had slipped from the protection of the quilt. Taking her hand, he felt desire stirring within him. As he looked at her lovely face, the noise outside dwindled to nothing, and hearing the jangle of bridles and the creaking of wagon wheels, he realized that the revelers had finally gone and left them with the sound of the wind in the pines. "Thank the Lord someone out there had a pocket watch and could tell time," he sighed, tracing his thumb over her hand. "It would be a shame to spend all our wedding night listening to that clamor."

Misty looked at his amazed expression and smiled, amused at his city ways. "It sure would," she replied saucily, "and somehow, I have the funniest feeling that you'd like to kiss me."

In the dim moonlight shimmering through the cabin window, she could see a grin race over his lips as he pulled her into his arms. "I've thought of nothing else for the last three hours," he said, his warm hands caressing her back with infinite tenderness.

The smoldering flame in his eyes made excitement swirl in the pit of her stomach and she told herself that she was the happiest woman in the world. Then, as he rained kisses over her face, she wrestled with the thought that she'd trapped him into the marriage—perhaps not intentionally, for she'd been a prisoner of their passion as much as he the night they lay on the rag rug, but afterwards she'd been wise enough to gamble on his basic decency—and there was no doubt that she'd organized the wedding in a flash. Even though they were married, she didn't feel completely secure in his love and wondered if he'd married her out of duty, or worse yet, pity. "Sometimes," she said with a soft sigh, considering her troubling doubts, "I wish I could close my eyes and shut out all the scary things about life."

He pulled back and looked at her, and she watched the play of emotions on his face. "There's some merit in that idea," he answered softly. With a chuckle he added, "And if you could temporarily lose your hearing, you might even shut out annoying shivarees, but then you'd also shut out all the good things, too. Things like the sound of burning logs and that peachy-pink color that lingers in the sky just before sundown and summer storms and patches of wild violets." He gazed at her, and it seemed as if he were looking into her very heart. "And things like this," he finished, his hungry mouth closing over hers.

A tremulous urgency ran through her and she encircled his shoulders in a gesture of surrender. She was vaguely aware of the sound of the whispering flames and the wailing wind, but her breath came hard and fast as she abandoned herself to a world of passion. As he explored her mouth in a deep kiss, she could feel him holding her tighter, shuddering against her. Gently, he slipped his tongue between her lips and thrust it in and out, making her moan with desire.

At last she eased her lips away from his and feathered her fingers down his corded back. "Love me, Raven," she whispered. "And take all my love, for I give it to you with all my heart."

Desire surged through her as he lowered his head, and when their lips touched once again, she sighed and relaxed into his cushioning embrace. He kissed her with an urgency that left her trembling, and surprising herself with her boldness, she pressed herself into the embrace, her tongue intertwining with his.

Giving in to a wild, primitive urge that had flared up within her, she pressed her fingers into his shoulders and skimmed her hands down his body until she found his aroused manhood. His immediate reaction gave her a sense of euphoria and she moaned and moved against him, her sensitive nipples brushing against his matted chest. The heavy beating of his heart stirred a sharp awareness deep within her, and she felt her body grow liquid with desire.

He placed a trail of tingling kisses on her neck and inched his way to her breast until she shuddered with passion and clasped his shoulder. With slow, teasing strokes, his tongue flicked over her aching nipple. Misty's heart pounded in her ears, but she was no longer the shy girl that had sat with him near the spring, and she craved the pleasure of his fiery touch.

Raven's heart thudded steadily as he kissed the throbbing pulse in her neck, then let her silky hair slide through his spread fingers. This was the tempting mountain flower that he'd desired for week after tortured week since he came to the Ozarks—and she was now his. How he'd longed for her. A reverent feeling stirred his heart as he cherished the thought that she was now his bride.

He moaned and, trembling with desire, fluttered kisses over her cheeks and eyelids before he slanted his mouth over hers once more. His better judgment told him that unseen trials lay ahead for them, but tonight he ignored those thoughts and concentrated on the sweetness of her kiss and the softness of her skin. She kissed him back with bold determination and the fire within him leaped higher until it seemed as if hot quicksilver was shooting through his veins. A torrent of desire now burst inside him with consuming urgency, and he leaned over her and lowered his body to hers, murmuring endearments. Once again he suckled each nipple in turn until she quivered beneath him.

Excitement flashed through Misty like sheet lightning, and she clasped his buttocks; then, shivering with anticipation, she opened her welcoming thighs. As his hard manhood slid into her at last, a sweet, aching pleasure spread through her abdomen, and she relaxed into the soft mattress, once again anticipating the moment of ecstasy she knew was to come.

With sure strokes, he began a slow rhythm, igniting a firestorm of erotic pleasure deep within Misty's loins. Sighing with delight, she met each of his thrusts, her body keenly attuned to his. She now yielded utterly to her building need, and the flame of love sparkled brighter and transported her to a realm of exhilarating sensations that left her heart pounding with excitement. Just when she thought that she would cry out in delight, a wave of overpowering desire rose from deep within her and she experienced the exquisite pleasure of throbbing release. Raven shuddered against her, joining her as their spirits soared to the hidden heights reserved for lovers.

Afterwards she whispered his name and he held her gently and kissed her hair as their passion ebbed away like a great tide. Warm and drowsy, she floated in the tranquil state before sleep, and she felt wonderfully content and peaceful. *I'm a married woman now*, she thought, a profound awe stealing over her. Although she didn't have a ring, she'd been married in a *real* church, by a *real* preacher, and no one could ever take Raven away from her, *no one!*

The second week of December, a blustery storm howled through Red Oak Hollow, bringing with it the worst snowstorm of the season. Outside, a shrill wind made the shingles clatter, but inside Misty's snug cabin, a cheerful fire burned, and Rollo, curled in a ball, slept peacefully in his box by the hearth. The lingering aroma of wood smoke and kerosene permeated the whole room, and on the table a lamp glowed warmly, pooling out golden light.

Misty, sitting across from Raven, studied his amused face with growing irritation. On the other side of the table, he read one of her homemade medical books in the quiet hours before bedtime. The corners of his mouth now twitched upward as he unsuccessfully tried to control little snorts of mirth. At last he closed his eyes and, tilting his head back, laughed deeply.

After he managed to control himself, he glanced at Misty; still chuckling, he said, "Listen to this. It says: *for a sprain take a dirt dauber's nest and make mud out of it with vinegar. Dab it on the sprain and bandage with a stocking."*

Misty reached across the table and snatched the book from his hand. "I know what it says— I've read it a zillion times."

He reclaimed the book, then, shaking his head, continued flipping through the pages. "And what does this mean?" he asked, looking puzzled. "A *speck*, a *dab*, a *middling*, a *wallop*, and a *whole bunch?*"

"Well, I declare," Misty huffed, "didn't that fancy medical school you went to teach you anything? Those are mountain measurements you just read." She sat forward and raised her brows. "Three specks is a dab, three dabs is a middling, three middlings is a wallop, and three wallops is a whole bunch."

Raven laughed again. "I've never seen such an outlandish accumulation of misinformation and superstitious beliefs," he muttered, a hint of censure in his tone.

Irritated with his superior manner, Misty sat back and started to speak her piece, then paused, transfixed by the play of lamplight on his face. The hard Ozark life had agreed with him, and if possible, he seemed more handsome than ever with his beard, making it easy for her to temper her anger and explain things to him yet again. "Most of the cures really work. There are reasons for all of them," she said defiantly. "And those that don't work at least ease the mind." She let her gaze roam over him. "And like I told you before—"

"The most powerful medicine lies in the mind," he chanted before she could even get the words out of her mouth. He stood and walked about the table and, after kissing her forehead, good-naturedly remarked, *"That,* my dear, is something you've yet to prove to me."

She crossed her arms and gave a heartfelt sigh. "Are all flatlanders as closed-minded as you?" she asked, blowing a dangling wisp of hair from her face.

He took her elbow and helped her to her feet, smiling lazily. "No," he responded, unfolding her arms and placing them around his neck. "Are all mountain girls as lovely as you?" A teasing gleam in his eyes, he lowered his head and began to nuzzle her neck with warm kisses.

She edged back so she could peer at his amused face. "Do you think you can change my mind about medicine by kissing my neck?" she countered.

He cupped her breast and grazed his thumb over its hardening nipple. "Well, no," he added in a low, rich tone that sent desire rippling through her, "but I *was* hoping to lower your resistance on other matters." He flashed her a devilish grin. "Why don't you get ready for bed?"

His expression was strongly sensual and he radiated such self-confidence that he was almost irresistable, even when she was angry at him as she was now. For a moment, she almost wished that he was old and ugly and hunch-backed so she could *stay* mad and really cross swords with him. Then she listened to her heart and told herself that she could always continue the argument tomorrow.

Masking her excitement with a little frown, she slipped from his arms, thinking she'd turn back the quilts on their bed. "Don't think you've heard the last of this," she warned, swishing away from him with a business-like air. "I'm just calling a truce for the night, you know."

Then as she passed the window, she noticed that she'd forgotten to pull the curtain and a chilly draft seeped in and ruffled the material. As she reached to close it, she spotted someone walking out of the dark woods into the swirling snowflakes, and she dropped her hand in surprise.

Through the misty night, she saw the figure pause to adjust a fluttering shawl, and with a spurt of alarm, she realized that it was a *woman* floundering through the mounded drifts as if her life depended on it. The woman, her breath a steamy cloud, fell to her knees, but struggled up, and as she fought her way closer to the cabin, a sick, worried feeling came over Misty. *The woman was Sloppy's wife.* Obviously some great tragedy had befallen her, for her every move bespoke desperation.

Misty, her legs trembling, turned about and looked at Raven, who now sat reading her book at the table once more. "Someone's coming," she cried urgently. "Sloppy's wife. Something awful has happened to her, I can see it in her face."

162

He rose and tossed the book aside. "Sloppy's wife? Why in the devil would she be coming here?"

"I don't know. But coming she is, and like Old Scratch is after her himself."

A concerned look on his face, Raven moved to her and peered through the frost-streaked pane; then, without another word, he shrugged on his jacket and left the cabin to help the woman. Through the window, Misty saw him stride to her and clasp his arm about her waist, helping her through the deep snow. Misty wondered if Sloppy had beaten his wife, and anger flew over her, but if that were the case, why was she coming here of all places? No. Something else had happened— something terrible.

When she heard footsteps crunching through the hard-frozen snow, she ran to the door and opened it, and Raven helped the sobbing woman into the cabin. As the door slammed shut, she fell against Raven and, looking as if she could scarcely walk a step farther, gave a piteous cry. Her face and hands were cold-reddened, and snow covered her head shawl and the shoulders of her shabby coat.

It was evident that their visitor's clothing was sodden throughout; pity surging through her, Misty gripped her arm and led her to the fire. "What's wrong? What's happened?" she asked as the woman collapsed on an old chair and threw back her wet shawl.

Sloppy's wife sobbed a moment longer, then, finally getting control of herself, looked up and blurted, "Tommy's got the winter fever. He's had chills and a croupy cough and he's been sick at his stomach. He's awful bad." She caught Misty's sleeve and clutched it tightly, her face drawn with despair. "He's burnin' with fever and I don't know if he'll last through the night. Save my son," she pleaded in a strangled voice.

A hard look passed over her face. "Sloppy said I shouldn't come—that I was makin' a fool of myself." Her voice broke. "But I can't stand by and let my boy die!" She trembled and looked wildly at Misty. "I didn't know where to go . . . what to do," she cried, a pulse throbbing in her throat. "Will you save my boy?" she asked with mounting anguish.

Chapter Nine

Sloppy jerked his cabin door closed, muting the sound of the wailing wind. "Why are you two here?" he demanded, his face contorting in rage. He glared at Raven, then glanced at the rifle he held in his hand. "There ain't nothing you can do, federal man!" He jabbed a finger at Misty, who felt her eyes water from the aftereffects of the stinging wind. "And there ain't nothin' that gal can do either." His whiskey-laced breath told Misty that he'd been drinking, and his food-stained longjohn top and filthy breeches repulsed her. Only her concern for the sick child made her bridle her temper and hold her tongue.

Sloppy scowled at his wife, who was just slipping off her sodden head shawl. "I told that woman not to bring you here. But she was stubborn, wouldn't listen." He swung his malevolent gaze back to Misty. "Get out, just get out right now, afore you start messin' with the boy!"

Misty felt as if she were trapped in a nightmare and couldn't wake up. She could scarcely believe that less than an hour ago she and Raven had been talking and laughing in her snug cabin, and now a small boy's grave illness had turned their lives upside down with shattering swiftness.

Sloppy's wife grabbed his arm. "Let the girl try," she wailed, her eyes glittering in the half shadows. "We can't do no more and we're gonna lose him!" She started sobbing again, and putting her hands over her face, she crossed the room to where her other children huddled in sagging iron bedsteads, their faces pale and frightened in the firelight. Catching her breath in desperate sobs, she sank down by one of her little girls and hugged the child against her.

Her sensibilities offended by the filthy cabin and its fetid odor, Misty stripped off her coat and laid it aside. Her fingers still tingled from the cold as she knelt by the single bed, and ignoring the Brewsters, who'd retreated into a corner to continue their argument, she steeled herself to her task. Removing a damp rag from Tommy's forehead, she studied his white face. When she put her hand on his brow, she noted that, as the mother had said, he was burning with fever. Pity pricked her heart for the boy, and deep in her soul she willed him to hold on and take courage.

She looked at Raven's face—his concerned eyes, tight lips, and the taut muscles working in his jaw. Still holding the rifle, he moved to the other side of the bed and gazed at the boy, whose labored breathing was rapid and high-pitched. With a great sinking feeling, she told herself that the expression on his face confirmed her worst fears—the boy was dying.

Her mind searching for possible cures, she grazed her fingers over the child's blue lips and, picking up his small hand, noted the bluish cast of his fingertips. "It's the winter fever all right. The worst case I've ever seen." She popped open her satchel and started rummaging through it, setting small bottles of possible cures on a keg by the bed.

"I don't know if there's a thing I can do for him," she confessed, staring up at Raven. "I've treated winter fever before, but the person was awake and could swallow. I can make the boy an herbal tea to bring down the fever, but I don't think he can raise his head to drink it. It 'pears he can barely breath."

"The boy's unconscious," Raven said dully. "And I'm sure he can't swallow at all," he added, placing the gun aside. He walked to her side of the bed and knelt on one leg beside her. "Can you hold that lamp closer, so I can examine him?"

Wordlessly, she picked up the kerosene lamp and held it close by the boy's milk-white face. By now Sloppy and his wife had returned, and they looked on with grim expressions. Gently, Raven felt each side of Tommy's neck, then opened the lad's mouth and turned his head from side to side. With a deep frown, he moved back and pulled the shabby quilt up to the boy's chin.

Misty studied his eyes. "What do you think?" she asked softly.

Raven stood and ran a hand through his wind-blown hair, still sprinkled with snow. "You may call it winter fever in the Ozarks, but in Saint Louis we call it diphtheria."

"Diphtheria?"

"Yes, and it's highly contagious. Since none of the other children is sick, I imagine the boy caught it from someone outside the family." He directed his gaze at the mother. "Has he stayed with anyone else lately?"

The woman sniffled into a ragged handkerchief. "Just my sister. I left him with her about a week ago. But she ain't sick."

A thoughtful look crossed Raven's face. "She must be a carrier. She probably doesn't even know she has the disease."

The woman came to his side, and with tear-filled eyes watched her son struggle for breath. "If you're a doctor like you say," she cried, transferring her gaze to Raven, "what can you do for him?"

Sloppy pushed her away from the bed. "He ain't no doctor. I done told you that before. It was just somethin' he told this fool gal here!"

As he pulled the woman across the room, again reviling her for bringing anyone to the cabin, an aching heaviness centered in Misty's bosom. "It hurts me to see the boy like this," she whispered, rising to her feet, "but if I can't get any tea down him . . . if he can't swallow . . ." She broke off, her throat aching with tears.

Raven nodded and put his arm about her, caressing her shoulder.

With a hollow feeling, Misty watched the boy valiantly struggling for breath, but obviously losing the battle with every moment that passed. "Why is he having so much trouble breathing?" she murmured, her voice raw with worry.

Raven let out a long sigh. "In severe cases of diphtheria, the windpipe begins swelling shut. That's what has happened here." He picked up the child's limp hand. "That's why his lips and fingertips are blue. He's starving for oxygen."

"We can't let him choke to death," she said, a chill of despair running over her arms. *"We've got to do something."*

Raven remained motionless as Sloppy and his wife returned to the bedside and the woman knelt to brush back her son's hair. "If we were in a proper hospital . . . if we had the equipment, a tracheotomy might be done," Raven muttered, almost as if he were talking to himself. He glanced about the cabin. "But here . . ."

Misty, feeling a tiny flicker of hope, studied his intent face. "How is it done?"

He rubbed the back of his neck. "A small incision is made into the windpipe, then a tiny tube is inserted so the patient can breath. Once the swelling goes down, the tube is removed and the incision heals."

Sloppy grabbed his arm. "Are you sayin' you want to cut my boy?"

Raven met his accusing eyes and felt a bitter contempt for the man that was so strong it almost overruled his other emotions. Then he glanced at Misty's hopeful face, and at that moment made the decision that he would try the operation. He knew his chances for success were slim, and his better sense told him he was being foolish, but somewhere in the back of his mind he kept hearing her words, *we've got to do something,* and in his heart he knew she was right. He looked back at Sloppy's scornful face. "Yes," he replied evenly. "That's what I'm saying. He's unconscious and he'll feel no pain."

Sloppy glared at him with flashing eyes. "Do you think I'd let you put a knife to his throat!"

he spat out contemptuously. "Do you think I'd allow it?"

Raven studied the man, repulsed by him, yet pitying him for his ignorance at the same time. "The boy will die if I don't," he answered calmly. "He'll choke to death."

"I don't believe you," Sloppy flared. "That's just more of your lies. Hell will freeze over before I let you touch my boy!"

Suddenly there was the loud metallic click of a rifle being cocked, and all eyes swung to the head of the bed, where Sloppy's wife stood holding the weapon Raven had discarded. Tears ran down her face and her lips trembled. "I'll pull this trigger if you don't let the doctor help our boy," she vowed, pointing the rifle at Sloppy's heart. "So help me God, I will! I've done lost one baby to winter fever, and I'll not lose another one!" She spoke through her strangling tears. "I've been knocked from pillar to post by you for nigh on to twelve years now, being half scared of you and hatin' you at the same time, and I vow on the grave of my dead baby up on cemetery hill that I'll kill you dead where you stand if you try to stop this man from savin' Tommy!"

Raven met Misty's wide eyes, and with a quick look warned her to stay out of the situation, for he sensed that something important was about to happen.

The woman put the rifle butt to her shoulder and stepped closer to her husband, her eyes sparking with pent-up rage. "They may hang me for killin' you, but it'll be worth it if it saves my boy," she said in a quavering voice.

Raven studied her, knowing she was dead earnest. It was one of those moments when a person knows in his soul what will happen, and he knew that the woman was drawing the line at risking her boy's life. He'd always thought of Sloppy's wife as weak and submissive, but he didn't think of her that way anymore—and what's more, he knew she had the upper hand.

Sloppy stared at her, his shocked face now turning angry. "He ain't a doctor," he finally spat out. "Can't you get that through your thick head!"

"I believe he's what he says he is, and I ain't listenin' to you no more. From now on," the woman ground out between clenched teeth, "I'm doin' my own thinkin' . . . about him and everythin' else!"

With a look of utter disbelief, Sloppy stood stock still. On the other side of the room the frightened children, who'd never seen their mother act in this fashion, whimpered and huddled together. Sloppy finally moved his mouth wordlessly and, seeming to almost shrink visibly, hung his head and shuffled to the hearth, where he flopped down in a chair and bent forward to hold his head in his hands. A kind of delighted shock rippled through Raven realizing that once the woman had summoned the courage to face up to the bully, he'd folded so easily.

Sloppy's wife lowered the rifle, but in her glittering eyes there was a determination that said she wouldn't hesitate to use the weapon at the slightest provocation. Tears glistening on her lashes, she laid the gun across a nearby chair, then fell to her knees beside Tommy's head. Raven felt a glow of victory for her, and knowing how timid she was, a kind of awe for the mother love that had spurred her to finally stand up for herself and her children. With Sloppy out of the way, the boy now had a slim chance at life.

Her face white with shock at what she'd just witnessed, Misty came to his side. "What will you need?" she asked quietly.

"Find the smallest, keenest knife in the house and hold it over the flames for a few minutes," he advised, looking into her frightened eyes. "Put it carefully aside, then boil some water and gather some clean rags." He glanced about the cabin looking for something he could use for a breathing tube. He spied a discarded writing quill lying on the table where one of the children had been practicing his letters. "Cut the smooth end from that quill and let it soak in some whiskey."

At the hearth, Raven stripped off his jacket and rubbed his cold hands to limber them up. While Misty hurried about the cabin following his orders, he rolled up his sleeves and scrubbed his hands several times with lye soap and hot water.

At last everything was ready, and a conveniently placed lamp flickered in the draft seeping around the window and washed feeble light over the boy's white face. Raven, his heart beating a little faster, picked up the sterilized paring knife that lay on its side on the table, and walked to the bed. He saw the mother kneel on one side of the boy's head while Misty knelt at the other.

Outside the cabin, a lonely wind howled through the pines and peppered grainy snow against the windows; inside the wretched shack, the children had finally gone to sleep, and near the fire, Sloppy sat like a man of stone, his eyes fixed on the snapping flames.

There was only the sound of the boy's labored breathing and the mother's quiet sobs as Raven pulled in a long, steadying breath. With a tightening throat, he studied the child's near-lifeless face, remembering how the boy had once beamed up at him when he'd returned the tiny carved horse to him at church. He gazed at the child's pale neck, and for a heartbeat the scene before Raven faded before his eyes and there was a sickness in the pit of his stomach. If he failed this boy, who would help him? Like a prayer, he sent all his hope and determination toward the child. Perhaps it was just a trick of his mind, but the lad's face seemed to relax and he sighed audibly.

With a thudding heart, Raven poised the shiny point of the makeshift scalpel against the child's throat and began the incision.

It was done.

Raven, standing by the cabin window, pushed back the shabby curtain and cleared a circle on the clouded pane with his fingertips. He watched dawn explode behind the top of the mountains, making the Ozark's dark pines stand out like lonely sentinels against the rosy sky. The storm had passed, leaving the hollow still and glistening white. Behind him, he heard the popping of the dying fire and felt Misty's presence as she sat with the boy. The exhausted mother had lain down for an hour of sleep, and the other children were not awake yet. He knew that Sloppy, his face an unreadable mask, still sat like a marble statue by the hearth.

Raven could scarcely believe he'd actually preformed a tracheotomy on a small child under the feeble light of a kerosene lantern. He remembered how relieved he'd been when he heard the boy take his first rasping breath, and anticipation rose within him as he considered the delicate life now hanging in the balance.

Would the child live? he wondered. There was a good chance that his ministrations had been too late—that even though the boy could now breath without struggling, and his fever had abated because Misty had rubbed him with snow all night, he still might not survive the crisis. With a rush of despair, he realized that the boy might yet slip away.

"Raven, he's waking up."

His heart contracted at the words; turning about, he met Misty's eyes. Her aura of desperation had faded, and her face was aglow with hope.

Raven moved to the bed and put his ear against Tommy's chest. "His heartbeat is strong," he murmured, his hopes rising along with Misty's. The child's pulse was even and his brow was cool. When the boy moved and groaned faintly, Raven walked around the bed; after contemplating his patient for a moment, a great, peaceful stillness washed over him.

It was at this moment that he knew the child would live after all.

He glanced at Misty and noticed the dark smudges under her eyes, her disheveled hair, the fatigue stamped on her face. His heart went out to her. He picked up an extra quilt from the foot of the bed and draped it about her shoulders to ward off the chill hanging in the drafty cabin. "Wake up his mother," he said, gently brushing back her tangled locks. "I think he's going to be all right."

Misty rose, her starry eyes soft and glittering with tears. Clutching the quilt about herself, she gazed at him for a moment, and he knew the words she was unable to speak.

While she went to the mother, Raven knelt on one leg by Tommy's side, clasped his hand, and held it firmly. There was a light in the small patient's dark eyes and a look of relief as a tear rolled down his face. From the keg where the lamp stood, Raven took a cup of water and, raising the boy's head a bit, held it to his lips so he could take a sip.

By this time, the mother was sitting on the edge of the bed. She cried quietly and kissed her son's cheeks. At last she moved her gaze to Raven, a kind of worshipful wonder running over her face. He stood and, putting the cup aside, looked down at her. "He'll sleep for hours now," he said, glancing at the boy, whose eyelids were already fluttering drowsily. "It's just what he needs."

He heard a whisper of a movement, and from the corner of his eye saw Sloppy rise from his place by the fire. His head bowed, he slowly lumbered to the bed. With his rumpled clothes and red-rimmed eyes, Raven thought he looked like a lost soul who'd just caught a glimpse of his way. There were deep lines etched on his brow and about his mouth, and he stared strangely at Raven. "I . . . didn't know," he whispered harshly. He glanced down at the boy, then dropped his grizzled head and walked away.

Whimpers rose from the cool shadows, and one by one, the children began waking up, some of the older ones sitting up in bed. Raven settled his gaze on Misty, and by her expression, he knew she understood that it was time for them to return to her cabin. As they began to gather their things, the boy's mother stood and clutched his arm. "Is he really goin' to be all right?" she inquired, her face filled with entreaty. *"Is he goin' to live?"*

"Yes," he answered quietly.

Still she looked as if she couldn't believe that her prayers had been answered. "Is that a promise?" she asked, increasing the pressure of her fingers.

Raven covered her hand with his. "No," he said slowly. "It's a guarantee."

Raven stood in front of the wash basin, wearing only his breeches and boots, and peered at a bit of cracked mirror as he trimmed his beard with a pair of scissors. Misty, garbed in a homespun russet gown, knelt by the hearth, making red-eye gravy to go with their morning bacon and biscuits. From Raven's vantage point, she looked mighty fetching in the lowcut creation that set off her bright hair and eyes and displayed each of her curves so temptingly. A warm glow welled up in his chest as he thought how she'd burrowed herself into his heart and how she meant more to him each passing day.

A week had passed since the night of the terrible storm, and Raven studied himself in the mirror, thinking he should look different, because he certainly felt different. Saving Tommy Brewster's life had given him more satisfaction than anything he'd done in a long time, certainly more satisfaction than prescribing nerve pills for Saint Louis socialites' imagined ills. Perhaps his good spirits had to do with the fact that he was needed in the Ozarks and he was touching lives here in a way he'd never thought possible. He only wished that he had more supplies and some sophisticated medical equipment so he could really help the mountain people.

When he heard the jangle of a harness and the creak of wagon wheels, he shrugged on a shirt, then strode to the door and opened it. Through a veil of snowflakes, he saw Lukie and Brother Jubal wheel into the clearing leading a line of wagons and mules and horses, all carrying grinning people, bundled up against the blustery weather. Some of the horses had jingling bells on their tack, which lent a merry holiday atmosphere to the procession.

Too stunned to speak, he watched the mountaineers as they dismounted or climbed from the wagons, all carrying wrapped bundles in their arms. Children and barking dogs gamboled and frisked through the powdery snow, and the wind carried snatches of laughter. Who could these people be and what could they want this early in the morning? he wondered, running a hand through his uncombed hair. Surely they couldn't *all* have ailments.

"Misty, come here," he called, hastily tucking in his shirt. "Look at all these people. What are they doing here?"

She bustled to the door, then smiled and clapped her hands. "Well, I reckon you've finally been accepted for what you say you are! Word gets around like wildfire in the hills, and it seems it got around about what happened the other night."

A trio of lanky mountaineers walked toward the cabin carrying brown jugs, and by the looks on their faces, Raven knew they'd already sampled their wares and were in no danger of freezing. "I still don't understand," he said in a puzzled tone. "Have they come to visit?"

Sonya Birmingham

Misty burst out laughing and clutched his arm. "No, they've come to give you a pounding."

He looked at her sharply. "A what?"

"*A pounding*," she came back easily. "See those bundles in their arms? Some are bringing pounds of butter, and others pounds of sugar or molasses or whatever they happen to have on hand. It's their way of saying they *like* you, that you're one of them now."

"But it's barely daylight."

She widened her eyes. "That doesn't matter. They're just getting an early start. The party is likely to run on all day." Another wagon rattled into the clearing, and a big smile broke over Misty's face. "Oh look, there's Uncle Fuzzy and Aunt Izzy all the way from Russell's Hollow," she informed him, pointing at a small man and a large lady, who now climbed down from their wagon, carrying musical instruments tied up in pillowcases. "We'll have some real toe-tapping music now."

Raven didn't have time for further comments, for Lukie and Brother Jubal led the visitors into the cabin, the men stopping to shake Raven's hand as they passed. With a nip of surprise, he recognized old Jasper and even one of the men who'd challenged him in front of the church building. He suddenly realized that here in the mountains, he'd learned more about human nature than he had ever thought possible. It seemed that until you proved yourself in the Ozarks you were nothing—and after you did, you were treated like a king.

Although Raven and Misty hadn't put up a Christmas tree yet, they'd decorated the cabin windows with fragrant mantles of pine and red berries, which gave a festive air to the proceedings. With whoops of laughter, the visitors threw their coats and hats on the beds, then deposited their bundles on the table. Raven's stomach growled as he saw hams and pots of honey, jam and jars of home-canned vegetables, baskets of sweet potatoes, pies and cakes, and several jugs of potent white lightning.

Stomping the snow from their boots, the last of the visitors closed the door behind them, and after everyone had found a place to sit or stand, Brother Jubal cleared his throat. From the way the crowd quieted, Raven expected he was going to say something important.

The old preacher pulled off his battered felt hat and, his lined face wreathed in pleasure, fixed his eyes on Raven. "A lot of folks have been talkin' about the way you saved that Brewster young'un's life the other night"—he scanned the men and some of them looked sheepish and dropped their eyes—"and a lot of folks figure they was wrong about you being a federal man—that you weren't treated quite right when you came here." He smoothed back his silvery hair and adjusted his spectacles. "Some of the boys came to me and asked reckon we could have a poundin'. I said as I reckoned how that would be as fine as frog hair—and well . . . here we be!"

Left speechless, Raven slipped his arm about Misty's shoulder and, hugging her against him, searched her beaming face.

A teasing smile raced over her lips. "Well, I guess you've proven you're not all vines and no 'taters," she said with a wink. "And if you give me a kiss, I'll give you the first silver dollar I see rolling up hill with spurs on it!"

Sonya Birmingham

With a deep chuckle, Raven lifted her from the floor and swung her about in a circle. Then he took her mouth in a breathtaking kiss while their guests shouted and clapped. As a physician, he'd earned several degrees, but in some strange way, this humble tribute meant more to him than all his gilt-edged diplomas. Here in the Ozarks his father's millions meant nothing. He'd earned these people's respect and affection for his integrity and his skill as a physician.

"Where's your fiddle, Uncle Fuzzy?" one of the men hollered. "Let's have some tunes!"

The old man untied the pillowcase he carried and pulled out a fiddle, and before Raven knew what was happening, the furniture had been pushed out of the way. Moments later Uncle Fuzzy and Aunt Izzy, who made a banjo ring for all its worth, began to play while other couples stared dancing. Urged on by shouts of "Put the fire to it!" the old man flashed his eyes and sawed out "The Devil's Dream" like a house on fire. Hardly more than five feet tall, he had a round belly that hung over his britches and shook as he drew his rosined bow across the fiddle strings with the speed of lightning. After "The Devil's Dream," he played "Soldier's Joy," and "The Arkansas Traveler," and two men joined him, one keeping time by blowing into a jug while the other played the spoons on his knee.

Then a tall mountaineer began dancing on the hearth stones, preforming something that looked like an Irish jig. The top half of the dancer's body remained almost motionless, but his legs worked like mad, and his feet tapped over the stones in a blur, preforming the double shuffle and cutting the pigeon's wing.

There was dancing and singing until twelve, when Misty and some of the other women unwrapped and served the food. After Brother Jubal said grace, everyone sat where they could to enjoy ham and vegetables, corn dodgers and ashcake; for dessert there were pies along with johnnycake and maple syrup.

After the feast, music shook the rafters once more, and some of the couples danced, accompanied by handclapping and shouted jests. Later someone stood up to pose riddles that everyone tried to answer, while the children played with Rollo or went outside to frolic in the snow. The merrymaking went on for a few more hours, then the visitors started to depart so those who lived a distance away could reach home before sunset.

With some amusement Raven noted that now that he'd been accepted as a doctor, everyone treated him with great respect, and at the threshold many of the people lingered to ask his opinion about their ailments. Some of the men weren't ashamed to yank up their shirts and show him *where it was a-painin'* or pull back their lips so he could see an aching tooth.

One youth put his arm about his pregnant wife, who lowered her eyes modestly as the pair stood before Raven. "Afore the winter's out, Lucy here is gonna have our first young'un," the man proudly proclaimed. "If it's a boy . . . and if you think its all right, we was studyin' on namin' him Raven." A toothy grin shot across the hillman's bearded face. "I reckon that's gonna be a right popular handle around this neck of the woods now."

Raven nodded mutely and shook the man's hand.

Before the visitors left, Misty wrote the names of everyone who needed care and told them when they could return to see Doctor Raven, as the mountaineers now called the man they'd once shunned. At the door, a little granny draped a heavy shawl over her head and, squeezing Raven's arm, wheezed, "I never doubted you was a doctor for a second. I could see you was a fine man by just lookin' at your eyes!"

When everyone was gone but Lukie and Brother Jubal, Misty made coffee. Then she and Raven sat down at the table with them to relax and reflect on the afternoon. As they were winding down by commenting on the funny things that had happened during the pounding, Bother Jubal leaned back and said, "I sure wish Ezra could have been here to play his guitar. I know how much he would have enjoyed it."

The words were no sooner out of his mouth than Lukie stood. A strange look passed over her face, and she hurried to the bed and searched her deep jacket pocket. "I plumb forgot," she apologized, a blush staining her freckled face as she offered an envelope to Misty. "When I was in town yesterday to pick up our mail, the man at the post office asked me if I'd bring this to you."

Misty rose, and Raven noticed that her hands shook a bit as she accepted the wrinkled letter. "It's from Ezra!" she exclaimed, her surprised expression melting into a look of concern. "I'd know that big scrawl of his anyplace." She ripped the end from the envelope and took out the pages, her eyes racing back and forth over them. "He says he's gonna get done at the saw mill a little early." Her cheeks a bright pink, she read on, then glanced up at everyone, a tremulous smile on her face. "He'll be home sometime around Christmas," she finished, her bosom heaving with excitement.

Brother Jubal chuckled and rattled his coffee cup in the saucer. "Well, that's real fine. I've been worried about that boy for some time now."

The letter fluttered to the table, and Misty met Raven's gaze with wide eyes. "Isn't that wonderful? Ezra's coming home early," she said, striving for a cheerful tone that only partially concealed her nervousness. "I want this to be the best Christmas ever. We'll need to go into Eureka Springs to get some special holiday fixings next week. I've got a big gunny sack of snakeroot that we can trade to Mr. Tanner at the general store."

Raven noted the tension on her face, but before she knelt by his chair, she camouflaged it with an over-bright smile. "You'll finally get to meet my brother," she added, running a trembling hand over his arm. "He's usually not fond of flatlanders, but I know he's bound to like you."

Raven studied her agitated eyes and understood that her natural eagerness to see her brother was tempered by concern over what he would think about their marriage. Obviously, when big Ezra Malone strode into the cabin, they would all have some long talks about the stranger she'd "jumped up and married" while he was gone.

And then, as always, there was the matter of the feud. With Ezra returning, he would be free to return to civilization with Misty. But first of all, he would have to tell both her and her brother who he really was. He only hoped he could explain things in a way that would minimize the shock they would experience. Feeling as if his emotions were caught in an ever-tightening vice, Raven put down his coffee cup, his light-hearted day taking a serious turn. It was funny, he thought, how a few words on a sheet of paper could change someone's whole mood. He realized that everyone at the table was looking at him strangely, and he tried to force a smile, but his lips just wouldn't work properly.

He'd painted himself into this tight corner, and at this particular moment he couldn't think of a single way to escape.

Chapter Ten

Raven positioned the gunny sack of snakeroot on his back and scanned the picturesque village of Eureka Springs, whose winding streets defied any kind of order or logic and followed the path of least resistance. Log cabins, softly lit against the dreary afternoon sky, perched upon jutting outcroppings, and tents and shacks clung to the limestone mountainside and nestled in great gorges. The whole town had a raw frontier look about it and seemed as if it had been thrown up overnight. In its dress of white, the spot reminded him of a crude Tyrolean village—without one level foot of ground. He shifted the heavy sack on his back.

Raven and Misty made their way up Spring Street, far above the place where they'd left their wagon and mule, and passed a livery stable and a saloon that emitted a tinkle of piano music. It was here that several mountaineers came through

185

the swinging doors and, with wide grins on their faces, ambled up to Raven and shook his hand.

Pride warmed Misty's heart as she stood there and watched the scene played out before her on the board sidewalk. Raven was now the most famous man in Red Oak Hollow and the surrounding territory. No flatlander had ever been more revered than the Saint Louis doctor who'd saved Tommy Brewster's life during the worst night of the year. His legend had grown, and many people without ailments wanted to meet him so they could tell their friends they knew the famous Doctor Raven. To these people, he was now one of them; he was a true hero—the man of the hour.

After the men left, Misty pulled her jacket more tightly about her, and she and Raven slogged across the snow-encrusted street. From there, the pair walked up a flight of crudely cut stone steps in the direction of Mr. Tanner's general store. A few hundred yards later, the wooden railroad depot appeared through the falling snow.

Misty looked at the depot as an engine hissed steam, then blew its shrieking whistle and slowly chugged away, pulling a string of rattling boxcars behind it. "I remember when they were laying those rails," she reflected, holding down her floppy hat against the wind. "The sound of the men driving the spikes echoed all through the hills. It was the biggest thing that ever happened to this little town."

"Let's go watch the train pull out," Raven suggested, eyeing her upturned face. Despite his troubles with his father, he felt pride surge within him as he looked at the large sign on the side of the depot reading *Missouri and North Arkansas*

186

Railroad Line. After all, it was Ezekiel's shrewd stock investments that had been the impetus for the railroad company, and that fact alone brought him a feeling of satisfaction.

Their footsteps crunching in the grainy snow, he studied the depot, whose main building towered two stories, while the first-floor contained a heated passenger waiting room with a ticket office. On closer inspection, he spotted a baggage room and platform sheds connected to the main structure. A separate freight depot stood alone, circled with wagons and stacks of boxed cargo.

Stung with a pang of nostalgia, he listened to the rattle of the departing train as it vanished into a cloud of enveloping snow. Glancing at the track, he realized that those long silvery rails connected Eureka Springs with Saint Louis, a place where many people were anxiously waiting for his return.

Under the depot porch, he saw a glassed frame on the wall displaying several timetables and a map of the United States. He stooped down to tap the large black dot that represented Saint Louis. "Look at this," he told Misty. "This is my home"— he ran his finger along a rail line marked in red— "and this is the route I took to get to the Ozarks."

She bent and stared at the map. "That little spot is Saint Louis? I've heard of Saint Louis all my life, but I thought it would be bigger than that."

Raven stood and laughed. "Well, it is. It's the gateway to the West—the jewel of the Mississippi." Despite his new acceptance in the Ozarks, he experienced his first real homesickness as he recalled the city he'd been so eager to leave, but now yearned to show to his new wife.

He hoisted the sack on his back, and they strolled on toward the general store. "Wouldn't you like to take a train trip there someday?" Raven asked in an appealing voice, his gaze falling on her doubtful face. "Saint Louis has everything. It's a great river port, and it has fine homes and department stores, famous theaters, cathedrals, even a symphony orchestra and one of the best newspapers in the United States."

Misty paused and placed her hand on his arm. "Does it have mountains and rushing streams and trees so tall you can't see the tops?"

He laughed. "No, but—"

"Is it filled with coons and deers and possums and birds singing their little hearts out?" she inquired, the wind whipping bright hair from beneath her hat.

"No, but—"

"Is the air so clear it sparkles and the water so cold it could split a stump?" she asked, blinking the snowflakes from her long lashes.

He expelled a frustrated sigh. "No, of course not, but—"

"Well if it doesn't have those things," she remarked loftily, rubbing her gloved hands together, "I don't want to go there." Raising her chin, she breezed off in the direction of the general store, seemingly dismissing the subject.

With a few swift strides, he was beside her. "You don't know what you're talking about. There's never been a place like Saint Louis!"

She cut her eyes at him. "You can say that again. And I don't care shucks about it."

He stopped and whirled her around to face him. "How do you know you don't like it when you haven't even seen it?" he prodded with

188

growing irritation. "Can you tell me that, miss know-it-all?"

"I've never been to hell either, but I know I wouldn't like it, and I'm not buying any train tickets to look it over." She tugged away, her eyes spitting sparks. "Don't worry, I know what Saint Louis is like!"

"No, you don't," he shouted, watching her swish ahead of him. "You've never been out of the hills."

"Aunt Izzy told me all about Saint Louis," she parried over her shoulder.

He strode to her. "Aunt Izzy used to live there?"

"No, but I know it's an evil place, and I don't want to pitch my tent toward Sodom and Gomorrah."

He burst out laughing. *"Pitch your tent toward Sodom and Gomorrah?"*

"Yep. Aunt Izzy has a cousin named Ida Bell."

"Oh, I see," he shot back, hardly believing the argument he was hearing. "Ida Bell lived there?"

He took her arm, and they crossed the street to the general store, whose false front was emblazoned with lettering advertising its goods. "No," Misty replied, her tone making it clear that she was getting a little annoyed with him. "Ida Bell has a niece who's married to a man in Berryville named Rip. Rip is friends with Luke Gallagher in Springfield. Luke once talked to a friend of his who talked to his second cousin once removed who talked to a fellow who sold cordwood. The cordwood man had talked to a businessman who made regular trips into Saint Louis on the railroad."

They stopped beside a deserted whittling bench. "Regular trips?" Raven echoed, trying to untangle the convoluted information she'd just dumped on him.

Her fingertips poking from the ends of her frazzled gloves, she put her hands on her hips. "Yep. Every two or three years that poor fellow had to back his ears and go into that Sodom and Gomorrah, whether he liked it or not."

Raven's mouth twitched upward at the thought of Saint Louis being compared to Sodom and Gomorrah.

She sighed and bit her lips. "You see, the businessman told the fellow who sold cordwood, and the cordwood man's cousin once removed told his friend, and his friend told Luke, and Luke told Rip, and Rip told his wife, and his wife told Ida Bell, and Ida Bell told Aunt Izzy, and Aunt Izzy told me." A big smile spread over her face. "You can't beat first-hand information like that. I'd never want to visit Saint Louis. I'm a mountain girl, and a mountain girl I'll stay!"

Raven tapped her on the chest. "That's ridiculous. You haven't the slightest idea what Saint Louis is like. You're an opinionated little mountain girl and—"

Leaving him alone with the sound of the wind in his ears, she entered the store.

"We'll need some candles for the tree and some raisins 'cause Ezra is awful fond of raisin pie," she called back, peeking over her shoulder. "Oh, don't let me forget to get some peppermint candy, too. Christmas just don't seem like Christmas without peppermint candy."

Raven, thinking that peppermint candy was the least of his problems, walked into the store himself and slammed the door behind him. On one side of the poorly lit building stood shelves of canned

vegetables, and on the other, in brightly labeled
tins, patent medicines such as Dr. Chaise's Nerve
and Brain Pills and Hostetter's Stomach Bitters.
The proprietor's desk and a covered showcase
of glittering knives and jewelry and fifty-cent
spectacles ran along the back of the store.

Misty picked up a can of Dr. Kilmer's Female
Remedy and Blood Purifier and frowned. "Would
you look at the price they've got on this?" she
commented disgustedly. She shoved it back on
the shelf. "It's a sin to the dogs. To tell you
the truth, I'd rather grind my own remedies
than buy this stuff." She circled her gaze over
the seemingly empty store, then meandered
toward the back. "Mr. Tanner . . . you here?"
she called out cheerfully. "Me and Raven have
some snakeroot to sell you."

As she entered the storeroom, Raven surveyed
the establishment, whose dim interior seemed
a jumbled mess. The storekeeper had recently
ground fresh coffee beans, and their aroma
mingled with the scent of tobacco, home-cured
hams, and leather saddles and boots. Walking past
a warm pot-bellied stove, Raven tossed his sack
of snakeroot on the back counter, which already
supported an open jar of peppermint sticks and a
tray of vanilla-scented chocolate fudge. He pulled
in a deep breath. What a wonderful potpourri of
mingled aromas, he thought, grudgingly admit-
ting he'd never visited a store in Saint Louis that
touched his senses this way.

With an impatient sigh, he resigned himself to
the fact that if Misty had her way, she'd never
see the glittering shopping palaces of Saint Louis.
How could he explain to her that as his wife,
someday she'd be forced to leave her beloved

mountains and actually live in the Sodom and Gomorrah she'd decided she hated with all her heart?

There were voices, and a thin man wearing spectacles and a white apron walked out of the storeroom, Misty at his side. A smile on his lips, he slicked back his thinning hair and stuck out a bony hand. "So, you're the Saint Louis doctor folks is talkin' about," he remarked, laugh lines crinkling from his twinkling eyes. "What can I do for you, Doctor Raven? I have whisky to ease the body and Bibles to soothe the spirit. I carry everything from diapers to dentures."

Raven tugged open the sack and poured some of the snakeroot onto the counter. "We won't be needing any of those things today. Misty said you often bought her herbs."

The storekeeper picked up a few of the roots and studied them intently, then whipped a pencil from behind his ear and scribbled on the back of a paper sack. Pursing his lips, he placed some snakeroot on a scale and scratched his head. "Yep. This looks like prime snakeroot to me," he wheezed, peering over his spectacles. "I figger I can give you twenty cents a pound for it," he ventured, tossing them both a speculative gaze.

Misty's face lit up. "You've got a deal, Mr. Tanner." She took Raven's arm and pulled him away from the counter. "*Come on,*" she whispered roughly, snatching up a handful of paper sacks. "That's the best price I ever got." She picked up a pound of coffee and tossed it into her open rucksack. "I think he's right partial to you. We better hurry before he changes his mind."

The old man cleared his throat and called out, "You two get what you want while I weigh out the rest of this snakeroot."

Together the pair scooped out raisins and sugar and everything they needed for Christmas, then poured the supplies into the paper sacks. As Raven rolled up the top of his baking powder sack he noticed Misty admiring a dress hanging from the ceiling to display it. Trimmed in lace, the rose-print garment had a black background, a tucked bodice, and a row of tiny buttons down the back. Misty's eyes glistened and she paused to brush the skirt against her cheek, her face bathed in pleasure at the splendor of the garment; then, noticing that Raven was watching, she blushed and knelt to scoop flour into her sack.

Later, when Mr. Tanner was tallying their goods, Raven spied a flash of gold glimmering up at him through the display case. Looking more closely, he saw a row of plain gold wedding bands resting in a velvet jewelry case beneath the glass.

"Is there anything else I can show you, Doctor Raven?" the shopkeeper asked respectfully.

Raven was aware that Misty had been watching him, and as his gaze strayed to her, her eyes shone with happy anticipation. "Yes, we'll be needing that dress you have on display, and one of those wedding rings before we leave—and a pound of peppermint sticks, too," he announced, still holding her eyes.

Misty's heart leapt. She'd never personally known anyone who'd been rich enough to own a gold ring, and she had never expected to have one herself. But it seemed that Raven was buying one for her, and that fact made tears prick her eyes. There was a kind of lazy amusement on his face now, and he was regarding her with a look that made her flush.

Lost in a haze of euphoria, she heard muffled words, and somewhere in the back of her mind she was aware that Mr. Tanner and Raven were talking and the storekeeper was giving him credit and saying that since he was a doctor, he could pay for the purchases later. Then the tray of rings was on the counter right beside the peppermint jar, and Raven had taken off her ratty glove and tossed it aside. He bent his dark head to kiss her hand, then slipped the ring on her finger and twisted it around to make sure it fit.

It fits perfectly, she thought, her heart pounding. She spread her fingers, and the ring shimmered before her eyes, its brightness no match for the glow inside her heart.

Raven gathered her into his arms and held her against his hard chest, caressing her back, and the excitement of getting the ring and her first store-bought dress made her temporarily forget how uncomfortable she'd been when he talked about going to Saint Louis. They were married, and even though he'd never said it, he surely loved her for he'd bought her a real gold ring.

He edged her away and smiled down at her with warm tenderness. "It isn't the kind of ring I would have chosen, but I suppose it will do for the time being."

Then and there, Misty looped her arms about his neck and kissed him long and hard right on the mouth, right before Mr. Tanner and Bill Wiggins, who'd just walked into the store and called out that he wanted to buy some liniment for his mule.

And for that moment, Misty forgot about Saint Louis being another Sodom and Gomorrah, and she forgot that she would ever have to go there and meet Raven's rich father. All she could think about was being the luckiest woman in Red Oak Hollow and Eureka Springs and the whole state of Arkansas.

Christmas Eve came to Red Oak Hollow with gusts of fluttering snow, but inside Misty's cabin, a warm, pink light crept out from the hearth to touch the edges of things and give them a soft, magical quality. Her hands pushing back her long hair, she stood looking at herself in the cracked mirror above the washstand as she tried on the new store-bought dress for the third time. Her locks were dark and glossy, her skin clear and white, and the happiness swirling within her had turned her green eyes the color of emeralds. The sateen dress clung to her lithe curves, and its long, lace-trimmed sleeves and full skirt gave her a sense of luxury she'd never known. Light from the kerosene lamp caught on her gold wedding ring as she brushed through her hair, and the band's twinkle made her feel as if there was a wild, sweet song playing in her heart.

Raven, who'd been wrapping presents, came to stand behind her, his hands going to her breasts and his head bent so that his warm lips nuzzled the side of her neck, making her joy soar to new heights. "You're mighty quiet tonight," he remarked softly. "What are you thinking about?"

"I was just thinking what a miracle it was that I was the one who found you on the road," she murmured. "How lucky I was."

He turned her about and gently stroked her hair. Not too long ago, he'd returned from outside with a bucket of pine cones to make the fire crackle and burn more brightly, and he still smelled of spruce and the cold outdoors. "Believe me," he offered, tenderly pushing back her locks, "it *was* a miracle . . . but the luck was all mine."

His words touched something deep within her, and the nearness and musky aroma of him sent her blood racing faster. When he brushed her lips with his, a slow languor stole over her, making her weak with longing and excitement. Rapture shooting through her like sparkling star dust, she clutched his shoulders, and as he deepened the kiss, her nipples strained against the sateen and ached sweetly. She knew she was passionately in love with him, wildly happy when he was near and desolate when they were separated, yet it still shook her heart when she thought of all the things she didn't know about him, and when he talked of going to Saint Louis, as he had during their trip to Eureka Springs, it frightened her to death.

With tender movements he now placed tiny kisses over her forehead and cheeks and regarded her with darkening eyes, an erotic fire glittering in their depths. A sweet warmth surged between her thighs because she knew they would soon turn down the lights and go to bed, but for now she searched for an excuse to stay up and enjoy the rapport they shared a little longer. Her body still tingling from his touch, she glanced at him through her lashes and whispered, "Let's open your present now."

He flickered a doubtful gaze over her. "Are you sure?"

She slipped from his arms and hurried to a little tree standing in the corner whose white candles shimmered with soft light. A few homemade gifts, wrapped in brown paper and saved twine, lay under its boughs, trimmed with strings of popcorn and cranberries. "Of course I'm sure," she answered, kneeling by the tree and searching among the presents.

For Lukie she'd worked hour after hour fashioning a broom from a split hickory sapling; for Brother Jubal she'd made a pillow from goosedown she'd saved all year; and for Billy Red Scarf—just in case she saw him—she'd made a box of fudge. She'd even hoarded a pint of honey for Rollo, but for Raven she'd saved her best efforts, a knitted muffler she'd worked on during the odd moments he was away from the cabin. Brimming with anticipation, she picked up his package and handed it to him, wondering what someone so rich would think of his first homemade Christmas gift.

"Here," she said, presenting it proudly, "go on . . . open it."

His gaze was as soft as a caress. "Thank you," he said quietly.

"It isn't much," she said with a grin. "Your best gift is gonna come a little later."

They laughed, and she felt a ripple of excitement as she led him to a chair by the hearth. A spicy scent floated on the air, for she'd finished her holiday baking, and all was in readiness for Lukie and Brother Jubal, who'd be coming for Christmas morn. Everything seemed so warm and cozy tonight—so perfect, she told herself, wishing she could preserve the moment forever.

Still, as she watched Raven unwrap the gift, she thought that despite the holidays, he'd been moody the last few days, and although he said he was pleased that Ezra was coming home, his manner didn't reflect it. And there was something in the back of his eyes that bothered her deeply. In her reflective moments, she considered Ezra's imminent return herself, feeling guilty that she hadn't summoned the courage to write her brother that she'd married while he was gone. Then, with a sigh, she told herself that this news would be better related face to face.

Before Raven finished unwrapping the muffler, they heard the thud of horse's hooves and the jangle of bridle bits outside the cabin. For a moment, fear welled up inside her, then she told herself that she was being foolish. Raven had now been accepted by his most ardent foes, and the rider could only be a friend. Of course—*it was Ezra!* she decided with nervous excitement. She rose to fly to the door, but Raven stood and, giving his head a negative shake, put his hand on her arm, then went himself.

As soon as the door closed behind him, she ran to the window and pulled back the curtains, spilling out light that made a pattern on the drifted snow. Through the swirling flakes, she saw a man dismount, and her heart sank, for the rider was too small for Ezra. No, this man was dressed in a fashionable winter riding coat with a fur collar, and he wore expensive boots and a fine hat. Although Raven stood stock still, staring at the stranger with disbelief, she sensed that he knew him, and when they clasped each other's shoulders, she realized that she was right.

For a moment, anxiety swept through her, for this man was not from her world, and by his expression as the pair stood talking, she sensed that the stranger was bringing news that would call Raven away from the mountains and shatter her happiness.

The snow whirled down faster and Misty's anxiety turned to fear, but her natural life force rose to meet the danger that she knew she must face. With a racing pulse, she snatched up her long shawl, threw it over her head, and ran from the cabin. The night air was cool and fresh, and the snowflakes felt icy against her cheeks as she walked to Raven and slipped her arm through his.

Upon her arrival, the men fell silent; then Raven encircled her waist and swept his concerned eyes over her.

Although the stranger was almost as tall as Raven and resembled him in a vague way, he had a soft, almost apologetic look about him that gave him a weaker appearance. The fine man stared at her with surprise; nevertheless, she detected warmth in his sad eyes, and with a rush of understanding, she suddenly realized who the visitor was—*he was Raven's bother*. With an aching heart, she instinctively understood that the thing Raven had been concealing since he'd arrived in the mountains was going to be revealed to her. He cupped her face and looked at her earnestly. "Misty . . . Warren has come all the way from Saint Louis to find me." Her fears confirmed, her heart turned over in her bosom, and she ached for the pain she saw etched on Raven's face as he added, "Let's go into the cabin. You aren't going to believe what I have to say."

Misty looked up into Raven's grim face, and her voice a mere whisper, she murmured, "*Your name is what?*"

He knelt by the chair where she sat and took her hand. "My name is Adam Davenport." He bowed his dark head, then gazed at her with full eyes. "That first day, when you asked me who I was, I lied." He tightened his fingers about her hand. "But I lied to protect you, sweetheart, to keep from hurting you."

Raven's eyes glittered with anguish. "I know it was wrong, and with every passing day, I felt worse about lying. It was a terrible mistake. I kept looking for ways to tell you, but something always came up, something always happened to keep me from doing so."

Misty was so stunned that she scarcely comprehended what was happening. Then, as his words sank in, she pulled away from him. With great physical effort, she stood, her legs trembling and her mind racing. Warren had gone to the stable to unsaddle and feed his horse, and she and Raven were alone. The cabin was deadly silent and cold, where only thirty minutes ago it had been filled with warmth and laughter. It now appeared dim and shabby and utterly sad.

To Misty it seemed as if Raven had pulled the very heart from her body and left an aching void in its place. She'd given him all her love and hopes and dreams, and with a sick feeling spreading through her stomach like ice, she realized that he'd lied to her and deceived her.

She'd wanted him so badly that she'd fooled herself into thinking that their match might work, but she now realized that he'd only used her for his pleasure and dealt with her as if she were no more than an ignorant child. She recalled the time they'd stood by his grandfather's grave and how evasive he'd been about the old man's last name.

For a moment she wondered if Ezra was right—if all the bad things she'd heard as a child about the Davenports were true.

Dizzy and light-headed, she glanced back and noticed the expression of compassion on Raven's face, and for some unexplainable reason this added to her pain. How dare he think he could treat her like this, then smooth everything over with a few citified words! she thought, her shocked hurt giving away to rising anger. She'd been a fool, and his deceit made her feel as if someone had smashed her life against the hard earth, breaking it into pieces.

Raven studied Misty's trembling form, noting that all the color had drained from her face. Her bosom rose and fell rapidly, as if she were struggling for breath. Regret knifing through him, he moved to her side, hesitated for a moment, then clutched her arms. She tried to pull away, but he held her there by sheer force of strength. Desperately, he tried to think of words to ease her hurt. "Forgive me. I should have told you, I—"

With a powerful twist, she pulled away. Tears glistening in her eyes, she placed her hands on her hips. "How could you have done such a thing?" she cried, quaking all over. She stared at him, her eyes shimmering with reproach. "Did you think I was so ignorant you could tell me what you pleased?" she added, her tone seething with humiliation.

Raven, knowing how he'd crushed her, bridled his temper and told himself he owed her his patience. "No, of course not. I know it was wrong, but I kept waiting—waiting for a better time to tell you," he explained in a strained voice.

Her delicate mouth hardened. "But you never found one, did you?" she queried, anger threading her words. With hot eyes, she raised her chin and met his gaze. "Were you going to wait until I met your father, or just ride off when you got tired of me warming your bed?"

"*No, dammit!*" he spat out, wanting to hold her in his arms and take away the pain. He raked a hand through his hair and, trying to rein in his emotions, studied her stricken face. "Warren has brought news that our father is dying," he said at last, noticing that her expression became more sympathetic. "John has suffered from heart trouble as long as I can remember, and a week ago he had a massive attack."

She moved to a chair and clasped the back of it, her eyes now calmer.

Raven paced the length of the cabin and back again, trying to walk off his nervous frustration, and as he thought of the father he'd never loved, a painful knot of emotions lodged in his chest. "I must go back and see him . . . see if there is anything I can do for him," he explained, glancing at Misty, whose slumped shoulders reflected her own inner turmoil. "If I can't help him, common decency demands that I try to make peace with him before he dies." An empty feeling washed through him as he realized that he had no natural affection for the man and only held a sense of duty toward him—a duty that now had to be fulfilled.

He paused, riveting his eyes on her. "I want you to come with me."

His request left Misty stunned and shaken. Although she felt a prickling of compassion for him, she was still so angry that her breath came in ragged gasps. "*You want me to go to Saint Louis?*" she asked in an incredulous tone, holding his gaze as she slowly sank to the bed.

After what he'd done, how could he ask her to go to the city, especially when he knew she despised the very thought of leaving the mountains? Confusion and despair and anger all coalesced within her in a great aching pain just beneath her heart. Closing her eyes, she chaffed her arms, thinking she'd never be warm inside again.

Then footsteps arose from outside, accompanied by a chill draft, and Warren entered the cabin and closed the door behind him. Quickly assessing the situation, he shifted his eyes in embarrassment. "I—I'm sorry," he stammered. "I didn't mean to—"

"Forget it," Raven said easily. He motioned him to a chair by the hearth. "You can tell me more about what is happening at home. Come and warm yourself by the fire."

Raven glanced at Misty, and from the look on his face, she knew he regretted the interruption. From his actions and the tone of his voice, she also knew that he loved and cared for his younger, somewhat hapless brother, and despite her anger, she couldn't help but admire the trait.

She now realized why Raven had waited until Warren took his horse to the stable before he revealed his shocking secret, and she was relieved that the young man had been spared the scene. She'd already welcomed him with food and hot coffee before he'd gone back outside, and in the short time she'd known him, she was impressed with his intelligence and kindness. She thought he looked much better now than he had earlier when he'd first arrived half-frozen and explaining how the people at the Eureka Springs livery stable had given him directions to her cabin, home of the famous Doctor Raven, who fit his brother's description so closely.

She'd never met anyone so appreciative of a kind word, and she knew enough about human nature to realize that although he was undoubtedly proud of his dashing older brother, he must be cold always standing in his shadow. At the same time she saw sympathy for her in his soft gray eyes and felt an instant comradeship with him. She now watched him take off his fine coat and muffler and sit near the flames while Raven stood, his bearded face imbued with emotion as he listened to his brother's story.

Barely comprehending their words, she stared straight ahead, trying to sort out her swirling thoughts. Moments later, she noticed the sound of distant hoofbeats. Alarm washed though her. *Ezra*, she thought, glancing at Raven and Warren, who were so absorbed in their conversation that they hadn't heard the almost imperceptible sound.

With escalating panic, she moved to the window and pushed back the curtain, searching the darkness. As yet she couldn't see anyone through the blustery snow, but dread raked over her as she remembered her huge brother's great strength and fiery temper, his booming laugh when he was amused, and the way his green eyes fairly struck fire when he was angry.

Then, in the space of a thudding heartbeat, she saw him ride into the clearing on his dappled-gray mare. He dismounted and lightly wrapped his reins about a tree limb, obviously anxious to see her before he led his horse to the stable. Her stomach knotting, she caught a glimpse of his tired face and, in the meager light spilling from the window, watched him take a Christmas present from his saddle pouch.

Panic spurted through her. Her legs scarcely holding her up, she whirled about, shaking with fear for Raven and his brother. Her mouth so dry she could scarcely speak, she cried, *"Ezra's here."* In the time it took her to move to Raven's side, the door banged back and big Ezra Malone strode into the cabin and latched the door behind him.

Chapter Eleven

Raven, feeling Misty tremble, pulled her against him and took a long measure of his new brother-in-law. A tall man of great bulk, Ezra wore a snow-sprinkled black hat, a heavy jacket, buck-skin breeches, and scuffed logger's boots. Lanky, reddish-brown hair hung to his shoulders, and a full beard covered the lower part of his harsh face. Raven could tell that under the shabby clothing, the man's shoulders were massive and his chest thick; he was almost solid muscle. Although the mountaineer's face held none of Misty's softness, it bore a family resemblance, and in his own way, the giant projected a rugged handsomeness.

Ezra's shocked, confused expression yielded to sudden fury. As he tossed the Christmas present on the table, his coat whipped back and a Bowie knife glittered at his side. His countenance turning plain mean, he glanced sharply at Raven; then, sailing his hat aside, he stepped closer. He was now so near that Raven caught his heavy masculine scent mingled with the aroma of the man's leather boots.

The logger's blazing gaze went to Misty, then dipped to her wedding ring before resting on her face. "Why are you wearin' that ring and fancy store-bought dress?" he jibed. He glanced at Warren, who still sat quietly by the fire. "I've never seen either one of these strangers," he stated, now fixing his eyes on Raven. "Who in the devil are they, and why has this one got his arm around you?" he demanded, his face hardening with suspicion.

Misty held herself proudly, but Raven heard her breath coming raggedly. "This is Raven"—her voice quavered—"me and him were married a while back." She tilted her head at the hearth. "The man by the fire is his brother."

Warren awkwardly stood, then blurted out, "Yes . . . I'm Warren Davenport."

Raven's heart sank, for he'd hoped to gradually introduce the idea that he was a Davenport. But now that the news was out, he could only hope for the best.

Ezra's face was blank and utterly unreadable for a moment, then rage swept over his features. *"Davenport?"* he breathed slowly. "There ain't no more Davenports in the hills. If there was, I would know about them."

Raven stepped slightly in front of Misty. "My grandfather, Ezekiel, was born here, but my brother and I are from Saint Louis." He remained silent as Ezra took in the information, then he continued speaking in an even voice, trying to stabilize the explosive situation. "I came here for a visit a few months back, but was attacked and left for dead. Misty found me and cared for me."

He straightened his back, determined to have the rest of it said and over. "When we met, I thought it would be best to tell her I was someone else." He paused for a moment. "I misled her." He glanced at Warren, whose face was clouded with apprehension. "My brother came to tell me our father is dying." He assessed Ezra's great anger, and despite it, knew the words he had to say. "I want to take Misty back to Saint Louis with me."

For a few seconds, the mountaineer stood stock still; then his mouth tightened with rage. *"You lied to her?"* he asked in a thunderous voice, his hands flexing into fists. "And now you want to take her from the hills?" he lashed out, smacking a fist into his open palm. "No, sir. I won't stand for it!" Defiance flooded his features, and his tilted chin challenged Raven to oppose him.

Misty knew her brother was almost beyond reason when he was riled, and her mind grappled for a way to bring down his temper. "Wait, Ezra! We have to talk about this," she cried out. "It isn't what you think."

Ezra's eyes snapped fire. "There ain't no talkin' to be done. You let in an outlander—a city man— and a Davenport at that. Did you lose every lick of sense you had while I was gone!"

When the woodsman reached out to grab Misty's shoulder, Raven interceded, putting out his arm to block his reach. The hillman's face hardened as he shouted, "Davenport, you die!" and drew back his arm and swung wildly, grazing the side of Raven's head.

In response, Raven shot a right to the man's jaw that knocked him to the cabin floor, but the mountaineer lumbered up and came at him, a solid chunk of flesh and bone. Ezra feinted a left hook, then looped a powerful right to Raven's jaw, sending him crashing against the table.

Before he could regain his balance, Ezra pounded him in the ribs. Seeing his brother at a disadvantage, Warren joined the fight, but Ezra pulled his knife swept it toward him. Misty cried out and rushed forward, but not before her brother moved again, slashing Warren's arm.

Sick with fear, Misty stepped back and saw bright blood flood his arm; at the same time, Raven scrambled to his feet and pushed Warren out of harm's way. Ezra now came at Raven with the knife, and by the wild light in his eyes she knew he was out of control.

Her heart racing furiously, she impulsively ran between them and grabbed her brother's arm with both hands. Tears stung her eyes, and she trembled inside as she struggled with him, crying, "Ezra, put down that knife!"

He threw her a furious glance; then, as her fingers tightened about his hard muscles, an amazed expression came over his face. Still clutching the knife, he visibly relaxed and finally let his arm fall to his side, breaking her grasp. With a fiery expression, he glared at Warren, then swung a hot gaze over Raven. "Get out. Just get out—both of you," he shouted in a choked voice. "I'll have no lyin' Davenports in my cabin." He drove his finger at Raven. "And I'll never let one carry my sister off to Saint Louis!"

Sonya Birmingham

Misty stepped back and studied her brother, who stood there like an enraged bear, his chest heaving with anger. She knew she'd never forget his face when he saw her grab his arm, and with a feeling of sinking despair, she also knew that things would never be the same between them.

Her eyes met Raven's as he examined his brother's bloody arm, and she saw outrage shimmering in their depths. Surely he must be disgusted with all Malones, including herself. But why should he be the only one upset? she thought, swallowing past the lump in her throat. All her dreams had been smashed and ruined, and suddenly all the joy she and Raven had ever shared turned to ashes.

He'd deceived her and spoiled their love as well as her relationship with her brother, who'd cared about and provided for her most of her life. She looked at Warren's wild eyes and blood-soaked sleeve, knowing the feud between the Davenports and Malones, which had lain dormant for so long, had just burst into flames once again.

Her throat ached with anguish; all the hurt, confused feelings she'd harbored since learning that Raven had deceived her surged up inside her like a scalding tide. Fighting an urge to break into tears of despair, she gazed at Raven evenly, at this moment both loving and hating him. "Yes," she said in a low, harsh voice, scarcely believing that the words were passing over her lips. "Do like Ezra says. Get your things and get out."

The old ticket seller in the North Arkansas and Missouri railroad station adjusted his spectacles and peered at Raven from the shade of his green visor, asking, "What will it be, sir?"

Raven shoved several folded bills under the barred opening of the ticket seller's stall. "Two tickets for Saint Louis—one way only."

The dried-up old man turned around for a moment, then slipped two pink tickets, along with some change, under the bars. "There you are, sir," he replied with a thoughtful blink. "Check your baggage with the porter." He lowered his spectacles and glanced at a big railroad clock above the waiting room door. "The train leaves at five-thirty on the dot," he added, swinging his gaze back to Raven. "That gives you thirty minutes to take care of your business in the Ozarks."

Raven put the tickets in his pocket. *Thirty minutes to take care of his business in the Ozarks,* he thought, walking toward Warren, who sat with a handful of other passengers waiting for departing trains. Thirty minutes to take care of his business, when by the turn of recent events, it looked as if it would take forever to straighten out his problems.

He recalled the three days since he and Warren had ridden away from Misty's cabin, thinking they'd been the worst in his life. He couldn't forget the stricken look on her face when he'd told her he was a Davenport, and a bundle of confused, depressed feelings knotted in his chest as he remembered her cold words: *Do like Ezra says. Get your things and get out.*

He'd managed to live through those three days attending to the things that had to be done. During the wee hours of Christmas morning, he'd applied an antiseptic to Warren's arm, then wrapped it with bandages while the nervous proprietor of Perkin's Boarding House looked on with wide eyes, holding up a kerosene lamp against the

211

darkness. Although the wound had bled profusely, it wasn't that deep, and Raven was sure that outside of a fine scar down his forearm, his brother would soon be as good as new.

After a few hours of fitful sleep, the pair had spent a dismal Christmas Day talking about Raven's Ozark experiences, including the discovery of Ezekiel's grave and the mystery of what had become of the fortune he'd taken with him. The following day Raven had tied things up in Eureka Springs, paying Mr. Tanner for Misty's ring and buying a decent set of clothes for himself with money Warren had brought from home.

And now, he thought, his heart aching, he was ready to return to civilization. But how could he go back without Misty, when she'd changed his life forever? It would be like leaving a part of himself here in the mountains.

With a hollow feeling, he sat down on the hard pine bench by Warren and stripped off his gloves. They sat there for a good five minutes listening to passengers' voices echoing through the large, near-empty hall and the sound of the hissing train, which was already building up steam.

An almost palpable tension rode the air, and at last Warren turned his attention to his brother. "I'm sorry I had to tell Papa where you were. I hated doing it like hell," he blurted out. "When you first left, he was so furious I thought he was going to have a stroke, but I still held out on him. Then last week, when he had this heart attack, the doctor said he might die soon." He sighed heavily. "That's when I caved in, and the next thing I knew, he was ordering me to track you down and bring you home."

Raven nodded, knowing that under the circumstances, there was no way Warren could have resisted their father's determined nature. "I understand," he calmly replied, letting his gaze wander across the station.

Warren hung his head for a moment, then looked back at Raven. "Lord, you look terrible," he suddenly remarked.

Raven cut his eyes at his brother. "Does it show that much?"

Warren gave him a lopsided grin. "Only to every man, woman, and child in this waiting room," he replied, giving him a questioning glance. "Do you want to talk about it?"

Raven leaned back against the creaking bench. "What is there to talk about?" he asked, thinking his feelings were still too raw to discuss. "I made a grand mess of things, and I have no one to blame but myself."

Warren moved his gaze over the shabbily dressed mountaineers in the waiting room. "I'm not so sure it was all your fault. These folks don't think like city people."

A heaviness centered in Raven's chest. "I agree. Going into the hills is like being swept a hundred years into the past." He visualized Misty's face in his mind's eye as she talked to him about medicine. "I've learned a lot here," he commented idly, feeling a strong tug of nostalgia.

A little smile rippled over Warren's lips. "Like what?"

"Well, for starters," Raven began in an amused voice, "slippery elm slime will cure the river ague, and for coughs and colds nothing is better than golden seal. And I'll bet you didn't know," he went on lightly, "that green persimmon salve is the best

213

healing potion known to civilized man." He lifted a brow. "It's made with strained persimmons fried in hog lard."

"Anything else?" Warren asked with a chuckle.

"Yes," Raven answered thoughtfully, his voice now serious, "money won't make you happy."

The light faded from his brother's eyes. "You and I have known that for years," he said quietly.

With a surge of loss, Raven sat quietly for a moment reassessing his months in the Ozarks and the new perspective it had given him on life. "These people may be mired in ignorance and superstition, but at least they know who they are."

Warren's half-smile held a flicker of sadness. "What do you mean by that?"

"During the last few months I've been wondering just who I am," Raven explained matter-of-factly. "I used to know. I was Adam Davenport and took office calls on Monday, Wednesday, and Friday, and went to Saint Mary's Hospital on Tuesdays and Thursdays for surgery. I attended balls every Friday and Saturday night during the social season, tried to avoid the pack of debutantes on my heels, and left early to play poker with my friends at Murphy's Bar on Eighth Street."

Warren's eyes kindled with interest.

"It wasn't the best of lives," Raven continued, "but it was *my* life and I knew who I was—a Saint Louis society doctor with a rich clientele. Then I came to the Ozarks and met Misty Malone and she gave me a new name. I grew a beard and became another person—Raven, a country doctor who tended the poor for bartered goods."

Warren regarded him for a quiet moment, then suddenly cut to the heart of the matter. "You love her, don't you?" he questioned point-blank.

The words slid past Raven without comment as he searched his soul, wondering what true love really was. "I'm not sure. I only know I don't want to be without her."

"Do you think she'd see you . . . talk to you?"

Raven reassessed his brother, giving him more credit for wisdom than he ever had. Of course, he'd considered the idea repeatedly the last few days, but to hear another person verbalize it made him reconsider it again. "I don't know," he finally answered. "Ezra's home and there are so many things that are different about us . . . things that are unsettled." He slapped his gloves against his thigh. "Things that I've only made worse."

Warren leaned back, another thought apparently crossing his mind. "She *did* come between you and Ezra, you know."

Raven, latching onto the words of hope, glanced at the big railroad clock and told himself that Misty was his wife and they'd shared a wedding vow—a vow to stand by each other no matter what. Then he suddenly thought of her saying that the heart was often smarter than the head. At this moment, his head was telling him that he was being utterly foolish, that he should get on the train and forget their star-crossed relationship, but something deep within him told him to heed his heart, which was advising him to go back to the cabin and try to work things out yet again.

When Raven stood, Warren gazed at him with a smile of approval.

"Meet me next Wednesday at the train station in Saint Louis," Raven said, handing him one of the tickets. Feeling a sense of urgency, he suddenly knew what he had to do. He had to see Misty. He had to try to explain how he'd only been trying to protect her when he'd made a terrible mistake and hurt her so deeply.

Warren also rose to his feet, his brows rising with amusement. "Don't be any longer, will you? Papa is calling for you, and I'm going to have a devil of a time trying to explain this arm and what's happened since you arrived in these mountains." He flashed his brother a wry grin. "And just wait until he hears some mountain girl has renamed you. The whole thing sounds like a fairy tale, and I doubt if he will believe me at all."

Raven looked down at him and tugged on his gloves. "Let's just hope this fairy tale has a happy ending," he replied, feeling a flame of hope for the first time in days.

The forest held the misty hue of winter and a fine sifting of snow powdered the rough ground as Raven galloped toward Red Oak Hollow. After the stuffy atmosphere of the railway waiting room, he rejoiced in the freshness of the woods and the sting of the wind on his face. Riding under the bare limbs which formed a canopy above his head, he recognized familiar landmarks but so far had met no other riders.

He was beginning to wonder if he would when he spotted a saddled horse cropping the short grass at the side of the road. His first reaction was one of caution, for he was near the place where he'd been attacked, and he reined his mount to a canter, then a walk. A warning sounded within him; then, with a snap of recognition, he realized the gray dappled mare belonged to Ezra. His insides grew taut as he nudged his horse forward, and from the concealment of a

huge oak leaning over the road, he searched the
territory ahead of him.

There, to his surprise, he saw two burly men
accosting Ezra beside the road. He remembered
Misty once saying that her brother liked to
ride into Eureka Springs on Friday nights, and
obviously word had reached the bandits' ears that
he was home and carrying a bundle of sawmill
money. The wind snatched away the voices of the
hard-bitten men, but as their mounts grazed over
the winter grass, one of them brandished a pistol
at their victim, demanding his money.

Ezra stalled, obviously not wanting to relinq-
uish his hard-earned pay, but when the bandit
jammed the gun into his belly, he slowly took a
packet from his jacket and handed it to the second
man, who stood with an outstretched hand.

For all of his surprise, one part of Raven's
brain remained cool and imperturbable, as if
this was merely a dream. His stomach tightened
and every nerve tingled in readiness. Without a
weapon, he had only one choice, and as the
man glanced down to slip the money packet
into his jacket, Raven's fingers worked surely.
Gathering his reins, he spurred his horse to a
dead gallop.

After that, events happened incredibly fast.

Their eyes large with terror, the white-faced
ruffians wheeled about and fixed their attention
on Raven, who plunged toward them at breakneck
speed. The bandit fired off a shot, but in his haste,
aimed poorly, and the bullet zinged past its target.
When Raven was almost on them, he jumped from
his horse atop the man with the gun, and the
action sent the weapon sliding over the winter-
burnt grass.

During that second, Raven met Ezra's eyes and instant understanding flew between them. He knew the mountaineer realized he was putting his life on the line for him. In the commotion that followed, the second man dropped the money packet, and Ezra was on him in an instant, pounding his fists into him.

The first bandit finally rose to his feet and swung back his arm for a blow that exploded on Raven's jaw. In return, Raven jabbed with his left and smashed his opponent's lips, splattering the man's jacket with blood. The stunned bandit staggered backwards, then dove at him, swinging powerful arms and hooking his ham-like fists into his side. Raven backed off, and the woodsman smashed a heavy left to his face, then drew back his muscled arm yet again.

Raven, knowing he must finish his opponent off quickly, blocked his left with his forearm, then caught him on the chin with a punishing right. A split second later, he threw himself at him, knocking him to the frozen ground.

With the last of his strength, the man wobbled to his feet only to meet a bone-jarring left to the cheekbone that left him on shaky legs. Raven now sent a blow into his belly, and as the bandit bent over, smashed a roundhouse into his jaw, which crunched bone and twisted the lower part of the man's face askew. The bandit went down like a sack of coal and sprawled on the ground, his chest heaving deeply.

With a rasping breath, Raven now glanced to his right and saw that the other bandit had knocked Ezra on his back. Before he could bat an eye, the man whipped a long knife from his boot and took deadly swipes at Ezra's throat, which Ezra barely managed to evade by twisting out of the way and grabbing at his attacker's arms. Not giving the action a second thought, Raven snatched up the discarded pistol and, aiming at the bandit's chest, fired away. The shot echoed through the hills, and for an instant a startled look flickered over the man's face. Then, dropping the knife, he toppled onto the earth beside Ezra.

Raven scarcely had time to gather his wits when the man he'd beaten to the ground crawled to his feet and pulled his own knife from his boot. His eyes shining with an insane light, he made a sound like an angry bear and, lowering his head, lunged forward, raising the knife at Raven. Again relying on gut instinct, Raven pulled the trigger, sending the man backwards to the ground as if he'd been pole-axed.

After the ear-splitting shot died away, he tossed the weapon on the ground, for moments oblivious to everything but the deep pounding of his own heart. The acrid scent of gunpowder still lingered on the chill air, but an almighty calm now pervaded the hills, and all he could hear was the sound of the nickering horses, which had skittered a short distance away.

On the ground where the body lay, a gold pocket watch had slid from the bandit's pocket. Raven, going over and picking it up, found it was his and realized that these were the same men who had originally attacked him months ago. As he bent on one knee and searched the man's clothing, footsteps scraped over the frozen stubble. Glancing up, he saw Ezra standing there, his face marked with astonishment. "Y-You killed them," he stammered in bewilderment. "You killed them both."

Raven said nothing, but went to the other bandit and, finding his ring on the man's hand, took it off and put it in his pocket. He still felt a little shaken by the swift, violent event, and if the truth be told, a little sad. Saving lives was his business, not killing.

Like a huge child, Ezra followed him and again repeated, "You killed them." With a slight movement of his eyes he indicated the other man. "You killed them quick as lightnin'." Raven glanced up, and although the light was almost gone, he could tell the shootings had struck some powerful cord within the big man. He studied him for a moment, then returned to his work. "There was no help for it," he said harshly. "I just reacted. They came looking for trouble and would have killed us both."

Rising, he locked gazes with Ezra, and from the tormented look in the man's eyes he knew a great struggle was going on within him. For a brief span, the woodsman just stood there dumbstruck; then Raven picked up the discarded money packet and handed it to him. He started to walk away, but Ezra clutched his arm, his disquiet apparent. "No," the mountaineer said, uncertainty creeping into his expression. "I've got somethin' to say, and it's fittin' that I say it now." A hint of tears glistened in his eyes. "Pa always taught me to stand up for the Malone name, and to me that meant keepin' the feud goin', but Pa taught me somethin' else, too—that when a man saves your life, you're beholdin' to him for the rest of your days."

Raven clasped his shoulder. "Ezra . . ." he began.

The huge man put out a spread hand. "Let me finish. You saved my life, and I'll always be beholdin' to you." As his words began to flow, a new composure settled on his face. "But it's not just this scrape that's changed my thinkin' about you. Misty and me have been doin' some talkin'. She's told me things that have happened—the way you stood up to Sloppy, and how you saved his boy—and how you seem to have real feelin's for the folks in these hills."

He hung his head, then raised it, his eyes filled with regret. "I was torn up the other night when I came home and the cabin was full of Davenports. And I reckon I went kind of crazy. But I've been doin' some studyin' on the situation, and I reckon since my blood and yours is gonna be mixed together, we should call off this feud."

He put his large hands on his hips and shook his head. "I never figured after all this time, I'd ever see a Davenport take a Malone's part. And I sure never thought I'd be the one to call an end to the feudin', but Pa always said sometimes it takes a stronger man not to fight than it does to fight."

Raven felt a warm satisfaction rise within him. Although it had taken a tragedy to break through Ezra's antiquated sense of tradition, he'd finally seen the senselessness of the feud and had summoned the power to throw off the hate he'd shouldered most of his life. Doubtless, he would wrestle with his conscience for months, and even years, before the matter rested completely easy in his mind, but he'd found the courage to begin forgiving.

As they walked toward their mounts, the shadow of a smile touched Ezra's lips. "By the way you was headed, I reckon you was ridin' out to see Misty. Why don't you go on? I'll throw these fellers over their horses and take them into Eureka Springs. I figure they're wanted men, and the sheriff will be right glad to see me."

A glint of warmth in his eyes, he paused and stuck out his callosed hand. "Sorry about your brother. Will you shake with me?" he asked, straightening himself with dignity.

Raven grinned and pumped his hand. "I'd be proud to."

Moments later, he watched Ezra walk away to gather the bandits' mounts, and as he swung atop his own horse, one question hammered at his mind: what kind of mood would Misty be in when he reached the cabin?

Misty, holding her tender emotions in check, raced her gaze over Raven's battered face and dabbed it with a healing potion. "Are you sure Ezra is all right? He isn't hurt?" she asked, fresh panic rising within her.

Raven clasped her hand and sat her down in the chair beside him. "He's bruised and scraped like me, but no permanent damage has been done." His understanding gaze clung to hers. "As I told you before, he took the bodies into Eureka Springs so the sheriff could identify them. We'll need to go into town later ourselves."

Misty dropped the wadded rag from her hand. She'd been thinking of Raven all day, but when he'd knocked on the door ten minutes ago, and she'd opened it and seen him standing there bruised and bleeding, with the shoulder seam of his fine suit ripped open, her heart had turned over in her bosom.

After he'd left three days ago, she'd made up a little speech that she was going to give to him he if he ever came back to the cabin. She was going to meet him with the rifle and tell him that he was a lying Davenport and a no-good city slicker who had taken advantage of her, and she'd thrown away her wedding ring. Besides that, she was going to tell him she'd forgotten all about him and never wanted to set eyes on him again! Then as the days passed, an incredible loneliness had seeped through her; she'd not been able to take off her ring, and she found she missed him terribly.

Even if she'd wanted to keep him out, one look at him in his present condition would have changed her mind. His story had made a chill race up her spine, and for the tenth time she thanked the Lord that neither he nor Ezra had been hurt.

As she rested her forehead on her spread fingers and took several deep breaths, trying to calm her nerves, he stood behind her and put his hands on her shoulders, massaging them. The masculine scent of him and the weight of his hands spread a comforting warmth through her body, easing the tension within her. Reaching upward, she clutched his hand. How she'd longed for him these past days and how she'd hoped he would return! From the perspective of a few days, how foolish her request that he leave the cabin now seemed.

In her heart of hearts, she knew she had been partly concerned for his safety earlier and only wanted to remove him from Ezra's threatening presence; still, she'd uttered words she never thought possible, and as soon as he'd gone, a sick feeling of loss had struck through her.

She and Ezra had discussed Raven at length during a sad Christmas day. Then her brother had gone about his business, catching up on chores and visiting old friends. As he talked to the other mountaineers, his opinion of Raven had mellowed, yet he'd been too proud to ride into town and speak with him.

Her hopes spiraling upward, she now released Raven's hand, then rose and turned about to face him. With a sense of powerful relief, she observed his tense face; noticing new lines etched there, she realized that he'd gone through his own torment the last few days. "And Ezra really shook hands with you?" she asked in a quavering voice, still scarcely believing it had happened.

He brushed back a lock of her loose hair. "Yes, he did, and I believe he genuinely wants us to get along. It seems as if our run-in with the bandits touched something within him."

Misty felt a new closeness to her brother. "Yes, a mountain man always feels beholden to someone who saves his life." Her mouth curved into an unconscious smile. "It's part of the code of the hills." She walked to the hearth and, crossing her arms, stared at the leaping flames, marveling at how this twist of fate had brought out a maturity in her brother that she hadn't known existed.

What a battle must have stormed within him when his rescuer had turned out to be a Davenport and he had to weigh his gratitude against his stubborn pride! Perhaps now he could understand that being a man also involved being able to receive a kindness as well as providing food and shelter and protecting the family name.

Raven moved behind her and lightly encircled her in his arms. "Are things all right between you two? I mean—"

She turned about, noting the questioning concern in his expression. "I suppose there's a love between us that can't be broken. It hurt him bad when I stepped between you two, but hour by hour and day by day his mood changed. He's never said anything about it—it's hard for him to talk about things like that—but I believe he's forgiven me. I can see it in his eyes." She grinned, thinking of all the times she'd anticipated Ezra's actions when they were children. "I know him so well, I can almost read his mind."

She looked down for a moment. "W-Why did you come back?" she stammered, feeling foolish, but knowing she had to ask the question anyway.

He lifted her chin with gentle fingers, and the fire in his eyes made a quiver course through her. "How could I stay away?" he asked, his face softening with emotion. "Warren and I were talking in the railroad waiting room—actually, I guess I was talking and he was listening." Their gazes met and held, and he brushed his long fingers over the side of her cheek. "Anyway, I knew I couldn't leave without seeing you again."

Her spirits fell that he hadn't told her that he loved her, but he'd thought enough of her to come back before he left. And he'd dared Ezra's wrath to see her—a brave act in itself. "I can't believe the feud is really over," she said, remembering the story he'd once begun by the honey tree and never finished. "By the way, what happened to that Romeo and Juliet couple? Did their story have a happy ending?"

Raven frowned. "No, not really . . . but we'll write the ending to our story, not Mr. Shakespeare. And I guarantee you, it will be happy." His eyes now became so intense that she felt a blush sting her cheeks. "That is, if you'll go back to Saint Louis with me," he stated, his voice taut.

Euphoria rushed through her; at the same time, she experienced a fear she'd never known. *Saint Louis*, she thought, barely able to comprehend the idea of such a huge city, filled with great buildings and elegant homes. How could she leave Ezra and Lukie and Brother Jubal and all her other friends? How could she talk to people who'd been born in mansions, when she'd been born in a log cabin? Why, it would almost be like trying to talk to those Frenchmen clear on the other side of the world; he might as well be asking her to go to the moon or a distant star. "For how long?" she finally whispered, fearing what she might hear.

She noticed a twitch in his jaw before he answered, "I'm not sure. Certainly until John recovers . . . or passes away." He heaved a great sigh and gently ran his hands over her shoulders, flushing them with warmth. "Things have never been good between us, and I think I should try to change that before . . ." His voice trailed off and finally faded altogether.

He'd touched her generous woman's heart, and she felt herself giving over to his way of thinking, even though she still trembled at the thought of leaving the mountains. "Where would we live?" she asked, biting her bottom lip.

"Since John is so ill, I think we should live there with him and Warren in the mansion on Garrick street. I can look after him that way."

She widened her eyes. "Is it a big mansion?"

He laughed softly. "The biggest in Saint Louis. It has three floors with twenty-five rooms and all the paintings and statues that John could buy and ship back from Europe. In fact, it looks something like a gloomy museum." Amusement played at the corner of his mouth. "When Warren and I were boys, we used to call it the mausoleum," he remarked dryly.

She chuckled a little. "The mausoleum? What does that mean?"

His expression darkened, but he shrugged lightly and gave her a forced smile. "Nothing much. It just means it's a fancy place."

By now Misty knew that Ezra wouldn't stand in her way and the decision to go with Raven rested squarely on her shoulders. She got a sudden flash of how much she'd be leaving behind: walks in the spring woods fragrant with flowers, will-o-the-wisps on damp nights, the morning mist fresh from the hills, and the flame of autumn, so rich it dazzled the eyes. A hollow, aching homesickness stole over her, and she hadn't even left the mountains yet.

"Well, what do you say?" Raven prompted, gathering her into his arms and massaging her back until a shudder of desire coursed through her. It was hard to pay attention with him so close, caressing her, and excitement swirled in the pit of her stomach. "I imagine we could get your things ready in a day or two," he whispered into her hair, pressing her more closely to him.

Craving his touch, she buried her face against his shoulder and gave a shuddering sigh. "I'm sure gonna miss my fresh air and spring water and having a hard bed every night." She frowned and, pulling back a little, looked him in the eye. "And being so citified, I'll bet they don't even have mountain medicines in Saint Louis. You know—things like ant eggs."

Laugh lines crinkled around Raven's eyes, and he rained kisses over her cheeks. "We'll open the mansion's windows and put boards under your mattress, but we'll just have to improvise where the ant eggs are concerned." He gave a low, throaty chuckle. "When a person is going to Sodom and Gomorrah, she has to expect some disappointments, you know."

"I'll have to bring Rollo," she insisted. "He'd grieve himself to death without me." She arched her brows. "And I'll want to take my doctoring satchel, too. A person never knows when she's gonna run across some sick folks."

Raven flashed a smile, and she noticed that his face held a look of deep relief. "Whatever you want," he agreed, lowering his head and feathering his mouth over the pulse in her throat.

Soon his lips sought hers in a questing kiss, moving across them with such an explosive effect that her blood rushed through her veins like hot quicksilver. Her senses reeling, she put her arms about his shoulders and an unexpected sweetness blossomed within her, like a wild rose opening its petals to the summer sun.

As the passionate kiss continued, Misty surrendered to a great rush of tenderness that warmed her all the way through, and her heart throbbing wildly, she realized that she was powerless to resist him. Even so, the realization that despite all her fears she'd agreed to leave the mountains left her a little light-headed. Lord above, she couldn't believe she'd said yes, *but she had*, and like her granny had always taught her, she must stand by her word.

In two days, she thought with a mixture of trembling dread and breathless excitement, Red Oak Hollow's best herb doctor would be on her way to Saint Louis.

Chapter Twelve

Three days later, Misty Malone sat in a dining car an hour and a half from Saint Louis and a million miles from her roots in the Ozarks. From her seat at a window table, she let her gaze roam over the plush car, now empty except for herself and Raven, and she could scarcely believe what she saw.

The special dining room on wheels was resplendent with velvet upholstery, hand-carved paneling, parquet floors, and elegantly appointed tables with fresh flowers. Overhead, a trio of crystal chandeliers tinkled cheerfully with every curve in the tracks.

"Everything is so fancy," she drawled, running her fingertips over the soft pile of the drapes. "It looks like something I saw on a poster in front of the railroad station one time."

Raven chuckled, then reached across the small

table and, covering her hand with his, caressed it with his thumb. The man who'd dressed in buckskin for months was now garbed in a starched white shirt, a new suit, and the best string tie Eureka Springs had to offer, making him a picture of fashion. Although he'd cut his long hair, Misty was happy he'd kept his beard because to her it made him look like a mountain man. "You'd better get used to it," he admonished in a firm voice. "It's yours now."

She slipped her hand from his and spread it over her bosom. *"Mine?"*

He grazed a knuckle over his jaw. "Well, in a way of speaking. It belongs to the Davenport family."

The train careened around a curve, and she glanced cautiously upward at a jiggling chandelier, then looked back at Raven. "From what Luke Gallagher told me once, this looks like the breakfast room of a fancy house of ill repute one of his friends saw in Fort Smith. How many of these dining cars does your pappy own, anyway?"

Raven laughed and shrugged his shoulders. "Actually I've never bothered to find out. I'll have to ask Warren about it sometime."

Just then, a white-jacketed steward approached and flourished a silver tray before Misty. "Pheasant, ma'am?"

She nodded at the man, and he lowered the platter and scooped a portion of pheasant and wild rice upon her plate, then served Raven. Afterwards the steward quietly left the dining car and closed the door behind him, leaving the pair with the sound of the clicking wheels.

Misty, feeling a tug at her skirt, glanced down to see that Rollo had finished lapping honey from a china dish and now gazed at her with imploring eyes. Chuckling, she reached for a small silver pitcher, refilled his bowl, and put the container aside. "I'll bet Rollo thinks he's died and gone to raccoon heaven," she told Raven. "He's always had to scrap for honey, and now he has a whole pitcher of it just for himself."

She now selected one of her three forks and tried to attack an artichoke that sat in her salad plate. Unable to dislodge the leaves, she looked at Raven and frowned. "How is a person supposed to eat this prickly thing? It looks something like a squashed pineapple, but it hasn't got any bottom on it."

He gently took her fork and laid it aside. "It's an artichoke. You're supposed to pull the leaves away with your fingers, then strip off the flesh with your teeth."

She widened her eyes. "Well, I'll be flamboozled. That doesn't sound too mannerly at all. I figured highfalutin' Saint Louis society folks ate everything with a silver fork and held their pinkies in the air while they were doing it."

Raven performed the operation for her so she could see how it was done.

She followed suit, and even made a little show of tossing the artichoke leaves aside, but deep within her she was scared stiff—scared that she would be a complete failure when it came to mixing with Raven's family and friends. Within an hour they would actually be in Saint Louis, and Warren would be at the station to meet them and escort them to the mansion.

The mansion, she thought with an inward shudder. Lord, what would happen when she arrived? Raven had been indulgent with the mistake she'd made with the artichoke, as he was with all her mistakes, but she had a feeling that everyone else in Saint Louis wouldn't be so forgiving, especially her new father-in-law.

As they finished the meal, Misty raised the tasseled shade, and in the darkness made out the shapes of trees and farmhouses and saw a host of bright stars sprinkled across the cloudless sky. The level land made her homesick for the mountains, and even now, a great lump formed in her throat as she thought of the emotional scene that had taken place earlier in the day at the Eureka Springs railroad station.

Ezra had dressed in his Sunday best to see her off from the hills. She remembered the resigned look on his face, the sheen of tears in his eyes, and the way his work-hardened hand had felt against her cheek when he'd kissed her good-bye, then hugged her so hard her bones had cracked. Then he'd turned and purposefully walked to his horse. She'd ached to call him back, to be with him a moment longer, but she realized that he'd left quickly to spare her a lingering farewell.

Lukie and Brother Jubal had been there too, and when the train's whistle split the air, she'd hugged them both, thinking her heart would break into pieces. Outside of her granny, she'd always thought Brother Jubal was the best person she'd ever known, and she and Lukie had been friends forever. And now she'd be denied the comfort of their familiar faces.

As the train had chugged away and the pair on the platform had become no more than a blotch of color, she'd been forced to quell the panic within her. And when the locomotive had clickety-clacked over a switch crossing and she'd lost sight of them altogether, she experienced a feeling of near despair.

Misty now steered her mind back to the present and watched moonbeams glimmer over a slash of gently curving rails that vanished into the darkness. Her heart thudded with anxiety, yet at the same time she felt a trembling anticipation for what lay ahead. In the back of her mind, she kept hearing Brother Jubal's last admonition: *Be yourself, child, and everyone who is important will like you.* That's just what she would do, she promised herself, her courage rising like a tide. She would be herself and let the good folks of Saint Louis take her as they would.

Raven thought how lovely Misty was with light from the little table lamp glinting in her auburn hair. She wore the same dress he'd bought her for Christmas, and the expectant look on her face tugged at his heart. He'd known how difficult it was for her to leave Eureka Springs this morning and how frightened she must now be as they neared Saint Louis. The incident with the artichoke had been amusing, but in his heart he realized that it was only a foretaste of things to come. She was bound to have a rough go of it in the city, and if he knew anything about John and the socialites he patronized, she was bound to be hurt.

She looked from the window again, then leaned forward and clutched his hand. "Look," she exclaimed, "I can see lights . . . lots of lights. Is that Saint Louis out there?"

"Yes," he answered quietly, wondering what it would be like to once again be that innocent, to feel that eager for adventure. He reached for a bottle of wine that sat in a silver ice stand near the table and, lifting his brows, caught her dancing eyes. "Wine?" he asked, positioning the bottle above her glass.

She threw him a look of gratitude. "Yes, I've never had anything but Aunt Izzy's dandelion wine before, but I feel all fluttery inside, like a whole net of butterflies have been set loose in my stomach."

He filled their glasses, glad he'd bought tickets for a hotel express car so she could get her first taste of city luxuries. "To new beginnings," he proposed, raising his glass aloft and giving her a reassuring wink.

Misty took a sip, then another, and chuckled lightly. "To new beginnings," she returned, her face aglow.

Raven saw her put down her glass, then hoist Rollo into her arms and stare from the window, her face registering her excitement as she smoothed back the raccoon's glossy coat. Lord, what a reception lay ahead for the pair of them! he told himself, picturing his father's reaction when he saw that he'd brought home not only a half-illiterate mountain girl but her pet raccoon as well.

He watched her eyes that now snapped brightly and was once again touched by her courage and self-confidence. Thank God she had those qualities in abundance, he thought with a feeling of relief.

If he knew anything about his father, she would need all the spunk she could muster.

As the locomotive slowly pulled into the green-domed Saint Louis railroad station, Misty stood beside Raven in the partitioned cubicle at the rear of the car, waiting to leave the train. They were alone, and with Rollo at her heels, Raven thought she looked small and vulnerable as she stared through the window, getting her first glimpse of the sprawling station. He couldn't help but notice her wide, frightened eyes. Trying to give her comfort, he gathered her to him and stroked her springy curls. "Well, Doctor Malone, here's the moment you've been waiting for. Don't worry, Saint Louis will love you, and you'll love Saint Louis. It's inevitable."

Her eyes speaking her gratitude, Misty tipped her face up to him. "I'm not quite as sure as you. Everyone is moving awful fast out there, and no one is smiling."

He kissed her forehead. "Well, I'm sure of one thing. If anyone can steal their hearts, it's you." Cradling her face, he traced his fingers behind her ears, then his lips touched hers in a soft caress. He was aware of her fresh scent and her beating heart, and a warm, full sensation rose within him as he silently vowed to protect her from all who would try to take advantage of her innocence.

Misty felt Raven's arms go tight about her, and as his lips moved over hers, heady seconds passed. The warmth of his caressing hand spread over her back, and a great inner excitement, created by both her sexual feelings and the drama of the moment, stirred within her. Then the train was slowing and grating to a stop, and Raven was lifting his lips and drawing back, his eyes warm and reassuring.

A porter walked through the car and hearing his cry of "All out for Saint Louis," she scooped up Rollo and held him against her bosom, shivering with anticipation. Just then a uniformed attendant yanked open the door from the outside, letting in a rush of cool air and the sharp scents of oil and soot and sulphurous smoke.

Raven escorted Misty from the train, and from her place on the platform, the station looked huge and cavernous. Even in the new coat Raven had bought her from Mr. Tanner's general store, she felt the penetrating chill of the winter air. Raven hailed a red-jacketed porter, and he soon brought Misty's dulcimer, medical satchel, and other pitiful possessions from the baggage car. Having nothing resembling a suitcase, she'd put her clothes into a large basket she'd once woven herself, then lapped the top together and bound a heavy twine about everything.

Her heart sank when she didn't see Warren in the noisy crowd, but Raven hoisted the huge basket by its twine and, putting a hand to her back, guided her into the station. "Let's walk toward the entrance and give him a little more time," he advised. "Knowing by brother, he'll probably be late."

Her satchel in her hand, Misty scanned the vaulted railroad station, impressed with how fine the passengers all looked, the men in well-cut suits and top hats, and the women in furs and plumed hats that made her new clothes seem dowdy and countrified. Together, she and Raven progressed through a maze of luggage toward the arched entrance, and she noticed that many of the travelers cast condescending stares at her and Rollo, who in her opinion was behaving very nicely.

Then, through an opening in the crowd, she spotted Warren, who wore a harried expression.

Raven, seeing him also, raised his arm and a relieved look flooded the younger Davenport's face. Upon reaching them, he took Misty's medical satchel, freeing her to reposition Rollo in her arms. "Sorry I'm late," he apologized, glancing at the huge clock at the front of the station. "Let's go to the exit. Nat is waiting with the carriage."

Outside the entrance, the noise subsided considerably and Misty felt a cooling breeze on her face. In front of the well-lighted station, clusters of horse-drawn vans and private carriages were positioned to pick up passengers and freight. With Warren in the lead, the trio threaded their way through the traffic until they came to an elegant carriage pulled by blooded bays, the finest examples of horse flesh that Misty had ever seen. Back in Eureka Springs, she'd once ridden in the Widow Smith's buggy, but she'd never even seen a vehicle as sleek as this landau with its top up, and it gave her the first inkling of how truly rich the Davenports were.

A black driver wearing a smart blue livery trimmed in red sat upon the box, and as soon as he saw them, he alighted to the street, a wide smile flashing on his face. "It's good to see you, sir," he said, looking at Raven with an expression of genuine affection. He shook his head and smiled again. "My, my, but it's been a long time since you left this old town."

Raven glanced at Misty. "This is Nat," he explained, making a quick introduction as he moved her toward the carriage door. "He'll be driving you about the city while we're living at the mansion."

With twinkling eyes, the driver swept off his cockaded top hat, revealing gray hair. He gazed at Misty kindly, seemingly unaffected by the fact that she held a raccoon in her arms. "Yes, ma'am. It'll be my pleasure, ma'am. It certainly will. Why, I haven't driven a lady since the first Mrs. Davenport went to her reward years ago." Interest sparking in his dark eyes, he ran his slim fingers over Rollo's head. "And if you need any help taking care of this young gentleman, I'd be proud to lend a hand." Raven handed the driver Misty's luggage, which he quickly disposed of; then, with nimble speed, he opened the door for his passengers and, after they'd entered, firmly closed it behind them.

Misty sank down upon the red plush seat over-whelmed by the magnificence of the carriage which rode so well it seemed to float along like a big rocking chair. The landau made a slow trot between the long line of carriages, then Nat had them out of the congestion about the railroad station. In a matter of minutes, they were on one of the large residential avenues, lit by soft gaslight.

Fascinating sights abounded on every block, and with her face turned to the window, Misty missed some of the conversation between the men, but she knew it had to do with their father, and she sensed the tension filling the fine carriage.

On the seat beside her, Raven stared from his window and recognized familiar landmarks that touched off a host of old memories. With an inward sigh, he wondered how he'd stayed away from home so long. Suddenly it seemed as if he'd been transported from a slow-moving backwater to a swiftly rushing stream, and he realized that he had a world of things to catch up on, most importantly his patients, whom he'd left in the care of a young doctor. Coming out of his reverie, he glanced at Misty, and amused by her air of excitement, he reached over and clasped her hand.

Misty felt Raven's fingers tighten about hers and threw him a smile. Then, so intrigued with the city that she couldn't take her eyes from it, she scooted to the edge of the seat and peered from the swiftly moving carriage once more. There were great houses aplenty, and the lights twinkling from the shore and bridges and reflecting off the great Mississippi made the trip go past in a blur.

Then the jingling carriage slowed, and when it turned onto a circular brick drive before an elegant Georgian mansion, her heart fluttered wildly. Rising three stories, the fine house was positioned well back from the fashionable avenue and surrounded by gigantic oaks that rustled in the evening breeze. Shadows flickered over the manicured lawn, but behind the building's Corinthian columns, arched windows shone with soft light.

After the landau stopped, brisk footsteps rang over the bricks, and Nat opened the carriage door and helped Misty to the driveway. Raven and Warren followed, and she heard the horses clatter away, but she was so stunned that everything seemed to be happening to another person. Warren moved to her side, and an uncomfortable look hovering on his face, he stared at the mansion. "I-I'm afraid Papa isn't up tonight," he stammered all at once. "He wasn't feeling well and retired early." As Raven placed his hand at her back, gently escorting her up the wide marble steps, she noted his glittering eyes and wondered why the news had displeased him so.

At the same time, irritation boiled up within

Raven. By his brother's expression, he realized that John, who usually stayed up until midnight, had elected to show his displeasure with his son and his new bride by being unavailable when they arrived at the mansion. It was very like him and an insult to them both, but Misty's sympathetic countenance told him that she didn't recognize it as such. Instinctively, he reached for her hand, deciding he would have to shield her from such slights, and found her fingers trembling.

Only Raven's presence gave Misty the courage to approach the enormous entrance door, and when it opened, revealing a large, raw-boned woman in black clothes, her heart turned over in her bosom. As they all stepped into the foyer, the opulence of the place washed over her, leaving her weak. Lit by a huge crystal chandelier, the hall was tiled in marble and boasted an ornate bureau and Grecian sculptures.

"This is the housekeeper, Mrs. Hawksley," Raven explained, looking at the middle-aged woman and tightening his arm protectively about Misty. Not knowing what to do, she smiled and put out her hand, but by the woman's surprised expression, she realized that she'd made a mistake and withdrew it. The housekeeper nodded, and with amused cynicism sketched on her stern features, she regarded Misty as if she were a beggar from the streets.

The woman stiffly helped Misty off with her coat; then, with a rustle of her taffeta skirt, she introduced the rest of the servants, who'd lined up on either side of the foyer.

Misty saw a fair, freckle-faced maid glance at Rollo and giggle. When Nat brought in Misty's basket suitcase, to be taken upstairs later, some of the other maids smiled and exchanged significant glances until Raven swept a quelling gaze over them.

Ignoring Mrs. Hawksley, he ushered Misty past her and extended his hand toward a curved staircase that led to the bedrooms on the second floor. "Since it's late and you've had a tiring trip, I suggest we retire for the evening."

Happy to leave the scowling housekeeper, Misty said good night to Warren, then walked toward the stairs, passing a drawing room on the left decorated with heavy furniture and dark colors. Seeing a huge arched door to the right, she impulsively asked, "Whose room is this?"

A dark look touched Raven's face. "That's John's room. It used to be a study, but after he had a heart attack and could no longer climb stairs, it was made into his permanent quarters."

They ascended the stairs, and Raven opened the bedroom door, revealing a rose-and-gold room, furnished with armoires, dressers, and enough velvet-upholstered chairs to fill an ordinary house. There was a magnificent canopied bed with rose hangings, and behind a French fire screen, flames crackled cheerfully. Although Misty knew hardly anything about money, she realized that the Davenports must be wealthy indeed to afford such fine furnishings. As soon as she put Rollo on the carpet, he scampered atop a silken chaise longue and, burrowing among the pillows, chirred contentedly.

Raven took Misty in his arms, his hand cupping her chin. "Don't let Mrs. Hawksley bother you," he said, his deep, comforting words rumbling up from his chest. "I don't think I've seen the woman smile since I was five years old." An amused expression flickered over his face. "And actually even then, it was more of a grimace than a smile."

Misty watched laugh lines fan from his eyes. "She didn't bother me at all," she said, secretly stinging from the reception she'd received a few minutes earlier.

Raven lowered his head, and his lips were firm and moist as they seared hers, stirring a soft, yielding passion within her. She was quaking, but she couldn't be sure if it was from the thrill his touch elicited, or the excitement of the evening. Even as he deepened the kiss, part of her mind kept thinking about the great arched door she'd seen and her father-in-law, who rested within the room. Feeling like a stranger in a distant land, she wondered if she'd be able to win his friendship, or be scorned and rejected simply because she'd been born in the mountains.

Trembling ever so slightly, she clutched Raven's shoulders, and putting one life behind her, she bravely embarked on another.

The next morning, there was a light rap on Misty's door. With a drowsy moan, she reached for Raven, and with a tug of disappointment found he was gone. Only now did she remember that he'd told her he had to leave early to see the doctor who'd attended to his patients while he was in the mountains.

Another knock issued from the hall. Still groggy, Misty sat up in the huge four-poster bed as the young freckle-faced maid entered her room, carrying Rollo in her arms. Twitching his whiskers, the animal leapt to the floor, then bounded to the bed.

"Mr. Adam brought him down early, ma'am,"

the girl explained, "and Nat let him have his romp." The maid glanced at the raccoon with a relieved expression, then brushed her hands over her long apron as if she wanted to wipe them clean. "Shall I bring your breakfast tray to the room, ma'am?"

"No, I wouldn't want to cause you the trouble," Misty replied in a sleepy voice. "I'll get dressed and come down."

After the maid had left, the ornately carved grandfather clock in the corner softly chimed nine-thirty and Misty blinked her eyes. She'd never slept this late in her life! With a rush of urgency, she pushed the raccoon aside and picked up Raven's robe, which he'd tossed at the foot of the embroidered counterpane.

Standing, she slipped on the oversized garment and padded to the dresser, tying the sash. As she tugged a brush through her hair, nervousness built within her, and she knew it was because Raven had told her he would introduce her to his father later this morning. Well, no doubt the man was already up at this late hour, she decided, putting the brush on the dresser. She'd just meet him and get it over with. After all, he was only a man, not a monster with a tail and horns! Why, if the old man hadn't eaten, she might even have a maid bring trays to his room so they could have breakfast together.

Once she'd made her decision, she ran to an armoire, pulled out her basket of clothes and selected some fresh underthings and the homemade dress she usually wore on Sunday mornings. Giving it a good shake, she snapped out the wrinkles and began dressing, trying to ignore her trembling fingers.

After closing Rollo in the bedroom, she hurried down the stairs and passed Mrs. Hawksley, who gave her a polite but chilly nod. Misty was tempted to ask the woman why she was being so standoffish, but this morning John Davenport was her first priority. As she stood outside his door, she wiped her damp palms on her skirt, then rapped and waited for an answer. She knocked twice more and heard nothing. Her heart stirring with a mixture of anticipation and dread, she turned the knob, and there was the click of a well-made lock as she peeked into the shadowy room.

On first sight, the chamber reminded her of the study it used to be, for there were dark paneled walls, a marble mantlepiece above a dancing fire, a writing-table, and a globe of the world. A huge four-poster bed, hung with green velvet curtains that shone in the light of a fringed lamp, dominated one wall. A wheelchair with a woven cane back sat in the shadows.

The sound of scribbling drew her attention to the occupant of the bed, a miserable-looking old man in a white nightshirt, who, illuminated by the chamber's poor light, was propped up against an assortment of lace-edged pillows. He held a pen in his hand, and a ream of papers lay on the silken coverlet before him. Her eyes locked with his, and if possible, it seemed that his expression turned even more sour.

For a moment she stood there stunned, not knowing what to do or say, until he pulled off his spectacles, tossed them aside, and bawled: "Well, since you invaded my privacy, come over here so I can get a look at you."

Misty shuddered inside that her father-in-law would speak to her this way, but screwing up her courage, she approached the bed for a bird's eye view of John Davenport. The fleshy man looked to be of medium height, and a tumble of silver hair crowned his head. A deep frown ploughed his brow, and sharp lines ran from either side of his beak-like nose to his tight-lipped mouth. All in all, it seemed as if he'd been pickled in brine and had never smiled in his life.

With a curt nod, he laid his pen aside and indicated a Victorian lady's chair beside his bed. With slow reluctance, she eased into the chair, and, as she clasped its arms, she detected the scents of medicines and whisky. Those aromas, mingled with the musty, unfriendly aura of the room, almost made her physically ill.

John glared at her in a disparaging manner. "Well, who in the hell are you anyway? Did Mrs. Hawksley hire a new maid?"

His brutal words stung Misty's sensibilities, but she decided she wouldn't let him intimidate her. "No," she replied, forcing back her hurt. "I'm Misty. I'm Raven's new wife."

John looked at her, she thought, as if she were a cricket that needed to be swept from the room. "His name is *Adam*. Can't you understand that?"

Misty scanned his harsh face, thinking that no matter what the old man said, she'd always call him Raven, for that was what she'd named him and who he'd always be to her. "I guess you already know what happened when your son got to the mountains."

"Yes, Warren came back from the Ozarks spouting some wild tale about his brother marrying a mountain girl," he sneered in a tone calculated to insult. "I couldn't credit it. Then, when Adam came in at five this morning to examine me, we had a long talk about you." He raked a fierce gaze over her. "He says that you brought a raccoon with you. I never could stand the smelly things."

"Rollo isn't dirty. He's clean, and smart too!" she shot back, defensively. "He won't hurt anything while he's here." Then in a calmer voice, she added, "Why, he could be a lot of company to you."

"Just keep him out of my sight," John ordered in a tone that chilled her to the bones. "I'll not have him poking about my room." He sat silently for a moment, then abruptly stated, "I hear you're a Malone."

Misty glanced down and took a long breath before meeting his hot eyes. "I *was* a Malone. I'm a Davenport now."

"Once a Malone, always a Malone," he snapped. "The Davenports have been feuding with the Malones for hundreds of years, and that will never change."

She raised her brows. "But they already have, Mr. Davenport. My brother, Ezra, and Raven ended the feud just a while back."

"Well, they should have kept it going. It might have kept you in the mountains."

It was impossible to insulate herself from his rudeness, but Misty told herself that he was old and feeble and probably didn't mean what he said. Still, he spoke with such vehemence that a silence fell between them. Trying to break the tension, she finally sat forward and asked, "You wanna have breakfast with me?"

"No, I do not want to have breakfast with you. Besides that, I've already eaten that tasteless mush that Adam said was good for my heart!"

Misty shifted uncomfortably. Making friends with John was going to be harder than she'd expected. Surveying the room, she noticed the closed green velvet drapes and half rose from her chair. "Would you like me to let some light into this gloomy old room? It's a nice day outside."

With a quick jerk of his head, he motioned her back into the chair. "No, leave the drapes closed," he ordered. "The light fades the carpets."

She sank back and ventured a small smile. "Seems with all your money, you could buy new carpets every week if you wanted to."

"I see you have no grasp of finance at all," he said sarcastically. "Money, my little mountain wildflower, is not to be wasted on carpets. It's for building railroad lines and buying art treasures." His face hardened. "If Ezekiel hadn't run off with all his money, I would have more to expand my empire."

"But there are things more important than money. Things like love and—"

"Hogwash! I'll put my faith in a silver dollar any day of the week." He leaned toward the night stand, which held a tray of medicines and liquor decanters, and fumbled for a bottle that was just out of his reach.

Misty rose and picked it up, along with a silver spoon that rested in a glass of water. She glanced at the bottle, then back at John. "Do you want me to pour it for you?"

He waved at her impatiently. "Go ahead," he answered as she opened the bottle and poured the medicine. "But it won't do a damn bit of good. The doctors are a pack of idiots just like everybody else." By the time he'd gulped down the medicine, Misty's hand was trembling so much that she dropped the spoon. When she bent to pick it up, he stormed, "Leave it. There are six maids in this house. One of them will pick it up!"

He crumpled one of his papers and threw it on the floor. Columns of numbers covered the sheet, and she guessed they concerned his railroad line. "I'm surrounded by servants and aides and not one of them has a brain, including my two sons!" the old man fumed.

He had himself in such a rage that Misty instinctively reached out to put a hand on his shoulder, but he roughly knocked it away. The thoughtlessness of the action finally brought a sting of tears to her eyes. "Let me help you," she exclaimed more harshly than she'd intended. "I've doctored lots of folks. Why, back in the mountains, I was an herb doctor and—"

"Yes, Adam and I had a long talk about your *medical abilities*," he interrupted. "And as as far as I'm concerned, it's all a passel of foolishness. There is nothing to mountain medicine but superstition anyway."

The humiliating comment cut Misty's pride, and she fell back a step, repulsed by the old man and his acid tongue. But she told herself that he was Raven's father and, as such, she owed him her respect. Perhaps he'd experienced a sleepless night or felt especially bad today. Still, somehow she had to make him realize how badly she wanted to ease his suffering and fit into this family.

"Look, Mr. Davenport," she began, her courage coming back in a rush, "I know you feel let down that Raven married me, and I know you think he could have done a lot better—that I'm not good enough for him. But I'll work real hard to learn city ways while we're here so you'll be proud of me. I'll study and have Raven teach me to speak better, and—"

"You ignorant little hillbilly," John shot out, cutting her off yet again.

No one had ever spoken words to Misty like that, and her throat tightened with tears.

John pushed himself up on his pillows, his eyes sharpening. "Don't you see that you're totally inappropriate to be Adam's wife? There's nothing in the Ozarks but poverty and ignorance, and I've worked all my life to better myself and forget that my father was as backward as yours. I'd chosen a refined socialite for Adam, and I can't believe he went back to the hills and married you! Hard-headed—that's what he is. He's *always* been hard-headed."

"That's enough," came a firm voice from the door. With a racing heart, Misty whirled about and saw Raven stride into the room, a stormy look in his eyes. When he put his arm about her, an ease flowed through her and she wanted to spill forth all her feelings and tell him how everything had happened. But her emotions were so tangled and confused that she couldn't speak.

"Go to our room, sweetheart," he said gently. "I'll come up later."

She hesitated for a moment, then Raven watched her hurry to the door with a pale face. Filled with compassion, he stood there until she'd left, then he moved to the drapes and jerked them open, pouring light into the darkened study.

Whirling about, he looked at his father, seething with rage. If the old man had been well and able to stand, he would have knocked him to the ground for what he'd just heard, but because he was old and sick and on the verge of dying, Raven had to take another approach.

Without a moment's hesitation, he stalked back to the bed and glared down at John's stony face. "Misty is my wife," Raven intoned in a steely voice, "and as such, I demand that you speak to her with respect! If we're going to remain in the house so I can attend you as you wish, you must accept the situation as it is."

John gave him a sour look. "You're the one who created the situation by marrying her," he answered tartly, "and you, dear boy, are also going to have to live with it." He wagged his head. "An ignorant mountain girl with a pet raccoon. Let's see how your elegant society patients take to that." His lips thinned with displeasure. "Who in the devil did you find up there to perform a wedding anyway?"

Raven paced about the bed, still so angry he could scarcely contain himself. "Just a kindly old man," he answered tightly. "Brother Jubal, they call him. He has a little church in the cove and—"

"Has he ever been to a seminary? Was he ordained by a bishop or anyone else of importance? Is he recognized by any organized religious group?" John demanded in one long breath.

Raven paused and looked him directly in he eyes. "No, as far as I know, he cannot fulfill any of your qualifications. He was a farmer before he felt the call to preach, but in his way, he's a saintly man and he's respected by all the community."

John twisted his lips into a cynical smile. "You still don't get my meaning, do you? Since this Brother Jubal isn't really an ordained minister, most civilized people wouldn't consider you married—and as a matter of fact you are not. A few words spoken over your head by some illiterate jack-leg preacher won't hold here in Saint Louis."

Raven stared at his father, wondering if he'd also had a small stroke when he experienced his last heart attack, for he couldn't believe what he was hearing.

As he paced about the room, trying to analyze the game his father was playing, John followed him with his eyes.

"Annul the alliance. Repute her," the old man continued, pushing himself up on one elbow. "If need be, divorce her. We'll have a top-notch lawyer handle the case."

Raven turned on his heel and took several steps toward him. "*No*," he retorted sharply. "Why should I do such a thing?"

"Because you can do so much better. Priscilla Lindsey has feelings for you. She always had. Fortunately, she and her parents didn't take offense when you left last October. I believe she still loves you."

"Her love for me exists only in your imagination. She didn't take offense because I never made her or her family any promises. *You* were the one who started the rumor that I was going to marry her. Can't you understand that?"

"But you should—"

"*No*. Attend to your own life and leave mine alone!" Raven ordered, interrupting his father for a change. "I'm quite capable of taking care of my own affairs."

John, leaning forward, swept the rest of the papers off the silken coverlet, and they fluttered to the carpet. "Yes, I know. That's why you ran away to the Ozarks and made such a poor match for yourself!"

Raven wheeled and started for the door, but half way across the room, he saw Warren enter, carrying a portfolio to show his father.

John glanced at the scattered papers, then glared at his younger son, whose white face revealed that he'd caught the last part of the argument. "Clean up this mess!" the old man ordered curtly.

Without a word of protest, Warren stooped and began picking up the papers.

Sickened by the sight, Raven rumbled, "Don't bother with that. You're supposed to be John's assistant, not his servant."

Warren ignored his words and, with trembling hands, neatly arranged the papers on his father's bed.

John stared at Raven, his gloating expression saying he'd scored another victory at the cost of his second son's pride. "If you must have that mountain girl around the mansion," he grumbled, "polish her up. Buy her some decent clothes, for starters. The way she's dressed now, she's an embarrassment to us all."

He glanced at Warren's bent head as the young man continued picking up papers. "Since you're so busy getting your medical practice back in order, have Warren take her to a shop tomorrow morning. He's of precious little use in the railroad business; perhaps he'll be more successful selecting women's clothes."

Not wanting to witness Warren's shame, Raven swiftly left the room, his only thoughts now directed at comforting Misty. As he bounded up the stairs, so mad he could scarcely think, he totally rejected all that his father had said. Then, as he cooled down a bit, he realized that the old man had been right about one thing. Misty did need city clothes. He remembered when she'd married him wearing her old boots and how he'd wanted to buy her a complete wardrobe one day—well, now was the time, he decided.

He thought about sending Mrs. Hawksley to assist her with the purchases, then scrapped the idea as he recalled the reception the woman had given Misty. Warren, on the other hand, liked her and the trip to the dress shop would get him out of John's presence for a few blessed hours.

He found Misty sitting cross-legged on their bed, staring into space. Her tumble of unruly curls gave her a vulnerable look, and her eyes held such innocence that they touched his soul. His protective instincts rising, he sank down beside her and cradled her head on his shoulder, then caressed her back, feeling a tremor run through her. "I'm sorry," he said in a warm, soothing voice, noticing a dampness where her head lay. "I wanted to be with you when you first met him. To prepare you for what—"

"No, don't apologize," she murmured, looking up and touching his face with cool fingertips. "He's sick and old and probably afraid of dying." Her eyes grew large and liquid and held a soft compassion. "Sometimes facing death makes the best of folks ill-tempered."

Raven wanted to tell her that John's personality had always been abrasive, but since she had to contend with him, perhaps it was best if she thought the best of him.

"I know I can make him like me if I try harder," she added, her face glowing with fresh hope. "We just got off on the wrong foot. Maybe I can find a game he likes or read to him or—"

Sonya Birmingham

"*Hush*," Raven ordered, a great tenderness welling up in him that almost left him speechless. There it was again, he thought with pride. That goodness, that fighting heart of hers, always trying to make the best out of a bad situation. He held her slight frame against him and let her take her comfort, and after she heaved a quivering sniffle, he eased her away and ran a finger over her cheek, wiping away a tear. "You're letting this trouble you too much," he whispered, smoothing his hands over her shoulders until they stopped quaking. "Just be yourself, as Brother Jubal told you. That's all that matters."

Unable to speak, she blinked her eyes and nodded, and he nestled her against him again and kissed the top of her head, holding her and caressing her until she was perfectly relaxed.

On that particular morning, Raven had never disliked his father more in his life.

Chapter Thirteen

The next morning as Misty left for the dress shop, she brushed past Mrs. Hawksley in the foyer and pretended not to notice the housekeeper's disdainful appraisal of her worn hat, fringed leather jacket, and long calico skirt.

Once outside in the thin winter sunshine, Misty pulled in a deep breath of cool air, glad to be away from the dark mansion, where everyone seemed to be sad and speak in whispers. Deep inside, she still ached from yesterday's battle with John, but she'd vowed to put the incident aside and make a new start. Obviously, appearance was of utmost importance to these city folks, and if they wanted her to dress like one of them, then she would comply.

A beaming Nat stood by the landau that glistened with shiny black paint and brass fittings. "Good morning, Mrs. Davenport," he called out.

"Yes, ma'am. It's a fine morning. It surely is." A slight hesitation in his eyes, he glanced at the mansion's entrance. "Where's Mr. Warren? I was told he was going with you."

"I didn't see him." Misty shrugged. "So I decided to go on by myself!"

"I don't know about that, ma'am. I—"

"It's all right," she responded matter-of-factly. "Raven said his brother is usually late. I imagine he'll take his own carriage and show up later."

Nat repositioned his top hat and laughed with relief. "Well, I suppose you could be right about that, ma'am," he replied, opening the carriage door with a little flourish.

"No," Misty said, walking toward the front of the landau. "I'll ride on the top side with you. If I'm going to be here for a while, I'd like to get my bearings and know my way around."

"But none of the ladies do that, ma'am," Nat exclaimed.

Misty placed her booted foot on the wheel and vaulted to the driver's seat. "I'm not any of the ladies; I'm me," she flung over her shoulder, "and I don't want to be scrunched down in that fancy contraption where I can't see."

Nat snapped the door closed, moved to the other side of the vehicle, and climbed up beside her, a troubled look on his face. "Yes, ma'am, if you say so," he replied, "but this is about the most peculiarest situation I've ever seen." He took the reins and slapped them gently on the horses' rumps. "Get along there, girls. We're going to buy Mrs. Davenport some new duds, so she'll be the prettiest lady in Saint Louis."

A gentle breeze stirred Misty's hair against her buckskin jacket as the carriage rattled away from the mansion. From her high perch, she had a wonderful view of her surroundings, and within minutes she could see the business district. Early-morning pedestrians strolled down the sidewalks and shop owners placed special displays in front of their stores, but whatever they were doing, everyone on the streets paused to take a long gander at the beautiful girl in mountain garb.

She leaned back and studied the street ahead. "You know, Nat," she remarked reflectively, "I don't know if I understand these city folks. People here seem mighty interested in what other folks think of them. Back in the Ozarks, I was welcome in any home in the cove, but around here I'm about as wanted as a frog in the water barrel." She heaved a great sigh. "John doesn't have any use for me, and that Mrs. Hawksley is as cool as a marble headstone."

"Oh, ma'am, you just haven't been here long enough," Nat said in an encouraging voice. "That's all that's wrong." He gently covered her hand with his own. "Give these city folks time and they'll warm up just fine."

Misty liked his friendly, relaxed manner, and feeling comfortable with him, she suddenly ventured, "We're rich, aren't we? Not little rich, but big rich—*really* rich, aren't we?"

"Ma'am," he said, a grin spreading across his ebony face, "we're the richest folks in all of Saint Louis. There ain't none richer."

They both fell silent as the horses clopped along pulling the fine carriage, but after a while, Misty shifted her eyes back to Nat and asked the question that had been tugging at her heart. "If the Davenports are so rich, then why are all the folks in that big mansion so sad?"

She watched tension gather around his eyes before he replied, "When the first Mrs. Davenport was alive, things was different. Oh, Mr. John always crowed and flapped around a lot, but he wasn't real bad. Then that sweet lady of his passed to glory, and it seemed to kill all the happiness inside of him." His face hardened visibly. "It made him kind of mean-like. Things was never quite right with him and his boys after that."

Misty silently digested the information, aching for the sad little boy that Raven must have been. Although she'd only heard bits and pieces about his life before they'd met, she now realized that, despite his wealth, she'd had the better childhood. She longed to ask Nat more questions, but from his veiled expression, she sensed that he'd temporarily closed a door between them.

A few minutes later, he eased the carriage to a stop in front of the most elegant dress shop in town, then alighted from the high seat and did a little dance step before extending his hand to help Misty from the box. She knew he was trying to lift her spirits and rewarded him with a grin. "I didn't know you were a dancer," she commented with genuine interest as she stepped to the pavement.

He offered her the warmest and brightest of smiles. "Ma'am, I was born dancing." Amusement twinkled in his dusky black eyes. "Now you just step in there and buy all the fancy duds you want. And while you're doing it, don't be forgetting we're the richest folks in Saint Louis!"

Misty nervously walked under the shop's awning, and as she stared at the looming door with its long oval glass, her composure crumbled like wet sand. Then, glancing over her shoulder, she noticed Nat's sharp but encouraging nod, and realized there was no retreat. Having no alternative, she pulled up her courage and twisted the door knob.

Once inside, Misty saw beautiful carpets stretching across the parquet floor, gold embossed paper covering the walls, and splendidly colored dresses hanging from golden racks. Stunned, she froze just inside the threshold; then, her heart pounding, she closed the belled door behind her. The jangle made her jump, but in a matter of seconds, a tall lady with graying hair appeared from the back and moved toward her like a great ship easing into port.

"Good morning, young lady," the woman sniffed, her gaze straying over Misty as if she didn't belong in the shop. "How may I help you?"

Misty's words tumbled out in a rush. "I'm Misty Davenport, and I was sent here to buy some duds—I mean *clothes*." She glanced down at her own humble garb, then looked up, comparing it to the fine lady's deep blue dress, trimed in lace. "I've never lived any place but Red Oak Hollow, and we don't have much of a call to dress up there."

The woman narrowed her eyes. "Did you say your last name was Davenport?" she queried, suddenly extremely interested. "Is John Davenport related to *you*?"

Misty nodded. "Yep. I'm married to his oldest son, Raven. His brother will probably show up later, but right now," she said, glancing toward the street, "I don't have anyone to help me pick out things but Nat." She turned and studied the woman's disapproving face, noticing the way her stiff white collar held her head rigid as a bean pole. "Do you suppose he could stand near your door so I could let him look at the gowns?"

"And who, may I ask, is Nat?"

"He's the carriage driver," Misty replied with a grin, "but he's real nice and—"

Shock flew over the clerk's face. "*I* can give you an opinion on your clothes," she snapped. "It won't be necessary for your driver to stand in front of our establishment for such a thing!" She flushed and, clasping Misty by the arm, pulled her toward the dressing rooms; at the same time, several shop girls appeared from the back, covering their mouths to muffle their giggles.

The saleslady threw a frown at the girls. "Bring out the maroon velvet and the green silk, and be quick about it," she ordered as she swept Misty into a curtained alcove and began peeling off her jacket.

It hurt Misty that the girls had laughed at her, but being trapped in the situation, she tried to save her pride by acting as if she hadn't noticed. Within minutes, the sheepish girls delivered the exquisite gowns and hung them in the alcove. And seconds later, several pairs of hands plucked away Misty's clothes until she stood in a shift and bloomers with her arms crossed over her bosom, feeling exposed and vulnerable.

She still wore her floppy hat and boots, and with a grimace, the older woman sailed the head covering aside. "*Now*," she said with a determined glint in her eyes as she pushed Misty onto a silken lounge and tugged at one of her boots, "we shall begin at the beginning." She darted her gaze at the girl who'd delivered the maroon gown. "Bring Mrs. Davenport a selection of our best corsets."

An hour later, a pile of lacy underthings and a dozen expensive gowns lay about the fitting room.

Misty looked at her reflection in a tall cheval glass, stunned with her appearance in a green silk evening gown. The creation's luscious color and stylish cut touched her woman's heart, but her mountain practicality rebelled at its extravagant cost. To make matters worse, she'd been cinched into three corsets—each one tighter—and pinched and prodded and stuck with pins, until her only thought was of escape.

When she heard Warren speaking to one of the shop girls, she tried to flee the dressing room, but the matronly saleslady, whose hair now fell in her face, held her tightly until she'd finished buttoning the gown. As soon as she was done, Misty rushed barefooted into the main shop. Warren was sitting on a French chair looking perfectly miserable.

His lips parting in surprise, he rose to his feet. "Sorry I'm late," he murmured apologetically. "I had to go downtown to get a portfolio for Papa. And . . . and . . ."

"And what?" she asked, wondering what the problem might be.

He took her hand and, turning her about, skimmed an appreciative gaze over her. "And you're beautiful," he stated in a warm voice. His eyes widened with amazement. "*Yes*, you should definitely buy this one."

"But this is like all the others," Misty murmured, peeking sideways at the saleslady and her assistants, who'd huddled into a whispering knot. "They've put a dozen dresses on me"—she rolled her eyes—"and you should see what I've got on underneath the dress. Why, they've cinched me into a contraption that's got my heart squeezed up in my throat!" She flicked at a ruffle on her evening gown. "When I get back to the

261

Ozarks, these clothes won't be worth shucks to me."

Smoothing the silk fabric over her hips, she paced about the shop, her bare feet sinking into the soft carpet. "This dress is as tight as a sausage skin," she complained, observing herself in a gilt-framed cheval glass. She met Warren's gaze in the looking glass, then bent her arm back and forth to demonstrate. "See? There isn't a bit of give in it."

He awkwardly cleared his throat. "Did you say, when you get back to the Ozarks?" he asked, studying her intently.

She turned and stared at his puzzled face. "Of course, didn't Raven tell you? We're just here for a visit until . . . until . . ." she trailed off, feeling embarrassed.

"Until Papa dies?" he asked.

She nodded her head, wondering if she'd said the wrong thing.

He looked at her blankly, clearly not understanding. "No," he replied softly, "he didn't tell me you were going back at all."

Misty's doubts and fears about coming to Saint Louis increased by the minute. It surprised her that Raven hadn't told his brother that they were just going to be in the city for a short while. Then, thinking she was being too harsh, she told herself that he'd simply been too busy.

The saleslady and her staff now approached, holding out feathered hats and encouraging her to buy them all. It was hard for Misty to think of herself as a lady of fashion and leisure, that she could go from buckskin to silk, from mountain child to fairy princess, in one trip to Saint Louis. And as the clerks' voices became a babble, indecision welled up within her. She stared at Warren, feeling helpless.

Taking her arm, he pulled her aside and said, "*Buy everything*. Money is no problem, and with the social season coming up, you'll need lots of gowns."

"But I can't work in them," she insisted, trying to move her arm again. "And compared to my loose mountain clothes, these tight-fitting gowns are about as uncomfortable as a passel of fire ants in a person's britches."

Warren grinned. "These aren't working clothes, they're *looking* clothes." That's what ladies wear in Saint Louis—looking clothes. Besides," he added, blushing a bit as his gaze strayed to her low-cut bodice, "if every gown suits you as well as the one you're wearing, you'll be a sensation."

Still unconvinced that one person could need so many clothes, she bit her lip and heaved a great sigh.

Apparently seeing that he would have to take the initiative, Warren gave the saleslady a nod of consent. "She'll take all the gowns and hats and underthings"—he glanced at her bare feet—"and while you're at it, throw in a selection of shoes and stockings as well."

The woman beamed. "Very well, Mr. Davenport," she replied, shooing the girls away to wrap the merchandise before he could change his mind. "Everything will be delivered later today!"

As Misty walked toward the fitting room, trying to ignore the giggling salesgirls, she thought that if she disgraced the Davenports now, at least she'd be doing it in style. Yet in a vague way, it rankled her that the clothes she'd worn all her life weren't good enough for these fancified city folk.

She looked back at Warren, capturing blue eyes that shone with laughter. "I'm telling you," she said, still refusing to believe her stay here would be longer than a few months, "when Raven and me go back to the Ozarks, these clothes won't do me a lick of good. The briars and brambles will catch the ruffles and pull every blasted one of them off!"

"On the box," said John with quivering jowls as he looked up at Raven, who stood by his bed that evening after dinner. "Mrs. Hawksley was looking from the window and saw your *wife*—and I use the word lightly—actually sitting on the box beside Nat when she left the mansion this morning."

Raven paced to the foot of the bed and studied his father's displeased face, anger rising in his chest. Couldn't the old man see that these spiteful reports on Misty's activities were just worsening their already shaky relationship? No, he probably couldn't, he answered himself, remembering that his father understood precious little about human relationships. "Well, she probably thought she could see better from there," Raven replied lightly, trying to control his wrath. "No great harm was done."

"No great harm was done? You're not concerned that everyone in this neighborhood saw her sitting there?" John returned, his voice rising testily. He wagged his head. "It only shows how unsuited she is to be your wife. We need to talk and decide how you can get yourself out of this embarrassing situation."

Raven felt as if a dam had burst deep within him, and his natural resentment spilled forth.

"No, we're through talking," he snapped, his voice crackling with authority. He narrowed his eyes and straightened his shoulders. "I'll not stand here and listen to you berate my wife." He met and held John's blistering gaze for a moment, then turned and walked from the room, feeling the same hot gaze bore into his back.

Emotions stormed through him as he strode about the foyer, trying to regain his composure. To him, Misty's mistake meant almost nothing, but he realized that others besides John would soon be talking about it, and unfortunately she would be the one to pay. As he calmed down, he remembered his promise at dinner to see her new clothes, and he jogged up the stairs, making a mental note to gently explain to her that here in the city manners were more regulated than in the Ozarks.

He blinked as he walked into their bedroom. Dressed in a feathery hat, a frilly shift, ribbon-threaded bloomers, and little else, Misty pranced about the chamber in high-heeled mules, examining the merchandise she'd purchased earlier in the day. Thinking that she looked like a little girl playing dress-up, he smiled inwardly, trying to repress his mirth. At the same time, he knew she had no idea how tempting she looked in her provocative dishabille, her rosy nipples showing through her thin shift.

Gowns, gloves, stockings, and underthings were draped over the chairs and chaise longues, and the bedroom looked like a lady's shop that had been hit by a Missouri tornado. Infected with her air of excitement, Rollo scampered about, chasing the colorful tissue paper Misty flung from the boxes.

A frown on her smooth brow, she walked to Raven and flounced back her hair. "Lord, what am I going to do with all these clothes? Warren told me to buy them, but there's more dresses here than I could wear in three lifetimes," she exclaimed. "And if someone had told me what city women wear underneath their clothes, I wouldn't have believed them!"

She carried a corset, and with a pained look on her face, she snapped it between her hands several times. "See this squeezing contraption? It has strips of whalebone that cut into a person's belly like hot knives. They put one of these things on me and cinched it up so tight I thought my heart would stop beating right then and there." She tossed it aside. "But did they stop? No, this old lady with the gray hair just kept on cinching *to get the proper Parisian shape*, she said. Well, I like my good old Ozark shape!"

He reached out for her hand, but she was off again, tossing plumed hats and silken shoes from their boxes. She stopped at the dresser and slipped several ropes of long pearls about her neck. "They said I needed these, too," she added, shaking the pearls. "Why, they darn near sold me everything in the store." She sashayed back to him and shook a finger in his face. "Let me tell you, that old lady was so skinny I don't think I could have hit her with a handful of corn, but she was strong. Strong and stubborn, too!"

Raven found himself smiling down at her, thinking that despite her protests, she was like a child on Christmas morning. He knew that a part of her adored the beautiful clothes, but he also understood that due to her mountain raising, another part of her considered them shamefully extravagant. He crossed the room, and from the tail of his eye saw her pause to attach a horse-hair bustle, which she got on sideways.

"Why in the world would a woman want to wear something like this tied on her rear end?" she asked with wide eyes. "It's hot and it's heavy, it bounces around like a five pound sack of potatoes—and it makes a woman's bottom look big as a wash tub." She picked up another bustle made of canvas and collapsible metal rods. "Look at this torture device," she said with disgust. "It has a spring in it so the bustle will fold up when I sit down." She dropped it into a chair and threw up her hands. "That's just what I always wanted—a spring attached to my butt."

She yanked off the first bustle, and finding a box of gloves, opened it and slipped on a pair made of white kid. "And look at all these gloves, and fans too," she added, opening a plumed opera fan and swishing it in the air. "This thing looks like the bottom of Granny's old goose."

Raven laughed, but he'd seen Misty in the mountains like this, and knew her well enough to sense that she was actually trying to entertain him. Something had happened to her today, he told himself, suspecting that her humorous attitude was covering another emotion. Whatever it was, he was going to get to the bottom of it. Loosening his tie, he threw it on the dresser, then walked to her and took her in her arms. "All right, you whirling dervish, what else took place at the dress shop today?" he asked, looking down at her and tracing his finger over her cheek.

Misty gazed up at him, startled that he knew her so well. "W-Why, nothing. What do you mean?" she stammered, innocently batting her eyes. How could she let him know that the shop girls had thought her so countrified that they'd actually laughed at her? she asked herself, a blush stinging her cheeks.

Trying to change the subject, she pulled away; looking for a diversion, she scooped up Rollo and put him in a large cardboard box padded with paper. She'd been stinging all day from the salesclerks' snubs, but had determined to put on a brave face for him. And she'd nearly done it too, she thought, stripping off her gloves and dropping them on a chair.

He came to her and turned her about, and with a surge of emotion, she impulsively looped her arms about him and, laying her head on his shoulder, melted against him. As his fingers traced wonderful little circles on her back, tension swelled within her, and she mentally relived her humiliation.

With gentle fingers, Raven lifted her head and searched her face. "Something happened today. Something you're not telling me about. Out with it, Doctor Malone. What happened?"

Unshed tears burned her eyes for a moment, then she blurted out, "They laughed at me. The shop girls laughed at the way I talked"—she swallowed hard—"and I heard them giggling about my clothes. This is the way their faces looked," she explained, pursing her lips and sucking in her breath to make her nose very thin. "They didn't think I saw them, but I did."

It infuriated Raven that the silly girls had laughed at Misty. He didn't want *anyone* laughing at her, but with a pang of regret, he realized that people being people, he should have expected it. Then, with swift certainty, he realized that what she needed was a teacher—someone to improve her grammar, introduce her to the fine arts, and instruct her in genteel manners. He made a mental note to find her such a teacher as soon as possible, but first he would have to gently broach the subject without hurting her feelings.

He grazed his hand along her bare arm, wanting to reassure and comfort her. "Well, to me, the sound of your voice is sweeter than the wind in the pines," he said sincerely, "and I've never seen a more delectable sight than Misty Malone in her buckskins." He noticed her face brighten up, and he gave thanks for her brave spirit and natural resilience. "What do we care what an old woman and some silly girls think?" he asked, stroking her hair and talking as if she were a cherished child. He kissed her on the tip of her nose. "And I hope those girl's faces freeze that way—skinny noses and all."

They both burst out laughing, and Misty snuggled up against him and whispered, "Maybe they'll even turn to pillars of salt."

He held her from him, studying her amused face. "Why, you little infidel," he said with an appreciative chuckle.

When he slipped the shift from her shoulder and began planting a row of kisses along her collarbone, his beard tickled her and, giggling, she asked, "What are you doing?"

He paused and gave her a look of mock seriousness. "Why, kissing your clavicle, of course. It's all your fault, you know. You have such a lovely clavicle, I couldn't resist the temptation."

They laughed, and he took off her feathery hat and sailed it aside before scooping her up and carrying her to the bed, where her mules slipped from her feet as she sank into the soft mattress.

He sat down beside her and cupped the breast whose nipple had been showing though the gauzy shift and tempting him ever since he came into the room. The light from the bedside lamp caught in her eyes, and they gleamed warm and inviting with golden highlights. And under the fine lawn he could feel her nipple swell and harden, and it struck sparks within him.

At that moment in her pearls and tempting shift, with her auburn hair loose and shimmering with highlights, he thought her the most beautiful woman in the world, and he temporarily put away all concerns about his father and his everlasting advice, and focused his thoughts on Misty and her alone.

His passions soaring, he stood and removed his clothes; then he tossed them aside, clicked off the lamp, and sank onto the mattress at her side. He raised himself on an elbow to move his gaze over her, and moonlight flooded through a bedroom window, silvering her and her great sweep of hair with a pale light.

Misty gazed at Raven's face, which was touched with the same soft light, and when he lowered his lips to hers, desire rushed through her like a tidal wave, making her heart pound crazily. As he deepened the kiss, tracing her lips with his tongue, then parting them to explore her mouth, she put her arms about him and pulled him tighter, her desire as strong as the first time they'd made love.

Secure in his sinewy arms, she forgot that she'd been an object of fun this morning and shivered as his hands moved over her like silken fire. When she sighed with passion, he gently broke the kiss, pulled the chemise over her head, and let it slide to the carpet. "I think we can do without this," he said. "And this too," he added, tugging off her silken bloomers and flinging them to the foot of the bed. His eyes glittered with hunger as he gathered her soft length to his own naked body and once again took her mouth in a deep kiss.

In the back of her mind she vaguely remembered that she was going to ask him why he hadn't told Warren they would soon be returning to the Ozarks, but lost in her passion, the intention didn't seem that important now. Questions and recriminations could wait until later. This was what she wanted, she realized in that secret place deep within her heart. To be his forever. Never could she ask for more than this.

Excitement swept though her at the feel of his hard frame against her, and warmth blossomed within her as he fingered her nipples and thighs and the sweetly aching place between them with exquisite tenderness. With firm but gentle movements, his tantalizing touch kindled the yearning within her to a fever pitch. And when it seemed that her pounding heart would burst, he positioned himself over her and entered her with a deep, powerful thrust that set her spirit free and spurred her need with every caressing stroke.

"You're so beautiful," he sighed tenderly against her ear.

Breathless, she clung to him, and clenching her fingers into his muscled back, she treasured the glory of that moment, wishing it could go on forever. She moaned with passion, and in silent answer he continued his movements with ever-building speed, sending a wild swirl of pleasure through her trembling body. Magic danced on the soft night air, and at last they crested into a fulfillment that left them exhausted but content. Her body touching Raven's, Misty lay with her head nestled against the crook of his arm and floated on the golden tide that comes just before sleep.

Gently he cupped her breast, caressing her nipple with his thumb; then, with great tenderness, he brushed his lips against hers. "I think I'll find you a teacher next week," he said lightly as if he were proposing a small outing.

Misty turned to look at his moon-silvered face. "A teacher?" she echoed drowsily. "Why do I need a teacher? Brother Jubal said to just be myself."

He kissed her forehead. "That's right and that's what you should do. All we're going to do is tie a few ribbons and bows on you."

She smiled, intrigued with the imagery. "Ribbons and bows?"

"Yes, we'll just make a few small changes," he said, raising himself on one arm and gazing at her with earnest eyes. "A teacher can help you learn the city way of doing things and help you appreciate the finer things of life. And a teacher can introduce you to all kinds of interesting people like Caesar and Augustus. Wouldn't you like to meet someone like that?" he asked running his hand over her body.

Misty pondered his words, wondering if this Caesar and Augustus he'd mentioned lived in Saint Louis. As far as appreciating the finer things, she thought she'd been doing that all her life. In the Ozarks, when the mist flowed down from the mountains in a white veil and the oaks trembled in the breeze, glinting like gold, the sight nearly took her breath away. And if all the city women wore clothes like those she'd bought today, she wasn't sure she actually trusted the city way of doing things. But with a big sigh, she realized that it was important to Raven, so she would try.

"*Well?*" he prompted.

"All right," she replied, her voice as soft as a baby's kiss, "I'll meet your city teacher and learn your city ways."

From his warm smile, she could tell he was pleased, and he kissed her and held her against him once more. At last he eased back so she could see his laughing eyes. "Why, I may have the woman even teach you a few words of French," he said with amusement. When she didn't respond, he grinned and trailed his long fingers over her cheek. "Your mind is miles away. What are you thinking?"

"I was thinking," she answered slowly, "that if Granny could see me speaking French with a spring on my butt, she'd turn over in her grave."

Chapter Fourteen

A week later, Misty sat at a writing table in the library, Rollo snoozing at her side. As she waited for her teacher, she rummaged through her medical satchel, and the fragrant scent of herbs made her think of the Ozarks and spurred a great pang of homesickness.

She could still smell the musty, damp odor of the mountain cabins, so unlike this library with its twinkling chandelier, carved furniture, and fine carpets. Many of her friends in the mountains were good, kind people with little of this world's goods, but happy with their simple existence. And with the tail end of winter blowing through the hills, a lot of folks would be sick and need her help.

But she wouldn't be there to assist them, she thought sadly. She'd be here in Saint Louis, sitting in this great gloomy mansion, dressed up like a useless doll in a maroon velvet dress, taking lessons so she wouldn't be an embarrassment to the Davenport family.

Suddenly, the sound of the tall library doors opening made her swivel her head around. Her teacher, a tiny woman carrying several large volumes, approached the writing table. She coughed, and from her watery eyes Misty could tell the woman had a cold.

"I'm Miss Sullivan," the teacher announced, a prim smile settling on her lips. A little sprinkling of gray frosted the woman's black hair, which was pulled atop her head in a tight knot. A white collar adorned her gray dress, and stiff lace peeped from beneath long sleeves to encircle her knobby wrists. Starched and ironed, thought Misty. Starched and ironed, if she'd ever seen it.

"All right, Mrs. Davenport, we can get started," the woman announced in a business-like manner. She laid her books on the table, then pulled a handkerchief out and dabbed at her nose. "I suppose you can at least read and write."

The insult stung Misty like salt in an open cut. "Yes, of course," she answered softly. "My granny taught me to read and reckon figures, too."

The teacher crossed her arms and paced about the writing table, a thoughtful expression hardening her severe face. "Very well, we'll start from there. You needn't have any nervousness. I'm here to help you," she explained, peering over her little spectacles. "Open the largest volume to page seventy-four and read the first column of type."

Misty picked up the volume on European works of art and did as she was told, but she had trouble pronouncing the larger words. When she'd finished and replaced the book, she knew the woman was not pleased.

"You have a terrible Appalachian accent, your voice is like molasses, and you pronounce *yes* as if it were a two-syllable word," the teacher announced bluntly.

Misty pressed her lips together. "I think Appalachian has something to do with the mountains," she said slowly, "and I know what molasses is, but what does that word *syllable* mean?"

"Never mind," the woman sighed. "I see we have a long road ahead of us." She pressed her hands on each side of Misty's face, squeezing out her lips. "Now repeat the vowels," she ordered matter-of-factly.

"*Tha whaot?*" Misty asked, scarcely able to move her lips.

"The vowels, the vowels," the woman said crossly. "Say *a, e, i, o, u!*"

Misty removed the teacher's cold, bony hands from her face. "Well, why didn't you say that in the first place?" she asked with a laugh. "A, e, i, o, u," she repeated with a heavy mountain drawl. She grinned a little. "Is this all these talking lessons are gonna be? Why, a five-year-old child could do this."

Miss Sullivan closed her eyes, and Misty noticed that her eyelids were quivering. "I think that today we should concentrate on sharpening your appreciation of the arts." She went to the writing table and turned a few pages of the book. "Dr. Davenport was most specific in his wish that you be exposed to the finer things," she added, piercing Misty with a keen glare. "Now look at this photograph of the *Mona Lisa*. It was painted by Leonardo Da Vinci, and it hangs

276

in the Louvre Museum in Paris. How do you like it?"

"Well, I like it just fine," Misty chirped, cocking her head and squinting her eyes, "but how did this Miss Mona Lisa lose her teeth?"

The teacher paled.

"Why, you can tell by the way this lady is smiling that she doesn't have any teeth. Old Man Potter back in Red Oak Hollow used to smile like that without opening his mouth, and he didn't have a tooth in his head."

Miss Sullivan gave a dry cough. "Why, I never heard of such a preposterous thing—the Mona Lisa without teeth!"

Misty walked about the table, trailing her fingers on its surface and studying the woman's startled face. "Does that Louvre Museum have any pictures of grizzly bears and panthers and things like that or just toothless ladies?"

The teacher motioned frantically. "Come here at once and focus your mind!" she ordered, turning a few more pages. "Look at this photograph of the *Venus de Milo* and tell me what you see. Give me your impression."

Misty surveyed the large photograph, then raised her brows. "Well, I'll be flamboozled. The poor lady's dress has slipped down around her hips, and she doesn't have any arms. Looks like the folks that was making the book could have at least found a statue with arms."

Miss Sullivan flushed. "Of course, it originally did have arms. They were broken away!"

Misty sighed. "I hope the part where you're gonna help me is coming soon," she said, "'cause I'm sure not getting the drift of this picture book."

Sonya Birmingham

Blanching, the teacher tapped her skinny finger on a photograph of Michelangelo's *David*. "This is in a museum in Italy." She narrowed her eyes at Misty. "Give me your first immediate impression so I can test your aesthetic sensibilities."

Misty chuckled. "Well, my first immediate impression is that he's naked as a jaybird."

"Perhaps you don't understand," the woman explained in a strained voice. "This is a statue of David from the Old Testament. He's holding a sling shot and contemplating his battle with Goliath."

Misty scanned the page again. "Granny always told me that David didn't have any fancy armor to fight Goliath, but I didn't know he fought him plumb naked. No telling what he could have done if he'd had some good clothes."

Miss Sullivan went beet red and burst into a coughing fit. With a great splutter, she clasped her handkerchief over her mouth.

"My goodness, you sure need something for that cough," Misty said as she kindly helped her into a chair at the writing table. Leaving the teacher wheezing, she rummaged in her medicine satchel until she found a bag of sharp--scented herbs hanging from a long cord. "Here," she said, putting it around the teacher's neck. "This concoction will ease that coughing."

The teacher leaned back in horror. "What is that foul-smelling thing? Get it away from me."

Suddenly there was a wild scrambling of fur and claws, and Rollo sprang from his hiding place and scrambled over the table, sneezing and shaking his head.

Miss Sullivan rose and, with a scream, threw up her hands, knocking her glasses sideways. She tossed off the herb necklace; then, grabbing her belongings, she made a hasty exit from the library, crying out, "Impossible, simply impossible!"

"Don't be afraid," Misty called after her, running to the door. "It's only Rollo. Sometimes he gets a might upset when he smells my cough remedy, but he won't hurt you." She stood on her toes and raised her arm. "You want to teach me some French now?" She started to go after the woman, but when Rollo darted down the hall, making his way toward John's room, her heart took a bounding leap. "Oh, no," she screamed. "Don't go into John's room. Don't go there!"

Even before she reached the room, she heard John shouting, "Get this confounded animal out of here or I'll send for a dog catcher!"

Breathless, she burst into the room just in time to see Rollo scamper over a table, knocking several articles of Delft china to the floor, where they shattered into pieces. Then he leapt upon a huge globe of the world, his claws shredding the painted leather covering. From there, he swung onto the expensive green velvet drapes and climbed up them in a few fast lunges. At the top, he struggled his fat little body onto the top of the wide cornice, then ran back and forth, growls and grunts coming from his black-masked face.

Near tears, Misty glanced at John's enraged countenance and thought he looked as if he might have another heart attack. At the drapes, she held out her arms, trying to coax Rollo down, but he wouldn't budge.

John struggled up on the pillows. "Call Nat from the carriage house and see if he can get him down," he yelled in a strangled voice.

Sonya Birmingham

As Misty ran from the room to look for a maid, she heard him add, "I want that demented animal caged!"

After finding a maid and giving her the message, Misty hurried back into the room, thinking she might calm down the old gentleman. "He's just a little animal," she said, rushing to John's bed. "He won't hurt you. He's just scared in such a strange place. I have some herbs in my satchel that might calm your nerves, if you'd just let me give them to you."

"No, no, no," John fumed, with flashing eyes. "Don't you see, I don't want any of your primitive *weed medicine?"*

A lazy drawl floated from the hall, and with a great sense of relief, Misty saw Nat enter the study carrying a long cane fishing pole. A wide-eyed maid followed him, wringing her hands. "Come on down here, little raccoon," Nat urged, moving to the windows. "Come on down, now," he crooned, trying to force Rollo to the edge of the cornice. "You know I won't hurt you none."

Rollo slapped at the pole and leaped away, but after considerable trying, Nat succeeded in positioning him where he had to grasp it or be forced from the cornice. When this happened, the raccoon instinctively clutched onto the pole and Nat lowered it to the floor. From there, Rollo leaped into Misty's waiting arms.

The maid rushed to John and tried to fluff his pillows, but he pushed her away and glared at Misty. "Get that insane animal out of here, put him in a cage, and confine him to the carriage house." As Misty and Nat hastily moved toward the door, he shouted, "Wait!"

Misty turned about with a pounding heart and looked at his red face. "Yes?" she asked in a quavering voice.

"Tell Adam to see me as soon as he returns from the hospital," he commanded. His eyes glittered with rage. "I have a lot to discuss with him!"

Six weeks later, Misty came out of the largest cathedral in Saint Louis and stepped into the light spring air, breathing a sigh of relief. The cathedral's warm, oppressive atmosphere had made her dizzy, and the sound of the blaring pipe organ still rang in her ears.

Raven was at her side, and her love for him was as constant as ever, but since they'd been in the city, she sensed that she was losing him. Thank goodness, after her afternoon with Miss Sullivan, he'd decided to teach her himself and spent time in the evenings improving her grammar and manners. Still, it seemed they'd lost some of the closeness they'd shared in the mountains, and today, when he'd appeared dressed for church services with a beardless face, it had saddened her deeply. In her mind, the action of shaving was a symbolic gesture, disowning his Ozark life.

With Raven's guiding hand at her waist, she walked toward Pastor James, who was garbed in a stiff clerical collar and a silken surplice. "We're very glad to have you here today, my dear," the cleric intoned, enclosing her hand in his. From the softness of the man's hand, a person would think he'd never done a day of work in his life, she decided, remembering Brother Jubal and his callosed hands.

As Raven escorted her over the well-kept lawn, she noticed the first crocuses nodding their heads in the breeze, but their beauty left her untouched. How dismal her world was! Rollo was now imprisoned in a cage in the carriage house and not allowed in the mansion, and although she visited him every afternoon, the happy, mischievous glint had vanished from his black eyes.

She knew how sad he felt, for she felt the same way.

A distinguished lady now approached them, and Raven stopped and inclined his head. "Mrs. Hillingsworth," he stated cordially, "may I present my wife, Misty?"

The gray-haired lady paused and peered through her spectacles. "Yes, I've heard all about her," she answered, flicking her gaze over Misty as if she were evaluating a piece of merchandise. "Where are you from, my dear?"

"Arkansas, ma'am," Misty replied in a shaky voice. "A place called Red Oak Hollow. It's in the mountains."

The lady stared at her for a moment, then commented, "Well, yes, isn't that interesting?" Turning her attention firmly to Raven, she patted him on the arm, then walked off, never looking back.

With a stab of pain, Misty knew that she'd failed again. She remembered the polite smiles she'd received when Raven had introduced her to other parishioners as they'd made their way up the church walk, and she remembered how quickly the people had dismissed her and turned away when she'd opened her mouth to speak. The socialites' chilly reception told her she was making slow progress, and their pitying glances revealed that they also thought the good doctor had married far beneath himself.

Raven, seeing a group of associates from the hospital, studied them with interested eyes, then glanced at Misty with a doubtful expression. Taking her in his arms and brushing a loose curl from her cheek, he swept a tender look over her. "There are some people over there I need to speak to. Would you like to come with me?"

Misty shook her head, experiencing a sudden shyness. "No, you go along," she replied softly. She managed a weak smile. "I'll be fine right here."

He paused for a moment, still looking unsure, then caressed her arm and walked away.

She watched him as he strode to the men, who all beamed and stuck out their hands. Soon a group of fashionably dressed young ladies migrated toward Raven, smiles lighting their lovely faces. From the babble of laughter and voices floating toward her, Misty heard a man ask, "Say, Davenport, when are you going to get back into circulation? I haven't seen you at a party in ages."

Tears filmed Misty's eyes. She knew why Raven had neglected his social life—his wife was just too much of an embarrassment to be brought along. Then, as the others drifted away, a particularly attractive blond girl approached him, making Misty wonder who she was. Raven paused to talk with the girl, who was garbed in a fetching pink gown that dripped lace and made her look like a porcelain figurine.

From where Raven was standing, he scanned Misty's sad face, then as etiquette demanded, he gave his full attention to Priscilla Lindsey, whom he hadn't seen since he'd returned from the Ozarks. As always, he was impressed with her creamy skin and apple-blossom cheeks and thought her delicate beauty was like a picture one might find on a bottle of face cream. "Priscilla," he said in greeting, taking her small hand in his, "it's nice to see you again. Have you been well?"

The breeze ruffled her hat's pink plumes against her cheek before she stammered, "Yes, thank you. I've been fine." She stared at him silently, apparently already at a loss for words.

Raven wondered where the conversation could go from here. Since Priscilla lived only a few houses down Garrick Street, he'd known her all his life, and for the same amount of time her pastel personality had left him untouched. Terribly quiet and shy, she'd never expressed an original thought or opinion, and the only one he'd ever seen her blossom around was Warren, who was almost as shy as herself.

How did one apologize for a possible social embarrassment? he thought, wondering if his father's meddling had left her the target of gossip. "I hope . . . I hope my trip to the Ozarks . . ." he began awkwardly.

Priscilla put her hand on his sleeve, her touch as light as a child's. "Please, you needn't say more," she interrupted, demurely lowering her eyes. "I understand."

Raven heaved a great sigh and studied her, thinking she was almost too fragile for this world. For years he'd suspected that she harbored feelings for Warren, but didn't know how to express them, and with his brother as tongue-tied as she, the situation was difficult indeed. But perhaps together they *would* be a good pair, he thought, setting a goal then and there to play matchmaker between them. "I was wondering," he began once more in a light voice, knowing he must finally ask the question he'd refrained from verbalizing for years, "how you'd feel about Warren escorting you to some of the balls this season?"

Priscilla's blue eyes lit up; a smile raced over her lips and she looked happier than he'd ever seen her. It was then that he realized he'd been right all along about her and Warren. He also realized that the blush riding her cheeks would probably be the closest confession of love that she'd ever make for his brother.

He transferred his gaze to Misty again, thinking that if possible, she looked even sadder, standing there in front of the cathedral all by herself. Taking Priscilla by the elbow, he decided to introduce the pair, knowing the blonde would say nothing to offend his wife.

Misty watched Raven clasp the girl's arm and, with a flicker of pain, turned away. How could she compete with someone as dainty and elegant as that? Why, the girl probably spoke French and a half-dozen other languages as well. Experiencing a great sense of inadequacy, she cast her gaze about, deciding that she couldn't stand there any longer.

The cathedral sat on a corner, and beneath a line of oaks just putting out light-green leaves, a host of fine carriages with uniformed drivers waited for the parishioners. She spotted Nat standing by the Davenport carriage, and with a heavy heart, she hurried down a flight of steps, still visualizing the socialites' cold faces in her mind's eye.

In the Ozarks, her life had revolved around daily survival and the feud with the Davenports, but her troubles there had been nothing compared to here, she sadly reflected. She'd tried for weeks to fit into the city folks' exalted world, but she'd failed. She could see it by the looks on their faces and the haughty lift of their brows.

Nat smiled and removed his hat. "Mrs. Davenport, you sure are looksome today," he said kindly, his dark eyes saying that he understood her anguish.

As he moved to open the carriage door, there was a noise behind her and Raven's hand grasped the brass handle. "Never mind, Nat, I'll get it," he said, helping Misty inside the low-slung landau and closing the door behind them.

She heard the reins snap as they rolled away from the cathedral.

"Now what was that all about?" Raven asked, measuring her with an appraising look.

Misty sank back against the velvety seat, feeling her spirits sink even lower. "What do you mean?" she returned, fingering the tassel of her reticule.

He widened his eyes and leaned forward. "You running off like that. I had people I wanted to introduce to you."

Misty tossed her reticule on the seat. "People like that pretty blonde?"

Raven looked astonished for a moment, then burst out laughing. "Yes, as a matter of fact. That was Priscilla Lindsey."

Misty experienced a spurt of anxiety, knowing this was the girl he'd mentioned in the Ozarks—the girl his father wanted him to wed. "That . . . that was Priscilla?"

He stared at her silently for a moment, his eyes glistening with amusement. "Yes, but she has no interest in me. I confirmed my suspicion today that she likes Warren, and I think he's in love with her, but they're both too shy to make the first move."

"Does your father know?" Misty asked, happy for the quiet young man whom she'd grown to like more each day.

The amusement slowly faded from Raven's eyes. "No. And he thinks so little of Warren, I doubt he would believe Priscilla has any interest in him."

They wheeled along in tense silence for a while, then Raven gave her a long, penetrating look. "You had no reason to feel out of place today," he said, his face showing his concern. "You were dressed as well as any of the other ladies, and a damn sight prettier than the lot of them. Don't you know that?"

"It doesn't have to do with clothes or looks," she replied, a growing tension inside of her. "It has to do with what a person knows and where she's lived—and to them I don't measure up."

Raven let out his breath in a rush. "You're a virtual stranger to them." He gave her a short smile. "They'll come around in time."

Misty opened the small wing window and let the cold air slough over her face, then fell silent as the horses clip-clopped over the long avenue. As church bells tolled the noon hour all over the city, she thought of the little log church back home. She could see it nestled in a grove of cottonwoods. She could hear its small bell echoing through the mountains.

Brother Jubal would be standing at the entrance shaking hands with all the men, while the women clustered together talking about what they were cooking for Sunday dinner. If she'd been there, she would have known every one of the hearty souls who spilled out onto the church yard, and they'd all greet her warmly, telling her of their aches and pains.

At that moment, a wave of homesickness spread through her that almost left her weak. "Raven," she pleaded, sitting forward and clasping his hand, "let's go back to the mountains. We've been here over a month and a half, and you said we were just coming for a visit," she whispered, her voice tight with emotion. "When I first came here, I was scared but I was also filled with hope and I thought I could make people like me. Now I don't know if I can."

Raven gazed at her sad face, thinking that for Misty to be this dispirited, the situation was worse than he thought. In retrospect, he would have handled things differently since they'd arrived here, like accompanying her to the dress shop; and Miss Sullivan had been a mistake on a grand scale. Compassion rose within him for her plight, yet he knew he had to be firm. "How can we leave," he asked, putting his hand over hers, "when John is still so ill? I'd hoped to make some kind of peace with him, but I've made precious little headway."

She looked at him with glistening eyes. "Don't you see he's just using the fact that he's sick to get you and Warren to dance to his tune?"

Raven had made the same observation himself, and he turned the problem over in his mind. "Yes, I know that," he replied evenly, "but what would you have me do? The fact remains that he's ill—desperately ill—and as a doctor I can tell you he only has a matter of weeks left."

She pulled away her hand, and sitting back, stared out the window, her face thoughtful.

Raven crossed his legs, thinking he had to help her adjust to city life before she became too discouraged. She needed a friend in the social world, just one friend—yes, that would help her more than anything else. She needed some quiet, sweet girl to take her under her wing and gently introduce her to society one tea party at a time, so she wouldn't be overwhelmed as she'd been today. Then it came to him all in a rush. Lord, as fantastic as it seemed, why didn't he ask Priscilla to help her?

Despite her shyness, her father's position put Priscilla in the middle of the social whirl, and John would be pleased to see her at the house and therefore would not oppose the plan out of sheer orneriness as he did most things. Knowing that Warren would happily oblige, he told himself he'd suggest that his brother ask both Priscilla and Misty to luncheon next week.

Pleased with this arrangement, he sat back with a satisfied sigh. Why, the arrangement would benefit all parties concerned, and the plan was virtually foolproof. After all, what could Misty do to upset one simple luncheon engagement with the two quietest people in town?

Chapter Fifteen

Outfitted in a soft blue day dress and sporting a feathered hat, Priscilla put her white-gloved hand on Warren's arm and gazed across the carriage at Rollo, who snuggled in Misty's lap. "Are-are you sure he won't bite?" she asked, a doubtful look flitting across her pale face.

Misty, sitting on the other side of the carriage, lapped another length of Rollo's new leash about her hand and smiled at the fair, blue-eyed wisp of a girl, deciding that as Raven had told her this morning, she was still half a child. Although she'd never met anyone as fragile as Priscilla, she was pleased that the girl treated her as an equal and sensed the possibility of a friendship between them. "No, he won't bite," she answered kindly. "Do you want to pet him?"

For a moment, there was only the sound of horses' clopping hooves, then Priscilla finally stammered, "Well, actually I-I've never touched a raccoon."

"Oh, go on," Warren laughed, reaching across the carriage to ruffle Rollo's head himself.

Ever so gently, the timid debutante leaned forward and trailed her fingertips over the animal's glistening back; then, relief flooding her face, she sank back against the seat.

Almost a week had passed since Raven had decided that Misty should meet Priscilla, and after introductions had been made at the debutante's mansion earlier that morning, Warren had suggested they all lunch at L'Orangerie, the city's finest French restaurant. Just being out with the pair lifted Misty's spirits considerably and gave her hope that with their help she might slowly win a few friends in the city.

Feeling better than she had in a long time, Misty looked at Warren and chuckled. "I'm glad I talked you into bringing Rollo. He's been locked up in that carriage house so long, he really needed some fresh air."

"Let's just hope Papa doesn't find out about it," he answered, drumming his fingers on the armrest. "I'm sure he wouldn't approve."

Misty settled Rollo beside her. "Why, he won't be any trouble. Nat can watch him while we're in the restaurant," she explained, swaying a bit as the carriage slowed and turned onto a street lined with fine shops and restaurants. "Afterwards, we'll go to the park. I've seen ladies walking their dogs there, and Rollo is as smart as any dog that ever lived."

When the landau came to a complete halt, Warren leaned back and frowned. "I just have a bad feeling about this whole thing," he complained with a sigh.

Misty scooted to the edge of her seat and laughed. "There's nothing to worry about," she said, trying to keep her tone casual. She ran her gloved fingers under the leash where it fit snugly about Rollo's neck. "This thing is as tight as a fat lady's stockings. Rollo will do just fine."

After alighting, Warren helped the ladies from the carriage, then gave the raccoon's leash to Nat, who stood on the sidewalk. Misty approached him and touched his arm. "Would you give Rollo a little walk before you put him back in the carriage?" she asked, eyeing his worried face.

He gave her a reluctant nod. "Yes, ma'am, *I'll try*. But I ain't never walked a raccoon before."

As the trio walked under the green-and-white striped awning leading to the restaurant, Misty decided that the tall corner building with bay windows looked like a palace. Inside the foyer, filled with palms and bouquets of sweet-scented roses, a maitre d' stood by an elegant desk holding menus.

Although Misty was dressed appropriately in a moss-green silk gown and a perky feathered hat, the magnificence of the restaurant overcame her and she paused in wonder, not knowing what to do. On the other hand, Priscilla seemed to be perfectly at ease. From his words, she knew John admired the girl's ladylike qualities, and when Raven had suggested they meet, Misty had experienced a twinge of hurt, for she guessed that in his own way he admired her too.

Somehow Misty made her way across the huge room, and with a bow of his silver head, the maitre 'd pulled out delicate tapestry chairs and seated everyone at a reserved table set with crystal and gleaming silver. In the background, the diners chatted amicably and there was the sound of pleasant piano music. From where she sat, Misty could also see the street, and with a glow of approval, she watched Nat walking Rollo down the sidewalk. She noticed that many of the pedestrians stopped to watch, but then strolled on, shaking their heads.

Warren scanned a wine list, then favored the ladies with a smile. "I say we forego red wine today and drink champagne. What do you say?"

Priscilla inclined her head in compliance while Misty answered, "That sounds fine to me. I've never been choosy about what I drink."

Looking puzzled, Warren ordered champagne, then peeked over the top of his tall menu at Priscilla. "How about escargots?" he suggested.

"Yes, that sounds very good," she replied in a silky voice.

Misty stared at Warren, realizing that Raven was right in his opinion that his brother was in love with Priscilla. But the girl was so quiet and shy, and displayed her feelings so little, that Misty didn't know if the socialite felt the same way about him.

Warren suddenly glanced at Misty, acting as if he'd almost forgotten she was there. "How does that sound to you?"

"I'm afraid I don't know what you're talking about."

"I was speaking French," he came back with a laugh. "I just suggested escargots."

"Escargots?"

"Yes, you know"—he slowly walked two fingers across the white tablecloth—"snails."

Misty couldn't have heard him correctly! *"Snails?"* she echoed, sitting forward a little.

"Did you say snails?" She cautiously moved her gaze about the restaurant, studying what other people were eating, then told him, "I knew folks ate strange things in the city, but it'd have to be awful hard times in the mountains before we ate snails," she continued, still outraged at the thought. "Just how much do they want for these fancied-up slugs?"

Warren checked the menu. "Ten dollars," he replied lightly.

She swallowed her breath. *"Ten dollars?* They're asking ten dollars for snails?" She tossed her menu aside. "Well, don't get them. They're slickerin' you bad at that price. No telling how much they'd want for a regular piece of meat."

Warren stifled a smile. "Let's just forget the escargots. Perhaps you'd rather have hor d'oeuvres—maybe Siberian caviar with lemon juice or a cold green-bean salad with truffles."

"Now what in the world is hor d'oeuvres?" she asked, feeling more confused by the minute.

Warren shot Priscilla an expressive glance, then turned to Misty again. "Hor d'oeuvres are appetizers," he explained patiently, "little things you eat to make you hungry."

Misty started to mention that if a person ate enough of these little things to make them hungry, they wouldn't be hungry at all, but instead she said, "Well, that's interesting. Now tell me about caviar and truffles."

"Caviar is fish eggs," Warren said. "Tiny, wee fish eggs they remove from the sturgeon, then smoke and salt." His face brightened up. "Would you like some?"

She stared at him silently, thinking things were getting worse by the minute. Why, the last time she'd used fish eggs it had been for bait. "I can answer that question in five words—*ab-so-lute-ly not*. Now go on and tell me about truffles."

"Truffles are a kind of fleshy, subterranean fungi—the blacker the better," Warren added in a soothing tone as if he were speaking to a child.

Misty widened her eyes. "A fleshy, subterranean fungi? Do you mean a *fungus* like a black mold that grows on trees?"

He shrugged and leaned back. "Well, technically truffles *are* molds, but they don't grow on trees"— he coughed a little—"I believe farmers use pigs to root them out of the ground."

She laid her napkin aside. "Does Raven know you eat things like this?" she asked, thinking they couldn't be good for anyone.

She was just going into a tirade about the evils of eating snails, fish eggs, and black mold when a movement on the street caught her eye. To her horror, a plump lady in a pink gown had strolled past the Davenport carriage, leading a poodle. When the dog spotted Rollo, it barked loudly and lunged against its leash. Despite Nat's frantic efforts, the raccoon lunged back. Soon the two animals snarled and struggled, trying to break their respective leashes.

With a surge of panic, she rose from her chair, her eyes still fixed on the scene outside. Warren turned about and looked in the same direction, then also shot to his feet. With a chorus of "*Oh, no*," they both hurried from the table, leaving a stunned Priscilla alone.

As they passed through the foyer, the maitre d' raised his brows, then strolled to the door, holding it open with one arm.

Sonya Birmingham

Once the Davenports were outside, Warren helped Nat hold the leash that the raccoon twisted and turned as he tried to free his head. Misty assisted the lady with the poodle, who kept yelling, "Call off that wild beast. Can't you see he's upsetting my Colette!"

A small crowd gathered to watch the noisy spectacle, and with a mighty snarl, Rollo finally slipped his head from the leash, leaving Nat and Warren to stagger backward and tumble to the street. With wild eyes, the animal then glanced around seeking sanctuary. The poodle, seeing his enemy free, went into frenzies, broke his leash, and raced toward him.

Rollo took off like a thunderbolt, and using the only available path in the gathered crowd, scampered past the startled maitre d' into L'Orangerie, the poodle at his heels. Misty and the maitre d' chased the barking, hissing pair inside the restaurant, arriving just in time to see the elegant diners rise to their feet and part like the Red Sea. Within seconds, Rollo darted under the tables, the poodle in hot pursuit. Shouts and screams rose to the high ceiling. Chairs overturned, dishes crashed to the floor, and tablecloths flew through the air. As if he knew higher ground was his best bet, Rollo leaped atop the grand piano, much to the amazement of the man who played it.

Warren now dashed into the restaurant and headed to the piano, where Misty held out her arms coaxing Rollo to jump. No quitter, the poodle raced about the base of the piano, barking wildly. From the corner of her eye, Misty saw the poodle's white-faced mistress stagger into the dining room yelling, "Colette, control yourself, my darling." She also noticed that Priscilla sat like a statue, looking as if she might melt and run through the cracks in the floor. But maybe, just maybe, Misty thought she spied an amused gleam in Priscilla's eyes.

Misty gave a loud whistle and waved her arms at Rollo. "Jump, jump!" she cried. With wild eyes, the frantic raccoon flew through the air and into Misty's arms, to the applause of the diners. Near tears, the plump lady in the pink dress snatched up her poodle, sank into a chair, and clutched the snarling dog to her ample bosom.

It was over, but L'Orangerie would never be the same again.

Three hours later, Misty and Warren stood at the foot of John's bed as he glared at them with fiery eyes. Misty believed that Priscilla had kept silent about their troubles at the restaurant and wondered how John had found out about the incident.

"Did you really believe you could keep it a secret from me?" the old man asked, his hot gaze boring into them.

Warren shifted his weight uncomfortably. "I asked the maitre d' to send me a bill for the damages." He dropped his head, then looked up with troubled eyes. "How *did* you find out?"

"One of my competitors was at the restaurant and was only too glad to relate the fiasco in detail," John replied with a glower. "No doubt you are now both the talk of the town—my nit-witted son and my ignorant daughter-in-law, who were lame-brained enough to put a raccoon on a leash and take him to the finest restaurant in Saint Louis!"

"It was my idea," Misty spoke up with a racing heart. "Warren didn't approve, and what happened wasn't his fault."

John focused on her. "I don't agree," he replied, drawing his craggy brows together. "Warren was in charge of this social expedition, and if he didn't have the sense to know better, he should have." He swung a hawk-like gaze back to his son. "Well, speak up," he jibed. "What have you to say for yourself?"

The color drained away from Warren's face. "I wanted to please Misty. She seemed sad, and the animal had been shut up for days, and—"

"*Weak*," John cut him off, jabbing his finger at him. "That's what you are and always have been. How do you expect to run a railroad and compete with men like Huntington and Crocker and Stanford when you don't have the backbone to say no to one uppity mountain girl?"

Anger spread through Misty like a blazing fire. Why was the man berating *Warren*? "It was my fault, *all my fault*," she cried, clasping the nearest bedpost until her knuckles turned white.

His face a mask of contempt, John glared at her. "Bah, I'm sick of you both. Get out, just get out of my sight!"

Warren opened his trembling lips to speak, then hung his head, turned, and slowly walked toward the door.

Misty decided that John was the meanest man she'd ever known, Back in the hills, Sloppy had been ignorant and stubborn and suspicious, but he didn't have the benefit of a fine education and a fortune as John did. The tongue-lashing he'd given his son was enough to break a person's heart, and she wanted to tell him so, but noticing Warren's

298

slumped shoulders as he left, she decided she should go after him.

As she picked up her skirt and hurried across the carpet, John called out, "If I see that raccoon outside of the carriage house, I'll have him shot. Do you understand?"

Misty paused and turned around dumbstruck.

A vengeful expression settled on his features. "I asked you if you understood?" he raged, his lips taut with fury.

"Yes, I understand," Misty ground out, biting her tongue so she would not say more.

Instantly she left the room and followed Warren's footsteps as he walked from a back entrance into the mansion's walled gardens. She paused at a set of French doors and watched him slump onto a stone bench, looking as if he didn't have a friend in the world. With a rush of compassion, she opened the doors and hurried outside.

In the garden, a breeze touched her skin and sunlight filtered between the oaks' yellow-green leaves, warming her cheeks. Early flowers—columbines, poppies, and daffodils—bordered the flagstone walks, and scattered about the garden, pear trees heavy with sweet blossoms brought into focus the sharper aroma of the fresh earth.

The cropped grass was like a soft carpet under her feet as she walked to Warren and sat down by his side. She studied his sad face, but having no idea how to ease his pain, simply rested her hand on his arm. "Was he always like this?" she asked at last.

He glanced up and sighed. "As long as I can remember. Nat and some of the other servants said he used to have a bit of tolerance, but

Mother died shortly after I was born. After that, it seems he lost every good quality he had."

For a long while she sat there, silently sharing his pain. Then, wanting to unravel the puzzle of this dark place, she softly ventured, "What was your childhood like? Were you happy at all?"

He looked at her with empty eyes. "There was some happiness when Ezekiel was here, but Papa constantly fought with him about money and finally forced him out. After the old man went back to the mountains, it was as if the sun had gone out. As children, Adam and I always had the best of everything—the finest food and the most expensive clothes—but something was lacking. I used to envy the servants' children, for they were so carefree."

Misty knew that the important missing ingredient in their young lives was love, pure and simple.

"I really think," Warren added, "that the Davenport family has too much money. It's been a curse rather that a blessing, and I often wish we were more like normal folk, who have their share of troubles but somehow seem to overcome them and go on with a smile on their faces."

He slumped over and buried his head in his hands. "I just wish I could be more like Adam. Even when we were children, he stood up to Papa." He gave her a sideways glance and laughed bitterly. "He always called him John. It made the old man mad as fire, but Adam wouldn't change, and he wouldn't change in his desire to be a doctor, although Papa pushed the railroad down his throat every day."

"Do *you* want to be in the railroad business?" she inquired, asking the question she'd wondered about many times.

His eyes shimmered with a pensive light. "Actually, I wouldn't mind if I could use my own ideas, but Papa will hear none of them and insists that I do everything his way."

Looking as if the weight of the world rested on his shoulders, Warren stood and walked to a garden wall bordered with a spill of lilacs that released their lush scent into the humid air. Misty, wanting to help him, trailed his steps and looked into his agitated eyes as he turned about. "Have you noticed how when Adam comes into Papa's study," he asked, "he always pulls back the drapes?"

She nodded, remembering how she'd tried it, and marveling that Raven had the courage to carry through the act.

Warren broke off a bit of lilac and gave the sprig to her, then shoved his hands into his pockets. "I tried it once and the old man almost snapped off my head." He hardened his jaw. "I just wish I had the courage to do it again—to rip open those drapes and let the sunlight flood into that dark place. How I'd love to stand up to him!" He raked a hand through his hair. "Actually, I think I'll never be happy until I do."

Misty slipped her arm through his arm, and they walked back to the mansion that stood before them like a gray prison. After talking to Warren she realized that he still saw himself as a child before his father, who'd skillfully manipulated him into the position with years of badgering and criticism so he could keep a tight rein on him. "You will stand up to him one day, you know," she said in an encouraging voice. *"You will."*

He paused and studied her with a melancholy frown. "But when? Lord, I'm twenty-five years old, and I haven't found the courage yet."

Misty, holding the lilacs to her nose, drew in their heavenly scent, then put the little sprig in his buttonhole and smiled. "When something becomes important enough to you, you'll find the courage." She ran her hand over his shoulder. "I promise you will."

At the French doors she stopped, and remembering something that Raven had said before they left the Ozarks, she looked at Warren. "What is a mausoleum?" she asked thoughtfully.

Surprise swept over his face. "Where did you hear that word?" he asked.

"A long time ago, Raven used it talking about the mansion."

He looked as if he were remembering a bad dream. "Yes, that's what we called this place when we were boys."

"Well," Misty prompted in a gentle voice. "What does it mean?"

He gazed at her with deep anguish, then slowly replied, "A mausoleum is a large and stately building that—that houses the tombs of the dead."

Misty's heart sank, for the term so aptly described this elegant mansion, whose inhabitants were so rich but so unhappy.

Trying to give Warren courage, she clasped his hand and gazed at his bleak face. "I think I'm beginning to understand the problem," she said softly. "But things are going to change."

*   *   *

The next day, the Davenport carriage slowed and entered the circular drive before the mansion, and Raven leaned back against the seat, puzzling out how a quiet luncheon had turned into a catastrophe. Of course, John had told him about it in excruciating detail last night, and afterwards he'd talked to both Misty and Warren, trying to put things into perspective. At least one good thing had come out of the debacle, he thought, trying to salvage something from the incident. Misty had met Priscilla and she liked her, and that fact would serve her well.

Still, Misty and Warren had so far to go! What was he going to do with them? he wondered with a long sigh, realizing that they both had a propensity for getting in trouble. Warren had as much difficulty as ever when it came to standing up to John, and Misty had run through his emotions at a shocking rate. Love, anger, frustration, compassion, tenderness—she'd touched them all. And despite his lessons, she was making painfully slow progress adapting to city ways.

In the mountains, she'd had her medicine to give her a sense of satisfaction, but here, she had nothing. Deep in his heart, he decided that she needed some responsibility to boost her self-confidence. He needed to teach her some very practical things—things like writing a check, which he was sure she'd never done before. Then, he advised himself, he needed to take a deep breath and give her a free hand with some matter to show his trust.

A renewed sense of hope rose within him as the carriage rocked to a stop and he got out, then entered the mansion and started searching for her. He found her in the library, playing her dulcimer at the writing table. She was so lost in the music that she didn't notice his presence and continued stroking the turkey quill over the strings. He stood there at the threshold, taking in her lilac gown and the fashionable arrangement of her hair, thinking about the girl who'd once been so happy wearing buckskins and running through the hills and was now surrounded by all the luxuries that money could buy, yet was bitterly unfulfilled. When the last note floated into the air, he entered the room and clapped his hands. "Very nice, indeed. It took me back to the hills. What were you playing?"

Upon seeing him, her face lit up, and dropping the quill, she rose to her feet. "That was 'Wild Mountain Laurel.' Do you remember it?"

He walked to her and took her hand. "Yes, I do. Have you been playing all afternoon?"

She picked up two letters that lay by the dulcimer. "No, I wrote Ezra today, and Brother Jubal and Lukie, too."

"Telling them all about Sodom and Gomorrah?" he asked in a dry tone.

A blush riding her cheeks, she looked up. "Something like that."

He released her hand and sat on the corner of the writing table, crossing his legs. "Tell me," he said, grazing a knuckle over his chin, "how much do you know about money?"

A smile lit her eyes. "Well, since I never had a lot of it—not much."

"Do you know how to write a check?" he asked, studying her puzzled face.

Misty wondered why he was asking her these questions. He was very close, and his gaze caressed her face, making her acutely aware of his presence. "No, I've heard of them, but I've never written one." She had no idea what he was about, but sensed that it was important and tried to pay close attention to everything he said.

He got up, took a checkbook from the writing table drawer, and wrote a check for a hundred dollars, made out to her. "Here," he said, giving it to her and tossing the checkbook on the table. "You can take this to the First State Bank of Saint Louis, and they'll give you one hundred dollars."

She giggled a little, liking the turn the conversation had taken. "Really, just for this little piece of paper?"

He smiled indulgently. "Yes, just for that little piece of paper. You see, that's the bank where the Davenports keep their money."

"All of the Davenports?"

Disarming her with a smile, he paced in front of the writing table, his hands clasped behind his back. "Yes, I have a separate account where I deposit checks from my medical practice. The business account for the Missouri and North Arkansas Railroad Line is there also." He gave her a sidelong glance. "Warren and I are both authorized to write checks on that account as well as John."

Raven had never mentioned financial affairs to her before, and she was so honored and excited that he'd broached the subject that she automatically blurted out, "How much money does John have?" before she remembered that the question was impolite and covered her mouth.

He paused and his eyes became serious. "Three million dollars," he answered quietly. "There was even more than that, but Ezekiel took several million with him and placed the rest in a trust fund for Warren and myself where John couldn't touch it." He searched her face. "Do you know how much money three million dollars is?"

She pulled in a long breath, stunned by the very thought of it. "That's as many dollars as there are stars in the sky," she replied in a hoarse whisper. "I never thought that one person, or even three people, could have that much money."

He walked to her and wrapped her in his arms, and as always, a pleasurable warmth washed over her. "When John leaves this world, all his assets will be divided between Warren and myself. Do you understand how rich that makes us? Can you comprehend it all?"

Misty knew she should reply, but actually she couldn't comprehend it all. To a person who'd lived off the land, bartering for things she couldn't grow or make, three million dollars didn't belong to her realm of understanding. All she knew was that she and Raven could never spend it all, no matter how hard they tried. "I don't know," she answered at last, her mind still grappling with the startling fact. "I'm just glad I didn't know you were this rich when I found you on the road. I would have been afraid to touch you!"

His mouth quirked up at the corner. "I'm glad you didn't know too," he replied, his voice tinged with mirth.

A horrible thought came to her mind, and she eased back in his embrace. "How does the bank tell our three million dollars from the other folks' money?"

He laughed a little. "Actually, they don't. The Davenport millions are all tumbled up in the vault rubbing shoulders with everyone else's money."

She blinked her eyes, trying to get everything straight. "So when I cash a check, I might get out some baker or carpenter's money instead of ours."

"That's right, but don't worry about it." Amusement softened his expression. "It will still come out of our account." He moved to the writing table and handed her his checkbook. "Here, write a few checks, so you'll know how to do it."

With a trembling hand, Misty wrote several checks for practice, and after he'd scanned them, he tore them up and threw them in the wastepaper basket. Becoming more interested by the moment, she picked up the checkbook and ruffled through it. "This just looks like a bunch of chicken scratching. How does a person keep track of all this money?"

He bit off a grin. "Actually this *chicken scratching* is a record of the money deposited and spent." He lifted a brow. "To keep a checkbook requires a good knowledge of math."

She glanced at his careful calculations and frowned. "I might have a little trouble with that," she said, remembering how she used to make a notch on the chicken house door for every dozen of her granny's eggs she gathered.

"Some people do," he replied, his mouth curving with tenderness.

She laid the checkbook aside, almost too bewildered to speak. "Why are you teaching me all of this?" she suddenly whispered.

He gathered her into his arms, and her senses stirred by the warmth of his body, she relaxed into his comforting embrace, enjoying the feel of his arms about her. "So you can become a person of business," he explained. "I'm authorizing you to write checks on my account, and next week I want you to go to the Collingwood Department Store and buy some new furnishings for our bedroom. Buy anything you like." He surveyed the library. "The Lord knows nothing has been changed in this place for fifty years."

Excitement surged through her. Surely he wouldn't give her this much responsibility. How could he trust the judgment of someone who'd been raised in a log cabin to buy *anything* for the Davenport mansion? Surely he'd send Mrs. Hawksley with her to monitor her purchases. "I suppose you're sending the housekeeper with me," she said weakly.

He smiled. "No. You'll have your own checkbook and Nat will drive you. Outside of that, you'll be on your own."

Misty stared at him, dazed and doubtful and a bit stunned by what she'd heard. Next week, she, Misty Davenport would possess her very own checkbook and be a real *person of business*.

Misty studied Nat's doubtful face as she tried to pull him to the entrance of Collingwood's Department Store.

He planted his feet apart and, making a firm stance on the sidewalk, shook his head. "No, ma'am, I think you're a might mixed up. I've never been in a department store with a lady like yourself." He widened his eyes and nodded at the carriage. "I'm supposed to *drive* you, not help you buy things."

"Oh, please come with me," Misty pleaded. "If you don't want to help me buy things, you can carry packages. I've seen other drivers doing that!"

With a wary frown, Nat scanned the busy street and, seeing that she was right, sighed heavily. "All right. Since this is your first time, I'll come in, but if you ask me," he said, scanning the store whose name was written above the door in huge brass letters, "this idea is just plumb crazy. Why, Mr. John would throw a conniption fit if he knew about it."

Misty, lifting the hem of her yellow silk gown, led him toward the department store's impressive entrance. "Mr. John will never know a thing about this—I guarantee you," she promised, giving him a big smile.

Once they were inside the huge doors, she adjusted her tiny chapeau while Nat swept off his top hat. A well-dressed man wearing a rosebud in his buttonhole, came up to them, eyed Nat, then gave Misty a concerned look. "Is there some problem with your carriage, ma'am?"

She blinked at the portly man, thinking he must be a little slow. "No. There's no problem at all." She slipped her new checkbook from her reticule and twisted it in her kid-gloved hands. "My name is Misty Davenport and I'm a person of business"— she cut her eyes at Nat—"and this is my man, Nat. We're here to buy some new bedroom furnishings for the mansion."

The man's jaw sagged. "Did you say you're *Mrs. Davenport,* ma'am?"

"Yes, that's right," she piped up, thinking that he was finally catching on. In a softer voice, she added, "You know, the Davenport family with three million dollars—the ones who own the Missouri and North Arkansas Railroad Line?"

The manager coughed, then escorted her and Nat from the stream of shoppers flowing in and out of the department store. With a gracious smile, he bowed his head, and with eyes dancing with eagerness, he announced, "I'm the manager of Collingwood's, ma'am, and if there's any way I can make your visit more enjoyable, please let me know." He flung a disparaging gaze at Nat. "But I'm afraid your help will have to wait—"

"Oh, no!" Misty interrupted him, taking the driver's arm. She spread her other hand over her ruffled bosom. "You see, I have these fainting spells and just fall right down on the floor sometimes, and he has to pick me up and carry me out of places."

Nat's mouth fell open, but he chuckled softly as the manager tried to make up his mind what to do.

Misty ruffled through her checkbook. "Are there any other department stores in Saint Louis, Nat?"

The driver scratched his head and nodded. "Yes, ma'am, there sure are. There's several more. The Paris was just built last year. It's over on River Drive, and—"

"The bedroom furniture is on the third floor," the manager cut in, sweeping his hand forward in a welcoming gesture. "I'll escort you there personally."

As they passed the men's furnishings, a rack of fur-trimmed coats caught Misty's eye. "Oh wait," she called to the manager. "I want to buy a coat for my husband. It'll come in real handy next winter back in the Ozarks. Elmer Frockmorton from over in Russell's Hollow used to make coats, but he passed away a while back. Besides that, the wolves are getting more scarce all the time."

The manager's lips trembled in a condescending smile. "These coats are not trimmed in *wolf* fur ma'am," he replied, caressing the fur collar. "They're trimmed in genuine Russian sable."

Misty brushed her hand over the collar. "Well, Raven's real even-natured. If he can't get wolf, he'll take sable and make do."

The man's expression crumpled. "But don't you want to know the cost?"

"Oh, that doesn't matter," she came back lightly, plucking a loose thread from her gown. "It won't make much of a dent in the Davenport millions."

Perspiration beaded the manager's brow. "Well, what size does your husband wear?" he offered in a shaky voice.

She glanced about, then pointed at a gentleman on his way from the store. "I'm not sure, but he's just that man's size." She gave the manager a bright smile. "Do you reckon he'd try one on for me?"

Seeing the customer departing, the manager ran after him and brought him back, whispering in his ear. Misty couldn't hear everything he said, but she did hear the words *eccentric* and *three million dollars*.

At the rack, the gentleman tried on coats until he found one that was just his size. "Forty-two," the manager said. "Your husband wears size forty-two." After a lingering stare, the innocent passerby walked away while the manager passed the coat to a clerk, giving him orders to wrap it up.

Misty scribbled out a check and handed it to the manager. "I was a little scared of this check writing at first, but there isn't anything to it." She chuckled deeply, really enjoying herself. "And I just love that little purring noise it makes when I rip out the checks."

Sonya Birmingham

As they advanced to the second floor, Misty went into a regular buying frenzy. She bought a new fiddle for Uncle Fuzzy and a banjo for Aunt Izzy, a rifle for Ezra, gowns for Lukie, and a Bible for Brother Jubal. She bought china, linens, lamps, and oil paintings for the mansion, always writing a separate check at each department and giving it to the clerk with a flourish.

As the packages were wrapped, she sent Nat to carry them to the carriage and gave a young man five dollars to stand outside and guard everything. By now the manager, who'd loosened his tie, carried a pad and pencil and wiped his brow occasionally.

When Misty paused to buy Ezra some boots, her gaze came to rest on a pair of patent leather tap shoes. "Nat, I've found a gift for you," she said excitedly. "Look at those shiny dancing shoes. They were made for you."

"Lordy, Mrs. Davenport. I have everything I need."

"Nonsense. John Davenport has three million dollars just moldering away, and some of it ought to be spent on dancing shoes. What size do you wear?"

"Ten, but—"

From the shelf, she pulled out a box of shoes his size and shoved them in his arms. "Try them on," she ordered, watching his face light up.

After Nat had put the shoes on, he pulled up his pants legs, looked at the shoes, and did a little shuffle step. "Them is sure dancing shoes, all right," he commented, a chuckle escaping his mouth. "They nearly dance by themselves."

Misty whipped out her checkbook. "Let him wear them," she told the manager. "He may want

312

to do some more dancing before we're through."
After she'd written a check for the boots and shoes,
she held up her checkbook and showed it to the
man. "Look, only three checks left. I guess we'd
better be getting up to that third floor!"

Nat came forward with a worried face. "I think
we'd better stop now, ma'am. The carriage is
already filled to the brim, and you've spent a
whole shebang of money."

The manager put out a spread hand. "Oh, don't
worry," he said, mopping his brow. "We can help
you with that. We have wagons and vans that can
deliver anything you want right to your home
without cost."

Misty linked her arm in his and strolled away,
delighted with the information. "Good. Then after
I buy the bedroom furniture, I'll buy some other
larger pieces like bureaus and maybe one of those
grand pianos like I saw in L'Orangerie."

The manager gave her a quizzical look, "I was
wondering," he said as they made their way to the
marble stairs with a worried Nat at their heels, "if
a person of business like yourself is familiar with
the credit system?"

Misty studied the man's eager face, astonished
that Raven hadn't mentioned such a thing. "No,"
she said in a interested tone. "Tell me all about
it."

Three hours later, Misty's carriage approached
the mansion, and she leaned back and sighed
with contentment, happy with her day's work.
The landau itself was full of packages, and she
had to peep over them to see from the windows.
There were packages on the box with Nat and
packages tied to the top of the carriage itself.

313

Misty crossed her arms and smiled, deciding she liked being a person of business. Raven would soon be home from the hospital, and she couldn't wait to tell him about her day. It was wonderful to write checks and rip off the little papers, hand them out, and see everyone scurrying about wrapping up things for her loved ones. And after the manager had explained the credit system and told her she could have anything in the whole store by just asking for it, she'd laughed with joy.

She supposed she'd spent a lot of money, but since she hadn't really *seen* any of it, it was almost like not spending it at all. Inside her head, she kept hearing Warren say, *"I think this family would be happier if we didn't have as much money."* She heartily agreed, and today she'd done something to remedy that situation.

When the carriage finally turned into the circular sweep of bricks before the mansion, she could see that some of the delivery vans, drawn by teams of horses, had beat them there and crowded the driveway. Peeking from the little round glass in the back of the landau, she spotted more delivery vans entering the driveway behind them.

With a feeling of excitement, she surveyed the lawn that teemed with frenzied activity. Fine tables, covered with padded blankets, littered the velvety grass, and shouting men struggled a grand piano up the mansion's steps. While some workers carried in mirrors and bookcases, others opened the backs of vans and laid ramps to facilitate the moving of heavy mahogany bureaus and tall secretaries.

When Nat stopped beside a big delivery van, Misty squeezed from the carriage, and glancing about, she noticed Raven driving his little open gig up the driveway, Priscilla at his side. Upon seeing the girl with Raven, curiosity stirred within her, for she wondered why the pair was together. On closer inspection, she noticed that a deep frown ploughed Raven's brow, and with a sinking heart, she got the distinct impression that he wasn't happy with what he saw.

Pulling up his horse, he whipped the reins about the brake lever, then jumped out and helped Priscilla alight from the gig. As soon as her feet had hit the ground, he strode to Misty and clasped her shoulders. "Good Lord, what in heaven's name is going on here?" he asked, running his eyes over her in alarm.

"W-well," she began softly, "I was just going to buy bedroom furniture like you said, but then I saw a coat I thought you needed, and the checks were making that nice sound when I ripped them off, and—" She bit her bottom lip, then held up her checkbook and gave him her best smile. "*Look*, I got rid of all the checks but one. Being a person of business, I thought I should save one for an emergency." She glanced down, then taking a deep breath, looked up at him again. "I bought the rest of the things on credit."

He stared at her with unbelieving eyes. No doubt about it, she thought, noting his deep frown, he wasn't happy with her *at all*. "What in God's name possessed you to do such a thing?" he asked in a stinging tone. "I told you to buy *bedroom furniture*, not a whole department store!"

Feeling as limp as a rag doll, she opened her mouth to speak, but could find no words.

After giving her a look of disbelief, Raven ran to a wagon and leapt upon it, attracting the attention of the workers, who paused and turned about. "You men, stop your work," he shouted through cupped hands. "All this merchandise must go back to Collingwood's immediately. I'll see your employer and settle this mess."

The murmuring men seemed puzzled and hesitated for a few moments, then began going into the mansion and bringing out pieces of furniture and carrying them to the vans.

Priscilla, looking like the perfect lady she was, stood by the gig under the shade of a lacy parasol, witnessing the spectacle. At the same time, Raven jumped from the wagon and went to talk to some of the confused workmen.

Despair spiraled through Misty. With an aching heart, she realized that she'd failed Raven's trust. Then a sound cut through her racing thoughts, and Nat appeared from around the carriage. He was barefooted, and his whole body seemed to sag downward. In his right hand, he held his dancing shoes, but when he extended them to Misty, she shook her head. "No, you keep them," she ordered, giving the shoes back to him. "Raven would want you to have them." Her next sentence almost stuck in her throat. "Well, I guess there's always something to be thankful for—nothing could get any worse than this."

Nat gazed toward the mansion, surprise flooding his eyes. "Lordy, ma'am. I hate to tell you, but I'm afraid it just did."

Misty turned about and, with a prick of shock, saw Mrs. Hawksley pushing John onto the lawn in his cane-backed wheelchair. A deep scowl stamped his angry face.

Chapter Sixteen

"I was bringing Priscilla home because she'd been working at the hospital," Raven said as he scanned Misty's puzzled face in the light flickering through the carriage window.

She blinked thoughtfully. "Priscilla has a job at the hospital?"

He grinned, for despite her finery she looked like a sad, lost child, and he realized that she was somewhat jealous of the young socialite. "Well, in a manner of speaking," he explained, touched by her relieved expression. "She works there every Thursday doing volunteer work. We both finished early today, and I offered her a ride home. I was going to drop her off first, but when I saw the mansion surrounded by delivery vans, I decided I'd better see what was going on at my own doorstep."

The storm was over. All the merchandise except

the bedroom furniture and Nat's dancing shoes had been returned, and Misty and Raven were now going for a late dinner, with champagne.

After his initial anger, Raven had felt a surge of protectiveness for Misty, especially when John started criticizing her. Putting his father in his place with a few sharp words, he'd decided that it would be best if he and Misty got away that evening to sort things out between them. Now as he looked at her stricken face, he knew she once again felt the sting of defeat and needed a victory more than ever. "Do you feel better?" he asked, brushing a loose curl from her cheek.

He felt the languid weight of her body against him. "Not really," she answered, drawing in a shaky breath. "I failed as a person of business, and I've begun to think there isn't anything I can do here—anything that matters."

There it was, Raven thought. She'd verbalized what he'd been wrestling with for days. With a mixture of pride and frustration, he considered her zest for life, her child-like eagerness to help people, and he knew she'd never be satisfied being simply a lady of leisure. But what *could* she do in Saint Louis that would give her a sense of fulfillment?

He turned another idea over in his mind, but considered not mentioning it, for the proposal might spark yet another failure. It seemed that when Misty Malone added her own unique touch to the affairs of mere mortals, she usually produced combustible results. Still, as he noted her slumped shoulders, he realized that he cared enough about her that he was going to take the risk. "You could always do volunteer work at the hospital, like Priscilla," he suggested, watching her closely to judge her reaction.

She stared at him with questioning eyes. "Just what does she do? Help the doctors?"

He repressed a smile, thinking of Priscilla doing anything other than being decorative. "No, she writes letters for the patients . . . gives them newspapers . . . cheers them up . . . simple things like that."

Misty rested against the carriage seat and listened to the creaking wheels and the rhythmic clop of the horses' hooves. For someone who could concoct over a hundred different healing potions from memory and didn't flinch at digging a bullet from a man's chest, the offer was a little insulting—but she'd be lifting people's spirits, which she knew was vitally important to their recovery.

"Mrs. Vanderhoosey is in charge of the volunteer program," Raven added, breaking into her thoughts.

"What a funny name!"

"Tell that to her husband," he replied quietly. "He's the chief-of-staff at Saint Mary's, and even though he's almost retired, he's a very important man." He gave her a wry smile. "His wife is one of those women who dominate everyone they know, including their husbands."

The carriage slowed, and from the amber blush of the lamps along the avenue, Misty knew they were in the section of Saint Louis where the fine restaurants were located.

"Well, what do you think?" Raven prompted.

She met his appraising eyes, slowly considering the idea. After her latest adventure, she relished his tolerance and was especially proud that he'd invited her to join him at his place of work. No, she thought, volunteer work wouldn't be like the doctoring she'd done in the hills, but at least she'd be doing something useful. Considering her present situation, what did she have to lose? "Yes," she murmured at last, giving him a big smile, "I think working at the hospital would suit me just fine."

His searching gaze roved over her as he gathered her in his arms. "Good," he answered, obviously pleased, "but there's one thing you must understand. Your job is to follow Mrs. Vanderhoosey's instructions, not diagnose patients or give them cures. And you must not interfere with hospital operations in any way whatsoever." His eyes darkened with intensity, and he trailed his fingers over her cheek. "Is that clear?"

She studied his serious expression, wondering why he should make her take a vow about something like this when she'd been doctoring folks all of her life. Didn't he have any confidence in her? Well, there was nothing to do but humor the man, she finally decided, remembering her granny's admonition that men sometimes acted like headstrong children. "It's clear as crystal," she whispered in an amused voice.

His face softened, and laugh lines crinkled from his eyes. "Mrs. Vanderhoosey visits Priscilla almost every week. I'll ask her to introduce you. If I know anything about her, the woman will have you working there in a matter of days." He put his hand behind her head and fluttered kisses over her face, and she felt his moist breath and the texture of his skin. "I'll take you to the hospital Saturday myself," he added softly. "I'll show you around, so you'll have an idea where everything is."

He gently shifted her in his arms and, holding her in a steely yet tender embrace, brought his lips to hers so that she was immersed in the scent of his spicy cologne. She sensed the fire of his passion as he dragged his lips back and forth across hers, then moved his mouth to the soft curve of her throat, making her gasp with desire. Breathing her name, he buried his fingers in the curls of her upswept hair and pressed her so closely against him that she felt his warmth and the beating of his heart.

Ever so gently, he eased back, and when he traced his thumb over her parted lips, a languorous tremor coursed through her. "Let's make this a short dinner," he suggested, the glint in his eyes making her pulse scamper with anticipation. "I think we have something important to do back at the mansion." His voice shimmered with passion, and his meaningful words heated her blood with excitement.

"We do?" she answered with a throaty chuckle.

He tilted a dark brow. "You bet. This doctor is prescribing a night of love for the two of us."

After a romantic dinner at the elegant restaurant, which fortunately passed without incident, they returned to the mansion, then closed the bedroom door behind them. In a playful mood, Misty twirled about, returning Raven's teasing gaze with one of her own. "I don't know about making love tonight," she said, running her fingers over his chest. "I think I'll have to check with my doctor before taking up any strenuous activity."

Raven chuckled deeply. "In my professional opinion, a little heavy breathing would be good for your lungs. In fact, I think it would be an excellent idea if you shed that binding garment right now"—he rubbed his chin and looked thoughtful—"no, I have a better idea," he said briskly, holding up his finger as if he'd just had a brainstorm. "I'll take it off for you."

Giddy from the champagne, Misty giggled and backed across the carpet, while he trailed her, extinguishing all the lamps but one small light that imbued the room with a rosy glow. She looked at him standing there, tall and appealing in the shadows, and felt overjoyed that they'd finally finished discussing her overspending. More important, after her defeated mood of this afternoon, the thought of working at a hospital filled her with happy expectation.

Raven discarded his jacket and tie, and with a wicked grin, took a few swift steps and pulled her into his arms. At first, she playfully beat against his chest and, laughing all the time, moved her lips out of the way as he tried to kiss her. Then, when he pressed her so close against him that she could feel the hardness of his manhood, her heart pounded; aroused by his passion, she put her arms about his broad shoulders.

"Well, tonight just proves that all the old sayings are right," he remarked, his eyes glinting with mischief.

She laced her fingers through the hair at the nape of his neck and raised a questioning brow.

"You know," he added, raining little kisses over her face, "remember the one about the best part of an argument is making up?"

"That was always one of my favorites," she said with a chuckle.

He brought his searching lips down on hers, letting her feel the warmth of his desire. Fueled by the emotion of their earlier tiff, their love-making that night was especially poignant, and what had started out as a playful romp quickly became more serious. With a wild fire, his tongue met hers and he urged her dress down around her shoulders, his fingers working at the back buttons, until her breasts spilled forth.

Deepening the kiss with thrusts of his tongue, he cupped one breast and grazed a thumb over its swollen crest, making her skin flush with warmth. He ran his open palm over one globe, then toyed with its sensitive peak, rolling it between his fingers until it hardened and ached sweetly.

At last, he broke the scorching kiss and, moving her away a bit, dipped his head and suckled her nipples with his firm lips. As he swirled his tongue over them, an ever building fire throbbed between her legs, and she was filled with an excitement that demanded release. When she thought she would swoon with need, he slid her dress and chemise down around her slender waist and, undoing her petticoat, inserted his hands at the top of her hips and eased everything down at once, until she stood in her corset and underthings.

He swiftly untied the bustle and tossed it on a chair, and minutes later, the unhooked corset landed beside it. Then, his hands warming her skin, he slid her bloomers from her hips, taking time to caress and knead her bare buttocks as he did so. When the undergarment slipped to the floor, she stepped free of the fabric at her feet, now nude except for her black stockings, garters, and shoes. Gently, Raven plucked the hairpins from her upswept hair; tossing her head, she felt her locks fall loose and cool about her bare shoulders.

Sonya Birmingham

His hands moved over her body possessively, and her heart fluttered as he scooped her up and eased her onto the bed. She closed her eyes and felt the give of the soft mattress and the coolness of the silken sheets against her bare skin. She lay motionless, at peace, her whole body taking on a languorous glow, yet tingling with anticipation.

Glancing at Raven, she saw him undressing, silhouetted against the soft lighting that burnished his huge frame. She was deeply touched at the perfection of his body—the breadth of his shoulders, his heavy arms rippling with muscles, and his chest, furred with dark hair that tapered to a trim waist and narrow hips. As her gaze dropped lower, she noticed his corded thighs and his aroused maleness, which made blood sting her cheeks.

He smiled as he sank beside her, then slipped off her shoes and rolled down both of her garters and took them from her legs. Shivers raced through her as his hands slid caressingly down her thighs and calves and he removed the silk stockings which made a soft, crackling sound when he tossed them aside. She trembled as his hands moved back along her ankles, up them to caress the flesh around her calves, skimmed over her knees, and roved tenderly along her upper thighs.

Her heart jolted as he leaned forward to kiss her mouth while his fingers lavished attention on her moist, inner flesh, sending shuddering need to the core of her being. She was bombarded with lush sensations as, slowly and lovingly, he teased her bud of desire, all the while exploring her mouth with his tongue until she thought she would die with the pleasure of it all.

At last he slipped into bed beside her and she was drawn to the warmth of his body as he embraced her, planting kisses on her closed lids and her cheeks, her ears, and the pulse in her throat. Soft feelings flooded through her, leaving her weak in his powerful embrace. Then, raising himself slightly on one arm, he brushed back her hair and, gazing into her eyes, murmured, "Sweet Misty, how my blood races when I hold you near."

Raven searched her exquisite face, so trusting, so pale in the diffused light. His heart burned at the sight of her—her dreamy eyes, her blushing cheeks, her gently curving mouth, as soft as a child's. His woman, he thought, shaken with the wonder of her. His gentle, child-like lover, so innocent in the ways of the world, but so wise of heart.

He caressed her delicately sculpted face, trying to ignore the questions swirling inside his head. He who'd always taken women so lightly was deeply concerned for this child of the hills. Would she ever lose her longing for the mountains and find fulfillment away from them? And what would happen if she was forced to make a permanent choice between the Ozarks and Saint Louis? Would she ever be happy here in the city?

Finding no answers to his troubling questions, he gave an inward sigh and pulled her to him until her breasts were crushed against his chest. Then he buried his face in her hair and explored the hollows of her back. She quivered beneath his touch and, relinquishing the last of her inhibitions, began a series of erotic caresses, cupping and stroking with a delicate touch and stirring within him a white-hot desire.

Misty's blood ran faster as Raven covered her mouth with his and caressed the tender folds of her body with his warm fingers. She felt her nipples tighten and grow pebbly beneath his palms, felt his silken touch at her secret crevices, felt the heat of his mouth moving from her lips to her breast once more.

As he lovingly drew at her aching crests and twirled his tongue about them, a warm flush rolled over her and prickles raced up her spine. She groaned with arousal as his fingers traced the cleft between her cheeks, then moved forward to tease the hair between the legs and explore her most intimate self, making her shiver at the wet, ripe sensation of it all. Ecstasy surged up from her core, and dizzy with voluptuous pleasure, she felt her seat of femininity swell and throb with a darting sweetness.

Now his tongue delved into her mouth and she trembled with pent-up excitement that was almost unbearable. His touch stirred some wild, carnal urge within her, until she surrendered to him totally.

As he leaned over her, she parted her quivering legs, and with a feverish longing, ached for him to enter her. Leisurely, slowly, with infinite tenderness, he continued caressing her, until she welcomed his hard length and melted against him.

"Put your legs about me, my darling," he whispered, brushing back her hair as he spoke.

They could feel the beat of each other's hearts, and as he rhythmically built their passion with sure strokes, Misty moved against him wildly, working toward a crest that lay tantalizingly moments away. They moved together with a glorious grace, up and up, higher and higher, into passion's dazzling realm. Misty, bathed in a flame of desire brighter than she'd ever known, finally exploded with a shattering ecstasy that rolled through her in tumultuous waves. With a gasp, she dug her fingers into his muscled back, savoring the fire of the moment.

Then, her passion unleashed, she fell downward from the heights until she floated to earth fulfilled and utterly satiated. Raven's arms tightened about her, and half-dizzy from the sweetness of it all, she gave a soft sigh and succumbed to the languorous peace enveloping her like a velvet cloak.

Raven opened the door of his office for Misty. "Well, I think you've seen most of Saint Mary's," he said. "I saved this bear's den until last."

Stepping into the beamed chamber, she swept her gaze over the book-lined shelves, the glowing gasoliers, the dark portraits of the former chiefs-of-staff, their faces set in stern lines. She took a deep breath; the place smelled of lemon polishing oil like the rest of the official rooms she'd seen, and pride glowed through her as she strolled about, trailing her gloved fingertips over everything in sight. This was Raven's personal realm, the office that claimed so much of his attention, and he'd brought her here to see it.

She was amazed at all the wonderful gadgets she'd seen today: stethoscopes, fever thermometers, tongue depressors, and even little hammers to test patients' reflexes! After twirling about in his swiveling chair, she rose to open a closet door, then clasped her throat as the white bones of a human skeleton gleamed from the darkness.

Raven walked to her side. "Oh, don't mind him," he said, laughter in his voice. "That's just Oscar. I keep him out of sight most of the time."

Misty gingerly traced her fingers over the skeleton's ribs. "Why, he's almost as skinny as Miss Sullivan." She tried to repress a giggle. "And he has the same kind of sparkling personality, too." As she worked the skeleton's fingers back and forth, she watched Raven's amused face. "It's good to see he's still nice and relaxed. I'd think living in a closet like that would tend to make a person real tense."

They both laughed, and Misty continued her inspection of the office, opening every drawer and asking Raven dozens of questions. He scanned her as they left the office and she sashayed ahead, still interrogating him as she moved around a nurse with a cart. "You know, when I'm doing volunteer work here," she rattled on, her green skirt swishing smartly, "I'm going to look this hospital over *real good*, so when we get back to the hills we can start something like it for the mountain people."

He shook his head, thinking she'd never run out of enthusiasm. "That's a wonderful idea, but do you know how much money it costs to build a hospital?"

She drew stares when she paused to peek into an empty examining room, but ignoring several nurses, she turned her eyes to Raven and shrugged. "We'll start small. There's not many people there, so we won't need a big hospital at first." She clutched his arm and gazed up as they continued, passing several slow-moving patients and their attendant orderlies. "Why, we could build it near one of the old Indian springs, so we'd have lots of good water for everyone."

They walked on and Raven gave an inward chuckle, thinking that Florence Nightingale could have cleared up the Crimean situation in half the time if she'd only had the Wizard of the Hills on her side.

"Now, have I seen *everything?*" Misty suddenly asked, stopping and looking at him with inquiring eyes. She looked up and down the crowded corridor. "I want to see this place from stem to stern."

He studied her glowing face, considering the situation. "Well, there *is* one more place—the children's ward. But I'm afraid it's very sad."

A tender look softened her eyes. "Why, I'm interested in that place most of all."

"Very well," he said, taking her arm. "Actually, there's a little girl there I'd like you to meet."

When they came to some glass doors, he opened them and, taking her elbow, escorted her inside. An antiseptic scent hung in the sparsely furnished ward and nearby a uniformed nurse in a long white apron tucked the covers about a sleeping child. "How is Sarah today?" Raven asked, pausing by the heavy woman's side.

She straightened herself and, looking at the end of the ward, shook her gray head. "The same, I'm afraid." A hopeless look clouded the woman's eyes. "She's been staring outside all day, just like she always does."

Raven thanked her; then, getting Misty's attention, tilted his head toward a little girl sitting by a window. She was a delicate child of five with large blue eyes and flowing brown hair that curled about her shoulders and hung over her simple nightgown. With a wistful look, she clasped her frail hands in her lap and surveyed the hospital's sloping green lawn. He noticed Misty's face light with interest as they approached her.

Hearing their footsteps, she glanced up, a smile racing over her soft lips at the sight of them. "Dr. Davenport," she murmured, "You've come to see me again."

Raven stooped and took her cool hand. "Yes, I've been thinking about you." He caressed her thin fingers, realizing that she'd lost more weight. "How have you been sleeping?"

The child trembled. "I had more bad dreams last night," she answered, her fingers plucking at the blanket that covered her legs. "I *hate* them, and they come all the time now."

Raven gathered her to him and patted her back, calming her. "Hush then, we won't talk about them any more," he soothed, feeling her slight body begin to relax. He eased her away, scanning her innocent face. "I have someone with me whom you'll like," he announced in a cheerful tone, glancing at Misty, then back at the girl. "This is my wife, and I've brought her here to meet you."

Compassion rose within Misty as she sank to a chair by the girl and cocked her head to the side. "My name's Misty," she explained, "and I'm from a place called Red Oak Hollow. It's so high up in the Ozark Mountains, the tops of the pine trees nearly scrape the sky."

Faint interest flickered in the girl's eyes. "You talk funny," she said, her voice scarcely above a whisper, "but you're real pretty . . . and I *do* like you."

Misty grinned. "All us mountain folk talk strange to city folk, but that's what makes us so interesting." She smiled and studied the child, who seemed as fragile as thistle down. "Do you know that I have a 'coon named Rollo that I brought all the way from the hills?" Sarah widened her eyes, hanging on her every word. "Why, he's so fat," Misty went on, "he waddles when he walks, and he pulls such shenanigans sometimes I nearly pop my gizzard string just laughing at him."

Sarah giggled. *"Pop your gizzard string?* I never heard anyone say *that."*

The pair talked with the child for another twenty minutes, and Misty told her so many funny stories that the girl's cheeks took on a rosy blush. When she and Raven were ready to go, he removed the blanket from Sarah's thin, scarred legs, then lifted her into her narrow bed and gently covered her. "You get some rest now," he advised, pulling the covers under her chin. He brushed back her hair. "I'll see you Monday."

Tears pricked Misty's eyes when she realized that the child couldn't walk, and a dismal feeling sat heavy in her stomach when she thought of leaving her there by herself. Fortunately, just as they walked away, the ward nurse approached to serve the girl a glass of juice. Feeling a tightness in her throat, Misty clutched Raven's arm, and when they were near the glass doors, she whispered, "What happened to poor Sarah?"

With a heavy sigh, he guided her between some orderlies and proceeded toward one of the hospital exits. "She was in a fire over three months ago," he explained, putting his arm about her. "Her parents and brother were killed, but the firemen were able to rescue her. Even so, her legs were horribly burned."

Sonya Birmingham

Misty glanced at his somber face. "But they're healed now—she should be able to walk," she insisted.

A brooding expression hardened his features. "Exactly. There is no medical reason she can't walk, but I guarantee you, she is unable to take one step."

As they left the hospital, a fresh breeze wafted over them, and the sounds of carriages and clopping horses rode the light air.

Raven paused on one of the marble steps, his face tight with concern. "She also has nightmares about the fire and has almost quit eating. It's as if she's given up on life."

"Does she have kin to take her in when she gets well?"

"Yes. Luckily, her grandparents live in the East. We sent word to them when the accident happened, and they've made arrangements for her to be cared for in their home. They should be arriving soon." A thoughtful look came to his eyes. "But I'm concerned about Sarah's well-being, even though physically she's fine."

Nat was waiting outside with the landau, and as the pair walked down the steps, the day that had been so pleasant for Misty took on an overcast hue. For the rest of the afternoon, her whole mind centered on Sarah's problem.

Mrs. Vanderhoosey peered over the top of her spectacles at Misty and asked, "And what of your family, my dear? Do you have any brothers and sisters?"

With trembling fingers, Misty set down her tea cup. "Well . . . I have one brother. His name is Ezra."

"How nice. And what is his occupation in Arkansas?" the lady inquired, idly fanning herself with a lacy handkerchief drenched in jasmine scent.

"He works at the saw mill."

Mrs. Vanderhoosey laughed. "What a quaint way to put it," she said, smoothing her long white gloves. "You mean he's in the lumber industry. He *owns* a sawmill?"

Misty glanced down, then met the great lady's probing eyes, determined to be honest. "No, he doesn't own the sawmill. He just works there . . . cutting logs."

Mrs. Vanderhoosey blinked rapidly. "Yes, I see." She sniffed distastefully. Seemingly at a loss for other words, she shifted her attention to Priscilla, who poured more tea into the matron's delicate china cup.

The ladies sat on the veranda of Priscilla's home, a Victorian mansion surrounded by leafy trees and well-tended lawns and flower beds. The wicker table before them held a dazzling silver service, and colorful cushions adorned their high-backed chairs.

Misty had seen pictures of Mrs. Vanderhoosey in the newspaper's social pages, but Mrs. Vanderhoosey *on the hoof*, as her granny would say, was a sight to behold. Several moles dotted the older woman's face, and today she wore a pale blue dress with ruffles running around the skirt and bodice, which made her look like a big, fluffy ball. A pearl choker and three additional strands of pearls encircled her neck, the longest hanging to her thick waist.

A ring flashed from every finger, and a large-brimmed hat decorated with three different shades of blue feathers topped her silvery hair. A gigantic burst of feathers cascaded from the crown, and to Misty it seemed as if the woman had a whole chicken sitting on her head. In fact, the feathery hat made her think of Albert, her old pet rooster back in the hills, and she'd have sworn some of the dyed feathers came from his tail.

When Mrs. Vanderhoosey squeezed Misty's hand, she felt the cold of her diamonds against her flesh. Evidently she'd recovered from the shock of Ezra being a lowly sawmill hand, for a smile wreathed her white-powdered face. "I've been waiting to meet Adam's wife. He's such a fine doctor."

Misty tore her attention from the fascinating chicken hat whose feathers fluttered in the breeze and smiled as Raven had instructed her.

"My dear," the woman continued in a serious tone, "Adam tells me you're interested in volunteering your services at the hospital. That's so generous of you." She nodded at Priscilla whose large Persian cat lay at her feet, a bundle of silky fluff. "Our dear Priscilla has assisted us for so long," she gushed, before appraising Misty again. "She passes out magazines to the patients, you know."

Misty wanted to tell the lady she could do more than that. Why, she could deliver a baby, or sew up an arm, or set a broken leg—but remembering Raven's warning, she merely smiled.

The maid brought out a three-tiered server of finger sandwiches and a plate of petit-fours and placed them on the table. Misty wasn't sure what to do, but she watched her hostess put a sandwich on her plate with a pair of silver tongs, then did the same. Mrs. Vanderhoosey chatted as they ate, most of the time with Priscilla, so all Misty had to do was smile between bites.

While the socialites talked, Misty felt the cat rubbing against her skirt before it nimbly leaped from the verandah. Having nothing in particular to do, she opened one of the sandwiches and, finding it contained smoked salmon, polished it off. When she tried to take another, others tumbled from the heavily packed server, starting a sandwich avalanche. What a shock the ladies would have when they discovered sandwiches scattered over the table! she thought, warmth stinging her cheeks.

She guessed it would be wrong to try to restack the server, but didn't know how to rectify her mistake. Then, with great relief, she spotted the Persian ambling across the lawn bordering the veranda, and while Mrs. Vanderhoosey and Priscilla continued talking, she cautiously tossed the sandwiches to the surprised cat, who devoured them all.

At last Mrs. Vanderhoosey turned about and, noticing half the sandwiches were gone, frowned with disapproval.

Misty grinned and rubbed her stomach. "I always was partial to salmon," she offered pleasantly. "And one of those little things don't even make a good bite."

Mrs. Vanderhoosey paled, but Priscilla came to the rescue with more tea, and after the socialite had taken several sips, she eyed Misty and managed a simulated smile. "I want you to come to the hospital next Thursday," she

Sonya Birmingham

ordered, already up to full steam again. "Some newspaper people will be there to photograph the volunteers and you'll make the society pages." She patted her arm. "I'm sure that will please your husband."

Misty knew the person it would please was John, who was always seeking a place in the social world.

"And, my dear," the woman added, once again squeezing her hand, "you and Adam are invited to my home Sunday night for dinner and dancing. Our darling Priscilla will be there with Warren and you'll meet my daughter, Estella."

"Well, I'm not sure . . ." Misty began.

"Nonsense, my dear," the woman cut her off sharply. "You must come. Everyone who is anyone will be there." Her eyes shone with happiness. "Why, the mayor of Saint Louis himself will be there."

Priscilla suddenly rose and, shielding her eyes, peered at the center of the velvety lawn where the huge Persian lay on its side like a bloated whale. "Now what in the world is wrong with that cat? Why isn't she moving? She's usually so lively."

Giving a relieved sigh, Misty looked at her and smiled sweetly.

"Yep, Red Oak Hollow is sure 'nuff back in the woods, all right," Misty said, scooting her chair closer to Estella and observing her plump face. "Why, some of the roads are so steep back that way, you can't get in riding a turpentined wildcat. And things are wild and woolly, too. Most of the time we just roof our cabins with shellacked bull hides and use their tails as lighting rods."

Dressed in a yellow evening gown that did nothing for her sallow coloring and lank brown hair, the Vanderhooseys' overweight daughter laughed at the bit of mountain humor.

Misty clasped her pudgy hand and, finding it cold, realized that being with a huge crowd like the one tonight was pure torture for the socially awkward girl. *Why, she's as frightened as a scared rabbit,* she thought, sending her a bright smile to lift her spirits.

When Misty and Raven had arrived earlier at the Vanderhooseys' home, she'd been awed, for this was the largest affair she'd ever attended, consisting of the city's aristocracy, including the mayor himself, a balding gentleman with a penchant for long speeches. Being taken aback, she'd talked mostly to Priscilla and Warren, who'd accompanied them to the party. Then she'd met Estella. After being ushered into the glittering dining room and seated by the homely girl, she'd concentrated on her most of the evening, trying to get her to smile.

Now as the dishes were cleared away and fragrant coffee was served, everyone's attention was riveted on the mayor, who sat back and spread his hands on the table, signaling another long story. When light from an overhanging chandelier glistened over his shiny dome, Misty nudged Estella and whispered in her ear. "If he'd let me work on that bald head of his, I could grow him some hair. I've got a potion made of slippery elm slime and rattle snake venom that'll raise fuzz on a rock."

For some reason Estella found the statement funny and stifled a giggle. Mrs. Vanderhoosey, again decked out in enough feathers to stuff a mattress, glared at her daughter, while her husband, a distinguished man with graying hair, scowled his disapproval.

Misty, who sat across the table from Raven, noticed his warning gaze and, suppressing her own mirth, pressed her lips together.

Raven rotated the stem of his wine glass between his thumb and forefinger, wondering what Misty had told the girl to make her laugh. As far as he knew, it was the first time he'd ever seen an emotional reaction from Estella, and he marveled at Misty's talent for making people feel at ease.

The mayor droned on, but Raven couldn't force himself to pay much attention, and despite his thoughtful mood, he studied Misty as she pretended to listen to the long-winded man. Every lady at the table was dressed to perfection, but in her cream-colored gown and long gloves, with her auburn hair decorated with white roses, she was a fresh wildflower among stiff, artificial blooms.

At last the mayor finished his tale, and with suppressed relief, everyone drifted into the drawing room to dance. As Raven escorted Misty into the large chamber, circled with settees and straight-backed chairs, laughter rippled through the group and there was the sweet undertone of a string ensemble. Misty frowned as she glanced at Estella, standing like a wallflower and looking self-conscious and very out of place. "Look at her all alone over there," she commented sadly. "The poor little thing looks as limp as a neck-wrung turkey. Does she act like this at all the parties?" she asked, her voice rough with worry.

Raven arched a brow. "I'm afraid so. Both her parents are keenly afraid she's going to become an old maid and have paraded her in front of all the doctors at the hospital, but with no luck."

Misty didn't have time to respond, for several of the young interns crowded about her, begging a dance, and as one of them led her away, concern rose within Raven as he recalled what he'd heard today and the effect it could have on their marriage. Mulling over the situation, he saw Warren enter the drawing room, and while Priscilla lingered to visit with some of the ladies, his brother approached him.

"Why the long face?" Warren inquired with a puzzled expression.

Raven watched the young doctor glide across the parquet floor with Misty, a blur of white tulle and roses. "Something happened at the hospital today," he confessed to his brother. "Doctor Vanderhoosey, who's retiring in a few months, said he was recommending me for the next chief-of-staff. If tradition is followed, the board will approve his recommendation."

Warren's countenance brightened, and he clapped him on the back. "That's wonderful news. You've always wanted that position and . . ." His voice gradually trailed off, and noticing his brother's eyes fixed on Misty, his expression sobered. "Oh . . . I see your problem," he muttered with a worried frown. "Have you told her yet?"

Raven met Warren's understanding eyes. "No, I haven't—and I don't know when I will. Tonight certainly isn't an appropriate time," he responded, shifting his weight and glancing around the room. "I need some time to sort things out before we talk."

At last the dance was over. Leaving Warren, he moved to Misty and, pasting a smile on his lips, took her in his arms. As they swept onto the dance floor, he studied her trusting face, considering the problem. The position of chief-of-staff was one he'd always coveted. It would enable him to make some much-needed changes at Saint Mary's. But Lord, how could he tell this innocent girl that he'd even considered accepting the situation when she lived only to go back to the Ozarks?

Since arriving in the city, they'd both focused on John's lingering illness, which had forestalled a confrontation about where they would live, but he realized that the time was imminent when they would be forced to make that important decision—a decision that would drastically alter one of their lives.

Raven watched the play of emotions on Misty's face as she turned in his arms and gazed at Estella, and he knew she was hatching some scheme. In fact, he could almost hear the wheels whirring in her head as she stared at the girl. "Now what are you planning?" he asked in a suspicious tone.

Misty noted his frowning face and quickly composed herself, giving him her most appealing smile. "Nothing. Nothing at all. Why, my mind is as still as a summer's dawn, and my thoughts are as pure as the morning dew."

When the dance ended, she took a last peek at Raven's dubious expression, then slipped from his arms, feeling a minimum of guilt. After all, there was no law that said she had to tell him *all* her business—especially when there was a good chance he wouldn't approve.

With great compassion for Estella, who now sat upon one of the straight-backed chairs placed along the wall, she nonchalantly strolled that way and sat down beside her. Taking her fleshy hand, she held it for a moment, then looked into her eyes. "Your mother tells me that you'll be doing volunteer work with Priscilla and me next Thursday at the hospital," she remarked.

A shy smile hovered on Estella's lips. "Yes, that's true. I will."

Misty squeezed her arm. "Well, honey, I just want you to know that I'm going to have a little gift for you that will cure all your sadness. You just meet me a little early Thursday and you'll get a surprise that'll make you so happy, the back of your dress will roll up like a window shade!"

Chapter Seventeen

On Thursday morning, Misty dressed in a plain white blouse and blue skirt and arrived at the hospital about ten o'clock, brimming with anticipation. Despite her vow to Raven to forego treating the patients, she'd brought her medical satchel, bulging with mountain herbs. Salving her nagging conscience, she told herself the satchel simply gave her added confidence. There was no way she'd break her promise—no way at all.

When she walked into the small room reserved for hospital volunteers, she saw just whom she was looking for—Estella. "Sit down right here and close your eyes," she suggested, clasping the girl's pudgy shoulders and guiding her to a chair. At this point, they were the only volunteers in the room, Mrs. Vanderhoosey having gone to another part of the hospital to check on supplies.

Misty popped open her satchel and pulled out

a small package wrapped in brown paper. "Go on and open it," she said with a smile. "It's that gift I told you about. I worked on it all yesterday afternoon."

Estella gingerly unwrapped the package, then the color drained from her face, for in her lap lay a dried sack of skin tied on a long red cord. "W-what is it?" she stammered, looking horrified.

Misty grinned, thinking these city folk were sure an ignorant lot. "Why, it's a love charm, of course." She shook the skin sack, making a rattling noise. "Y'see, this is a dried pig bladder just chock full of special herbs mixed up my own special way. Back in the hills, Elviny Huffsetter used to make love charms like this to catch the men, but she didn't know what to put in them so they always failed."

Estella shrank back and stared at her with frightened eyes.

"Why, this charm has *everything* in it," Misty went on, "mullein, tansy, yellow puccoon, and about a jillion other things. And I added some mandrake dung on the seventh day of the seventh month by the light of the full moon to make it extra powerful. You're sure lucky that I brought all these herbs with me from the Ozarks," she finished, draping the cord about Estella's neck.

She knelt down beside the girl and spoke in a confidential tone. "Now this is what you do to catch a fellow. Just pick out your man, then make a wish on the charm before you go to sleep. In less than a month, that man will be hanging around your door, plumb lovesick from yearning for you. After that, you'll be able to wind him around your finger like a wet noodle, then wedding bells will be ringing as fast as double-geared lightning."

She rose and scanned Estella's pale face, wondering why she looked so dumbstruck. Snapping her satchel together, she decided that the shy socialite was just too overcome to thank her properly for the gift that would undoubtedly change her life. At the door she glanced back at Estella, who sat in stunned silence. "There's no use wasting good time. Tell your mother I went on to see some of the patients. She can catch up with me later and let me know what I'm supposed to do."

Still as white as the hospital walls, Estella slowly nodded her head.

With a touch of worry, Misty left the room and paced down the corridor, thinking it was good that she'd made the love charm extra strong. In the back of her mind, she recalled her promise to Raven not to interfere with the hospital staff or its patients, but at the same time she felt an almost irresistible urge to use her doctoring skills. And it felt so good to be of use again—so good!

As she turned a corner, she met Priscilla, a vision in pink silk. Almost bumping into each other, they both laughed; then Misty surveyed the girl and, making a quick decision, took her hand. "Come along with me," she coaxed, "we can get a lot of work done before Mrs. Vanderhoosey even gets started."

"But I've always just done what she said," Priscilla protested. "I've never just started doing things by myself. I-I—"

"Don't worry," Misty replied in a soothing tone. "I know where everything is. We'll visit the grown-ups first, then get on to the children's ward, 'cause they need us most of all."

"But I—"

Misty clasped Priscilla's arm and, ignoring her feeble pleas, escorted her to the ladies' ward, where she breezed in and swept her gaze over the patients, who all eyed her with curiosity. Noticing charts attached to the end of the beds, she picked one up and looked at Priscilla. "Let's see what's ailing these folks," she suggested in a concerned voice. "You read me the charts, and I'll tell each person how to get better."

Priscilla bit her bottom lip. "But I really don't think that's our job."

"Oh, go on," Misty urged, pushing the chart into her hands. "I'm just talking. Talking can't hurt anyone, can it?"

"Well . . . I suppose not," the girl replied hesitantly. With a pained expression, she began reading in a whispery voice. "This lady has severe diarrhea and is dehydrated."

The woman struggled up to see what was going on, but Misty eased her back against the pillows. "What you need," she said in a kind tone, "is some ragweed tea." She studied the woman's puzzled face. "None of these doctors told you that?"

With wide eyes, the lady shook her head, prompting a deep sigh from Misty. "Well, I'll be flamboozled. I'd have never thought these city doctors couldn't cure a simple case like this."

For a second, she visualized Raven's frowning face, but by now she was so engrossed in her work that she easily pushed the troubling vision aside. "Next patient," she said, marching on and cutting her eyes at her assistant.

"This lady has a badly sprained ankle," Priscilla informed her.

Misty examined the bandages, warning the woman, "If those wrappings aren't soaked in hot salty vinegar, they should be."

An elderly woman with rheumatism slumped in the third bed, and Misty popped open her satchel and presented her with a tiny vial of skunk oil to apply at her leisure.

Before leaving, she examined a pregnant woman in the first stages of labor. "Honey," she tenderly advised, brushing back the woman's damp hair, "if you can get one of these city doctors to put an axe under your bed, it'll cut your pain considerably, and if your husband will nail an alligator head above your bed, it'll sure speed things along."

The woman groaned and shook her head in compliance.

When Misty and Priscilla had been on the ward for almost half an hour, a nurse arrived and, catching a bit of their conversation, shot them a glare that let them know they were unwelcome.

On the way to the men's ward, Priscilla hung back, a worried expression settling on her face. "I think we should go back now," she offered, tension lacing her voice.

Misty sighed. "I say we go on. There's lots of sick folks here, and the doctors probably appreciate all the help they can get."

When they arrived at the men's ward, the surprised patients hastily pulled sheets over themselves. Here they followed the same procedure, with Priscilla reading the charts, while Misty crossed her arms and paced about the beds, thoughtfully considering the cases. For a man who'd cut his leg in a building accident, she prescribed chimney soot mixed with coal oil; for a case of pneumonia, a hot poultice of hopvine leaves; for anemia, a dose of sulphur and black strap molasses; and for hemorrhoids, bittersweet berries in lard.

By now it was eleven-thirty, and orderlies in white uniforms entered the ward, pushing creaking carts with stacks of lunch trays. Examining one of the trays, Misty put a hand over her heart. "Look at that," she told Priscilla. "They're giving that poor man ham and he has blood poisoning. A child would know that pork angers the blood in cases like that." With an air of efficiency, she took the tray from the startled man's hands and switched it with the tray of another, who was a diabetic and had a light meal of soup and fruit.

After Misty switched several more lunches, one of the orderlies approached her and tugged the tray from her hands. "Madam, what do you think you're doing?"

"Saving lives," she shot back quickly.

Deep into the argument, she brushed back her damp hair and, glancing about, noticed that all the windows were closed. Suddenly turning her attention from the food to the temperature, she marched down the ward, opening windows to let in a cool draft of air. At that moment, a large nurse appeared and strode toward her with a pointed finger, ordering, "Madam, close those windows instantly."

Misty put her hands on her hips. "How do you city people expect these folks to get better when you feed them the wrong things and shut them in with no fresh air?" As Misty threw open more windows, the nurse followed, slamming them down, the pair making *swish-bang, swish-bang*

347

sounds that reverberated through the long hall.

Misty, seeing that her efforts were not appreciated and noticing that Priscilla was about to cry, motioned to her. "Come on. Let's try our luck on the children's ward." She looked at the nurse's frowning face. "There's no use trying to help folks who don't appreciate it."

Priscilla blotted her shiny brow with a handkerchief and hurried to catch her leader. "Don't we need to find Mrs. Vanderhoosey?"

"Oh, she'll be fine," Misty answered with a negligent shrug. "We'll probably run into her anytime now."

Carefully pushing open the glass doors of the children's ward, she entered, but noted that Priscilla hung back, standing just inside the threshold with a frightened look on her face. At the end of the ward, Sarah was sitting in a wheelchair gazing from the window. Hearing Misty's footsteps, she turned about, and a large smile raced over her face. "You've come back," she cried, holding out her arms. "I've been waiting for you."

Misty hugged her; then, scanning the rest of the children, she noticed a dozen of them sitting up in their beds, most with dried chicken-pox spots on their faces. From their condition, she realized that none of them was seriously ill and thought that a little exercise and fresh air would improve their health. "How would you kids like to play some games?" she asked, pushing Sarah to the center of the ward.

Grins spread across their faces and many of them laughed out loud. "Fine. All of you stand at the end of your bed. We're going to play Simon Says," Misty ordered, watching them already tossing back their covers, eager for the game. "Simon says take two steps forward," she playfully commanded. With a chorus of giggles, the children walked to the end of their beds and took two steps forward. "Simon says rub your belly," came the next order. The children rubbed their stomachs, including Sarah, who actually giggled.

Misty spied some cleaning supplies in the corner and, walking to them, picked up a feather duster. After plucking out some turkey feathers, she stuck them in her hair, much to the amusement of the children. "All right," she chirped, strolling past the little patients and also putting feathers in their hair, "now we're going to play Indians." She wrapped a blanket about their shoulders and the children took blankets from their beds and did the same. "It's a beautiful day outside. Do you want to take this tribe outside for some sunshine?"

Cheers rose to the ceiling.

"Here's what we'll do," she directed, organizing the children into a long procession, "we're going Indian-file down the corridor, then outside onto the lawn."

She pushed Sarah to the ward entrance and looked back over her shoulder to see that the children all had blankets about them. "Now remember," she warned, "be careful and walk slow."

As she led the procession from the ward, she glanced at Priscilla and, knowing the idea was just too much for her, suggested, "Why don't you stay at camp and watch for raiding parties while we're gone?" She paused a moment in afterthought. "If you see Mrs. Vanderhoosey, tell her I'll be back in fifteen minutes. We won't be outside long."

With a bewildered air, Priscilla nodded her head in compliance.

In a matter of seconds, the Indian tribe was outside, and Misty led them over the sloping lawn. Happiness twinkled in their eyes, and healthy color stained their cheeks as the noisy procession snaked about the hospital grounds, winding around trees and bushes as they searched for paleface wagon trains.

Carefully judging their strength, Misty ordered them to sit about her as she relaxed on the grass telling Indian stories peppered with colorful details that left them enthralled. She was on her fourth tale when a flash of yellow feathers snagged her attention. Swinging her gaze to the side, she saw Mrs. Vanderhoosey marching across the velvety lawn, her face set in determined lines. Priscilla followed on her heels, daintily holding up her skirt and clutching a hand to her bosom.

Suddenly, a large, freckle-faced lad of ten also saw the socialite and stood, waving his arms and calling out, "Ambush, ambush—circle the pale-face squaw and her scout!"

The children shot to their feet and, following the boy's lead, circled Mrs. Vanderhoosey and Priscilla, shouting and giving wild Indian yells, the tails of their white gowns fluttering behind them.

With a great sinking feeling, Misty rose and ran after them, trying to calm them down, but by this time they were in a frenzy and raised such a ruckus that hospital windows shot open, revealing startled faces.

Mrs. Vanderhoosey tried to battle her way through the whooping tribe, but they now held hands and foiled her every effort, cheering and playfully jostling her from one side of the circle to the other. Priscilla clasped her hands together like a dying saint and wilted to the grass, her pink skirt billowing out around her.

When Misty thought that things couldn't get much worse, she noticed a buggy pull up in front of the hospital, and to her horror she saw several men get out with writing tablets in hand, followed by others carrying heavy photographic equipment. One of the laughing men pointed to the Indian attack and nudged his companion, who began arranging the tripod for his bulky camera. Only then did she remember the meeting that Mrs. Vanderhoosey had scheduled for the newspaper reporters to interview the volunteers.

Knowing the scene before her could not be recorded for posterity, she ducked under the children's arms and waved, trying to shout above them. Just then Mrs. Vanderhoosey teetered, and Misty tried to steady her, but not before the woman's feathery hat slid over her eyes, temporarily blinding her.

There was a galaxy of flashes and shouted instructions, and with a feeling of doom, Misty realized that her efforts had been too late. She arranged Mrs. Vanderhoosey's hat so that she could see, at the same time noticing the blank expression in her eyes. Giving up the older woman as a lost cause, she rushed to Priscilla, helped her to her feet, and tried to brush her grass-stained skirt. "It's all right," she crooned, caressing the girl's trembling hand. "Everything will be all right."

Even as she spoke, she knew she lied, for the Indians had now reverted to the wild and

351

raced for the bushes, some of the smaller bucks' naked backsides flashing from their open hospital gowns. Chaos, total and complete, ruled the moment.

Then, her throat swelling with anxiety, Misty spotted a flock of white-coated doctors moving over the green grass like God's own avenging angels. Dr. Vanderhoosey was with them, but in front of them all, a deep frown creasing his brow, his lips turned down, and his hands clenched into fists was Raven, looking like the mighty Archangel Michael himself. Although he carried no fiery sword of vengeance, she could have sworn little sparks shot from his eyes.

Misty, wishing she had a dose of purple nightshade, which she knew produced instant death, waited for him to arrive, her heart pounding like a bass drum.

The next morning, Misty looked at Raven across the breakfast table and in a quavering voice asked, "Would you please pass the salt?"

With a deliberate movement of his hand, he placed the crystal cellar in front of her, never uttering a word.

She passed it over her eggs, and from the corner of her eyes, studied his dark countenance. They'd exchanged heated words at the hospital, but last night after he'd finally arrived home after working until ten o-clock, he hadn't spoken to her, only brushing past her on the stairs on his way to bed. She knew he was still furiously angry with her for breaking her promise, and she realized that for some reason he was damming it all up inside of him.

Reflecting on the situation, she tried to choke

down a bite of dry toast. She knew they wouldn't get over this incident as easily as they had her overspending, for she couldn't blame her mistake on inexperience. Her debacle at the hospital yesterday was no light matter, but a great rift between them and it filled her with despondency.

They continued to eat in icy silence, the sounds of their scraping flatware only emphasizing the tension between them. Then, as their eyes met, Misty felt threatening tears. "Well, why don't you say it?" she prodded in a tense voice, her silver fork slipping from her fingers and clattering against the plate. *"Just say it."*

Raven sent her a look that chilled her heart. "Say what?"

"Say what you're keeping inside you," she shot out, tossing her napkin on the table. "Say I broke my promise. Say I made a stupid mistake. Just say something!"

Raven stood and regarded her, deciding that she looked like a frightened child. But Lord, how angry he was when he found out what she'd done! he thought, shoving his hands into his pockets and pacing about the table. With embarrassment, he recalled his colleagues' expressions when he came into their offices unannounced and interrupted them as they were discussing his wife. And when one of the nurses told him that Misty was leading the children outside, a great knot of hot frustration had gathered in his chest.

Misty, meeting his gaze, sank back in her chair. "I know I made a few mistakes yesterday, but—"

He turned, not believing what he'd heard. *"A few mistakes?"* he echoed, widening his eyes and slowly moving to her side. "Do you call prescribing all kinds of wild cures and taking children from the hospital *a few mistakes?*" He stared at her, watching her wilt before him. "Besides that, you involved Priscilla in your wild escapades."

Misty looked at his scowling face, feeling an unwanted pang of jealously. But how could she help it when he'd brought up Priscilla yet again, and in that tone that said she was so revered that her name shouldn't be sullied? Wild speculations now darted through her head. Was Priscilla attending affairs with Warren just so she could be with Raven, who always showed her the greatest respect and courtesy?

"But I didn't harm anyone with my cures," she came back defensively. "I was just talking."

His face hardened. "What about the ruckus you made switching the lunch trays?"

Her spirits plummeted even further. Obviously he knew everything. "You heard?" she asked with quivering lips.

Reproach glinted in his eyes. "Of course I heard. You were the talk of the hospital. Never since I've been there have I heard a person or an event discussed as much as you." His mouth dipped down at the side. "I heard about the windows too," he added roughly. "And Estella was crushed that you presented her with a dried pig bladder full of weeds so she could *catch a fellow*. Her mother said she actually cried."

Pain welled up in Misty's heart. "She didn't like it? I worked a long time on it and made it extra powerful." She stared at Raven's stormy countenance, scarcely believing that Estella had been offended by the gift. Then, greatly abashed, she dropped her head and murmured, "As for the rest of the day, I'd felt useless so long that when I did get a chance to be around ailing folks, I just got this urge to help them any way I could." She looked up with a contrite expression. "I have to admit, I could have given everything more thought, but I was feeling the healing fever so bad, I just couldn't help myself."

Raven studied her sad countenance and, sitting down beside her, put his hands on her shoulders, realizing that at the time she'd actually believed she was doing the right thing. One part of him wanted to hold her and protect her, while another part of him bristled with anger, especially when he thought about her breaking her promise. In one respect, he blamed himself for giving her the responsibility, but who in his right mind would have dreamed that she would have done such things?

She looked at him with pleading eyes. "I know that I got a little carried away with the children—"

"Taking the children from the ward is more than getting a little carried away," he cut in. "You endangered their lives and—"

"But most of them just had chicken pox and were nearly well," she insisted. "I looked over the others real good and made sure they all had blankets around them."

"The point is that you didn't know about their cases. Moving them might have hurt them."

She spread her hands. "But it didn't, did it?"

Raven sighed. "No, luckily not. After they were all rounded up, outside of a few scraped knees, they were fine, but they were not in your charge. You interfered with their doctors' orders for them to stay in bed."

"But the fresh air did them good. I could see it

in their eyes and their faces. It perked them up. It helped them!"

"Only temporarily. After you took them outside, then what happened?"

"What do you mean?"

"Just answer my question—then what happened?"

Misty frowned. "Well, at first everything was fine; then one of the boys saw Mrs. Vanderhoosey and started yelling"—she blinked her eyes and looked as if she were reliving a nightmare—"then things started to go wrong."

"Exactly," he replied, scanning her perplexed face. "Don't you see that if you hadn't led the children from the ward, none of this trouble would have happened in the first place?"

She sat there silently, a thoughtful look on her face. "I was just trying to help them," she whispered, staring at him with big eyes that pulled at his heart.

"I know you were trying to help, but you broke many rules, and rules are necessary if a hospital is to run smoothly." Still Misty did not speak, and he silently cursed the differences between them that had brought them to this pass. Hearing the sound of creaking wheels, he stood, and irritation welled up within him. He knew that his father would soon be appearing in his wheelchair, no doubt with another complaint.

In a matter of seconds, John had wheeled himself into the dining room, garbed in a paisley silk robe and wearing leather slippers on his feet. His face bore its usual sour expression and a folded edition of the morning newspaper lay on his lap. He threw a sharp gaze at Misty, then fixed his eyes upon his son. "I'd like to speak to you alone, if you don't mind," he announced tartly.

When Misty rose to leave the room, her face was pale and drawn, and she hurried past Raven without looking at him.

John shoved the paper toward his son. As soon as Raven opened it, he added, "Take a look at that. There's an accompanying story too, featuring your beloved bride. She made the paper all right"— he paused meaningfully—"but not the society pages."

Raven scanned the paper, noticing a photo of Misty and Mrs. Vanderhoosey taken the moment the matron's hat had slid over her eyes. Priscilla was in the background of the photo, slumped on the grass, covering her face with her hands. An accompanying article mentioned that one of the hospital volunteers, a prominent doctor's wife, had taken the children from the hospital yesterday. It briefly described the fiasco that had followed.

Anger flew over Raven that the photo and article had been printed in the first place, and he knew that Dr. Vanderhoosey would be furious. Then, despite the seriousness of the situation, he felt amusement at the sight of the feathery hat over the socialite's eyes. Lord, he'd thought the woman was going to take wing for years—perhaps this set-down would put her more in touch with reality.

"*Well,*" John prodded. "Didn't I tell you it would happen?"

Raven threw the paper on the table. "I don't know what you're talking about."

John's eyes flashed. "Oh, I think you do. Didn't I tell you she'd embarrass us all?"

Raven glared at his father, wanting to silence

him. "Don't worry," he said a little cynically. "You're not responsible for her actions. Your social standing hasn't been besmirched."

"I don't agree," John retorted. "As long as her name is Davenport, her actions *do* affect me." He clenched the arms of his wheelchair and shook his head. "She'll never fit in here. She hasn't the breeding or the maturity. You should have never brought her here."

Anger darted through Raven. Although he had his own doubts about Misty's ability to adapt to his way of life, he didn't want to hear his father criticize her.

John's gaze sharpened. "I'm sure that everyone who is anyone has cut us from their social list after reading this morning's paper. We need to think of a plan . . . do something spectacular to restore our social standing."

Raven was so irked with his father's obsession with society that he was organizing a blistering rebuttal to the proposal when he heard the outside door suddenly slam shut. His thoughts flying to Misty, he stormed past John and strode to the foyer, regret lodging in his chest. Once outside the mansion, he saw Nat assisting Misty into the landau, and from his brief glimpse, he noticed that she carried her dulcimer. When Nat climbed up on the box and headed the carriage in the direction of the local park, Raven guessed that she intended to escape there for some privacy, as she'd done before.

Entering the mansion, he returned to the dining room, where to his great relief he found his father gone. As soon as he sank to his chair, he pushed his plate of half-eaten food aside, frustration hammering at his brain. The possibility of being the new chief-of-staff of Saint Mary's had put a fresh perspective on his life and given it new meaning. And to be perfectly honest, he realized that he now thought of himself as Adam and not Raven, and Lukie, Brother Jubal, Ezra, Sloppy Brewster, and Billy Red Scarf seemed like characters from a book he'd once read.

Pain tore at his heart as he contemplated his life with Misty. As evidenced by her mistakes yesterday, the things that had made her charming in the Ozarks—her creativity and spontaneity, her sense of unbridled adventure, the way she thumbed her nose at convention—made her a misfit in Saint Louis society. Again and again his father's words resounded in his head: *She'll never fit in here. She hasn't the breeding or the maturity. You shouldn't have brought her here.*

While a part of him denied it with all his might, another part wondered if there wasn't a grain of truth in the message. Had he been short-sighted and selfish in insisting that she accompany him to the city?

How long could this impasse go on between them? he wondered, rising from the table.

Almost a week later, Misty tossed an opened envelope on Raven's desk, as he sat there reading mail before dinner. "Why didn't you tell me?" she asked, her voice rough with indignation. "Why didn't you tell me that you were being considered for the next chief-of-staff at Saint Mary's?"

She looked at his implacable face, waiting for him to answer. How it had hurt her when she found the letter on his desk just an hour earlier and, thinking it was only another invitation, had opened it out of idle curiosity to read the words:

Sonya Birmingham

You yourself understand what an important role is taken on by the wife of the chief-of-staff, who must be above reproach in every matter. The board hasn't made a final decision, but many members feel that although you are qualified, your spouse's shortcomings would make your appointment as the next chief-of-staff an unwise decision.

There had been other words. Words describing her as charming but *inappropriate*, lovely but *unschooled*. It stung Misty that the board had judged her actions without her knowledge, but it wounded her more that Raven had kept the news about the appointment from her. Demanding an answer, she put her hands on her hips and met his hot gaze.

Irritation rose in Raven's chest that she had opened his mail, until he remembered that he'd asked her to scan their invitations. Judging by the size of the large envelope, the mistake now seemed more understandable. With a sinking feeling, he removed the pages and read them, thinking he'd been expecting something like this and knowing he would have done anything to keep Misty from seeing it. "I didn't tell you," he began, slipping the pages back into the envelope, "because I saw no need to upset you when the event might not come to pass."

A frown flitted over her face. "I remember a time back in the Ozarks when you didn't tell me that you were a Davenport either. Are you sure this wasn't something along the same line?"

Raven pushed back his chair and stood. "No, of course not," he replied sharply, tossing the envelope on the green blotter. He walked in front of his desk and crossed his arms. "I knew you'd be worried when you heard about the appointment . . . afraid that it would keep us here when you wanted to go back to the mountains. Why should we discuss something that might not happen, when it would obviously upset you?"

Misty's eyes sparked with emotion. "Well, what would have happened if I hadn't been *charming but inappropriate, lovely but unschooled?* Would you have accepted the position if they'd offered it to you?"

He met her questioning gaze. "They may yet offer it to me."

"You didn't answer my question."

Raven blew out his breath, wondering what he could tell her that wouldn't upset her more than she already was. "I don't know," he finally confessed, holding out his arms. "I simply don't know." Then, noting her stricken face, he walked to her and took her in his arms, feeling her stiffen a bit. "If the hospital had offered me the position for a certainty, I would have come to you and we would have made the decision together."

Misty scrutinized his tense features, knowing she should have been satisfied with the answer, but a little devil of pride kept whispering in her ear, telling her that she'd been set aside, overlooked, dismissed, and generally treated like a half-witted child. With a wiggle, she slipped from his arms and walked about the library, trailing her fingertips over the books. The swish of her petticoats cut through the strained silence until she turned around and said, "Don't you see it hurts me when I have to read a letter to find out about your personal business?"

Raven had managed to hold his temper so far, but her last words nettled him so that he walked back to his desk and, picking up a handful of letters, shook them at her, noticing the surprise in her eyes. "Well, never let it be said that I kept any of my other correspondence from you. Here's a letter that I brought home from the hospital today. It's from a lady to whom you prescribed one of your outlandish cures," he said, opening it and tossing the pages on the desk. "She made a written complaint to the hospital, and they passed it along to me."

He moved behind the desk and pulled a memo from his jacket pocket, seeing her face pale. "Here's a memo from the head nurse of the female ward, stating that you were a general nuisance and asking me to monitor your actions." He tossed it aside, instinctively knowing he was going too far, but unable to stop. "And here's a message from Mrs. Vanderhoosey," he added, taking yet another note from his vest pocket. "She says that your services won't be needed in the hospital volunteer program any longer."

He shoved it away, then opened the lower drawer. Taking out another letter, he placed it on the blotter. "I've been hiding this piece of correspondence for two days. It's from the parents of one of the children you took from the ward. They're so upset that I've contacted a lawyer to handle the situation."

As soon as Raven was finished, he slumped into his chair, regret welling up within him. Misty's pale face and trembling lips told him that he'd said more than he should and he wished that he could recall every word. Yet at the same time, a kind of sweet relief surged through him that he'd cleared the air between them. He wanted to hold her in his arms, but realized that her pride wouldn't allow it.

He watched her back toward the library doors.

Misty stared at his grave face, shocked by what she'd heard. She knew that she'd made many mistakes while she was here, both in the Davenport household and in society, but she'd blithely gone on her way, doing what she thought best while Raven had been picking up the pieces behind her. Swallowing back her tears, she tried to compose an explanation, but her lips moved silently. And all at once she felt immensely weary. All she wanted was to rest in the privacy of her bedroom.

Rushing from the library, Misty suddenly realized that all the things she knew in the Ozarks— her great skill with herbs, how to give hope to a struggling patient, and how to console a dying one—meant absolutely nothing here. To these city folk, she was an ignorant outcast, a meddlesome, uneducated bungler, an object of fun and ridicule.

The thought that Raven might also put her in this category filled her with pain such as she'd never known.

Three days later, Raven came home from the hospital one rainy afternoon, and pausing in the foyer to give his hat to the butler, he heard a conversation floating from the drawing room. He recognized his father's deep tone and also a light feminine voice, and upon entering the chamber was surprised to find Priscilla visiting with John, who felt well enough to be up and about in his wheelchair.

Seated upon the camel-backed sofa, she rose as soon as their eyes met. "I think I should be going now," she announced, a blush staining her cheeks.

She pulled on her white gloves, then turned and took John's hand. "It's good to see you feeling so well. I hope your progress continues."

He beamed and patted her arm. "Thank you for dropping by, my dear. Come and visit anytime."

As Priscilla slipped past Raven, she modestly lowered her eyes. Moments later, he heard the sound of the entrance door closing and moved to a grog tray to pour himself a drink. Swirling the tinkling ice in his glass, he looked at John and saw a satisfied smile purse his lips.

"Well, what did I tell you?" the old man stated triumphantly.

Raven, knowing he was in for another lecture whether he took the bait or not, sank to the sofa and studied his father's radiant face.

"It's plain as the nose on your face," John announced, rolling himself toward the sofa. "Priscilla's in love with you." Raven started to rise, but his father put out a beseeching hand. "Wait and hear me out," he ordered, annoyance crossing his face. "She came here on the pretext of visiting me, but only a blind man could have missed her blush when you entered the room."

Irritation flared within Raven. Since his argument with Misty, there had been a strain between them, but they were working out their problems and this wild claim was the last thing he wanted to hear. "The girl blushes at everyone," he stated flatly. "It meant nothing."

Annoyance clouded John's eyes. "No, you're wrong. She's obsessed with you. Why else would she always be at the house? I'm not fool enough to think she simply comes here to pay me social calls."

Raven sipped his drink, vexed with his father

beyond words. "You're right about that. She does have an ulterior motive for being here," he replied, observing John's expectant face and relishing the reaction that he knew was to come. "She's in love with Warren."

The older man gave a delayed gasp, then laughed. "*Warren?* For God's sake, why would she be in love with him? What is there about him to attract a woman?"

Drink in hand, Raven fluidly rose and paced away from the sofa. "If you haven't noticed," he replied, glancing over his shoulder, "he's highly intelligent and has a good sense of humor."

His face set in hard lines, John stared at the wall. "Impossible," he retorted gruffly. "I know the girl has attended a few social functions with him, but it was only to be near you." He swung his hard gaze back to his son. "There is absolutely nothing about Warren that would interest a debutante like Priscilla!"

Raven started to mention that their quiet personalities were just alike, that they enjoyed many of the same things, and they'd known each other since they were children—but knowing that his father saw Warren only through his own prejudiced viewpoint, he realized that the statement would be useless. Pulling his brows together, he placed his drink on a table and turned to go, but John leaned forward and caught his gaze. "*Wait,*" he demanded curtly. "I have something of importance to tell you."

Raven stood silently, ready to leave the room as soon as possible.

With narrowed eyes, John pulled a letter from his suit jacket. "I've invited a very important guest to dine with us in a few weeks," he announced, tapping the letter in his hand, "and I received an affirmative response today." Anticipation brightened his countenance as he slipped the envelope away. "I met the man in school here in Saint Louis years ago. And he now has great influence in the railroad industry that may enable me to obtain that stretch of land I've been wanting for years. It could mean extra millions for the Missouri and North Arkansas Railroad line." He slapped his hand on his leg. "Believe me, all the rail mavens would give anything to have this man's ear, but I've beat them all out."

Raven, who always steered clear of his father's business, searched his confident face, sure that a request was coming. "And why are you telling me all this?"

John's lips twisted in exasperation. "Because I need your help—and Misty's help, too," he confessed, obviously distressed that he'd been forced to make the admission. He leveled a measured gaze at his son. "I want her to plan a fashionable dinner party for the man. Invite at least fifty guests—the very cream of Saint Louis society. I want her to serve the finest food, the best wine that money can buy. And I want the man to be entertained as he's never been entertained in his life."

Resentment boiled up within Raven, for he didn't relish putting Misty through the strain of such an event. "And why can't Mrs. Hawksley preform this social miracle for you?"

John shifted in his chair. "Mrs. Hawksley does well enough with everyday meals, but she hasn't the imagination to engineer a social event of this magnitude," he reflected sarcastically. "And it's the principle of the thing. An affair like this should be undertaken by the lady of the house, not hired help."

"Don't you think you're asking quite a lot of Misty?"

John turned to him, sending him a black stare. "No, not at all," he snapped, looking up with a sour smile. "It's her duty as my daughter-in-law. The little baggage has dragged the Davenport name through the mud with her escapades, but I'm offering her a chance to redeem herself. Don't you remember I said we needed to do something spectacular to restore our social standing? Well, this is our golden opportunity. After this dinner party, the old biddies will form a new opinion of their hostess. I expect Misty to do it, and I expect her to do an excellent job."

Anger sizzled through Raven that his father was trying to manipulate them both to raise his social prestige, but he knew that once the old man got an idea in his head, it was impossible to change his mind. Giving the dinner party some thought, he decided that if the event was inevitable, perhaps it would help Misty feel more useful. And after all, she really wouldn't be doing it alone, since he would be reviewing all her plans. "I'll tell her what you said," he offered stiffly, turning to leave the room. On the threshold, he paused in afterthought and looked back at his father's expectant face. "And who might this esteemed guest be?" he asked out of idle curiosity.

John smiled, and if Raven didn't know him better he would have thought there was actually a twinkle in his eyes. "That's the sweet part of it all," he replied, his voice full of pride. "Our guest is Benjamin Prescott Longstreet, the esteemed governor of Missouri."

Chapter Eighteen

"The governor of Missouri?" Misty echoed, her eyes flying wide open. She placed her hairbrush on the dresser and put her hand over her heart. "The governor of Missouri is coming *here?*"

Raven, wanting plenty of time to discuss John's surprising news, had waited until bedtime to tell her, and he thought she looked very desirable sitting there in her sheer nightgown, showing a dazzling display of bosom as the lamplight struck red highlights in her hair. For a moment, he regarded her whimsically, deciding that he hadn't seen her look so dumbstruck since she found out that he was a Davenport.

The rain had increased, and for moments there was only the sound of the drops pounding against the mansion's roof as she sat there too startled to speak. Then, tossing back her gleaming hair, she stood and moved toward him, the light outlining her lush figure through the thin material. "Are you sure of this?" she asked, in a quavering voice.

He clasped her shoulders and moved his hands down her arms, feeling the silky fabric slide under his fingers. "Yes, he's coming here in two weeks, and he's coming for dinner. In fact, John has requested that you plan an elaborate party for him."

When his words hit her full force, the color drained from her face and she gave him a look of utter disbelief. "After what has happened, I'm surprised he'd ask me."

Raven studied her amazed expression, wondering if the responsibility was too much for her. She was fresh from a bath, and as he drew her to him, holding her close, she smelled of a light rose scent. They hadn't made love since her day at the hospital, and with her soft, creamy breasts and her eyes glistening with surprise, she looked very ripe and lush indeed. "It isn't necessary for you to accept, you know," he said, still rankled that John felt it was her obligation to take on the responsibility.

She stared at him wordlessly, then slowly blinked her eyes. "What would I have to do?"

He looked down at her, touched that she would even consider such a challenge. "Yours would be a job of organization. Mrs. Hawksley has given dinner parties here before. You could look over her menus and expand them . . . add your own special touch. You would need to hire musicians as well as extra servants for the evening, visit a florist, and make arrangements with a printer for invitations." He smiled tightly. "With the governor coming, I doubt that you would receive many regrets." When she gave him a blank stare,

Sonya Birmingham

he added, "The decision is yours, but if you do accept, you would have help along the way."

Misty met Raven's cool appraisal, still shocked that she was going to meet the governor of Missouri and even more stunned that she was being asked to arrange a dinner party for him. Since their argument, there had been tension between them, but for her part also a new determination to shoulder her part of the marriage. Although the thought of planning a dinner party for the governor frightened her, she also realized that this would be an opportunity to do something right for a change. And most of all, it would be a chance to prove to Raven just how sorry she was for causing the ruckus at the hospital. Surely, with people to guide her along the way, she could accomplish what now looked like an impossible feat. Her heart beating a little faster, she let out a long breath. "All right," she whispered, "if it will help the family . . . I'll do it."

She relaxed under his approving gaze, feeling a new intimacy between them. When he gathered her to him, she could feel the warmth of his hands through the thin fabric and a wave of passion surged through her. Then he slowly bent his dark head, and for the first time in many days, his lips found her trembling mouth. As she twined her arms about his neck, returning the kiss, she listened to rain drip from the eves and, enveloped in his musky, masculine scent, shivered with anticipation.

Gently, he loosened the first few buttons on her deeply scooped nightgown and tugged it over her shoulders so that it slid to a silken pool at her feet. In turn, she untied the sash of his robe and, as it fell open, hungrily nuzzled his chest, savoring its clean, faintly salty tang. He swept his warm hands over her shoulders and down the small of her back, his lips nibbling at the throbbing pulse in her neck and finally moving lower to draw on her hardened nipples. Misty's knees weakened, and excitement ran through her like lightning.

Eliciting her moans of delight, his tongue now flicked teasingly over her lips, then plunged deeper, sending a sweet fire through her body. Easily scooping her into his arms, he deposited her on the soft bed, and as the mattress gave way beneath her, she felt the cool, silken coverlet on her bare skin.

Misty watched him shrug off his robe and let it fall to the carpet, and with a fluttering pulse, she eyed his wondrously muscled body outlined against a curtain of soft, golden light. She saw his well-defined muscles flexing beneath his flesh, the sleekness of his belly, the power of his corded arms and thighs. As her gaze strayed lower to a region half lost in the shadows, she felt her cheeks heat with warmth. Opening her arms, she welcomed him into her embrace, hungry with a demanding need that only he could fulfill.

Passion raced through Raven like quicksilver, and spurred by hot desire, it seemed as if he could never slake his passion for her. Lying there with her creamy arms outstretched, she looked so desirable that he wanted to immediately feel himself surrounded by her warmth; yet, at the same time, he longed to stir her with gentle touches and soft words until her fire matched his own.

Taking on a rosy hue from the glow of the lamp, her delicately proportioned body stood out against the pale coverlet, and with a feeling akin to awe, he noticed the perfection of its glistening curves and planes. In the diffused light, Raven focused on the soft tangle of curls between her legs, and at that moment experienced a fiery need to taste the silky smoothness of her white thighs. He sank onto the bed and feathered soft, nibbling kisses from her arches to her calves; then, with tender yet urgent caresses, feathered his way upward, enticed by the sweet, musky aroma that sloughed over him.

His touch struck a fire within Misty, and with a caught breath, she traced his hard shoulders as his strong hands clutched her hips, lifting and supporting her. She let her head fall back and leaned into this new caress, twining her fingers in his thick hair as she raised herself to his warm, moist lips. As he lavished damp kisses upon her most intimate places, a pleasurable heat glowed through her and she pulsed with a savage ecstasy she'd never known.

She gasped as he lowered himself onto her and fitted herself against his body, experiencing a great yearning to be one with him, in spirit as well as flesh. Instinctively she slipped her legs over his waist, and he entered her with a long, slow stroke, then began an urgent, ever-building rhythm while she arched herself to meet him.

With the faster pace, a keen sense of excitement streaked over her, and she felt as if she might faint with passion at any moment. Tightening herself about his long hardness, she moaned for surcease while at the same time trying to prolong her rapture as long as possible; he masterfully controlled his tantalizing strokes until, with one mighty thrust, they both crested into shuddering fulfillment. Aglow with exaltation, she cried out his name, and he whispered endearments into her ear until their passion eddied, leaving them gloriously content.

As Raven held Misty by his side, gently caressing her shoulder, she heard the murmur of the rain and, sighing deeply, drifted into the first stages of sleep. Warm and secure, she felt as if she'd come home after a long journey—as if everything was now right with the world again.

A week later Misty entered John's dark study and found him propped up in bed reading papers that Warren had brought. "I thought you might like to see this menu for the governor's dinner party," she offered in a light tone. As she walked toward him, the scent of the musty room left her weak, for she associated it with its owner and his almost palpable dislike for her. "I've also added a list of wines that we could serve," she continued, pausing at his side and watching light flicker over his hard features.

He scowled, and without a greeting, motioned her to the chair beside his bed. Snatching the menu from her hand, he adjusted his spectacles and began reading under his breath.

With Mrs. Hawksley's help, she'd gone through a list of recipes; then, after a brief explanation about wines from the butler had made her own choices. She now crossed her fingers under the folds of her skirt, hoping her father-in-law would approve her hard work.

"Tomato soup, green salad, standing rib roast, buttered peas, layer cake," he muttered dully. He pulled off his spectacles and tossed them on the coverlet. "No. Don't you see, this is all too common." He shook his head vehemently. "And you have the wines all wrong. You should serve a sweet, sparkling wine with the dessert, not a dry wine."

Misty's heart sank. After all her efforts, she'd displeased him. Scanning his angry face, she sometimes felt he would find fault with anything she did even if it was perfect.

He shoved the menu at her. "Work on this until you have it right and put some effort in it this time." He frowned at her before picking up his railroad papers again. "Have you sent the invitations and hired the musicians?" he questioned crossly.

Misty steeled her nerves, determined not to let him intimidate her. "The invitations are out," she answered, keeping her voice strong, "but I—"

"Don't tell me you haven't hired musicians yet," he interrupted, not giving her a chance to finish her sentence. "Priscilla should be planning this party, not you. She'd know how to handle everything with ease."

The anger that Misty was holding back suddenly flew out. Why must she constantly be compared to Priscilla, and must she always be reminded that where breeding was concerned she was bitterly lacking? She stood and, hastily rolling up the menu, moved to the foot of her father-in-law's bed. She saw his expression of mockery, and pride sparking within her, she stated, "I know you think your son would be better off married to Priscilla, but he isn't. He's married to me." Her pulse racing a little faster, she decided that if she was ever going to stand up for herself, it would be now. "And you must accept that fact, just as I must accept the fact that you are my father-in-law."

"If I know anything about it, you rushed Adam into a quick marriage before he had a chance to think about it," John stated, his voice full of reproach.

Guilt twisted through Misty, for if the truth be told, she *had* arranged a quick marriage and recalled her doubts about her actions at the time. Raising her chin, she now stood silent, staring at John's accusing face, finding no words to defend herself. Would Raven have married her if she hadn't arranged the affair? she wondered miserably. Her spirits plummeting, she recalled that as many times as they'd made love, he'd never told her that he loved her. Was his attraction for her merely physical, and had he brought her to the city simply because he enjoyed sleeping with her? Worst of all, was he saving his confession of love for Priscilla or some other socialite who was his social equal?

Experiencing a sinking sense of insecurity, she met John's cold eyes and felt all the power she'd mustered flow from her body, leaving her limp. This was to have been her great moment, the time when she finally established her place with her father-in-law, but he'd bested her once again, leaving her with no reply. Even as she ached to defend herself, there was nothing she could do but turn to leave the room.

As she walked toward the door, her confidence at low ebb, new doubts about her marriage and her husband's love swirled in her head and she heard John's quiet laughter behind her.

The evening of the governor's dinner party finally arrived, and standing among her guests, Misty could see nothing but a kaleidoscope of color and the glitter of jewels. Although the guest of honor had yet to make his appearance, the elite of Saint Louis chatted amiably in the huge drawing room, their voices mingled with soft music provided by a string ensemble playing in the corner. Except for visiting Sarah, Misty had worked on the dinner party all week, and as she gazed at the crowd, hearing light laughter and the tinkle of ice against crystal, she could scarcely believe she'd planned such a genteel event.

John's accusation that she'd pressured Raven into a quick marriage had damaged her self-confidence considerably, but with great tenacity, she'd engineered the affair in spite of the old man. Nevertheless, her father-in-law's indictment pricked her tender conscience like a thorn, and still not confident in Raven's love, she'd kept the painful allegation to herself.

She now watched Raven while he moved around the room, being the perfect host. Radiating vitality and magnetism, he was attentive to the ladies and jested with the men. As he worked his way toward her, affection surged within her. "You look beautiful," he said, putting his hand at her waist and gently moving her away from a nattering guest. "I'm sure you'll hear those words often tonight, but I wanted to be the first to tell you." She smiled and ran her gaze over him. His black hair gleamed in the light of the chandeliers, his eyes glinted with warmth, and he looked particularly appealing in his dark evening clothes. "Here," he said, offering her his own glass of champagne, "sip this while we talk to more of our guests."

Raven introduced Misty to guest after guest, and she drew in her breath at the magnificence of their clothes and recognized the names of many important people. The ladies' smooth shoulders and creamy pearls, their long white gloves and gold bangle bracelets, set a tone of dignity and refinement and made her wonder if she was light-headed from the champagne or the excitement of the evening. No wonder Raven had suggested that she buy her moss-green gown with its high bustle and lavish trim of silk roses, she thought, adjusting the frothy skirt that trailed behind her.

She let her gaze circle the room and pause on individual faces. Priscilla, exquisite in lavender, talked to Warren, and across the room, Doctor Vanderhoosey and his wife visited with friends. The matron displayed a pirate's ransom in pearls and gestured dramatically as she talked to a group of doctors from Saint Mary's. When Misty captured her eyes, she frowned and turned away, making it plain that only the governor's presence had lured her here. With a pang of disappointment, Misty noticed that everyone from the hospital had ignored her all evening, but she passed it off with a sigh, attributing it to the day she'd scandalized them. She also spotted John dressed in his finest and seated in his wheelchair. He talked with guests, but as his eyes fastened on her, she knew she would be judged for the rest of the evening.

Then when the room seemed filled to overflowing, the butler cleared his throat and in a stentorian voice announced, "His honor, Benjamin Prescott Longstreet, the governor of Missouri!" There was a burst of applause, and Misty's heart beat a little faster as Raven escorted her toward the distinguished man, who stood at the threshold of the drawing room garbed in evening attire.

She knew the lifelong bachelor had once been a colonel in the Confederate Army, unlike most Missouri officers, who fought for the North. As his name suggested, he was a dashing man of six feet or better, displaying a military manner and sporting a soft beard and mustache. His dark eyes twinkled with kindly intelligence, and his long gray hair was combed back and ruffled on his coat collar in the manner of many of the old war heros. Even at this distance, she detected a genuine friendliness that seemed to radiate from the stately gentleman.

John rolled himself toward the guest of honor, and after introductions had been made all around, the governor took Misty's hand and brushed it with his lips. "Ma'am, I wish to thank you for your gracious invitation."

Misty's spirits rose as she heard a distinctive Southern drawl in his voice.

John, his face filled with anticipation, quickly cornered his guest, and as the pair talked, she noted a glazed expression in the governor's eyes. If her father-in-law couldn't tell, she could see that the man was bored. All the other guests kept a respectful distance, and glancing at Raven, she wondered how they would rescue the governor.

At that moment, the gentleman looked at her and smiled; leaving John, he moved toward her. "Ma'am," he said gently, "if dinner is ready, I'd be obliged if we could be served. And as we go in, perhaps you could introduce me to some of your other guests." He took Misty's hand and, laying it on his arm, grinned at Raven. "Sir, my old daddy, God rest his soul, told me always to sit by the prettiest lady at the party, and I've found that to be unfailingly good advice. If you'd be so

378

kind, I'd like to steal your lovely little wife this evening. After all," he added, his face marked with amusement, "she'll be yours for the rest of your life, while I'll be blessed with her presence for one night alone, charmed as it may be."

Raven smiled and inclined his head, and by his demeanor Misty knew that things were going well. She and the governor made their way toward the dining room, followed by Raven and John, and there was the swish of taffeta and the floaty sweep of chiffon as ladies stepped forward to be presented. Misty sensed that in his own way, her courtly escort was assisting her; with the help of his easy Southern charm, her anxieties lessened.

As they entered the huge dining chamber, the guests trailing discreetly, she glanced about just to assure herself that everything was perfect. Three tables had been put together in a U-shape and covered with the finest embroidered linen. The tables were set with expensive silver and crystal and interspersed with flickering candelabra and bouquets of red roses that perfumed the air.

With quiet murmurs, the smiling guests checked the place cards that were displayed on silver holders, then settled themselves in their chairs. People still poured into the room, and as the governor seated Misty at the head table beside himself, John positioned himself on the other side of the man and shot a warning glance at his daughter-in-law. Her heart lurched; then, looking at Raven, who sat two seats down from his father, she spied his nod of approval and relaxed a bit.

Raven scanned his wife and the governor of Missouri and experienced a spurt of pride. Evidently, the gallant old gentleman had an eye for a pretty lady, and tonight, with her rosy cheeks and sparkling eyes, Misty was indeed a vision of beauty. So far he hadn't seen her make one mistake, and it seemed that she'd thought of everything. He himself had reviewed all her plans, including the French menu, which he knew was superb, and it looked as if Misty Malone would finally come into her own tonight.

The meal began as waiters in black served *potage crecy,* and one delicious course followed the next. As Raven ate, occasionally pausing to speak to the lady sitting beside him, he stole a glance at his father and knew the old man was nettled because the governor was focusing his attention on Misty and not himself. When she laughed and clasped the governor's hand, Raven met her shining eyes, which were brimming with happiness, and he knew she was really enjoying herself.

Misty moved her gaze from Raven's pleased face and focused her attention on the governor again. He'd just told her an amusing story about the Civil War, and his eyes gleamed with nostalgia. "Those were the days," he said with a sigh. "The fellowship of brother officers, the thrill of battle, testing my mettle . . ." He swept his gaze over the guests and frowned. "All this is just filling up time."

Misty didn't take offense, for she understood what he meant. He wasn't impressed with pomp and circumstance like John, and she knew he didn't stand on ceremony or judge a man by what he owned. She understood because she felt the same way.

When the waiter started to pour the governor more wine, the old gentleman put his spread hand over his glass, then cast a questioning look at Misty. "Dear lady, by any chance would you have some Tennessee sipping whiskey in the house?" Laugh lines fanned from his eyes. "I never cared much for these weak-kneed French wines, no matter how expensive they are."

Misty immediately ordered whiskey, and when it arrived, the waiter set down a snifter and served the guest of honor, then left the bottle sitting on the table.

"Yes, sir," the governor continued, after taking a sip and smacking his lips. "Now this is more what the doctor ordered." He chuckled and covered her hand with his. "This ambrosia has the sweetness of mountain moonshine."

Misty searched his face. "You're not from the hills, are you?"

The governor laughed warmly. "Well, in a roundabout way. My grandparents were mountain people, and they lived so far back in the Ozarks they hardly saw the light of day."

Misty's heart lurched. "Well, I'll be flamboozled! I knew there was something I liked about you," she confessed, leaning toward him. "I guess you can't tell, but I'm from the mountains, too. A place called Red Oak Hollow."

The old man chuckled and refilled his glass. "Actually, I did detect the lilt of the hills in your voice, and may I say it only makes you lovelier." He sipped the liquor with appreciation. "My granddaddy made wonderful moonshine that tasted a lot like this. Being from the hills, I'm sure you know what I mean. Would you taste a thimbleful and see if you agree?"

Misty nodded, thinking that although she wasn't much of a drinker, it was only the polite thing to do. After the governor had filled her glass with more than a thimbleful, she tasted a bit of the fiery liquid, then placed it aside, agreeing with him. She'd been very circumspect in all she'd done this evening and, with surprise, had detected some looks of disapproval, but easily dismissed them. After all, the governor was happy and that was all that mattered.

"When I was a boy, I used to spend my summers with my grandparents," the old man rambled on. He smiled, his eyes taking on a dreamy look. "Outside of my army days, it was the best time of my life."

From that moment on, the governor of Missouri and Misty Malone were soul mates, talking about the Ozarks with great relish as they laughed and drank more whiskey. In high feather, they discussed the best recipes for moonshine, the best way to butcher a hog, and the best cures for a mangy hound dog. All the while the old man automatically refilled their glasses.

As her spirits rose, Misty was aware that John and Raven, as well as Warren and Priscilla were staring at her, but she was having so much fun she scarcely noticed their looks of concern. And why was Mrs. Vanderhoosey nudging her husband? she wondered with mild irritation. Caught up in the spirit of the moment and the glow of the whiskey, she and Benjamin Prescott Longstreet might have been the only two people in the room.

After a dessert of chocolate mousse, she and the governor had a last shot of whiskey, and he helped her from her chair. As they left the table and adjourned to the drawing room, she suddenly realized that John hadn't had a chance to discuss the railroad land with his guest of honor, but deciding she didn't know how to remedy the situation, she put the matter aside.

The governor claimed her for the first waltz, and while they danced, he told her another funny anecdote and she burst out laughing, eliciting the raised brows of half the guest. Raven danced with Priscilla, and with a twinge of worry, Misty noted her radiant face, thinking she'd never seen her look happier in her life.

When a new dance began, Raven swept Misty into his arms and frowned down at her. "It seems you and the governor are getting along famously," he said, holding her a little tighter. "What were you two doing—exchanging recipes for sour mash?"

Surprised at his scowl, she giggled and laid her head on his shoulder. "How did you know what we were talking about? The governor said his granddaddy always added ten pounds of sugar when he was thinning the mash, and I told him Uncle Fuzzy swore that was too much. He never used more than six pounds of sugar to a barrel in his life." She lifted her head and gazed at his angry eyes. "I guess I'm a little tipsy all right, but the governor just kept refilling my glass."

A warning cloud settled on Raven's features. "A little tipsy? From where I sat, I wondered which one of you would slide under the table first."

Knowing that a lecture was coming, Misty sighed inwardly, but suddenly the dance had ended, and her spirits lifted when she saw the governor walking toward them. Before Raven could say another word, the man bowed gallantly, then took her hand and led her away. As she stared back through a rosy haze, she noticed that Raven stood with feet apart and arms akimbo, and she wondered why he should be upset.

The governor kept up a light, happy conversation while they danced. "Remember those old mountain songs they used to play back in the hills?" he asked, his voice threaded with longing.

Misty laughed, and hearing the fiddles and banjos ring in her memory, leaned back in his arms. "I sure do. There were dozens of them, all written to set your feet dancing."

The old man paused in the middle of the dance floor, his face aglow. "Do you really know the steps to those old dances? Do you think we might do one?"

Misty met his eager eyes, wanting to make him happy. "Of course we can,"—she surveyed the dignified musicians as they played a Viennese waltz—"but I'll have to talk to the conductor."

She hurried to the corner where the string ensemble played on a slightly raised platform, and the surprised conductor turned about, anxious to please the lady who'd engaged his group. As she conversed with the man, she saw Raven watching her with a speculative look while John scowled his displeasure.

When the musicians had finished the waltz, the conductor conferred with them, and at first there was much talking and confusion. Moments later, the first violinist stepped forward and, rosining his bow, beamed at Misty. Then the man who'd just finished the silkiest of waltzes burst into the "Arkansas Traveler," to be joined moments later by the other musicians.

Suddenly the room was filled with a fast, pulsing music that seemed to lift Misty's feet from the floor. She joined the governor and began to dance, clopping her heels to the beat of the music. Raven gazed at her anxiously while his father rolled to his son's side and, with a flushed face, engaged him in deep conversation.

The musicians played with gusto, and Misty lifted her skirts and danced faster and faster while the governor clapped his hands and tried to follow her steps. Gradually all the guests circled about them, their faces pale with surprise. A few of the men smiled, but the women looked aghast and fanned themselves rapidly, whispering among themselves. As the music reached a fever pitch, Misty kicked off her shoes and let out a rebel yell that sent the governor into gales of laughter.

After the dance was over, the circle disintegrated, and the governor took Misty's hand and brought her to Raven and John. "I'll tell you what," he said, eyeing John, "I haven't had such a good time in many a year." He gazed at Misty fondly and patted her hand. "*Spunk*, that's what this little lady has. And if you don't mind me saying so, she's damn entertaining, too. If you two gentlemen will escort her to my next social, we'll talk about that railway land."

John spluttered and stammered but didn't seem to be able to say anything in return. He shook hands weakly; then, throwing Raven a look that said he should make his excuses, he rolled himself toward his room.

Filled with geniality, the governor transferred his gaze to Raven. "Unfortunately sir, I must take my leave now. I have an important session with the legislature tomorrow." A smile spread over his lips. "Hang on to this little mountain flower of yours, Davenport. She's one in a million, and if I were ten years younger, I'd steal her from you myself."

Benjamin Prescott Longstreet gave Misty a courtly bow and kissed her hand. "Thank you, my dear, for a most enjoyable evening." He winked at her. "And when you see your Uncle Fuzzy again, tell him it's ten pounds of sugar to a barrel, not six."

As Raven escorted the governor into the foyer, Misty noticed pleasant looks hovering on the guests' faces, but as soon as the distinguished man had left the drawing room, the smiles fell from the socialites' lips like dry leaves.

Seeing a woman glare at her bare feet, Misty put on her shoes, then walked to the foyer to say good-bye to the guests who now streamed from the drawing room, ignoring her as they bade hasty farewells to Raven. Puzzled by their expressions, she couldn't believe how quickly the party had broken up—and just when she was having fun. Raven evaded her gaze, and as a line of carriages moved about the huge driveway, he left the foyer to help an elderly lady down the steps to her waiting brougham.

When Warren walked past, escorting Priscilla home, he gazed at Misty with astonished empathy. And as she stood on the threshold, now alone except for the haughty butler, she caught a scrap of conversation from two women as they hurried away.

"Have you ever had such an evening in your life?" the first lady asked.

The second shook her head. "No, I see what you mean about Dr. Davenport's wife. I'm sure that little hillbilly witch doctor has completely ruined his practice."

Pain stabbed through Misty, and she held on to the edge of the great door to steady herself. *So this was what her guests secretly thought of her.* A mist filmed her eyes as she realized that all her work had gone to waste and that her carefully planned affair had ended in shambles.

After Raven handed the older lady into her carriage and it wheeled away, he turned on his heel and jogged up the steps. His face set in grim lines, he brushed past Misty with cool dignity, and she resisted an urge to call him back.

She leaned against the door, her heart breaking, and watched him stride toward the library.

Raven grasped the whiskey decanter and, pouring himself a drink, blew out his breath in pent-up frustration. How he'd longed for Misty to have her moment of victory—and she'd been so close! he thought, regret knifing through him for her lost triumph. At this moment, he should have been holding her in his arms congratulating her. Instead, everything had gone terribly wrong and he'd watched her lose all the social credibility she'd struggled so hard to achieve.

With a sense of great sorrow, Raven sipped the whisky, then lowered his glass, having no taste for it at all. Hearing the sound of footsteps, he turned about, and there she stood just inside the library doors, a lock of hair falling over her brow. As beautiful as ever, she projected the quality of a lost child, and despite his irritation, her loveliness touched a vulnerable spot within him. He tried to control his rising anger as he watched her walk toward him, projecting a contrite air that pricked his heart. They were both silent for a moment; then he took her elbow and searched her troubled face. "Do you care to explain what happened?" he asked hoarsely.

A blush crept over her cheeks. "I'm not sure. The governor and me were talking, getting along real good, then he wanted some Tennessee sipping whiskey. A little later, I found out that his grandparents were from the Ozarks, and after that everything was like a blur. We talked and laughed, and talked some more, and drank a little more whiskey, and—"

"Governors and war heros may drink Tennessee sipping whiskey until they're pie-eyed," Raven cut in. "But ladies don't imbibe, especially in public."

"But he asked for my opinion about the whiskey," she said, in a strained voice, "and it pleased him, too."

He sighed deeply. "You may have pleased the governor, but you shocked everyone else senseless. You should have taken one sip at the most."

Surprised hurt flooded her face and she walked away from him.

Following her movement across the room, he placed his drink on the desk. "And ladies don't take off their shoes at dinner parties," he announced, feeling his temper flare. "And above all, ladies don't let out rebel yells."

His accusation hung heavily in the air, and forcing back her tears, she looked at his stony face. The liquor and excitement of the moment had loosened her tongue and all at once she blurted out, "Oh yes, *the rules*. I forgot the rules again. Anything is fine here as long as a person doesn't forget the rules. Folks here can *do* anything they want, or *insult* anyone they want, as long as they don't forget the rules and do it elegantly." Hurt that he would criticize her, she was overwhelmed by emotion. "I've tried to accept that, which is a real trick if you can do it—but somehow my heart just keeps getting in the way."

A muscle flicked in his hard jaw. "All anyone asked of you were a few changes."

She could sense the barely controlled anger seething within him and knew she was on dangerous ground, but her pride forced her to speak. "You once said we were just going to add some ribbons and bows, but it's come to much more than that. I feel like I've been forced to change just to impress people—to keep from embarrassing the Davenports." Trembling with frustration and chagrin, she walked toward him again. Her heart beat a little faster as she took in his stern expression. "Don't you see, you can't force someone into a mold like they were a piece of wet clay? Don't you see how wrong that is?"

Irritation played over his face. "You're overreacting. No one asked you to sell your soul to the devil—just to polish your manners. You're the same person inside."

She drew in a shuddering breath. "But I *won't* be if I stay here much longer. I feel like I'm being buried alive."

He regarded her with blazing eyes. "So that's where we're at? Going back to the Ozarks again?"

"And why not?" she answered, her voice breaking. "When I came here, I thought it was just for a visit, but now it seems we're here to stay. I haven't seen you make any plans to go back after your father passes away. I've never heard you talk about it, and I doubt if you've even thought about it. Why, I'll bet you're still hoping the board will overlook my mistakes so you can get that chief-of-staff position."

He assumed a secretive expression, and she wondered what he was keeping from her. Had the board offered him the position already? she wondered with growing unease.

"I made you no promises when we left the Ozarks," he said matter-of-factly. "Have you forgotten that this is my home?" He strode away, his gaze sweeping over the elaborately decorated chamber. "Look about you. You're living in a palace, and you wear the finest of clothes. What do you find lacking?"

She moistened her lips, trying to gather her thoughts. "I'm lacking nothing in worldly goods," she conceded, "but I'm lacking something more important. I'm lacking purpose and meaning here."

"Being my wife doesn't fulfill your needs?" he asked coolly.

Misty looked at his demanding eyes. She knew that she'd drunk too much, but strangely her mind had never felt clearer and she harbored a burning need to express herself. "Of course, that means the world to me, but there are other parts of my life too," she answered quietly. She smoothed back her straying locks, choosing her words. "Back in the hills there are people depending on me to help them stay well."

"Don't you think one doctor in the family is enough?" he retorted, his countenance hardening.

Her instinct warned her to hold her tongue, but a powerful spirit rose up to deny it. "No, I don't," she answered in a choked voice. "And I'm tired of being a lady of leisure. And I'm weary of doing things that don't matter and saying things just for manners' sake."

Raven gazed at her anguished face and noticed a pulse throbbed at the base of her throat. Moved by her child-like honesty, he gathered her soft warmth to him, trying to understand her. "Go on," he prompted in a quiet tone. "Tell me what is in your heart."

She swallowed convulsively. "*I miss the hills,*" she said with great passion. "I miss Ezra and Lukie and Brother Jubal. And I miss the hidden meadows, and the scent of the rain coming over the mountains, and the morning dew sparkling in the sun." She glanced downward for a moment, then met his gaze again. "And I miss the magic," she confessed softly.

Amazement touched Raven's heart that she was still so emotionally immature. He could understand her missing the mountains and her family, and even understand her desire to practice her herb medicine, but *magic* was another matter altogether. He'd given her books to read and discussed the importance of believing only what one could prove scientifically, but with all his work she hadn't changed one whit. Irritation burst within him, and in his heart he suspected that if the truth be told, she still believed in lightning-struck toothpicks. "What magic are you talking about?" he asked dryly.

Her eyes became large and soft. "The magic of *loving* and *believing.*"

Somewhat put off by her attitude that all spiritual qualities were limited to the hill folk, he answered, "Believe it or not, those qualities can even be found in Saint Louis."

Misty searched his frowning face and continued, now too far into the perilous conversation to retrieve herself. "I'm not so sure. I understood you in the mountains. In the mountains we laughed and talked together, and everything seemed right and good. But sometimes I don't know who you are anymore," she whispered in a tight voice. "Sometimes I think you've lost your spirit as well as your laughter here."

Disbelief flashing on his face, he strode to the window and, pulling back the drapes, stared at the darkness.

Misty looked at his broad back with a fluttering heart, and when he slowly turned about, his countenance was hard and fixed. "I've had very little to laugh about," he challenged, with crossed arms. "Your whole life in the city has been one disaster after another. You demolished the best restaurant in the city. You bought a whole department store full of furniture that had to be returned. And you turned Saint Mary's Hospital upside down." He strode toward her, his brows drawing into a frown. "And if you haven't noticed, tonight you made a laughing stock of yourself before the aristocracy of Saint Louis. Can't you get through one event without causing a sensational scene?"

The words hurt Misty more deeply than anything he'd ever said, and tears scalded her throat. But at the same time relief spread through her that all their cards were on the table. "Yes, I know I've made some mistakes here," she began in a broken voice. Then as she noted his angry eyes, her spirit rebelled that she was being forced to defend herself when she'd tried her best to fit into a world that didn't want her. "But they were honest mistakes made out of ignorance," she announced, changing the tone of her voice. She tapped her chest. "And I made the mistakes because I care more about people than rules— *and I always will.*"

Raven's eyes glittered icily. "A very dangerous way to live your life, my love," he remarked coolly.

"The heart is fickle, but reason and logic will never fail you."

She saw his handsome face through a mist of tears. "To Hades with reason and logic," she said hotly. Fuming with anger, she hurried to the library doors, then paused on the threshold and turned her gaze back to him. "You know, I was wrong about this place," she cried, her voice quavering with emotion, "Saint Louis isn't Sodom and Gomorrah—*it's hell.*"

So saying, she left the room and ran up the sweeping staircase.

Chapter Nineteen

Misty woke up the next morning thinking of the Ozarks. She'd been dreaming that she was picking herbs, and the dream was so vivid that she could smell the herbs' sharp scent and feel the cool mountain breeze on her cheeks. Lukie was there, and they'd laughed and talked, and Misty had once again felt the great sense of contentment that she'd missed so desperately since leaving the mountains. Now, as consciousness flooded back, terrible despair assailed her.

Sunlight crept between the half-closed drapes and wavered across the bed, and realizing that Raven was not there, she eased up and looked about her, missing him dreadfully. Pain pulled at her heart when she saw the smooth sheets and uncrushed pillow. He hadn't slept there at all. After storming up the stairs the night before, she'd gone to bed and fought back her tears, thinking he would join her later. But after hours of tossing and turning and regretting her hot words, she'd fallen asleep alone. She'd grown used to his warm body and loving hands, and his absence left a hollow place inside her.

Sighing, she sat up and shook back her hair, wishing she could relive the whole of the past evening, especially her conversation with Raven. Then, as she spotted his dark evening clothes draped over a chair, she wondered if he might have slept on the leather sofa in the library. She slipped out of bed, clinging to a thread of hope. Perhaps if she hurried down, she could catch him before he left for the hospital.

After opening the wardrobe, she tossed off her gauzy nightgown and selected a simple blue day dress. Her head ached dully as she dressed, a painful reminder that she and Benjamin Prescott Longstreet had almost finished a bottle of whiskey. In the clear light of day, she was astounded that she'd imbibed so heavily and began to see the past evening from Raven's view point. If she could only catch him and explain things, she thought, leaving the bedroom without even bothering to brush her hair.

At the bottom of the curving staircase, she heard the clatter of dishes and saw Mrs. Hawksley supervising the cleaning of the dining room. One sharp glance from the woman told Misty that her latest escapade was known to the entire household staff. With warm cheeks, she looked away and hurried to the library.

The darkened room remained as it was from the night before, Raven's untouched drink still sitting on the desk. Sweeping her gaze about the chamber, where light filtered in through the partially opened drapes, she could tell that he was not there, and her spirits plunged even lower. Evidently, he'd been so put out with her that he'd already gone to the hospital without even saying good-bye.

With a heartfelt sigh, she drifted toward the desk, then traced her fingertips around the rim of the liquor glass, recalling pieces of their argument. After her overindulgence, the whiskey's aroma almost made her sick, and she started to walk away, but just then, the corner of an envelope placed under the blotter caught her eyes. Only the tip of the envelope was showing, but against the green blotter its whiteness sprang out, tempting her mightily.

Her fingers trembling, she picked up the opened letter; seeing that it was from the hospital and addressed to Raven, she pulled out the pages and began scanning them. Her heart turned over as she read: *So after long and painful consideration, the board has decided that your wife's actions make it unadvisable to appoint you as the next chief-of-staff. The appointment will go to Doctor Thompson.* Tears flooded Misty's eyes; blinking them back, she checked the date and saw that the letter had arrived last week. No wonder Raven's countenance had been veiled when she'd mentioned the position last night! He'd lost what he coveted so dearly—and all because of her—but he hadn't said a word about it.

Shaken, she placed the letter on top of the blotter, then closed her eyes. She now knew why all the doctors from the hospital had looked at her so strangely last evening and why Mrs. Vanderhoosey had turned her back. And at that moment she recalled the words she'd heard from the gossiping women as they left the mansion: *I'll bet Doctor Davenport's little witch-doctor wife has completely ruined his practice.*

Misty put a hand to her mouth. When word that the chief-of-staff position had been given to another doctor filtered down to Raven's patients, she was sure that some of them *would* leave him, thinking him incompetent. And if that wasn't enough, her actions would stamp him with a scandal that would be hard to live down. At that moment, her life since she'd arrived in the city passed before her eyes in a sickening haze, and she relived all her mistakes, this time seeing how embarrassing they must have been to Raven.

With a sense of sinking defeat, she left the library and started back to her bedroom to sort out her whirling thoughts. As she passed John's room, she saw that the door stood ajar, and wondering how he was feeling, she peered into the shadowy room. Although his lamp glowed softly, an untouched breakfast tray sat on his bedside table and he slept tangled in the covers. In repose, his ashen face had a pale, utterly defeated appearance, and he seemed very ill indeed.

Slowly approaching the bed, she thought of all the cruel things he'd said to her and how he'd tried to tear down her confidence by insisting that she'd rushed Raven into wedlock. Nevertheless, he looked so ill that she instinctively reached out to brush his cheek; then she held her fingers still, realizing that he wouldn't want her to touch him. When she moved back her hand, she accidentally brushed against some of the breakfast dishes, making a rattling noise.

John groaned and, opening his bleary eyes, focused them on her. Slowly pushing himself up on his pillow, he smoothed back his tousled hair. "Well, are you pleased with yourself?" he asked in a sleep-thickened voice.

Misty stared at his humorless face, having no idea what he was talking about.

"Because of you," he went on, his voice gaining strength, "I've lost my chance to talk to the governor about that railroad land."

She smiled, wanting to encourage him. "No, you haven't. Didn't you hear him asking us to his next social? You can talk to him then."

"That means nothing at all," John answered with a resentful expression. "The governor's socials are large crushes. A guest is lucky if he merely gets to shake hands with the man." The lines deepened around his mouth. "No, last night was my best chance to influence him, and I lost that chance because of you."

Misty met his disapproving gaze. "I'm sorry," she said. "Truly sorry. I-I didn't know how to make him talk to you."

John scowled. "As my daughter-in-law, you should have steered the conversation toward the railroad business or directed some comments my way, instead of ignoring me."

Her lips trembled and she couldn't speak.

John moved a speculative gaze over her. "But knowing your background, I suppose I couldn't have expected anything else." A cruel smile twisted his lips. "The truth be told, I'm not so sure that you *are* my daughter-in-law."

The words hit her like a physical force, and she assessed him, wondering what he could be implying. "What do you mean?" she asked, feeling a heaviness in the pit of her stomach. "Raven and me were married in a church . . . by

Brother Jubal." She nervously brushed back her hair. "Everyone in the hollow was at our wedding. They saw us. They heard our vows."

John lifted his brows. "And who is this Brother Jubal?" he asked in a quietly insulting tone.

"Why, he's the preacher in Red Oak Hollow," she answered, wondering what he could be talking about. "He's preached there for over twenty years. Everyone knows him. They love him and he's a good—"

"Is he an ordained minister?" John cut in, his eyes freezing on her. "Was he ever ordained by a bishop or anyone of authority?"

Misty stood mute, for she'd never even considered such questions. In Red Oak Hollow, religion wasn't a matter of certification, it was a matter of the heart, and in that respect Brother Jubal fulfilled every qualification. "I'm not sure what you're getting at," she whispered.

John gave her a smug smile. "I'm simply making the point that unless a man is an ordained minister, he has no right to marry a couple. I know all about these old backwoods ministers. They suddenly feel the call to preach and put themselves in the business." He jabbed an accusing finger at her. "But that doesn't make them ordained or legal."

She'd never even considered that she and Raven might not be married, but as she looked down at her wedding ring, aching doubt seeped through her.

"If you ask me," he speculated, "Adam just went through a meaningless ceremony to pacify you. Legally you aren't even a part of this family."

"But that's not true," Misty shot out. "Raven and me *are* married."

"Only in your eyes, young miss. I seriously doubt if the wedding would stand here in Saint Louis if we put it to the test." He pursed his lips. "Why, I suspect you can't even produce a marriage license."

A heavy weight dropped on Misty's shoulders, for just as he said, she *couldn't* produce a marriage license. All she could do was stare at him, her words of protest lodging in her throat.

He sat forward, his face flushing. "Your position as Adam's wife is shaky at best, and in truth, no more than a sham. Can't you see how much he thinks of Priscilla? She's the one he really loves."

Humiliated, Misty stared at the carpet while her father-in-law voiced her innermost fear. She couldn't argue that Brother Jubal was an ordained minister, for she knew that he was not. Her mind reeling with doubt and confusion, she edged away from the bed while John snapped, "You're nothing but an ignorant little hillbilly who had the good fortune to seduce a man who is your better!"

Tears stung Misty's eyes, and she started to run from the room. Then a fierce pride sprang up within her as she realized that this was the second time John had thrown the words at her. And in so doing, he'd insulted not only her, but all the mountain people she'd ever loved.

Taking a steadying breath, she held her ground and spoke in a strong, clear voice. "I may not have three million dollars, but my inheritance is greater than yours because it's the Ozark Mountains and the White River rushing clean and clear. And I don't need high-placed friends to make me feel important, because my love for healing is like a fire in my heart that will give my life meaning if I live to be a hundred years old!" Feeling a passion that left her shaken, she moved closer to him and held his eyes. "And if loving God's mountains and caring for the good people he put in them makes me a hillbilly, then I'm proud to bear the name!"

John's face remained as implacable as ever, but deep relief washed through her, leaving her weak, for she'd finally spoken her mind, holding nothing back. She controlled her threatening tears by sheer force of will, then turned and walked from the room with great dignity. Only when she was in the hall, safely out of John's sight, did she raise her skirt and race up the stairs, wanting to be as far away from her father-in-law as possible.

How she'd wanted him to like her, and how she'd tried to please him! She only wished she could have touched his spirit or brought him even a moment of joy—but she hadn't. With a heavy heart, she realized that she felt not hate for him, but pity, instinctively understanding his poverty of spirit. With all his millions, he'd striven for something so fleeting as social acceptance while ignoring his sons' pleas for love.

Once inside her bedroom, she leaned against the door and, trembling all over, tried to master her emotions. Her mind working fiercely, she began untangling her thoughts as if they were bright strands of embroidery thread. Because of her, John had lost a chance at a great business opportunity, but more important, she'd cost Raven a position he coveted above all else. With a stab of anguish, she realized that as long as they were married, she would keep on embarrassing him and pulling him down. Perhaps John's bitterness held a nugget of wisdom, she thought with a pain so deep it almost took her breath away. No matter how much she loved Raven, she wasn't suited for him, and no matter how hard she tried, she wasn't good enough for him either. He needed a wife like Priscilla, someone who could meet society with no qualms about her behavior.

Her confidence shaken by John's accusation, she spread her hand and looked at her wedding ring, shining in the morning light. With a pang of sentiment, she remembered the day Raven had given it to her at Mr. Tanner's general store. On that frosty winter's morning, she'd fancied herself the happiest woman in the whole state of Arkansas. And she had been, but she didn't know all the trials that were waiting for her here in Saint Louis, she thought, feeling a single tear slide down her cheek.

Memories flooding her mind, she remembered the freezing afternoon she'd found the frost flower. How thrilled she'd been when she made a wish on it, for that wish carried all her hopes that Raven would stay in the mountains and love her. With a sad smile, she recalled the day they were wed and how she'd sworn to love him until the Ozarks were flat and the great White River ran dry. And she *would* always love him, she vowed, her hand quaking a bit. Love him with all her heart and soul until she drew her last breath. And loving him that much, how could she bear to ruin his life?

Her heart beating a little faster, she slipped the ring from her finger and laid it on top of the dresser, thinking how small and lonely it looked there on the lacy scarf all by itself. *Raven will know*, she whispered to herself. He would understand as soon as he saw the ring. He would know that she was setting him free to live his life without her holding him back and embarrassing him.

He would know she'd gone back to the Ozarks.

An hour later, Misty walked to the carriage house. Feeling comfortable for the first time in months, she wore a long skirt, a homespun blouse, and her floppy mountain hat. Her dulcimer under her arm, she carried her basket suitcase, packed to bursting with belongings she'd brought from the hills. In her way, she'd already said good-by to John, and she knew Mrs. Hawksley really didn't care to have words with her. After searching for Warren and not finding him, she decided that perhaps it was best, for he would just try to convince her to stay. Now she just had to ask Nat to take her to the railroad station and say farewell. Swallowing the lump of emotion in her throat, she didn't know which task would be harder.

Nat was polishing the landau, and upon seeing her, he straightened up and his lips parted. "Oh, Mrs. Davenport, what are you doin' now?" he asked, the crumpled rag falling from his fingers. "I sure hope you ain't doin' what I think you are." He took the dulcimer and basket suitcase from Misty and set them aside, gazing at her with astonishment.

"I reckon I'm doing just what you think I am. I'm shaking the dust of Saint Louis from my feet and going back to the mountains." She met his worried eyes, fighting back her own emotions. "Will you drive me to the railroad station?" she asked in a broken voice. "If we hurry, I can be gone from here before anyone misses me." The carriage house smelled of leather and horses, and only a faint light penetrated the dusty windows, but even in the gloom she could see his look of disapproval.

"No, ma'am. I'll do about anything you say. But I can't be doin' that. What would Mr. Adam say?" Dressed in his livery pants and a white shirt with rolled-up sleeves, Nat swept the back of his arm over his brow. "Oh, this is bad news. Yes, sir, real bad news if I ever heard it!"

Rollo's cage sat on one of the carriage house shelves, and Misty went to it and started unwiring the door. Upon seeing her, the racoon chirred happily, and as soon as the door was open, he jumped into her waiting arms. Feeling a little flicker of happiness for the first time that morning, she held his warm body against her, catching the familiar scent of his fur.

She walked back to Nat, then sank down on the steps of the carriage, looking up at his troubled face. "I think the mountains is where Rollo and me belong, don't you?" she asked, smoothing back the animal's glossy coat.

From the open door, a shaft of light poured in the building and washed over Nat, highlighting his lanky body and the pained look in his eyes. "No, Mrs. Davenport, I think you belong here with Mr. Adam," he answered, giving her a long, steady look. "He's your husband, and he'd be grieved terrible if you left him."

Misty met his earnest eyes. "He might miss me a little at first, but we both know he'd be better off without me." She cut her gaze to the side before looking back at him. "I've just been in one scrape after another ever since I landed here."

Nat blinked his eyes. "Well, I don't deny we've had some interesting times since you came." He chuckled and rubbed a hand over his gray hair. "And the Lord knows we cut a swath through that department store, all right,"—he knelt on one knee beside her—"but Mr. Adam thinks the world of you."

She pressed her lips together. "I guess you didn't hear about last night?"

An uncomfortable look passed over his face. "Yes, ma'am, some of the kitchen help was sayin' you and the governor was feelin' real fine, but you don't need to be leavin' for that little dab of trouble."

Still holding Rollo, she ambled away, then turned and looked at him. "But that's just it," she added, feeling tears well up in her throat. "I'll always be in *a dab of trouble* here because I don't think like these city folks."

Nat rose, a perplexed look in his eyes.

"I've got it all figured out," she explained, with a sigh. "I think with my heart and not my head. That worked all right in the hills, but all it's done here is get me into a mess of trouble." She tapped her toe against an empty polish can, sending it rolling over the floor. "And I can't follow the rules for shucks."

Nat laughed good-naturedly. "You just haven't met enough people."

"Oh, I've met a passel of people," she insisted, pacing back and forth beside the carriage, "but they didn't cotton to me much. To them, I'm just like a piece of furniture that doesn't fit, no matter where you put it." She looked at his kindly eyes. "I'm tired of trying to fit in where I'm not wanted. And I'm tired of trying to admire statues with no arms on them, and learn the names of old pictures, and eat buttered-up snails." On the verge of tears, she waved her arm, then let it fall loosely to her side. "And I'm tired of wearing stiff, uncomfortable clothes and being cinched up and having a dad-blamed spring attached to my butt!"

Nat widened his eyes. *"Ma'am?"*

She paused and heaved a long sigh. "Never mind," she said in a softer voice. "I was just talking." Then, feeling an overpowering wave of homesickness, she searched his compassionate face. "And Lord, I'm nearly dead with longing for the hills, *I miss them so much!*"

Nat clasped her shoulders. "But Mr. Adam needs you here," he advised roughly.

"No, he needs someone like Priscilla, someone who knows the rules and doesn't mind staying with them. He needs a *real* lady."

Nat's eyes flashed. "Oh, ma'am, don't be sayin' that," he urged, now taking her hand. "You're the finest lady I've ever known. Why, the rest of them can't hold a candle to you. You care about people, and if you ask me, that's what bein' a lady is all about."

Her throat tightened, and for a moment she couldn't speak. In her mind, a lady was someone who did things gracefully, a person who didn't cause *sensational scenes*, as Raven had called them. And a real lady couldn't possibly have made as many mistakes as she had, or experienced as many setbacks. After finding her voice, she covered his hand with hers. "Will you take me to the station?" she pleaded in a choked voice.

He let out a long, audible breath. "I reckon if I don't, you'll just find another way to get there."

She swallowed hard and whispered. "Have you still got your dancing shoes?"

"Yes, ma'am," he answered in a shaky voice. "I've still got 'em, but after today I don't figure I'll be doin' much dancin'."

She stood there silently, knowing she'd miss him terribly and feeling thankful for all he'd meant to her. "Will you say good-bye to Warren for me?"

He tightened his jaw and shook his head.

"And you won't tell Raven about our talk, will you?"

He placed a hand on her arm. "If your heart is set on leavin', I'll take you to the station and stay till the train pulls out," he answered, his face drawn with tension, "but don't be askin' that of me."

She lowered her gaze, then nodded. "All right," she said quietly, glancing up again, "I won't." At that moment, she remembered Brother Jubal's advice to just be herself and anyone who was important would like her. Well, she thought, with a flicker of irony, she'd followed that advice and gained the unqualified friendship of Warren, Nat, Sarah, and the governor of Missouri—a mixed but noble assortment of friends, who in their own way were all important people.

She scanned the sleek carriage and thought of the day she'd been so ignorant that she'd ridden on the box and didn't know any better. Now she just didn't care. "Nat," she ventured, "I'd like to leave town in style with my head held high, and I don't care who sees me." She ran her fingertips over the landau's glittering brass fittings, then glanced at him. "Could me and Rollo ride on the box with you going to the station—just for old time's sake?"

Nat's dark eyes misted up. "Yes, ma'am. I'd be proud if you did."

An hour later, Raven threw down his pen and pushed back his desk chair. His eyes heavy with drowsiness, he stood and strode about his hospital office. His eyes ached and his temples throbbed, and scraping a hand over his stubbled jaw, he knew he wouldn't be able to keep his mind on his work a moment longer. After pacing about the library and giving his argument with Misty deep consideration, he'd gone upstairs to talk with her and found her lying still and breathing deeply. By the look of the tangled sheets, he knew she'd had difficulty falling asleep and didn't want to wake her. On the other hand, he realized that he wouldn't be able to sleep himself and had changed clothes and come to the hospital, turmoil eddying through him.

Through the wee morning hours, his desk lamp had glowed in the darkness as he reviewed routine forms, his mind only half focused on his work. As dawn broke, he'd extinguished the lamp and rubbed his bleary eyes. Knowing Misty wouldn't be awake yet, he'd doggedly plunged ahead with his work, ignoring the aching knot of tension between his shoulders. All night long her words, *I feel like I'm being buried alive* resounded in his head, and knowing she was now awake, a deep yearning to see her welled up within him. Now all he could think of was going home and somehow working out their seemingly unsolvable problems.

Even as he shrugged into his jacket, he told himself that he couldn't let their relationship be damaged by bitter words and stinging accusations. Somehow, some way, they had to forge a plan to share the same world harmoniously. Then, as he reached for his hat, swift footsteps resounded outside his door, and all at once the nurse from the children's ward burst into his office unannounced. An amazed expression marked her face. "Come quickly, doctor," she blurted out, so excited that she dispensed with a greeting. "It's Sarah. You must see her."

Raven put down his hat. "What happened to her?" he inquired, slightly alarmed.

The nurse shook her head. "I can't explain now," she called over her shoulder, already out in the corridor again. "You'll just have to see for yourself." Several steps ahead of him, she waved her hand. *"And hurry."*

Raven followed the woman down the corridor, maneuvering around the staff, who pushed rattling carts stacked with breakfast trays. Near the door to the children's ward, the nurse reached for his arm. "I'm so glad you were in your office," she said, her voice laced with anticipation. "Sarah wanted me to find you." A smile leapt to her eyes. "And I knew you'd want to see this."

Inside the ward, white-gowned children stood in clusters, their attention drawn to the end of the room, where Sarah held the footboard of her bed with one frail hand. Her face lit up when she saw Raven, and with slow, shaky steps, she walked toward him. As she put one foot in front of the other, narrowing the distance between them, the wide-eyed children murmured with awe.

After his argument with Misty and a sleepless night, Raven's emotions were already strained, and a lump formed in his throat. When the child was only a few feet from him, he beckoned with open arms, and she took a last awkward step, throwing her arms about his neck. "See," she announced proudly, her eyes sparkling with stars. "I can walk again."

He trailed his fingers over her radiant face. "And so you can," he replied, happiness rising in his chest like a warm tide. He realized that the girl still needed therapy to walk with ease and would have to remain in the hospital weeks longer, but she was past her first great hurdle. Her mind had been freed, and she'd summoned the courage to challenge life again. He caressed her back, scarcely believing the miracle he'd witnessed. "Tell me, how did this wonderful thing happen?"

She gave a little shrug. "I don't know," she replied with a childish grin. "I just woke up this morning and knew I could walk. So I got out of bed and did it!"

Savoring the momentous event, he swept his hands over her arms, then looked at the nurse who stood beside them. "What has changed? Has another doctor seen her? Was a new medication prescribed?"

A quiet smile flickered over the woman's mouth. "The only other *doctor* who has seen her is Mrs. Davenport."

"Misty?" he asked, a spark of wonder in his tone.

"That's right," Sarah chirped, capturing his attention again. "She's come to see me almost every day."

He laughed and caught her hand. "And what happened when she came here? What did you two talk about?"

"All kinds of things," Sarah answered, cocking her head to the side. "Then, just a few days ago she brought some paper and colored pencils and we drew pictures of the fire."

A cord struck deep within Raven, and he cupped the girl's upturned face. "Tell me about these pictures," he asked softly. "What did you do with them?"

"Misty put them in a little box and tied it with a string. Then she took me outside in a wheelchair." She looked pensive as she recalled the scene. "She had a spade like people use to make flower beds, and while I watched, she dug a hole. Then we buried the box together."

"Tell me the rest," he prompted, already guessing what he was going to hear.

"Misty told me we were burying the fire forever. She said that I wouldn't dream about it anymore, and she told me that one morning I'd wake up and I would be able to walk again." She smiled brightly and flung out her hands in happiness. "And that's just what happened."

Raven had suspected that Sarah's problem was centered in hysterical paralysis, but he was awed by Misty's skill. How clever she'd been! It had taken someone who could think like a child to handle the case, but on a deeper level it had taken the faith of a child to cure the little girl. At that moment, a great stillness settled in his soul, and with a flash of insight he now completely understood Misty's words that the most powerful medicine lay in the mind.

Sarah touched his stubbled jaw. "When is Misty coming to see me again? I miss her."

Raven forced back his emotions. "I know . . . me, too," he whispered.

There was the noise of a door opening and footsteps behind him, then Raven heard: "I'm afraid I've got some real bad news for you, sir."

At the sound of Nat's distraught voice, Raven whirled about, still holding Sarah in his arms. Blinking his eyes, he saw the driver standing just inside the children's ward. He held his hat in his hands, and from his anguished expression, he carried the weight of the world on his shoulders.

His mind still filled with shock, Raven strode up the mansion's sweeping staircase and entered his bedroom. Out of habit, he moved his gaze over the empty room, which was clean and in order, but without Misty so cold and empty that it left him shaken. The memory of their argument pierced his heart, and he longed to hold her in his arms and make things right with her. He knew there wouldn't be another train for Eureka Springs until tomorrow morning, but realizing he could start packing, he moved to the dresser. As he opened the top drawer, Misty's small wedding ring glittered in the sunlight, and with a twinge of anguish, he picked it up and held it in the palm of his hand.

Instantly he understood that she'd left the ring to say that he was free—free to find another woman who would fit into his city way of life. Leaving the ring was her admission that she'd failed, and the only place she could find solace of heart was the mountains. In that dark moment, a feeling swept over him that left him feeling sick and leaden inside. If only he'd handled things differently, he thought, realizing that he'd been so busy establishing his practice again that he'd never replaced the simple gold band with a more expensive diamond ring. And there had been so many other mistakes he'd made with her, like depending on others to guide her when he should have put his work aside and made her his first priority.

As he slipped the ring into his pocket, his mind churned with worrisome questions. Yes, they'd quarreled, but it was unlike her to leave without saying anything or at least leaving him a letter. With a twinge of despair, he knew that she had to be terribly upset to take such a drastic step, and he wondered if his father had said anything to her.

His temper rose with his suspicions as he left the room and jogged down the stairs. At the threshold of his father's room, he saw John lying in bed propped up against a mound of pillows, reading some papers.

"Misty is gone," Raven announced bluntly as he strode toward the bed. "What do you know about it?"

The old man yanked off his spectacles, his eyes gleaming with surprise. "So she's gone, hey?" he retorted with a pleased expression as he placed the papers aside. "To answer your rather rude question, I know nothing about it, but I won't say that I'm sorry."

Anger coursed through Raven, for he knew his father was lying, and he assessed the old man, wondering what was going on in his head. "Did you see her this morning? Did you talk to her?" he prodded.

John tossed his spectacles on the coverlet. "Yes, I saw her," he confessed in a harsh tone, "and I talked to her, but I won't be held responsible for her actions."

Anxiety coiled in the pit of Raven's stomach, and he strode away from the bed, then gazed at his father again, determined to pry the truth out of him. "What did you say to her?" he demanded, a sharp edge to his voice.

John scowled. "If you must know, I mentioned that because of her irresponsible actions, I'd lost my chance to influence the governor." He gave a dry laugh. "And I also brought up the subject of your missing marriage license, among other things."

Raven stared at him, hardly believing what he was hearing. After their argument, the last thing Misty needed to hear was John's embarrassing accusation. Anger exploded inside of him as he realized that John had finally got his way by playing on Misty's sense of honor. Although he hadn't touched her physically, the man was guilty of emotional assassination.

"Yes, I see what's happened now," Raven said, stalking to the foot of the bed. "Sensing that her spirit was at a low point, you pounded away at her confidence, making her feel she was a complete failure with no right to wear the Davenport name. No wonder she left!"

His father lowered his brows. "Be thankful for the blessing you have received. The girl was totally inappropriate for you, and if you didn't have sense enough to realize it, thank God she did. Let her go and be done with her!"

Raven's heart pounded with rage, and he had to use all his discipline to simply remain in one spot. How dare John verbally assault Misty in such a way! he thought, clenching his jaw. He was so infuriated that he cared little about his father's feelings. "Damn you," spat out, rancor hardening his voice. "Damn you and your meddlesome ways!"

A tense silence burned between them; then there was a sound at the threshold that demanded Raven's attention. Warren, his face white, lingered at the open door, seemingly gathering his courage. He glanced to the side, obviously realizing that he'd arrived at the worst possible time. "I'm sorry," he murmured apologetically. "I'll come back later."

Raven walked toward him. "No, stay," he said, pausing a few feet in front of him. "Perhaps you can help. Misty has gone back to the Ozarks."

Warren's eyes widened and darkened. "I'm sorry . . . terribly sorry."

Raven searched his pale face. "Did you speak with her this morning?"

His brother shook his head. "No, I didn't. I left early this morning, but I never would have gone if I'd known she had that in mind." His eyes delivered a message of sorrow; then he glanced over Raven's shoulder at his father. "I'll come back later . . . at a better time," he suggested.

He turned to walk away, but John fixed him with a hard stare. "No, stay here," he ordered crossly. "I've been waiting for those new reports all morning. Where in the hell have you been?"

Raven walked to the windows, but from the corner of his eye, he noticed that his brother looked directly at John. "I've been at Priscilla's," Warren replied, his face suffused with color.

John's eyes sharpened. "On a week day, when you should have been working? Why in the devil for?"

Warren glanced down. "I really don't think this is a good time. I—"

"Oh, go on. Spit it out!" John ordered. "What did you come about?"

Warren pulled in a long breath; then, with a new composure, he walked to the bed. "All right, if you must know, it concerns what I came here to tell you."

"And what is that, pray?"

Raven noticed Warren's beaming face. "Priscilla has agreed to be my wife," Warren announced, his voice gaining depth and strength. "I asked her last night at the governor's party, and she said she would give me her answer this morning. We're to be wed as soon as possible."

Raven stared at his brother and, despite his own troubles, felt a rush of pride. Using his own initiative, Warren had courted and wooed Priscilla, finally winning her hand. No wonder the girl looked so radiant last evening!

"Good God," breathed John. "I never would have believed it."

Warren stiffened. "No, you've always believed only what you wanted to see," he observed in a confident tone Raven had never heard before. "You've always been totally blind where Adam and I were concerned."

Raven didn't know what had happened to Warren, but he liked what he was seeing. For the first time in his life, his brother was speaking freely and standing up to the man who'd always belittled him. Evidently Priscilla's acceptance had given rise to the courage that was always lurking just below his mild manners.

John's mouth turned downward. "Snap at me, will you, you young pup? Do you really think you'll be able to make a go of this business on your own?"

Warren's eyes glinted with righteous indignation. "Yes, actually, I do—after I make some

416

changes," he shot back, straightening his back and seeming to grow in stature. He glanced at the drawn drapes. "The first change being to let some light into this gloomy mausoleum!" With a manly stride, he walked to the drapes and pulled them back, flooding the room with golden sunlight. Then he turned about, his eyes glinting with a fire that Raven had never seen. "This is only the beginning. From now on, you will give my ideas equal consideration with your own. And I'll no longer tolerate being no more than your glorified delivery boy. If we are to work together, you must respect me."

John flushed and spluttered, searching for words he could not find.

Satisfaction streamed through Raven, and he gave thanks that Warren had found the courage to stand up for his rights. With his brother's keen mind, he knew that he would now be an equal match for John and would finally be treated with the courtesy he deserved. With an inward smile, he turned to leave the room so he could finish his packing. He was just at the door when he heard his father throw back the bedding, and he instinctively turned around to see what was happening.

"If you go after that little baggage, it's all over between us," John called, struggling his legs out of bed. "Do you understand me? I'll send for a lawyer today and have a new will drawn up," he fumed, color blotching his face. "You'll be out of it altogether and receive nothing at all!"

Raven coolly regarded the old man, who was trembling visibly. "Do you think I give a damn about that?" he blurted, spilling out his heart.

"Do you think I want a dollar of your money, which is so stained with heartache and grief that it reeks to the high heavens?"

Perspiration broke out on John's brow, and staring at his oldest son with glassy eyes, he turned ashen.

Warren walked from the windows to the bed. "If you did such a despicable thing, I'd share my part of the inheritance with him anyway. And knowing how you want your rail dynasty to continue, I hardly think you'd leave everything to charity." In a kinder voice, he added, "Don't you understand that you can't manipulate and bully us anymore? Don't you understand that we've both broken free of you?"

From his position at the door, Raven could almost see his father crumbling as he was finally faced with total opposition from both of his sons—a thing he had never imagined possible.

John trembled with anger, and a large vein stood out on his forehead. He tried to speak, but only made gasping sounds, spittle foaming on his lips. Then as he began sweating more profusely and slumped against the pillows, Raven quickly moved back to the bed, realizing that he was having another heart attack.

Warren knelt on one leg, riveting his startled eyes on his father. "What's happening?" he asked in a roughened tone.

Raven put his ear against the man's chest and listened to his weak heartbeat degenerate into a useless quivering that prevented blood from being pumped through his body. "He's having a heart attack—and I'm afraid this one will be massive."

John's eyes fluttered open and he moaned weakly. "There's a sharp pain behind my breastbone . . . and I'm dizzy and sick to my stomach," he muttered in a voice hardly more than a whisper.

"I know, just rest easy," Raven answered, gently wiping his brow with his own handkerchief. Realizing that there was nothing he could do to halt this huge attack, he poured his father a spoonful of medicine and slipped the liquid into his slack mouth in an attempt to ease his pain. Then he simply held him in his arms, trying to comfort him.

With a stricken face, Warren caught his brother's eyes. "Should I go for someone else? Is there anything else to be done?"

Shaken himself, Raven frowned, letting him know that there was really nothing more they could do but give their father companionship in his last moments. Putting his ear against John's chest once more and hearing a useless gurgling, he knew he only had a few moments of life.

Seemingly understanding the same thing, John looked at Warren, whose eyes glistened with tears. Then he turned his head and clasped Raven's arm with trembling fingers. He gazed at his oldest son with a wild, desperate expression and tried to put out a blue-veined hand. "I-I love . . ." he began with a raspy breath. But before he could finish the sentence, his voice trailed off, and dropping his hand, he became a dead weight in Raven's arms. He put his ear to his father's chest, and when he heard nothing at all, tears swelled in his throat.

Gently he brushed his hand over John's glassy eyes, closing them; then he laid him against the pillows and gazed at the man who had given him life, yet at the same time tried to strangle that very life force out of him since he was a small boy. He realized that in his own way his father had loved him, but John's love had been a possessive, smothering love with numerous strings attached. Nevertheless, he shouldered a sense of loss and shock at the death of his parent, and at the same time felt deep regret that his father couldn't have been a happier man.

He glanced at Warren, who held his head in his hands, and knew he was dealing with his own loss and misery.

Raven looked at John's waxy face, again knowing that his father had been trying to tell him that he loved him, but had lost his struggle with death before he could finish the sentence. How sad, he thought, that the man had tried to rush out the confession on his last breath, when they should have heard the message as young boys.

With a deep, life-altering realization, he suddenly knew why he hadn't understood love better, and why he'd never told Misty that he loved her. With all of his advantages, no one had ever spoken the golden words to him! Despite his wealth, how utterly impoverished his life had been, while she'd reveled in the warmth and love of all who ever knew her.

Tamping back his grief and pain, he vowed to find her. Feeling as if a band of iron had just broken from his soul, he now realized what he had to do to claim his heart's ease.

Chapter Twenty

Four days later, amid the clatter and smoke of the Saint Louis railroad station, Raven paused on the steps of a hissing train bound for Eureka Springs. Clad in black mourning clothes, Warren and Priscilla stood on the platform looking up at him, a warm light in their eyes.

"Tell Misty I miss her!" Warren called, raising his hand in farewell.

As the train whistle shrieked and the locomotive began pulling out of the station, Raven waved back. "I will . . . take care of yourselves while I'm gone."

Enveloped in an air of warm intimacy, the couple joined hands and smiled their last good-byes.

Raven remained on the steps, holding Warren's gaze and sending his silent thanks for his help. What a transformation his brother had made, he thought, noticing his new manner that bespoke confidence and authority. Ever since he'd stood up to John, he'd put aside his temerity and come into his own . . . come alive.

Once the train was completely out of the green-domed station, Raven entered the almost empty passenger car. Knowing the demands of the mountains, he'd dressed casually and packed only a small rucksack that he now passed to a waiting porter, who stowed it on a rack above the seats. As the locomotive picked up speed, Raven sank onto a leather seat and laid back his head, considering the crisis he'd just endured.

He'd experienced a passionate longing to leave for the mountains the morning after his father had died, but decency had demanded that he arrange services for John, then stay to attend the largest funeral the city had ever seen. Warren had stood steadfast by his side greeting distant kin and old friends who'd come to pay their last respects, and in her own quiet way, Priscilla had also been a surprising fount of courage.

Throughout the ceremony, Raven's heart had felt like a heavy stone in his chest, and one thought had hammered at his head, overpowering all others: he must find Misty, sort out the trouble between them, and bring her home. After the last houseguest had left and the last wreath had been taken to the cemetery, he'd heaved a great sigh of relief, knowing he was free to leave. His father's lawyer had told him that, as expected, the Davenport millions would be divided equally between himself and Warren, who'd now inherit the burden of managing the Missouri and North Arkansas railroad line. But with his sharp mind and Priscilla's love and support, Raven was sure his brother could summon the courage to meet the monumental task.

As the train moved farther away from Saint Louis, Raven let his mind wander back to last October, when his only thought had been escaping John's insistence that he make a society marriage. How much had changed since then. Misty had introduced him to her own unique philosophy and turned his perception of himself upside down, leaving him to wonder who he really was—Adam or Raven.

He closed his eyes and thought of all the folks he'd known in the mountains. Undoubtedly Ezra would be there, not completely understanding the situation between himself and Misty, but extending his brawny hand in greeting. Lukie would cover her mouth and giggle, and Brother Jubal's face would light with warmth and friendliness. And perhaps he'd see Sloppy Brewster or even catch a glimpse of the elusive Billy Red Scarf.

And so many things had been settled since he'd returned to Saint Louis. Warren and Priscilla had found each other, and John had gone, but Raven knew that his legacy still lingered on, for resentment lay in his heart that his father had driven off Ezekiel, who'd died a lonely death by himself. For that he could not yet quite forgive John, try as he might.

Then, feeling a presence near him, Raven opened his eyes and saw a tall, lanky man standing in the aisle. "Mind if I take a seat?" the old fellow asked. A rough country type, the bearded fellow was clad in an old-fashioned suit and a battered hat and looked eager for company. Pulling a plug of tobacco from his pocket, he cut

off a chew, then sat down across from Raven.
"Want a chaw?" he asked, popping the tobacco
in his mouth.

When Raven shook his head, the man began
an account of his trip to visit a sick relative in
the city.

"I'll tell you what," he said five minutes later,
scratching his belly. "I'm sure 'nuff glad to be
leavin' this here Saint Louis. It's the unfriendliest
place I've ever seen, and everythin' in it is sky
high," he added gruffly. "Yes sir-ree-bob, I'll shore
be glad to get back to them hills. This city is a
regular hotbed of sin and iniquity. Why it's a
regular . . ." He paused and frowned, trying to
think of the correct term.

Raven sat forward. "Sodom and Gomorrah?"

The old fellow laughed and slapped his leg.
"Yep, that's just what I was thinkin' of. How did
you know what I was goin' to say?"

Raven rested back against the seat. "Just a
guess."

The old man rambled on for another thirty
minutes, just giving Raven time to nod every so
often. When he'd finally run down, the hillman
fixed his eyes on him and tugged his ear. "Say,
young feller. You never told me your name.
Who are you and what's your business?" he
asked with the open curiosity of the mountain
folk.

In his present emotional condition, the words
hit Raven with the force of the train carrying him
to the Ozarks. After all, every man should know
his own name and his own business. That was
the nub of his whole problem—he couldn't be
both Adam and Raven and hold Misty's love. In
her own way, that was what she'd told him when

she'd said that sometimes she didn't know who he was anymore.

And in that second, sitting on the rattling train with the old fellow gazing at him expectantly, he realized from the bottom of his soul that Misty would never follow the rules or fit into city life. She'd always think with her heart and believe in her kind of magic. Moreover, her success with Sarah had taught him that her special brand of medicine had true healing power for the spirit as well as the body. At the same time, he recalled the thrill he'd experienced when he'd saved Tommy Brewster's life. And as he remembered the pounding the hill folks had given him, he realized that he'd never felt such love and gratification in connection with his professional life.

Suddenly everything was as clear and plain as the inquisitive glint in the old man's eyes: Raven was going to take Misty back to the city, but to find happiness, he should be taking himself to the mountains—*to stay.*

Straightening his back, he finally addressed the patiently waiting man. "My name is Raven . . . and my profession is healing," he said softly, as if he was understanding the words for the first time himself. After making the confession, warmth rushed through him and new hope stirred within his heart.

The old man chuckled. "So you're a doctor. Well, why are you goin' to the hills, then?"

Raven let out a long breath. "To correct a mistake I made a while back . . . if I can," he answered with deep conviction.

Early summer had flushed into the Ozarks in a soft green tide, and that afternoon Misty walked through the verdant woods on an herb-picking expedition. The air was light and soft, and sunlight radiated toward the earth in golden streams as she and Rollo made their way back to the cabin with a bucket of snake root. Ezra had ridden into town for the day, leaving her alone with her poignant memories of Raven, which she presently turned over in her mind, hardly aware of her surroundings.

She now realized how swiftly she'd left the city, just up and taking off without speaking to anyone but Nat. In her haste, she'd not even left Raven a note, and she regretted the pain she'd undoubtedly caused him. Then, with deep anguish, she thought that perhaps he'd just be relieved she was gone.

After she'd returned home, Ezra had told her that Raven would come—but he hadn't. And Lukie and Brother Jubal had told her he would come—but he hadn't. Now, almost a week later, she accepted the fact that he would never come. She'd never see his smile again, never hear the deep voice that thrilled her so, never feel his warm hands gathering her to him.

She paused under an oak and listened to a warbling bluebird as she waited for Rollo, who trailed behind. Tilting her face up to the warmth that filtered through the leaves, she leaned against the tree and drifted into her thoughts once more. If she'd left to make Raven happy, why couldn't she take comfort in the joy that he must now feel? And why did making him happy make her so miserable? she wondered, recalling that tears had moistened her eyes most of the way home.

Her life had come full circle. When she'd first met Raven, she'd been riddled with doubts and insecurities about fitting into his world; later, when she arrived in Saint Louis, she'd harbored the hope that she could make the adjustment to city life. Now she understood the truth: she was just a little mountain girl who'd been fortunate enough to cross paths with a rich, powerful doctor. Her whole life in the city was nothing but a long charade. Millions of dollars, Raven's father, and the whole of Saint Louis society stood between them—not to mention their own beliefs about life and medicine.

Walking on, she gave herself a mental shake. She'd made her decision and now she must summon the courage to stand by it. That was the best thing for both of them. She tried to focus on the delicate green of the trees and the wild violets that dazzled the eye; but try as she might, her thoughts kept drifting back to the magical days of last October when she'd first met Raven.

She remembered the spring they'd visited after they robbed the honey tree. How thrilled she'd been to show him her world, and what joy had coursed through her as his mouth first brushed hers. A strange sweetness permeated her thoughts, and she experienced a great longing to see the spring again. And that's just what she would do, she decided. Later today she'd visit the spring, and there with the splash of the water stirring her memories, perhaps she could recapture some of the joy that had been hers when her whole world was bathed in a rosy glow.

Her spirits rising a bit, she saw her cabin; then, somewhat startled, she discovered a visitor sitting on her porch patiently waiting for her. *Why, of all things*, she thought with a snap of recognition— it was Billy Red Scarf. She hadn't expected to see him, but the surprise made her happy.

427

Now what in heaven's name could the old man want?

Later that day, Raven galloped toward Misty's cabin, his whole being full of glowing expectation. When he caught a glimpse of the cabin's roof, his heart leaped; then, as he rounded a bend, he spied a figure walking down the dirt road toward him. Dressed in overalls, a weather-beaten hat, and brogans, the hillman trudged along carrying a gunny sack on his back. Even on first sight, he could tell the man was old, and there was something strikingly familiar about his gait. The wizened fellow walked with the same limp that had belonged to his grandfather years ago, and as true recognition set in, Raven's throat went dry and he blinked, not believing what he was seeing.

As incredible as it seemed, the old fellow was the picture of Ezekiel; he had the same height and the same bristle of wiry gray hair sprouting from beneath his shabby hat. Raven slowed his horse and dismounted, and as the reins dropped from his hands, his heart began pounding against his ribs.

With slow steps, he walked toward the man, searching his face, hoping against hope and praying at the same time. And as he closed the distance between them, the old gentleman stopped and let his gunny sack fall to the ground. Then a smile like the rising sun broke on his lips.

Ezekiel, Raven thought, the name bursting in his mind like a fiery comet. A sudden mist clouded his vision. Yes, it had to be him, for it could be no other. Hadn't he seen that smile in his dreams for years? His throat aching with emotion, he now strode toward the old man and embraced him, knowing for sure that he was his grandfather. "You're alive," he murmured hoarsely, running his hands over the mountaineer's stooped back to assure himself that he wasn't holding a specter in his arms.

Sobbing and laughing at the same time, Ezekiel clutched him tightly, and for a moment Raven simply held his grandfather, trying to comprehend the miracle that had just happened.

At last, he held Ezekiel away and studied the moist eyes that peered from beneath bushy brows. His weathered face creased with surprise, the old man pulled off his hat and shoved a gnarled hand through his hair, making it stand out at wild angles. He and Raven burst out laughing for a moment; then, half out of breath, Ezekiel exclaimed, "Lord, I'm so glad to see you, my heart is pumpin' fit to bust. If you ain't a sight for sore eyes, I don't know what is!" His country voice rang with the lilt of the hills, and just hearing it brought back Raven's dearest childhood memories.

"You came to take Misty back, didn't you?" Ezekiel asked with a wise grin.

"No, I'm here to stay in these hills," Raven stated, euphoria rising within him.

The old man's eyes glinted with a bright spark of life. "Somehow I had a feelin' in my bones you'd end up here," he said with a grin. Then his face sobered. "I know you think you're seein' a ghost, but you ain't," he said, his voice threaded with regret. "I shouldn't a tricked you, and I hated doin' it, but I figured there just weren't no other way."

To Raven the whole experience still seemed distant and far away, and he felt as if he was viewing a play rather than holding Ezekiel in his arms. After receiving the letter about his grandfather's passing and seeing his grave with his own eyes Raven had accepted his death. How the confrontation had an unreal, dream-like quality about it, and his stunned mind struggled against the reality before him.

Then, observing Ezekiel's guilty expression, something clicked in his brain, and suddenly he realized that the old man had faked his own death to escape the pressures of city life. A second later, he understood why Billy Red Scarf had seemed so familiar to him even at a distance. He and Ezekiel were one in the same person.

"You sent the letter that said you'd died, didn't you?" he asked in an incredulous tone.

Ezekiel wiped an arm over his brow and clapped on his hat. "Yep. That was me that done it, all right. And I fixed up that grave and marker with my name on it, so if John come snoopin' around beggin' me to sign over more of my money to him, he wouldn't find me."

With a determined expression, he held Raven's arm. "I set up those trust funds for you and Warren, then put the rest of my fortune in a Fayetteville bank where John couldn't spend it on some more of them fancy pictures he was always buyin' to impress people. At first I just came up here to get a rest from his everlastin' carpin', then I got to thinkin' how I'd never have to bother with him again if he thought I was dead."

A pained look darkened his face. "Of course, it grieved me to leave you and Warren, but I knew that with me gone there'd be no more wranglin' over money." His voice cracked with emotion.

"And I thought that some day I might meet up with you again."

Raven stared at him, still hardly believing what he'd heard. The old man had falsified his own death, not only because of John's relentless requests for money, but also to protect his grandsons' inheritance.

Ezekiel turned and pointed a thick-jointed finger toward the hazy hills. "When I came here, I was so sick of life I just moved into one of them Injun caves up there to hide out for a while. Then livin' there got to be a habit, and I got the place fixed up right comfortable." He chuckled and scratched his hairy ear. "I heard a feller showed up here claimin' to be a doctor that looked like you, but folks said you was callin' yourself Hepplewhite. When I saw you up at that grave last October, I was hiding in the bushes and nearly had a heart attack. Then I spied that Malone girl comin' up the hill, and I reckoned you were sweethearts. It was then I figured out why you was using that false name. Me bein' a Davenport and her bein' a Malone, I couldn't just bust out of the brush and spill the beans."

Raven chuckled and patted his shoulder, realizing that Ezekiel had acted as his guardian angel all last autumn. "I'm glad you didn't," he said, remembering the day the old man had trailed him and Misty along the ridge, then given Sloppy a surprise party he'd never forgotten.

Sorrow darkened Ezekiel's eyes. "I was achin' to tell you I was alive, but with you sparkin' a Malone, I thought it was best if I just stayed dead as far as everyone was concerned." He looked over his shoulder at Misty's cabin, then transferred his attention back to his grandson. "After you two got

431

married, I heard that you and Ezra had ended the feud, but quick as lightnin', you and Misty took off for the city and I thought I'd never see you again."

As Raven digested the information, the old man added, "A day or so ago, I heard that Misty had come back and I couldn't stand it no longer. I had to come talk with her and see how you were doin'." Amusement gleamed in Ezekiel's eyes. "She was a might surprised to find out that Billy Red Scarf was your grandpappy, but after she got over the shock, we visited all afternoon." He cut his eyes at the gunny sack on the ground. "She gave me a whole mess of food and herbs and things to take back to my cave. With the feud over, I'm thinkin' of buildin' me a little cabin and lettin' everybody know who I really am."

Knowing he would always take care of the old man, Raven put his arm about his grandfather's shoulders and told him that Warren would be married soon, then gently related the story of John's last days and the fashionable funeral that so many socialites had attended. Together the pair walked to the place where Raven's mount patiently cropped grass. Tears sparkled in Ezekiel's rheumy eyes as he pulled a large red handkerchief from his overalls and blew his nose. "Did John ever change any?" the old man inquired in a tremulous voice.

Raven regarded his sad face, wishing he could tell him another story. "I think he wanted to at the end . . . but it was too late."

Ezekiel shook his head. "Somethin' happened to him when we went to the city," he lamented. "With me the railroad was just a game, a way to make a little money, but making money and high-toned

432

friends got into John's blood and turned him into somebody I didn't know." His shoulders slumped in resignation. "Well, maybe he'll find some peace now. The Lord knows he never did when he was alive."

He hung his head for a moment, and Raven could tell he was getting control of himself; then, roughly clearing his throat, the old man met his eyes. "Looky here," he offered, valiantly holding back his emotions. "I don't know what's got crosswise with you and Misty, but I reckon you better hightail it to that spring she took you to when you first came here. We both left the cabin together, and she took off in that direction a few minutes afore I saw you riding down that road."

His voice hardened with purpose. "If you ask me, she's the kind of woman a man would want to hold on to with all his might."

Raven rode past Misty's honey tree, and as he saw the little clearing near the spring, he dismounted and wrapped his reins about a low-hanging oak limb. Striding over the forest floor, he made his way through the shadowy woods where the air carried the scent of fresh pine. Early summer blossomed in all its glory now, and thinking it was a pleasure just to be alive, he proceeded through a patch of yellow buttercups. When he heard the gurgling of the spring, his heart stroked faster.

Quietly, he approached; then, standing on a low bluff, he looked down to see Misty lost in thought as she relaxed on a log while Rollo chased a butterfly. Dressed in a long gingham skirt and a loose white blouse with a drawstring top that exposed one shapely shoulder, she splashed pebbles into the water, then sat back, sadness passing over her features.

With a rush of warmth, he gazed at her delicately sculpted face and willowy body, wanting to go to her but instinctively holding back as he watched her movements. He smiled when she smacked her arm where an insect had bitten her, then in a voice calculated to carry over the sound of the water, he said, "If you'll treat that sting with some fresh-dipped snuff, Doctor Malone, it'll feel a lot better."

Shock flashed on Misty's face and she slowly rose, her hand flying to her mouth. Then her eyes sparked with joy and her lips blossomed into a smile. "Well, if it isn't the Saint Louis-Big-City-Doctor come back to the Ozarks!"

Misty's erratic heart jumped in her bosom, and she could only stare at him as he hurried toward her, rushing down the gently sloping bluff. A white linen shirt lay open at his throat and tan breeches molded his slim hips. *He's finally come*, she thought, her mind reeling with disbelief. A few feet away, he spread his arms and she ran to him, her pulse racing madly. As he gathered her to him, she felt his hard chest and beloved warmth. Then his mouth found hers, leaving her knees weak.

His lips devoured hers, his tongue flicking over them while his hand caressed her hair. He seared kisses down her neck and bare shoulder and his hands slid over her body, pulling her more closely against him. *"Raven,"* she whispered, shuddering with relief and a passion she thought she'd never know again.

He cupped her face, and seeing that his eyes burned with desire, she reached up and ran her trembling hands through his crisp black hair. A moan burned her throat as he tenderly probed her mouth once more, making her breasts feel ripe and swollen beneath her loosely woven blouse. Her breath coming in tattered gasps, she pressed against him, and as his fingers spread over her breast, a hard shiver ran the length of her.

For breathless moments they kissed and caressed each other like hungry children rediscovering forgotten delights. Then at last she eased back, and blinking away tears of joy, whispered, "I met your grandfather today and found I already knew him."

Raven nuzzled her neck, and as he moved to her earlobe, she felt his warm breath on her cheek. "I know . . . I just left him," he muttered, now planting light kisses over her face.

Buoyed by her giddy pleasure, she found the courage to speak the words that lodged in her heart like sharp stones. "I'm sorry," she murmured, her eyes filling with moisture. "Sorry I ran away without saying good-bye." She swallowed and clasped his shoulders. "And I'm sorry that you lost that position at the hospital. It was all because of me, and—"

He put a finger over her lips, then gently flicked away her tears with his long thumb. "And I'm sorry, too—sorry that I even considered a position that might come between us. And actually, Doctor Malone," he announced with a twinkle in his eyes, "I came all this way not to chastise you for reading my mail, but to make you a proposition. I wondered if you would consider going into practice with me—here in the mountains near Eureka Springs."

A heady joy unfolded within her, for this was what she'd always wanted. "But I'm not like everybody else, and I never will be," she murmured in shaky haste, scarcely believing her ears. "I can't follow the rules, and I don't think like you, and we're so different and—"

Raven brushed his lips over hers, quieting her. "I know . . . and that's what I like about you. I wouldn't want you to be like everyone else"—he gave her a lopsided grin—"and lately I've come to understand that rules were made to be broken." A smile hovered at the corner of his mouth. "I've worked with doctors who thought like me all my life and hardly learned a damn thing from them—but with you, there are new and surprising revelations every day!"

Still stunned by his offer, she sighed, thinking she couldn't be understanding him. "But what will you tell them at Saint Mary's—and what about John?"

Raven's face darkened. "I'll tell them I'm leaving Saint Mary's." A sadness gathered in his eyes. "And John is gone."

Shaken by the news, she stood silently, remembering the last time she'd seen her father-in-law and the hot words they'd exchanged. After all their struggles, it seemed strange that everything should be over between them so quickly, and he was now no more than a memory. Then, even in her shock, she remembered that Raven had once told her he was gravely ill and could go at any time. Truly grieved for the man she held in her arms, she traced her fingers over his muscled back. "I'm sorry," she offered quietly. "I didn't want things to be as they were. I wanted to be his friend."

Raven ran his hands down her arms, and in his eyes she saw understanding. "I know," he came back softly. "I know . . . and it's over now."

For a moment he held her against his thudding heart, and as he stroked her hair, she thought of Saint Louis and remembered Sarah. "Someone else has been on my mind," she said, leaning back and holding his shoulders.

A smile returned to his dark eyes. "Yes, I imagine you're thinking of Sarah. Due to your efforts, she can walk now," he answered, a tinge of wonder in his voice. "She has a ways to go, but because of you, what once seemed impossible is now possible."

A deep contentment spread through Misty, leaving her awed. Guided by love and intuition, she'd struggled to find a way to unlock the girl's mind, and she thought of her every day, wondering if the much-wanted miracle had happened. Now to know that it *had* happened warmed her with the greatest satisfaction possible.

Raven sent her a tender gaze. "Something else happened after you left the city. Warren was finally able to make his stand, and he and Priscilla are due to be married in a few weeks."

She blinked in astonishment. "*They are?*" With the perspective that comes with hindsight, she felt a little foolish for ever suspecting that Raven and the shy socialite were interested in each other. And she now realized that Raven had only been aiding his brother's case all along.

"Well, what do you say to putting on this ring again?" he prompted, slipping her wedding band from his pocket and holding it in his palm. "I don't mean to press," he advised with a chuckle, "but I really need to get a commitment soon." He glanced over his shoulder, then gave her a playful look. "Why, I wouldn't be surprised to see

Benjamin Prescott Longstreet ride up on a white charger, dressed in a Confederate uniform, ready to sweep you off your feet." She laughed softly, and his gaze penetrated her heart. "And after all," he added, his face now serious, "I couldn't let that happen to the woman I love with all my heart and soul."

As his declaration sank in, an exaltation rose within her that lifted her spirit to the stars. These were the words she'd yearned to hear. He did love her—*he really did*, she thought, dizzy with happiness. Then, with a profound understanding, she realized that her wish on the frost flower, made so long ago, had finally come true because in her heart she'd never stopped believing it would.

He pressed his lips on her palm. "We'll add a diamond setting to this when we visit the city," he explained, slipping the ring on her finger. "That is, if you'll accept it."

A grin tugged at her mouth. "You know, I never cared much for diamonds," she said in a throaty voice, "but I'm right partial to plain gold bands. They're good and strong and solid all the way through—just like the man I love." There was a lump in her throat and tears blurred her vision. "And I'm going to hold onto that man 'till the Ozarks are flat and the White River runs dry—and I'll put a mark on any gal that comes between me and him that won't rub off!"

He held her face in his big hands, and the look in his eyes took her breath away. "I finally know who I am . . . and I've come home," he whispered huskily, "come home to you where I belong."

In the dying light, she met his passionate gaze and circled her arms about his shoulders. When he lowered his head, she melted against him and he took her lips in a kiss singing with fire and poetry and wild desire. Amazement flooded her heart as she realized that they were together again—together at last.

Raven held Misty away from him and met her dreamy eyes. He remembered the first time he'd come to this spring tired of life and only believing in things he could see and touch. Even then when they'd first met, she'd told him there was a magic in the mountains that floated in the air, a magic that offered weary souls their heart's ease. How right she'd been, for he now believed in things he couldn't see or touch, wonderful things of the spirit—and guided by her wisdom, he now understood that the heart *was* often wiser than the head.

Skimming his fingers over her face, he drew her to him, cherishing her above all else. "You never did answer my question, sweetheart. How about starting a clinic with me here?" he gently prompted.

She threw him a sidelong glance. "Well, I'll go into the situation on a trial basis," she answered, her voice husky with mischief. "But the first time we run out of ant eggs or lightning-struck toothpicks, I'll be gone faster that a scalded cat."

Raven chuckled and kissed her forehead; then he tilted her chin so he could look into her lovely green eyes. "One more thing, Doctor Malone," he ventured, his voice as gentle as a whisper and as tender as the dusk that now settled over the misty mountains. "My heart is broken with love for you, and I think I need a consultation. What would you prescribe for such a malady?"

Misty straightened up and tapped a slender finger across her lips. "For a patient with that condition, Doctor Raven," she slowly answered, looking as if she were giving the problem great thought, "I'd prescribe bitter-root tea and a hard rubdown with horse pee, followed by a roll in hot hickory ashes." Her eyes danced. "Oh, yeah," she murmured, trailing her cool fingers over the side of his face, "and a lifetime in my loving arms."

Lifting her skirt and swaying her hips, she sashayed away from the spring, slanting him a provocative look.

He moved after her, and as they clasped hands and ran into the woods, their laughter floated through the hazy blue hills.

AUTHOR'S NOTE

I wish to express my gratitude to the people of Arkansas who greeted me so warmly when I traveled to the Ozarks. As the world has changed, the age-old wisdom and traditions of the mountaineers have served them well. Their great insight, individuality, and wit are truly refreshing, and I hope that someday every reader will be able to personally experience the magic of the Ozarks.

Although many of our modern medicines are based on herbal remedies, they are prescribed by modern doctors. All of Misty Malone's cures were actual remedies during the late 1800s, but medicine has advanced far since then, and as Misty herself might say, only a dang fool would use them now.

The character of Benjamin Prescott Longstreet was based in part on the actual governor of Missouri in 1886, John Sappington Marmaduke, a grand old gentleman of the South and venerated Civil War hero.

Bestselling Author of *White Apache's Woman*

When half-breed Jess Robbins rides into Cheyenne to chase down a gang of cattle thieves, he is sure of three things. The townsfolk will openly scorn him, the women will secretly want him, and the rustlers will definitely fear him. What he doesn't count on is a flame-haired spitfire named Lissa Jacobsen, who has her own manhunt in mind.

Dark, dangerous, and deadly with his Colt revolver, Jess is absolutely forbidden to the spoiled, pampered daughter of Cheyenne's richest rancher. But from the moment Lissa stumbles upon him in his bath, she decides she has to have the virile gunman. Pitting her innocence against his vast experience, Lissa knows she is playing with fire...but she never guesses that the raging inferno of desire will consume them both.

_3601-0 $4.99 US/$5.99 CAN

Winner of 6 *Romantic Times* Awards!

Cassandra Clayton could run her father's freighting empire without the help of any man, but without one she could never produce a male child who would inherit it all. When Cass saved Steve Loring from a hangman's noose, he seemed to be just what she needed—a stud who would perform on command. But from the first, Steve made it clear that he wanted Cass's heart and soul in the bargain. Although his sarcastic taunts made her dread the nights she must give him her body, his exquisite lovemaking made her long to give him all that he asked—and more!

_3345-3 $4.99 US/$5.99 CAN

Remember When

ROBIN LEE HATCHER

Bestselling Author of *Forever, Rose*

"Robin Lee Hatcher writes lively, tempestuous romance!"
—*Romantic Times*

Certain that her destiny doesn't lie in her dull hometown of Homestead, Idaho, Sarah McLeod wants to shake off the town's dust and see distant lands. But as long as her ailing grandfather needs her, fantasies of exotic cities and dashing noblemen have to wait. Then Jeremiah Wesley returns from years of wandering around the world, looking for a steady job and a peaceful home. He is the last man Sarah thinks she'll ever love. Yet as she gets to know Jeremiah, she finds herself dreaming less of a far-off prince—and more of a virile lover only a heartbeat away.

_3683-5 $4.99 US/$5.99 CAN

Sage NORAH HESS

Winner Of The *Romantic Times* Lifetime Achievement Award!

"Norah Hess not only overwhelms you with characters who seem to be breathing right next to you, she transports you into their world!"
—Romantic Times

Jim LaTour isn't the marrying kind. With a wild past behind him, he plans to spend the rest of his days in peace, enjoying the favors of the local fancy ladies and running his bar. He doesn't realize what he is missing until an irresistible songbird threatens his cherished independence and opens his heart.

Pursued by the man who has murdered her husband, Sage Larkin faces an uncertain future on the rugged frontier. But when she lands a job singing at the Trail's End saloon, she hopes to start anew. And though love is the last thing Sage wants, she can't resist the sweet, seductive melody of Jim's passionate advances.

_3591-X $4.99 US/$5.99 CAN